COMPOSERS OF THE
TWENTIETH CENTURY

ALLEN FORTE, *General Editor*

THE MUSIC OF CLAUDE DEBUSSY

RICHARD S. PARKS

Yale University Press
New Haven and London

Set in Baskerville types by
Keystone Typesetting Inc., Orwigsburg, Pennsylvania.
Printed in the United States of America by
Vail-Ballou Press, Binghamton, New York.

Library of Congress Cataloging-in-Publication Data

Parks, Richard S., 1942–
    The music of Claude Debussy / Richard S. Parks.
        p. cm.—(Composers of the twentieth century)
    Bibliography: p.
    Includes indexes.
    ISBN 0–300–04439–9
    1. Debussy, Claude, 1862–1918—Criticism and interpretation.
I. Title.   II. Series.
ML410.D28P24   1989   6 5 4 1 6
780′.92′4—dc19   89–31406
                                                        CIP
                                                        MN

10   9   8   7   6   5   4   3   2   1

For Ros'y

CONTENTS

ACKNOWLEDGMENTS

The work that culminated in this book began in 1977. Twelve years is sufficient time to accumulate many debts from those who have aided me in diverse ways.

First, I wish to thank Allen Forte, whose encouragement and support have never wavered throughout this long project. He is a teacher, colleague, and good friend whose work I admire deeply and regard as a standard of excellence in music scholarship. We first discussed my work on Debussy in the summer of 1980 during an NEH seminar that he conducted, and I attended, at Yale University. I thought my goal was a theoretical-analytical study of Debussy's piano music, but during the following year he convinced me that the scope should be broadened to encompass all genres, and although this expansion delayed the project's completion by several years, it also gave me time to develop new ideas and better analytical techniques. His reactions to an early draft of the material on text expression were subsequently incorporated into part 3 of this book. On numerous occasions we discussed material and organization, to my considerable benefit. Allen has always shared freely of his expertise and ideas on everything from microprocessors to his own significant work on Debussy.

I am indebted to several libraries which allowed me to study Debussy autographs in their possession. In particular, I wish to thank the staffs of the Pierpont Morgan Library (especially Rigbie Turner), the Département de la Musique de la Bibliothèque Nationale (especially François Lesure), the Music Division of the Library of Congress (especially Wayne Shirley), the Spaulding Library of the New England Conservatory of Music (especially Geraldine Ostrove), the Sibley Music Library of the Eastman School of Music (especially Ross Wood), and the Humanities Research Center of the University of Texas, Austin (especially Cathy Henderson).

I would like to acknowledge the material and moral support I have received from two universities. Wayne State University, my academic home from 1974 to 1983, generously awarded me three research grants for Debussy work in 1977, 1981, and 1983; one assisted with a preliminary study, one freed me for a summer of research and provided supplies and clerical assistance, and one provided funds for travel. My present university home, the Faculty of Music of the University of Western Ontario, provided much of the computer hardware and software that enabled me to create camera copy for most of the musical examples and figures.

It remains to thank several people who have aided me in diverse ways. The musical examples were produced on Noteprocessor, a computer music editor, and I am grateful to the author, Stephen Dydo, for his ready availability, advice, and assistance.

It has been a great pleasure to work with Jeanne Ferris of Yale University Press, whose cordiality and enthusiasm matches her skill and expertise. I am grateful to Harry Haskell, my manuscript editor, whose sensitivity and keen judgment have made the text more graceful and perspicuous.

Charles M. Joseph read an early draft of part 1 and gave me reasons to reconsider its general thrust as well as its details. Gail Dixon read and discussed several papers that served as preliminary essays for parts 1 and 5. Several individuals have helped with proofreading the text, but, in this regard, special thanks must go to Leslie Black and Gail Dixon. (I retain responsibility, of course, for any errors that remain.)

Finally I must thank Rosemary, my wife. At certain times this commission would have resembled a punishment more than an opportunity were it not for her. She helped to design most of the musical-analytical examples and figures, and her elegant autography turned my incoherent sketches into efficacious schemata. More than once these transformations, and her observations about them, revealed features to me that had been obscure. In particular, I am indebted to her for clues regarding the use of instrumentation in the Sonata for flute, viola, and harp discussed in part 5. She has helped as well with myriad tedious chores that largely go unnoticed but are essential to an undertaking such as this. For all of this I am grateful, but no less for her unflagging confidence in me and in the importance of this project.

PREFACE

What is the nature of Debussy's musical medium and resources, and how are they employed to generate his musical surfaces in all their richness and diversity? This is the fundamental issue that shapes this study. It engenders a number of subsidiary issues of varying importance, which may be summarized as follows:

What are the nature and extent of tonality in Debussy's music? This topic, which is concerned less with the *nature* of pitch-class materials than with their *use* in fulfilling an imperative that transcends styles and style periods, is treated in part 1, "Aspects of Tonality."

What is the nature of the pitch-class materials themselves? What are their inherent properties as exploited by Debussy? How and to what extent are they organized in ways other than those that we usually associate with the term *tonal* (and to which the term *atonal* is often attached)? Do the "atonal" properties of Debussy's music have anything in common with those employed by other composers of works that are more often characterized as atonal (such as Bartók, Berg, Schoenberg, Scriabin, Stravinsky, and Webern)? Part 2, "The Pitch-Class Set Genera," is devoted to these topics.

What is the relationship of pitch-class materials to extramusical imperatives? Songs and dramatic works occupy a major place in Debussy's catalog and played pivotal roles in his artistic growth. The relationship among music, text, and dramatic scenario is therefore crucial. It is the subject of part 3, "Text Expression through Pitch Materials."

The fourth issue concerns two aspects of form in Debussy's music: *morphological form*, which is manifest in features and devices that generate patterns through the temporal disposition of musical materials; and *kinetic form*, which is manifest in qualities of vitality and mutability. Related questions include: What creates patterns and what is their nature? What kinds of musical continuities and discontinuities conspire to define formal partitions and hierarchies? How do hypostatic and kinetic form interact—that is, how do they support and conflict with each other? These questions underlie part 4, "Aspects of Form."

Part 5, "Aspects of Structure in Orchestration, Meter, and Register," addresses the structural roles played by other nonpitch parameters—in particular, orchestration and instrumental effect, meter, and register. Space does not allow treatment of all musical parameters, but these three are accessible without lengthy speculative-theoretical introductions.

Analyses of a limited number of Debussy's works introduce and illustrate each of the above issues, followed by chronological surveys that embrace all genres.

Throughout Debussy's career, new compositional techniques did not merely succeed one another; they accreted. This book is structured similarly; the issues accrete, as do the analytic approaches that address them, and issues raised in one chapter may be deferred for further discussion. Thus, the subject of text expression arises briefly in part 1, though comprehensive treatment is postponed until part 3. Part 2 continues to examine tonal relations alongside its main topic of pitch relations considered from a set-theoretic perspective. Part 3 continues to examine tonal and set structures alongside its study of text expression; a stage work discussed in part 5 includes consideration of musico-dramatic features as well as those directly related to orchestration, meter, and register. Since the book's perspective widens continually, analyses of individual works often become progressively more comprehensive, and many pieces discussed in early chapters return for further consideration in the light of other issues. This will not help readers who want quick analytic insights for a specific work and find them widely dispersed, but it is necessary for the most effective presentation of my argument. Moreover, since I intend to examine Debussy's music and compositional technique in general, my focus must be on the whole of his work. Those interested in specific pieces will find help in the Index of Works, but information about a single piece may be obscure when read in isolation, since I assume that the reader has followed the general analytic argument from the beginning.

I have eschewed historical commentary to concentrate on the music's intrinsic character and internal dynamics—a subject that is largely neglected in the existing literature. To have done otherwise would have expanded greatly the book's already intimidating bulk. Besides, the vast and rapidly growing historical and critical literature devoted to Debussy includes many fine studies on both general and specific topics.[1]

Even a book-sized study cannot discuss more than a fraction of Debussy's oeuvre as thoroughly as it deserves. No doubt every reader will find favorite pieces omitted or given short shrift, including many that provide illustrations as efficacious as those I have chosen. Even so, a goodly portion of Debussy's catalog receives attention in these pages: representative piano works from the three books of *Images, Children's Corner*, Préludes, and Douze études; orchestral works including *Prélude à "L'après-midi d'un faune," Nocturnes, La mer*, and *Images pour orchestre;* stage works including *Pelléas et Mélisande, Le martyre de Saint-Sébastien*, and *Jeux;* chamber works including the String Quartet and the Trio for flute, viola, and harp; and a number of songs.

I have never harbored an illusion that I could write the "complete" analytic study of Debussy's music. Instead I have concentrated on those aspects that particularly interest me and that have heretofore been neglected. I have long felt that pitch materials remain open to more sophisticated treatment, as do the structural roles of such things as orchestration, register, and meter, and the source of the affective power of Debussy's music in works with texts. I assume that the reader has been exposed already to the conventional notions of harmony, tonality, and form apropos of Debussy and needs no recapitulation of these ideas here.

ANALYTIC METHODS AND STYLE CONVENTIONS

Two of the analytic approaches invoked for this study occupy at present a favored position in the mainstream of theoretical studies: Schenkerian tonal theory and pitch-class set theory. Certain features of Debussy's music respond well to Schenkerian analytic principles, and so I have employed them, mindful that Schenker formulated his ideas with a different repertoire in mind.

Set-theoretic notions have proven invaluable for explicating other aspects of Debussy's pitch materials, and here I must acknowledge the contributions of scholars—too many to name—who have toiled in this field during the last thirty years or so. I am especially indebted to the work of Allen Forte, who has contributed much to the growing store of concepts and information and compiled most of it in a very compact source.[2] I have also had to devise ways of solving certain problems that have not been adequately addressed in the literature. Set theory has not often been invoked for the study of music in which diatonicism plays so large a role, and no one has developed a way to treat the phenomenon of specific pitch-class references for atonal pitch fields, diatonic or otherwise, that is comparable, for example, to what the notion of "scale" is to "key" in tonal theory.

My investigation of form and structure in nonpitch parameters has pushed me into territory whose charting is at best sketchy. In this I have been aided substantially by the work of Wallace Berry.[3]

New analytic approaches (and extensions to old ones) are introduced when needed. I have not consolidated them into a single chapter because these theoretical discussions exist for the answers they provide (rather than to make Debussy's music the grist for their mill), and the present arrangement assigns greater priority to the music and to the issues.

Abbreviations

A number of abbreviations are used repeatedly. Less familiar ones are introduced in parentheses following the first use of the full term (for example, "pitch-class (pc) set"); thereafter only the abbreviation is used. More conventional abbreviations appear without the preliminary full reference; interval names, for example, are indicated by standard short forms: M3 for major third, m3 for minor third, and so on.

Integer notation is employed throughout, where C = O, C# or Db = 1, . . . , B = 11. Integers may also indicate interval classes (ics), where ic 1 = one or eleven semitones, ic 2 = two or ten semitones, . . . , ic 6 = six semitones. They are used, as

Example 0.1. Register designations

well, to indicate the number of semitones that separate adjacent pcs in successive-interval arrays. Typographical conventions help to distinguish between these uses: pc integers are always separated by commas; ic integers are always preceded by "ic" or "ics"; successive-interval-array integers are always separated by hyphens. The content of a pc set is always cited with integers arranged according to Forte's definition of "normal order";[4] that is, integers appear in ascending order such that the smallest possible interval separates the first and last integers.

When it is necessary to reference specific pitches, the designation c^1 is assigned to middle C (ex. 0.1). The pitches from middle C to B a M7 above also carry the superscript "1"; the next higher octave begins with c^2. The octave below middle C carries no superscript; the second octave below middle C employs upper-case letters; the one below adds the subscript "$_1$", and so on. Pitch classes are referred to by upper-case letters (for example, "C" and "D♭").

Other Conventions

Most musical examples are pc reductions that eliminate performance directions (such as slurs) and rhythmic detail; the horizontal placement of notes, however, usually reflects their relative temporal positions, and bar lines provide additional aid for comparison with scores. Registers are generalized to bring notes onto the grand staff, but relative registral positions (highest versus lowest notes) are retained. Only rarely are portions of original scores reproduced completely; it is assumed that the reader will have access to the scores.

PART I
ASPECTS OF TONALITY

ONE
HARMONY AND VOICE LEADING

Tonality does not determine all pitch relations in Debussy's compositions, and many pieces manifest it through nontraditional means. There are, however, a number of structural features whose effect can be characterized as tonal and which recur across his oeuvre, contributing in large measure to his idiosyncratic style. Some may be accounted for by means of a Schenkerian perspective, while others require alternative means of addressing pitch-class (pc) hegemony.

We cannot characterize Debussy's music as tonal, implying links with that repertoire of which such composers as Mozart and Brahms are representative masters, without recognizing that the nature of his tonality is markedly different from theirs.

Throughout these pages I use the term *tonality* to describe pitch materials, processes, and contexts that project into prominence one or more pcs to a significantly greater extent than (or at the expense of) other pcs. I assume that tonality is a property that arises from a composition's internal conditions, though external factors may facilitate its recognition (such as cognitive habits acquired through experience with the eighteenth- and nineteenth-century tonal repertoire).

Because the nature of tonality is both specific and relativistic, we will examine several compositions that represent the range of Debussy's treatment. We will determine how and to what extent they are tonal, and consider those features that combine to emphasize a pc or group of pcs under the particular set of conditions specific to each piece. We will find that the pcs that are accorded tonal prominence sometimes form unconventional constructs as an alternative to the scales and triads traditionally associated with key and tonality in earlier repertoires.

This chapter shows how principles of harmony and voice leading embodied in the tonal repertoire of the eighteenth and nineteenth centuries contribute structure to Debussy's music as well. It also identifies some crucial ways in which his practice is at odds with that repertoire. Given these objectives, Schenkerian theory seems a logical tool for examining tonal relations in Debussy; indeed, a literature on the subject already exists.[1] However, one must avoid the trap of modifying the Schenkerian model when confronted by a repertoire that Schenker rejected—a

3

trap to which Oswald Jonas alluded in his introduction to Schenker's *Harmony,* where he criticized Felix Salzer's attempts to modify Schenker's concept of the *Ursatz.*[2]

THE SCHENKERIAN MODEL AND DEBUSSY'S MUSIC

Many characteristics of common-practice tonality so eloquently revealed by Schenkerian theory simply are not to be found in Debussy's music. Perhaps most conspicuously absent is the *Urlinie;* one rarely finds structural soprano lines that begin on members of the tonic triad and descend, across the work, to the tonic itself, though a few rather early compositions (such as the "Arabesques" for solo piano) pose exceptions. The absence of Urlinie descent has a parallel in the absence of structural harmonic fifth-relationships. After the early works especially, one rarely finds dominant-tonic closure in a structural sense. In Schenkerian terms, this means that bass arpeggiation is not an integral feature of underlying structure. Linear progressions are far less common than in the works of eighteenth- and nineteenth-century masters, as is the multilayered concatenation of contrapuntal-harmonic relationships which normally accompanies them. In Debussy, linear progressions tend to be of the simplest sort and of only local significance.[3] Structural levels are few and uncomplicated; a foreground and one or two middleground graphs will generally suffice to represent the tonal matrix, even for rather lengthy pieces. Also, there is a disparity between foreground and deeper levels that favors the former in richness of relation. We look in vain for many of the features that contribute to structure and cohesion in the music of Debussy's immediate and more distant antecedents: the myriad contrapuntal and harmonic relationships nested within each other in an intricacy of structural levels, the transformations of deeper-level voice-leading progression into passages of charm and artifice, the extended linear and interval progressions that interconnect formal units and structural elements across time and musical space. All the same, many artifacts of tonality can be found. Linear progressions and bass arpeggiations do occur, though normally they constitute prolongations of small scale rather than large, and foreground diminutions are as copious as their middleground counterparts are scarce; in particular, arpeggio and neighbor-note diminutions saturate Debussy's surfaces and often control events over longer spans.

Two interrelated features that mark Debussy's departure from the tonal models of his predecessors are his use of chromaticism and of harmonic sonority for its own sake.

In Schenkerian models, chromaticism is always relegated at some level to a subordinate position vis-à-vis diatonic structure, which it serves to tonicize or enrich (through inflection or modal mixture). Thus, despite the complication it imposes on musical surfaces, chromaticism ultimately affirms (rather than obscures) diatonic structure by pointing up the diatonic basis from which it departs. In Debussy, chromaticism functions differently; it does not always tonicize, nor enrich in the Schenkerian sense of mixing alternative scale steps drawn from parallel keys (though it is enriching in the sense that it expands and supplements diatonic pitch content). An E, for example, is not necessarily lowered to Eb in order for it to inflect towards D, nor to invoke a comparison with its diatonic alternative; instead, it may simply appear as one of many available pcs.

Related to Debussy's treatment of chromaticism is his use of harmonies for their own sonorous value. He often employs chromaticism to create dominant-seventh, leading-tone-seventh, dominant-ninth, and French-augmented-sixth sonorities that cannot be associated with their usual scale-step functions as dominant, leading-tone, and dominant-preparation harmonies (though the dissonances these harmonies incorporate are usually accorded special treatment in the foreground voice leading).

The following examples illustrate these points. The first four briefly survey harmony and voice leading throughout Debussy's oeuvre; the fifth demonstrates the vestigial influence of harmony and voice leading in works that are more apt to be characterized as "non-atonal."

FIRST "ARABESQUE"

Although most sources give 1888 as the date for the two "Arabesques,"[4] the style of these pieces suggests that they were composed earlier (the very square and blatantly articulated phrasing, for example, and the pervasive use of traditional harmonic progressions and cadences at phrase and period endings).

Conventional Features

While it is typical of his very early works, the first "Arabesque" is exceptional in Debussy's oeuvre for its adherence to certain traditional tonal and formal conventions. Figure 1.1 provides a formal plan and example 1.1 contains foreground and middleground voice-leading graphs for section 1 and the first three phrases of section 2 (mm. 1–50).

Formal conventions include the composition's clear phrase and period construction: four sections plus coda, each subdivided into phrases and periods, which expose six distinct motives or themes (labeled on the figure with lower-case letters). Although four-bar phrases are the norm, "irregularities" abound, wrought by extensions and elisions. But clarity of construction is evident throughout in the consistent use of harmonic-melodic closure, with gradations in weight that reflect the formal plan's hierarchy.

Of special significance among the work's structural tonal conventions is the presence of a complete Urlinie (from scale degree 3, g#²), with replications at lower structural levels (see mm. 95–99 in the middleground graph of example 1.2 and, for lower-level descents to tonic, mm. 17–18 and 23–38 in example 1.1). Structural descents to the tonic are rare in Debussy (though other examples may be cited, among them the second "Arabesque" and "Clair de lune" from *Suite bergamasque*). It is tempting to conclude that this feature is characteristic of his

FIGURE 1.1. Formal plan for the first "Arabesque"

Section	Subdivision	Measure		Tempo changes
Section 1 (A) (38)	Introduction	1	(5)[a]	andantino con moto
				ritard
	a	6	(4)	a tempo
	b	10	(7)	
				ritard
	c	17	(9)	
				ritard
	d	26	(13)	a tempo
Section 2 (B) (32)	e	39	(4)	un peu moins vite
	e	43	(4)	
				mosso
	f	47	(4)	
				ritard
	f	51	(4)	mosso
	e	55	(4)	a tempo
	e	59	(4)	
Section 3, transition (8)	e¹	63	(4)	risoluto
	e¹	67	(4)	ritard
Section 4 (A) (27.5)	Introduction	71	(5)	1° tempo
				ritard
	a	76	(4)	a tempo
	b	80	(7)	
				ritard
	c	87	(7.5)	a tempo
	c¹	95	(4)	
				(2/4 bar)
Section 5, coda (9)	a	99	(9)	
		108		

[a](number) = measures in 4/4 meter

Example 1.1. Voice-leading graphs for the first "Arabesque," mm. 1–50

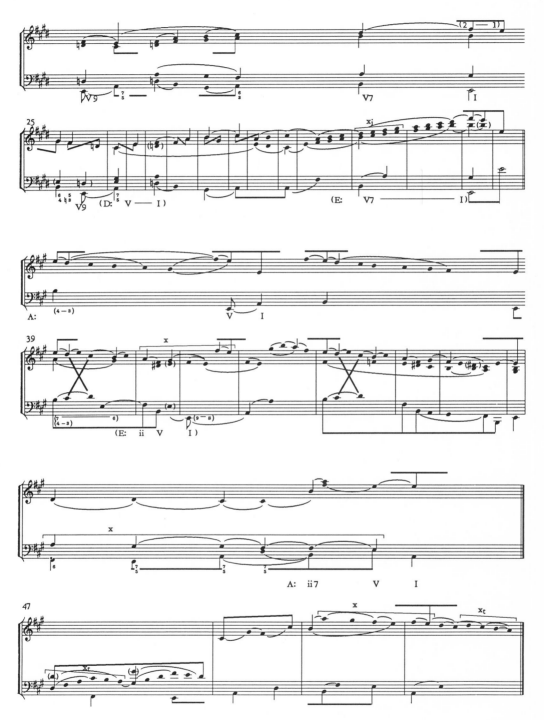

Example 1.1. *Continued*

Example 1.2. Deep middleground voice-leading graph for the first "Arabesque"

early style and constitutes an important tie with tonal convention that he would subsequently abandon. But a look at an early song, "Nuit d'étoiles,"[5] indicates that it is not so simple, for there Debussy resolutely avoids, at each opportunity, the obligatory descent to the tonic by returning to the head tone (again, scale degree 3).

The first "Arabesque" is replete with passing diminutions and linear progressions that control local events and those of longer spans. Examples of the latter may be found in mm. 17–26, which contain stepwise parallel sixths in the outer parts. Passing diminutions span octaves in mm. 1–4 (in the bass) and 39–40 (in the soprano), and a twelfth in mm. 34–37 (in the soprano). The outer-voice octave couplings in contrary motion in mm. 1–4 complement each other and expand the registral space from a sixth to a twenty-first.

An important structural motive occurs at all levels (labeled "X" in the voice-leading graphs): a tetrachord whose most prominent form is initially stated in mm. 5–6 (a^2–$g\sharp^2$–$f\sharp^2$–e^2, identified in the middleground graph of ex. 1.1).[6] It is easily seen in the foreground of mm. 17–18 (same pitches, ex. 1.1) and in the deep middleground of mm. 95–99 (ex. 1.2). It occurs in many transpositions throughout the piece, as in the bass's foreground octave progression in mm. 1–4, which is partitioned into two tetrachords by a change in figuration (ex. 1.1; transposition forms of the motive are labeled "X_t,") and in the middleground of mm. 46–49 (ex. 1.3). It also occurs in the foreground diminutions of mm. 47–49. It links formal units, such as the Introduction and Theme A at the beginning of section 1 (refer to figure 1.1 and the middleground graph of example 1.2). The new section in chordal style that begins in m. 39 reveals several occurrences, including ascending

Example 1.3. Voice-leading detail for the first "Arabesque," mm. 46–50

and descending tetrachords at various transpositions; some of these may be seen in the foreground graph of example 1.1.

All chromaticism serves either to tonicize or enrich the underlying diatonic tonal structure. For example, the striking change to the remote key of C major in mm. 63–69 of transitional section 3 can be understood as a harmonic modal mixture that prolongs the structural E in the bass (ex. 1.2).

Unconventional Features

The first "Arabesque" exhibits a number of unconventional tonal features. To begin with, while there are indeed numerous linear progressions, the middleground is relatively impoverished compared with eighteenth- and nineteenth-century masterworks. Also, the emphasis on neighbor-note motion throughout the work leads, at times, to novel voice-leading harmonies (the V^9 of V, for example, at m. 25). In m. 39 there is a voice exchange of C for D—notes that lie a step apart (a device associated more with composers of the next generation)[7]— and such exchanges recur several times thereafter.

The subdominant scale step occupies a special role in the first "Arabesque" (and, as we shall see, in the rest of Debussy's oeuvre). The composer constantly exploits its potential for functional ambiguity vis-à-vis the tonic (where E–to–A can mean I–IV or V–I). The subdominant is tonicized in mm. 39–62 (emphasized graphically by a change of key signature from four sharps to three); within this section, E, acting now as dominant, is itself tonicized by the reinsertion of D♯ (mm. 40–41, 44–45, and especially 59–62), a feature which only heightens the ambiguity that surrounds these two pcs. The subdominant also initiates the descending tetrachordal motive, a^2–g♯^{2}–f♯^{2}–e^2.

Although the head tone is initially articulated (in m. 7) at the register in which the Urlinie descent finally occurs, it is prolonged throughout most of the piece in a higher register (see ex. 1.2, mm. 6, 15–85, and 97–99); indeed, one could imagine the piece ending in this higher register (in which case the initial placement of g♯^{1} in m. 7 would serve as a delaying prolongation). While Debussy thus observes obligatory register, the effect is of an afterthought, and his handling of this tonal convention may serve more to indulge his fondness for assigning a prominent motive (here the descending tetrachord motive "X") to a specific register, only to change it as a harbinger of an important formal event—in this case, the composition's conclusion.

And while there is an Ursatz setting an Urlinie, the head tone is by no means obvious. Indeed, the descending tetrachord a^2–g♯^{2}–f♯^{2}–e^2 is so prominent, and a^2 so well supported by the dominant, that one may be tempted to infer b^2 (5) as an implied structural antecedent (though subsequent events do not confirm such a reading).

STRING QUARTET

The quartet was completed in 1893,[8] the same year in which *Pelléas et Mélisande* was begun, and shows a level of maturity well beyond adolescence. Example 1.4 provides voice-leading graphs for two passages.

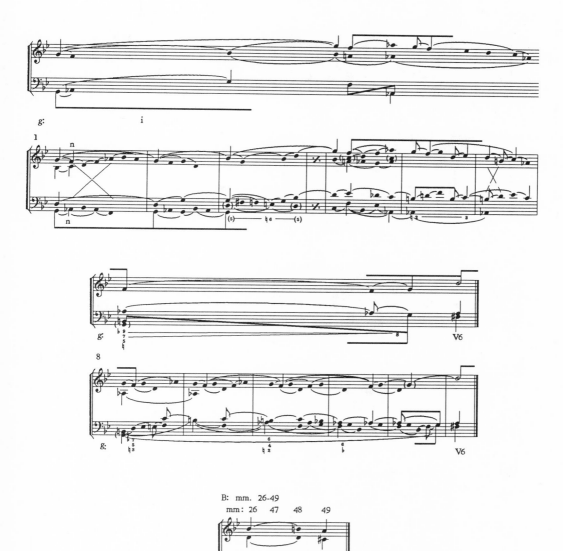

Example 1.4. Voice-leading graphs for the String Quartet, I

Example 1.4. *Continued*

Mm. 1–13

The G minor tonic triad provides structure for mm. 1–12, prolonged by complementary ascending and descending octave couplings in the top voice that extend
the neighbor-note prolongation of g[1] and are supported by neighbor-note motion
(to Ab) in the bass (seen in the deep-middleground graph of ex. 1.4A). The
elaborated tonic then proceeds to the dominant major, which controls the next
section of the piece (not shown).

The foreground is saturated with neighbor-note motion, and the prolonging
sonority is the same as that of the middleground: a § chord on Ab (ex. 1.4A
foreground, m. 1). This prolonging sonority is certainly an unconventional
choice. Its subtonic root does not tonicize, and the chord's minor third invokes a
form of mixture that is quite remote. While the relationship between these tonic
and prolonging harmonies is in itself hardly an innovation, the emphasis that
Debussy accords it by embedding the altered chord in a main thematic element is
uncommon.

Conventional diminutions fill the foreground. Arpeggiation and neighbor
notes predominate, though there are some passing motions (mm. 6–7) as well as
voice exchanges. The tonic triad is projected clearly in mm. 1–4 and elaborated by
neighbor-note motion in mm. 5–7; thus, the prominent foreground neighbor
notes reflect those of the deeper middleground.

The conventional aspects of this passage's voice leading are often overshad-

owed by unconventional features, such as the prolonging sonority already mentioned, and the avoidance of resolution for the tritone, B♮–F. Another is the
disproportionate length (compared with their resolution in m. 12) accorded the
seventh (F) and ninth (A♭) in mm. 8–12 relative to G in the bass. The chromaticism
(♮3,♭7,♭9) effects a dominant-ninth *sonority* without invoking a dominant-ninth
function. The issue of implied function is settled amicably; ♭9 resolves, ultimately, in
the direction of its inflection (a♭ to g), as does ♮3 (b to c¹) before it is replaced by b♭
(in m. 10). But the treatment of this V⁹ reveals a composer whose infatuation with
sonority for its own sake tempts him to override stronger relations in the realm of
harmony and voice leading.[9] Moreover, the unusual neighbor-note sonorities in
this passage receive additional emphasis through their placement in positions of
syncopation, which clutch the listener's attention.

Yet another unconventional feature is found in m. 5, whose falling fifths serve
no imperative of voice leading, but merely enrich the color of the musical surface.

Mm. 26–49

The second passage (mm. 26–49), whose voice leading is more complicated,
presents an altered and extended reprise of the first. It begins by prolonging the
tonic while presenting the initial thematic material, but a harmonic reinterpretation of the theme brings significant changes. The tonic is prolonged harmonically,
in mm. 26–32, by a preaffixed progression (g: VI–V¹³–i) whose members are
richly elaborated by neighbor-note motions chromatically adorned (ex. 1.4B,
foreground). The unfoldings of mm. 32–38 (combined with additional chromatic
elaborations) show the composer's reliance on tonal means for expanding his
materials. The special importance accorded sonority over diatonic voice-leading
imperatives is evident in the unusual chromatic harmonies that provide middleground structure for mm. 34–47.

Debussy handles foreground details with care: a seventh usually resolves
stepwise in the direction of its inflection, as does at least one member of a tritone;
if not, such tones continue into the next harmony where they are reinterpreted as
more stable chord members (a♭, the seventh of the chord in m. 47, for example, is
retained in m. 48, where it is the third of the chord, g♯ [spelled enharmonically as
a♭]). But this apparent concern for foreground details belies a more casual treatment of voice leading at deeper levels, since the reinterpretation (rather than
resolution) of a dissonance forces the listener to abandon customary voice-leading
expectations. Consonant reinterpretation of a dissonance may well ease the tension that an experienced tonal listener senses, but it also thwarts the ability of such
tensions to communicate the presence of crucial intervals that carry special voice-
leading roles. If middleground dissonances help the listener to chart tonal journeys over longer temporal spans, reinterpretation (rather than resolution) renders those journeys less comprehensible. Debussy's unorthodox treatment of
dissonances (which are projected strongly by syncopation and chromaticism)
provides aural surfaces that resemble familiar tonal territory, but the deeper
relations they conceal reveal the environment's foreignness.

Bars 34–47 are intricate tonally and further illustrate the way chromaticism reflects Debussy's disregard for middleground voice-leading imperatives in favor of surface sonority. The chromaticism of the parallel six-three chords in the middleground inflects eventually towards the applied dominant of A, but the way is certainly convoluted, since d^1 and f function first as neighbors to, respectively, $e\flat^1$ and $g\flat$ (in m. 39), and then as neighbors to $c\sharp^1$ and e (in mm. 48–49; see ex. 1.4B, middleground).

The sparseness of structural levels in both passages contrasts sharply with the complex chromaticism of their voice leading, and linear progressions are conspicuously absent. The result is a rich musical surface that lacks the dynamic quality of forward motion to which we are accustomed from our experience with earlier tonal music.

Many features familiar from earlier tonal repertoires are readily found in these quartet passages: register interplay and obligatory register operate throughout; unfolding, connecting, and neighboring motions are ubiquitous (though Debussy's idiosyncratic chromaticism often obfuscates). The greatly increased complexity of the second passage, in particular, and the radically different harmonic interpretation of the opening motive and tonic prolongation, attest to Debussy's considerable grasp of tonal possibilities.

From a Schenkerian perspective, tonal anomalies occur at all structural levels: the unusual use of mixture in the first passage, the lack of linear progressions in the middleground, and the prolongation of scale degree 1 (a tone that can go nowhere) as first primary tone for both passages.

"LA FILLE AUX CHEVEUX DE LIN"

The autograph fair copy for "La fille aux cheveux de lin" (Préludes I) carries the date January 1910, seventeen years after the quartet.[10] The piece was discussed thoroughly by Adele Katz, who speaks of the pervasiveness of neighbor-note motion, in particular around $D\flat$ ($D\flat$–$E\flat$–$D\flat$), frequently complicated by register transfers.[11] I will discuss features that she overlooked.

Example 1.5 presents a foreground graph of mm. 1–4 and a middleground graph of the entire composition that shows the main structural notes and some passing diminutions. The opening, mm. 1–4, reveals a third-progression (coupled with a register transfer), $d\flat^2$–$c\flat^1$–$b\flat$, that connects the head tone with an inner voice (ex. 1.5, foreground). The difficulty of hearing the register transfer at the beginning of the progression is eased by practice with the preceding neighbor-note motion, which is also disposed between two different octaves. The plagal cadence in mm. 2–3 supports the third-progression.

The piece is replete with neighbor-note motions around $D\flat$, complicated by frequent changes of register; this Katz has already observed, as well as the manner by which the opening measures' surface discloses the principle of deeper-level neighbor-note motions. The vertical lines in the middleground graph of example

Example 1.5. Voice-leading graphs for "La fille aux cheveux de lin"

1.5 indicate formal divisions (phrases) rather than bar lines. The graph reveals that the neighbor-note motions are correlated to the formal plan. The bass clearly emphasizes G♭ as tonic, but not through structural bass arpeggiation; instead, four bass notes—G♭, E♭, C♭, and A♭ (in mm. 22–23)—are projected strongly and repeatedly by interior, foreground authentic cadences, and of the four, G♭ is projected most often.

There is irony in the way "La fille aux cheveux de lin" employs foreground dominant-tonic closure while avoiding background closure altogether. The absence of Ursatz bass arpeggiation has a correlate in the absence of an Urlinie descent (the first primary tone, D♭, is also the last).

Although the voice-leading graphs reveal hierarchic organization, wherein certain noncontiguous tones crucial to the key are projected in a manner that implies structural roles for them, the lack of structural progress makes clear that despite its suggestive surface, "La fille aux cheveux de lin" is not organized pervasively according to Schenkerian models. The emphasis on the subdominant, which is projected conspicuously by the plagal cadence in mm. 2–3 and is even more prominent in the pedal of mm. 28ff., confirms the special role accorded this scale step and chord among Debussy's tonal resources.[12]

"NOËL DES ENFANTS QUI N'ONT PLUS DE MAISONS"

This song, Debussy's last, was composed in 1915.[13] (Example 1.6 displays foreground and first-middleground graphs for portions of the song and deeper middleground graphs of the entire piece.) Its voice leading is intricate, and the neighbor-note motions that are integral to Debussy's style abundantly pervade all structural levels. There are linear progressions (in mm. 1–11 and 20–27) as well as the arpeggio and neighbor-note foreground diminutions so common in Debussy. Indeed, all of the pitch materials can be accounted for by means of harmony and voice leading.

Yet although the piece is emphatically tonal, it lacks such crucial elements as the Urlinie progression and bass arpeggiation; instead, the tonic chord itself, prolonged by neighbor-note motion, serves as the most remote level of structure. This unusual, deeper-level neighbor-note prolongation occupies mm. 36–59 (ex. 1.6, deep middleground especially, and detail 1).

Two gestures from the opening measures adumbrate the composition's prominent tonal motions: the interrupted neighbor-note figure in m. 3 (a^2–g^2–[ ]–a^2), and the double-neighbor-note motion of mm. 3–4 enriched by modal mixture (ex. 1.6, detail 2).

The graphs reveal many other tonal features familiar from previous works, including more exchanges of notes a second apart (see ex. 1.6, foreground, m. 7).

"Noël des enfants qui n'ont plus de maisons" accords great prominence to interplay between subdominant and tonic. This is seen in the recurrent 5–6 and 3–4 neighbor-note motion over the bass (ex. 1.6, foreground, mm. 4–6 and 12–13); in mm. 40–43, where, having modulated to E♭ major, IV (A♭) becomes the temporary goal of the bass; and throughout in the application of mixture between scale steps A and D (to be construed as i–iv/IV or ii–v/V?)—a novel exploitation of ambiguity of function between tonic and subdominant.

Register interplay is often crucial. The upper-voice third-progression (e^1–f^2–g^1) in mm. 1–8 is complicated by register transfer, and octave shifts occur frequently in the bass (as in mm. 14–15, where the ascent from D to d helps clarify the function of E as a neighbor note to D, not vice versa). Tonally perplexing mm. 57–59 may be heard as shown in example 1.6, deep middleground, and detail 4), where c♭^{1} originates as a member of the six-three chord above e♭ in m. 40 (detail 3) and descends (returns) to neighbor-note B♭ before the latter resolves to the tonic, A.

This song resembles the passages from the String Quartet and "La fille aux cheveux de lin" in its emphasis on neighbor-note motion complicated by chromaticism, its paucity of linear progressions, and the absence of structural bass arpeggiation and Urlinie descent. Although harmony and voice leading control pitch materials throughout, in "Noël des enfants qui n'ont plus de maisons" (even more than in the other pieces examined), this control is concentrated in the foreground, rather than middleground and background.

All of the pieces examined so far exhibit comprehensive organization of their

Example 1.6. Voice-leading graphs for "Noël des enfants qui n'ont plus de maisons"

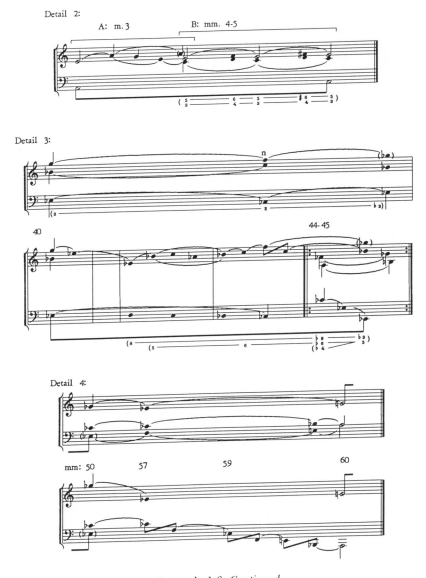

Example 1.6. *Continued*

pitch materials by means of harmony and voice leading (albeit this organization is irregular compared with Schenkerian models). But although they span Debussy's entire career, these works are not truly representative. Most of his works after 1889 do not manifest this form of pervasive tonal control; still, tonal features occur in abundance. We will consider one example.

"POUR LES DEGRÉS CHROMATIQUES"

Also composed in 1915,[14] "Pour les degrés chromatiques" (Douze études II) manifests tonal harmony and voice leading far less than the preceding examples. Even so, it illustrates the extent to which these features penetrate all of Debussy's writing.

Bars 1–4 unfold the A minor tonic chord through an implied polyphonic fabric compressed into a single line (ex. 1.7A): in the highest voice, e^2 passes to c^2 via eb^2 and db^2; c^2 passes to a^1 via bb^1 in an inner part; the third, a^1-c^2, passes back up to c^2-e^2 via b^1-d^2. Bars 11–14 contain a recurrent theme that unfolds a D minor triad (subdominant of A minor) elaborated by neighbor-note and passing diminutions.[15]

Measures 43–46 unfold the D minor triad again (embedded in the same theme as mm. 11–14), but over the fifth of the chord in the bass. The theme's harmonization, however, unfolds a five-three chord on A, which contradicts the D minor triad (ex. 1.7D).

For these passages, tonal analysis that invokes the Schenkerian model raises as

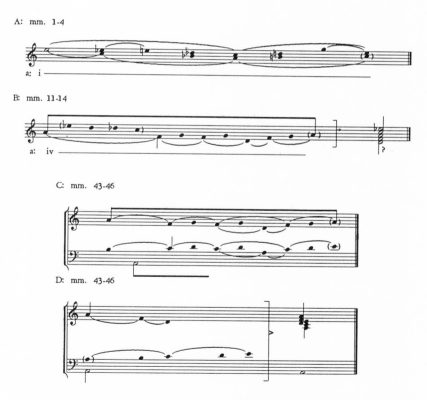

A: mm. 1-4

a: i

B: mm. 11-14

a: iv

C: mm. 43-46

D: mm. 43-46

Example 1.7. Voice-leading detail of "Pour les degrés chromatiques"

many questions as it answers; nonetheless, remnants of voice leading and fore-ground diminutions remain.[16]

Debussy's earliest compositions conform to Schenkerian models in many re-spects, while embodying eccentricities that point toward his stylistic evolution. Harmony and voice leading offered Debussy his first means of control over pitch materials, and he continued to write pieces in which conventional tonal operations play a major role long after he had developed highly sophisticated alternatives.[17] His forging of interconnections between harmony and voice leading, on the one hand, and other musical and extramusical elements such as form on the other, shows his sense of organicism and his concern to integrate nonmusical and musical elements.

Debussy's idiosyncratic manner of handling tonal operations included a pref-erence, in foreground diminutions, for neighbor notes and arpeggiation, features that control events of longer span as well. He exhibits a fondness for remote forms of mixture as a source of chromatic alteration, and he uses chromaticism to create harmonies whose sonorities belie their functional associations from earlier tonal repertoires. These features of early works adumbrate his subsequent exploration of new means for generating and controlling pitch resources, means that we will explore in part 2.

Remnants of harmony and voice leading are commonplace even in pieces that are not strongly tonal—including "radical" works that are more likely to be characterized as atonal—and this indicates the extent to which such features pervaded Debussy's thinking. As we shall see, his evolution entailed a reformula-tion of tonal principles that made them compatible with new means of generating novel music.

Debussy's predilection for the subdominant is manifest in many ways: in voice-leading elaborations around the tonic that consist of $\hat{5}-\hat{6}$ neighbor-note motions; in linear motions directed towards the subdominant; and in the tonicized-fourth scale steps often encountered as structural anchors for passages and large sec-tions. His awareness of the subdominant's potential for functional ambiguity vis-à-vis the tonic is manifest in pairings that capitalize on their susceptibility to conflicting interpretations (I–IV versus V–I).[18]

Two features that suggest the direction of Debussy's subsequent innovations are his avoidance of structural bass arpeggiation and Urlinie descent (in pieces whose foregrounds are replete with conventional diminutions) and his separation of sonority from scale step. The absence of *Ursatzformen* has a profound impact on a work's inner and outer dynamics, and opens the way for other means of control. His use of bass arpeggiation to support linear progressions at lower structural levels indicates a willingness to employ this feature to assist in internal partition-ing while denying it the power to exert its dynamics and deep-level voice-leading imperatives over the piece as a whole. The detachment of sonority from scale step, accomplished through a freer use of chromaticism (which rejects voice-leading imperatives associated with structures whose basis is diatonic), signals a new principle for relation, one that arises from intrinsic intervallic properties rather than extrinsic interval associations.

Where does this lead? If voice-leading imperatives no longer serve to distinguish referents from their subjects, does this mean that there are no referential pcs other than fleeting surface associations projected by foreground diminutions (which are often contradictory)? Or are there other means of imposing priority for a selection of pcs in a given pc field, means that would allow for the exploration of sonorities' intrinsic intervallic properties both familiar and novel? These questions are the subject of the next chapter.

TWO

TONALITY IMPOSED THROUGH
OTHER MEANS

There are features other than harmony and voice leading that contribute to the strong tonal character of some pieces and that reside, to some extent, in less overtly tonal works. All of them accord prominence to a pc or group of pcs. These features include quantitative means of emphasis, invariance within a fluctuant pc field, qualitative means of emphasis, linearity, and implied emphasis by association with familiar harmonic conventions. "La fille aux cheveux de lin" may serve as the first example, since its suitability for Schenkerian analysis (demonstrated in chapter 1) facilitates comparisons with that model.

"LA FILLE AUX CHEVEUX DE LIN"

Quantitative emphasis entails reiteration, agogic accent, and dynamic accent (including unison and octave doublings). *Invariance* in a fluctuant pc field constitutes a special form of quantitative emphasis.

Consider the first eleven measures of "La fille aux cheveux de lin" (ex. 2.1). Pitch classes 10,1,3,6 predominate; in fact, they serve as referents in these bars as well as for the piece as a whole.[1] Important pc collections that emerge in these opening measures include: the arpeggiated major and minor triads in mm. 1–2 and 8–9 (pcs *6,10,1* and *3,6,10* [referential pcs are italicized]); the pentachords that encompass the pc content of the triads in mm. 1–2 and 3–4 (*10,11,1,3,6* and *10,1,3,5,6*, respectively); the pentachord formed by the soprano line in mm. 5–6 (*6,8,10,1,3*); and the septachord of mm. 10–11 (*5,6,8,10,11,1,3* = the G♭ major scale). The referential tetrachord, *10,1,3,6* appears as the seventh-chord that contains the aforementioned triads in mm. 1–2 and 8–9, and it forms the bass line of mm. 5–6. These constructions account for most of the composition's pc content, though others appear as well. It is easy to see (and hear) that pcs 10,1,3,6 are favored over others in the pc field of mm. 1–11: they are often assigned longer durational values (pc 1 is sustained in m. 1, for example, as are pcs 6,10,1 in mm. 3–4); they are frequently doubled in octaves (pcs 1,6 in mm. 3–4 and 10–11); they form the invariant subset shared by all of the larger collections cited above,

Example 2.1. Referential pc saturation keyed to phrase divisions in "La fille aux cheveux de lin"

including the three pentachords, the G♭ major scale, and the tetrachord; and each of the six triads in mm. 5–6 retains at least one (and usually two) of the pcs as invariants. Although by mm. 10–11 it is readily apparent that G♭ major provides both key and tonic triad, it is not yet clear in mm. 1–2, which accord E♭ the same measure of prominence as G♭, B♭, and D♭; it is easier initially to accept E♭ as coequal to the other three pcs.

Qualitative emphasis projects pcs into prominence through disposition and context: first, last, highest, and lowest notes; notes accented by metric placement or dynamic stress (an overlap with quantitative emphasis); notes isolated from others by remote register placement or pauses; or pitches that lie on either side of a skip in an otherwise stepwise line. *Linearity* is a special form of qualitative emphasis in which notes that serve as boundary tones for stepwise motions assume greater prominence. In mm. 1–11 of "La fille aux cheveux de lin," pcs 10,1,3,6 are made prominent by their placements as first and last notes of phrases and motives, as highest and lowest notes within phrases, and by placement in positions of metric accent (for example, on the first beats of mm. 1–4 and 8–11). Linear motions in mm. 1–11 and across the piece as a whole were discussed earlier in connection with voice leading, and it is hardly necessary to point out that pcs from the referential tetrachord serve as origin and goal for each of the linear progressions and neighbor-note motions in mm. 1–11.

Implied emphasis through familiar associations occurs when familiar tonal harmonic conventions point to a pc (or group of pcs) as a goal. An example would be Debussy's use of authentic full and half cadences for formal punctuations. There are many in "La fille aux cheveux de lin": mm. 3–4 (full plagal); mm. 9–10, 15–16, 18–19, 23 (all full authentic); and m. 27 (half). Each implies a temporary tonic that acquires special prominence, at least momentarily. As I have demonstrated elsewhere,[2] such associations can mislead, as when a sonority that carries a strong tonal association thwarts the expectations it engenders. For example, the parallel dominant-seventh sonorities of "La cathédrale engloutie" (Préludes I), mm. 64–66, confound tonal implications since they do not resolve in voice leading, but function as complex acoustic doublings—not unlike an organ mixture stop.[3]

In its entirety, "La fille aux cheveux de lin" provides an example of invariance as a manifestation of quantitative emphasis where the feature is both form defining and vivifying. The work exhibits selective saturation by pc referents 10,1,3,6, in which the proportions of referential to subsidiary pc content vary markedly from one passage to the next but in an orderly fashion. This may be seen by comparing the percentages of referential pcs struck within each phrase and section (ex. 2.1 and table 2.1).[4] Overall, referential pcs predominate, accounting for about 70 percent of the notes struck, but proportions vary greatly from phrase to phrase. As the piece proceeds towards its midpoint, the proportion of referential pcs tends to attenuate, falling to 47 percent in mm. 15–16 and 50 percent in mm. 19–21. This trend begins in the sixth phrase (mm. 14–15) and holds through the ninth phrase (mm. 22–23). A reprise of pc content in mm. 24–27 restores the

TABLE 2.1. Saturation of "La fille aux cheveux de lin" by referential
pcs 10,1,3,6

Formal plan	Measures	PCs articulated	PCs 10,1,3,6	%	Totals (%)	
Theme	1–4	27	24	89		
	5–7	42	30	71	149 : 114 (77)	
	8–11	54	39	72		
	12–13	26	21	80		
Contrasting material	14–15	33	18	55		
	15–16	17	8	47		
	17–19	27	15	56	198 : 107 (54)	571 : 402 (70)
	19–21	58	29	50		
	22–23	63	37	59		
Reprise	24–27	98	91	93		
	28–32	37	32	86		
	33–34	54	31	57	224 : 181 (81)	
	35–39	35	27	77		

referential tetrachord to dominance (93 percent), and the thematic reprise that follows (mm. 28–32) sustains the tendency. Trends of fluctuation within each larger division mirror that of the piece as a whole, as saturation by the referential tetrachord first diminishes and then increases.

These tendencies are form defining in two ways. First, the proportional decline in referential pcs struck after m. 13, and the subsequent rise at m. 24, coincide with a turning away from the opening thematic material and the eventual reprise; contrast and return in the thematic domain are thus reinforced by the change in the mix of pc content. Second, to the extent that we perceive a high degree of saturation by referential pcs as stable, and a low degree of saturation as unstable, the cyclic fluctuation that occurs across the piece as a whole and is replicated within each of the three large divisions engenders a dynamic process which is both distinct from and coordinated to the formal plan.[5]

Doubling and registral placement also emphasize the referential pcs[6]: doublings in mm. 3–4 and mm. 10–11 strongly favor pcs 6,10,1; it is less obvious that referential pcs are the chord members most often doubled in mm. 5–6, 8–9, and 12–13.

For most phrases, referential pcs assume positions as highest and lowest notes. See, for example, the registral extrema in mm. 1–3, 5–7, 12–13, and 19–22. Exceptions occur in mm. 15–16 (pc 11 in the soprano), mm. 24–27 (pc 11 in the bass), and mm. 28–32 (pc 11 in the bass), the latter at a crucial formal juncture (pc 11 is struck just before the reprise of the opening theme) to which it draws attention. The highest note in the piece is pc 6 (g♭[3] in m. 36, not shown in example 2.1) and the second highest is pc 3 (e♭[3] in m. 21). The lowest note is pc 6 (G♭ in mm. 12–13). Doubling and registral prominence are also assigned to nonreferential pcs, usually in passages where quantitative emphasis is on nonreferential pcs (which the doublings reinforce; note pc 11 in mm. 15–16, pc 0 in mm. 19–21, and the registral emphasis accorded pc 11 in m. 16).

"VOILES"

Composed in 1909,[7] "Voiles" (Préludes I) has attracted the attention of many authors who have noted its use of whole-tone and pentatonic materials and expressed doubts regarding its tonal aspect.[8] Perhaps its enigmatic tonality is better addressed by recognizing pc relationships that depend less on harmony and voice leading. To begin with, pc content in "Voiles" tends to depart from and return to the whole-tone hexachord 0,2,4,6,8,10. Three referential pcs (6,8,10) are emphasized through invariance and linearity while nonreferential pcs are withheld, suppressed or projected, in coordination with the formal plan.

"Voiles" falls into three large sections (fig. 2.1) defined by key-signature changes at mm. 42 and 48, and by internal homogeneity of theme and texture. The first section's contrapuntal texture features a series of ostinati and lines doubled in octaves. The second section is heterophonic and idiomatically combines pianistic glissandi with extremely brief motives. The third section synthesizes these glissandi with the contrapuntal texture and ostinati of the first section. Because distinguishing characteristics of the first two sections conjoin in the third, the overall tripartite plan is more accurately described by the scheme A–B–A/B than by the familiar A–B–A.[9] The disposition of pc materials supports the formal plan: the outer sections employ a single form of the whole-tone scale (0,2,4,6,8,10), while the middle section uses exclusively the black-note anhematonic pentatonic scale (6,8,10,1,3). Pitch classes 6,8,10, are invariants whose significance as referents is quickly established: pc 10 is ubiquitous in the bass ostinati, where its register is fixed as Bb_1; pcs 6 and 8 consistently appear as initial notes of motives (stemmed on the graphs) and as goals of musical motions (connected by slurs). Example 2.2 excerpts representative passages from the beginnings of formal units which it renotates to distinguish referential from nonreferential pcs in the same manner as example 2.1.

The first large section is itself subdivided by the new theme at m. 23, coupled with a new inner-voice ostinato, and by a return of earlier material in m. 33. The pc content again supports this partitioning: among the nonreferential pcs, 0,4 predominate over 2 in mm. 1–22, 0,2 over 4 in mm. 23–32;[10] and 2,4 over 0 in the third subdivision (mm. 33–41; see ex. 2.2, A–C).

The middle section (mm. 42–47) signals a change in pc content as pentatonic pcs 1,3 replace whole-tone pcs 0,2,4. Again, although referential pcs 6,8,10 are predominant, nonreferential pcs 1,3 are also stressed. In the glissando of m. 42, for example, referential pcs 8,10 provide the figure's first and last notes, but pc 3 serves as the first and lowest note of the glissando itself, and pc 1 is the highest (and loudest) note.

FIGURE 2.1. Formal plan for "Voiles"

Division		Measures	
Section 1 (A)	(a)	1	(41 measures)
	(b)	23	
	(a)	33	
Section 2 (B)		42	(6)
Section 3 (A/B)		48	(17)
		64	

The last major change in pc materials at m. 48 effects a transition: pc 4 is withheld from the glissando runs, and then pcs 1,3 are exchanged for pcs 0,2 a semitone away.[11]

FANFARE TO "LE CONCILE DES FAUX DIEUX"

This marvelous fanfare, which precedes "Le concile des faux dieux" (*Le martyre de Saint-Sébastien* III), falls into three main divisions, of which the first and last divide into two subdivisions each (fig. 2.2). These formal junctures are defined by changes: the transposed return of the opening material at m. 17; the rapid changes in harmony combined with an increase in pc content, dense texture, and

Example 2.2. Referential pc saturation in excerpts from "Voiles"

FIGURE 2.2. Formal plan for the fanfare preceding
"Le concile des faux dieux"

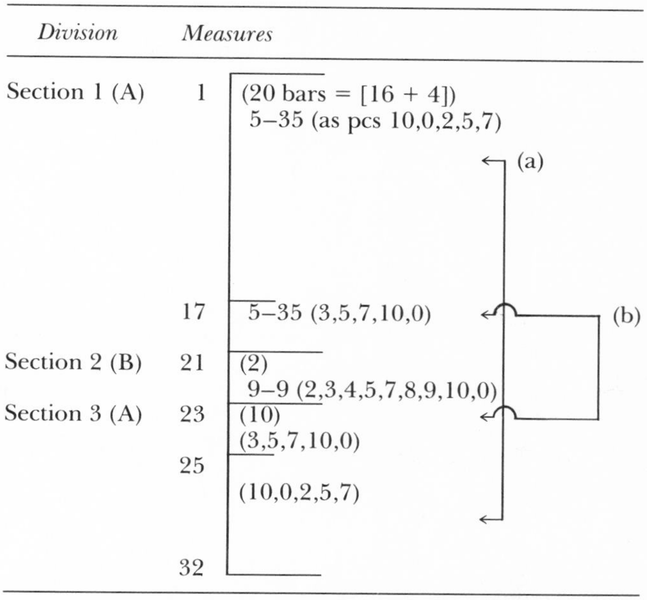

Division	Measures	
Section 1 (A)	1	(20 bars = [16 + 4]) 5–35 (as pcs 10,0,2,5,7)
		← (a)
	17	5–35 (3,5,7,10,0) ← (b)
Section 2 (B)	21	(2) 9–9 (2,3,4,5,7,8,9,10,0)
Section 3 (A)	23	(10) (3,5,7,10,0) ←
	25	(10,0,2,5,7)
		←
	32	

tutti instrumentation at m. 21; a return to the original texture and reduced pc content of m. 17 at m. 23; and a return to the original pc content at m. 25. The formal plan's proportions are asymmetrical and the middle section, in particular, is disproportionately brief (barely two measures).

Pitch materials correlate closely to the formal plan. The large outer sections employ pcs 5,7,10,0 enriched by either pc 2 (outer subsections, mm. 1–16, 25–32) or pc 3 (second and penultimate subsections, mm. 17–20, 23–24). The brief middle section employs nine pcs: 5,7,10,0; plus 2,3; plus new pcs 4,8,9. (Example 2.3 A–B shows representative excerpts to demonstrate fluctuation in pc saturation.) Pitch classes 5,7,10,0 are favored throughout to such an extent that they serve as tonal referents. They appear first and last, and they saturate the piece; they are reinforced by octave doublings in the brief middle section, where their hegemony is threatened by the sheer numbers of added pcs; and they account exclusively for the pc content of the concluding bass ostinato. As in "La fille aux cheveux de lin" and "Voiles," the pc focus of this fanfare changes in tandem with the degree of saturation by the referential tetrachord. And as in both preludes, this fluctuation is both correlated to the formal plan (which it supports by tying fluctuation to points of subdivision) and independent of it (in its dynamic cycle of stability-instability-stability engendered by the departure from and return to referential pc saturation).

An important processive feature of Debussy's can be seen in the way certain pcs are at first withheld and then gradually acquire prominence as the work proceeds. Insignificant at the beginning, pc 0 is important by m. 9, and by mm. 10–16 it is as crucial as any pc. In similar fashion, pc 2 (present from the beginning) is conspicuous in mm. 14–15 and is the only pc in m. 16. Pitch class 3

A: mm. 1-10

B: mm. 17-19

C: mm. 21-24

D: mm. 25-28

Example 2.3. Referential pc saturation in the fanfare preceding "Le concile des faux dieux"

does not appear until m. 17, but it is rearticulated ever more frequently through-out mm. 18–20. The middle section, which introduces pcs 4,8,9, mainly reserves octave doublings for familiar pcs from the first section's hexachord (10,0,2,3,5,7).

Linear connections are sparse; indeed, the referential tetrachord's saturation of the pc field precludes linearity as a tonal device, since, at least in the outer sections, some pcs needed to fill skips between members of the tetrachord simply are not available.

"LA FLÛTE DE PAN"

Composed in 1897–98,[12] "La flûte de Pan" (*Chansons de Bilitis* I) falls into seven sections defined by pauses and changes in thematic-harmonic materials (mm. 6, 7, 17, 22) or by reprises (mm. 12 and 27).

The distribution from section to section of referential versus subsidiary pcs is depicted in the excerpts from each section that comprise example 2.4A. Pitch classes that serve as referents for the song as a whole are notated using open noteheads; pcs that function as temporary tonal referents are identified by stems, though their noteheads are filled.

Three or four pcs predominate within each section through reiteration, agogic accent, doubling, register isolation, and placement as first, last, highest, lowest, and registrally isolated notes (see table 2.2). While it is convenient to think of them

TABLE 2.2. PCs emphasized within
each section of "La flûte de Pan"

Section	PCs			
1		3,	8,	11
2		3,	8,	11
3		3,	8,	11
4		3,	8,	11
5	1,		6,	10
6	0, 2, 4,	7		
7		3,	8,	11

as forming tonic chords in various keys—G♯ minor (8,11,3), F♯ major (6,10,1), and C major (0,4,7, with pc 2 as an auxiliary tone)—these are not "keys" in the traditional sense, either because the appropriate scales are incomplete, or because the weight accorded pcs unrelated to the designated key renders its ascription equivocal. Aspects of harmony also militate against unambiguous key associations. In section 2, for example, for which pcs 8,11,3 serve as referents, the prominent harmonies are C♯ major and E major. As example 2.4A shows, the pcs that fulfill referential roles for each section do so because of quantitative and qualitative emphasis accorded to them rather than to other pcs. Example 2.4B summarizes the changes in tonal referents across the song. (Register placement in the example is abstract, and voice leading is not implied.)

Linear motions that connect and point towards referential pcs are abundant, except in mm. 15–16. These two bars occur just prior to the beginning of section 5, coincidental with the change of referential pc content from 8,11,3 to 6,10,1, and they are "transitional" in the sense that the referential role of pcs 8,11,3 is weakened in preparation for their replacement in m. 17 by pcs 6,10,1 as temporary referents. Measures 15–16 eliminate pcs 8,11,3 as foci for linear motions and temporarily assign more prominence to nonreferential pitches; this opens the way for pcs 6,10,1 to assume referential roles for the next section—an active process in which one group of tonal referents replaces another gradually, rather than abruptly. It is not unlike the progressive process observed in the fanfare from *Le martyre de Saint-Sébastien,* where pcs are introduced gradually and accorded increasing prominence.

Pitch classes 6,10,1 appear frequently in sections 1–4, but their contexts suppress rather than project them. (They occur less often and for shorter durations than pcs 8,11,3 and are placed in the midst rather than at the boundaries of

Example 2.4. Referential pc saturation in "La flûte de Pan"

linear motions.) In section 5 the situation reverses as context projects pcs 6,10,1 and suppresses 8,11,3. As preparation for section 6, where pcs 0,2,4,7 are to serve as referents, pcs 4,7,2 emerge prominently at the end of section 5 (especially mm. 20–21). Pitch classes 10,1 supplement the pc content of section 6 but do not assume significant roles. Section 7 marks a return to pcs 8,11,3. Pitch classes 5 and 9, which appear persistently but sparely throughout (as E♯ and A), have a role independent of the tonal scheme.

The seven sections set the poem's four stanzas. Formal junctures do not always coincide with those of the poem; they often overlap, so that the flow of text and music is punctuated by junctures in one or the other dimension or both, by turns. (Figure 2.3 aligns the poem with the formal plan.) This does not preclude inter-connections between text and music, however. Besides many obvious examples of text expression (for example, the triplets of mm. 8–9 suggest "trembling"), there are more fundamental connections, such as the changes in pc content that align with the poem's marked changes in sense and mood. After m. 17, where the text turns from the girl's narration of her encounter with Pan to the intrusion of the mundane world, pcs 8,11,3 are replaced by new referents 6,10,1. A few bars later, at m. 22, as she draws closer to that mundane world (she contemplates her mother's reaction to her absence), a new set of referents appears: 0,2,4,7. Given the aforementioned affective connections between pc referents and text, the return to the original referents in the instrumental coda helps to re-draw our attention to the sensual focus of the first three stanzas. As a constructional principle, these changes in referents invite comparison with changes of key in music that is more conventionally tonal. The practice of establishing correspon-dences between text and tonal referent is not especially innovative; it does, how-ever, show Debussy subtly accommodating a new way of handling tonal focus to old imperatives of text expression.

Subtle also are the reciprocal relationships between the song's proportions and the pacing of bar-line metric changes (table 2.3). The disproportionately brief second section (four bars) coincides with the poem's first vividly sensual meta-phor: "joined with white wax that is as sweet on my lips as honey."[13] The abrupt-ness of the change and the brevity of the passage attract attention. The change of metric pattern in section 6 (4,3,3,3,3 reversed to 3,3,3,3,4) acknowledges the abandonment of Pan's sensual world for the mundane world that the girl's mother represents.

In "La fille aux cheveux de lin," quantitative and qualitative emphasis conspire with harmony and voice leading to raise four pcs (10,1,3,6) to the status of tonal referents.

Harmony, voice leading, and other traditional harmonic conventions do not define tonality in "Voiles," but qualitative and quantitative principles do, includ-ing the retention of invariants that comprise the tonal referents (6,8,10). These invariants, moreover, reflect the whole-tone and diatonic characteristics that are embodied by turns in each of the piece's three sections.

The fanfare from Le martyre de Saint-Sébastien reveals an important processive feature in its gradual introduction of pcs and increased emphasis accorded to

FIGURE 2.3. Formal plan for "La flûte de Pan"

Division	Measures	Text alignment (in stanzas)
Section 1	1	(16)[a]	1. Pour le jour des Hyacinthies, il m'a donné une syrinx faite de roseaux bien taillés,
Section 2	6	(4)	unis avec la blanche cire qui est douce à mes lèvres comme le miel.
Section 3	7	(16)	2. Il m'apprend à jouer, assise sur ses genoux; mais je suis un peu tremblante. Il en joue après moi, si doucement que je l'entends à peine.
Section 4	12	(16)	3. Nous n'avons rien à nous dire, tant nous sommes près l'un de l'autre; mais nos chansons veulent se répondre, et tour à tour nos bouches s'unissent sur la
Section 5	17	(16)	flûte. 4. Il est tard; voici le chant des grenouilles vertes qui commence avec la nuit.
Section 6	22	(16)	Ma mère ne croira jamais que je suis restée si longtemps à chercher ma ceinture perdue.
Section 7	27	(16)	
	30		

Reprises

[a]Durations of sections measured in quarter notes

TABLE 2.3. Metric scheme and formal
units for "La flûte de Pan"

Section	Length[a]	Metric scheme[b]
1	16	4,3,3,3,3
2	4	4
3	16	4,3,3,3,3
4	16	4,3,3,3,3
5	16	4,3,3,3,3
6	16	3,3,3,3,4
7	14	4,4,3,3

[a]Measured in quarter notes
[b]The unit of pulse is the quarter note.

them subsequently. As in "Voiles," its tonality is more readily revealed through quantitative and qualitative means of emphasis (including invariants) than through harmony and voice leading.

"La flûte de Pan" evinces a more complex treatment of tonal referents. The presence of secondary referents, assigned to internal formal subdivisions, contributes to the hierarchy among referents, and between referents and subsidiary pcs. This song embodies many features cited in the other examples, including the processive feature of gradual and systematic replacement of tonal referents—features that confirm the extent to which quantitative and qualitative emphasis (rather than harmony and voice leading) impose tonality on the pitch materials.

Since it is an earlier work than the other examples, the tonal complexities of "La flûte de Pan" cannot be ascribed to sophistication acquired through experience; more likely they arise in reaction to the subtle complexities of the text, which demand a complex expression. Wenk implies that Debussy's vocal pieces exhibit more daring and innovation than do his contemporaneous instrumental works.[14] To the extent that this is true (it appears to depend on the texts, better poetry receiving decidedly more remarkable musical settings than mediocre poetry),[15] it reflects the importance he assigned to text expression—the necessity for congruence between music and text, not only in superficial matters, but in aspects of structure and process as well.

ADDITIONAL ASPECTS OF TONAL FOCUS

The remainder of this chapter addresses some special aspects of tonality that are related but tangential to quantitative and qualitative emphasis, and are not addressed by voice leading and harmony. Each example isolates a single feature: the first two offer innovative reformulations of variation technique in which tonal referents play an important role; the remainder illuminate the special place occupied by the subdominant in Debussy's music, in particular its relationship to that quality which is often characterized as "modal."

Tonal Referents and Variation Technique

Prélude à "L'après-midi d'un faune." Composed in 1894,[16] only one year after the String Quartet, the *Prélude à "L'après-midi d'un faune"* marks a step in a different direction in its avoidance of traditional formal procedures in favor of an innovative reformulation of variation technique. The piece consists of a series of seventeen passages based on the same fundamental shape: a direct descent in predominantly stepwise motion followed by a rapid ascent to (or near) the initial pc. Except for the original and final statements, the descent is always harmonized by two chords, one for each of the boundary pitches. The referential boundary pcs are 1,7; the referential timbre is solo flute; there is no referential harmonization (there cannot be, since the original version is unharmonized). The composition's inner dynamics entail a series of variants on this fundamental shape whose modifications become progressively more radical and engage most elements, including harmonization, referential pcs, boundary interval, register, timbre (in-strumental assignment), and rhythm. The process culminates in m. 55 (whose variant is the furthest removed from the original flute theme), after which its course reverses as subsequent variants regress towards a close counterpart of the original version in m. 94. The last variant (in the horns) invokes an entirely new, lower register and harmonizes each note of the descent; though its surface differs markedly from the source theme, its similar rhythmic contour and chromatic, stepwise motion tie this variant to its model.

Example 2.5 catalogs the variants. Five of them reharmonize the original boundary pcs (1,7); the remainder transpose one or both (mm. 23, 31, 34, 37, 55, 63, 79, 83, 86, 90, 100, 107). The motive is passed to other instruments on nine occasions, and the boundary interval is frequently altered, either compressed (to a P4, D4, or m3) or expanded (to a P5). Throughout the composition's series of

Example 2.5. Harmonic settings of motivic boundary pitches in *Prélude à "L'après-midi d'un faune"*

permutations, only the motive's essence—the stepwise descent and ascent between two pcs at least a third apart, and the use of two harmonies for its setting—remains invariable.

"Pour les sonorités opposées." More than two decades separate the *Prélude à "L'après-midi d'un faune"* from "Pour les sonorités opposées" (Douze études II),[17] yet the two share a connection in the principle of presenting a rather free series of variants. But whereas in *Prélude à "L'après-midi d'un faune"* the subject of variation is a melodic contour and its setting in harmony, in "Pour les sonorités opposées" the subject is a pc and its setting in (or, more properly, against) harmonies.

Pitch class 8 saturates the etude, withheld only twice (in mm. 53–58 and 71–73) for only nine of ninety-five measures. Pitch class content, doublings, and register distribution are shown in the reduction of example 2.6 (which shows pc 8 throughout in open noteheads); table 2.4 summarizes pc content by phrase and section. The scope and variety of sonorities generated is remarkably diverse.

The only conventional sonority that enfolds pc 8 is the E major triad (which is outlined in the motive of mm. 31, 59, and 68); all other sonorities "oppose" pc 8 with dissonances. The composition's vitality derives from the constant shifts in the nature of this opposition (its specific pc manifestation from moment to moment) and in settings that range from the E major triad (of which pc 8 is a consonant member) to sonorities that exclude it altogether (those of mm. 53–58, for example).

The piece ends on a tetrachord whose function is rendered ambiguous by the doublings and register assignments of its pcs. Is it to be understood as a C♯ minor tonic triad with an added seventh, or as an E major tonic triad with an added sixth? Various key-signature changes imply modulations, and G♯ minor, C♯ minor, and E major take turns as plausible keys. But even as they point to key and tonal center as operational principles, these tonal allusions oppose one anothers' primacy; as a consequence, the enigmatic nature of tonality in "Pour les sonorités opposées" leaves open the way for pc 8 to assert its special kind of primacy, not as a tonal center in the usual sense, but as a solitary constant in an ever-changing pc field.

The example and table illustrate the ubiquity of pc 8 and the remarkable variety of its settings. While other pcs recur often—especially pcs 4,5,11 (compare the tallies in table 2.5 to those in table 2.4)—none appears as often as pc 8. Table 2.5 shows the proportion of saturation among pcs for the piece as a whole, but saturation varies considerably from section to section (as is shown in table 2.4). Pitch class 5, for example, appears nearly as often as pc 8 in section 1, as do pcs 5,10 in section 2, pcs 3,11 in section 3, pcs 1,6, in section 10, and so on. "In "Pour les sonorités opposées," changes in pc saturation contribute to formal definition in the same way that changes in motivic materials are form defining; the association of a specific pc content with a specific location helps to distinguish formal boundaries.

The composition's title is a clue to the source of the etude's dynamism in the conflict between a stable element (pc 8) and its fluctuant harmonic setting.

What links the *Prélude à "L'après-midi d'un faune"* to "Pour les sonorités op-

Example 2.6. Harmonic settings of pc 8 in "Pour les sonorités opposées"

posées" is Debussy's rather free conception of variation, which eschews morphological aspects of musical materials in favor of processive ones. His "themes" are not merely harmonic progressions, nor melodic contours, nor specified durations. In *Prélude à "L'après-midi d'un faune"* the constants are two (unspecified) notes that define the boundaries of a motion. The second tone is lower than the first (to what extent is unspecified), and each is harmonized (but the chords are unspecified). In the more radical "Pour les sonorités opposées," a principle of opposition uses harmony as a medium for a constant (pc 8), which is placed in a

TABLE 2.4. PC content of sonorities keyed to the
formal plan in "Pour les sonorités opposées"

Division	Measures	PC content
Section 1	1	8,9
	4	0, 4, 8, 11
	5	2, 5, 8,9
	6	2, 5, 8
	7	0, 5, 8, 10
Section 2	8	2, 5, 8, 10
	9	4,5, 8, 10
	10	1, 5, 8, 10
	12	0, 5, 8, 10
	14	2, 4,5, 8
Section 3	15	3, 5, 8, 11
	15	1, 5, 8
	16	3,4, 8, 11
	25	3, 6, 8, 11
Section 4	31	4, 8, 11
	33	0, 5, 8, 10
Section 5	34	0, 2, 5, 8
	35	2, 5, 7,8
Section 6	36	1, 4, 8,9
	36	3,4, 8, 11
Section 7	38	4, 6, 8, 10,11
Section 8	53	0, 5, 9
	59	4, 8, 11
Section 9	60	1,2, 6, 8, 11
	62	0, 2, 5, 8
Section 10	63	3, 6, 8, 11
	65	1,2, 6, 8,9
	65	1, 3, 7,8, 10
	66	1, 6, 8
Section 11	68	4, 8, 11
	69	0, 5,6, 8,9
	74	1, 4, 8, 11
	(75)	

series of pc settings. These pieces by no means account for all of Debussy's ideas
on the subject of variation. As we shall see, *Jeux* and the Sonata for flute, viola, and
harp are among his late essays of this type. A precursor is the String Quartet, in
which variation technique plays a central role.[18]

TABLE 2.5. Tallies of pcs in sonorities
from "Pour les sonorités opposées"

Pitch class	Number[a]
8	30
5	16
11	12
4	11
2	9
0	8
1	8
10	8
6	7
3	6
9	5
7	2

[a]Number of sonorities in which each pc is
found (see table 2.4)

The Subdominant Harmony and Scale Step

As a Component of Tonal Motions. The subdominant often pairs with the tonic to form boundaries for middleground tonal elaborations, and the reduced role of the dominant (evident in the absence of bass arpeggiation) further elevates the subdominant to a position of great importance. In view of the increased emphasis accorded the subdominant in nineteenth-century tonal relations,[19] Debussy's treatment of this harmony and scale step should be regarded as a logical extension of tendencies already set in motion by his tonal antecedents.

"Des pas sur la neige" (Préludes I) provides good illustrations. It begins (mm. 1–4) in D minor with an ostinato in the d¹ register that unfolds the root and third of the tonic (ex. 2.7A); mm. 5–6 employ subdominant and tonic chords as boundaries for a descending passing motion in the D-register. In mm. 26–27 the opening ostinato recurs, but initially harmonized by the subdominant triad, for which the tonic serves as a goal (ex. 2.7B). The last three bars consist solely of alternating first and fourth scale degrees (mm. 34–36), following arpeggiation of the subdominant under the familiar ostinato in mm. 32–33 (ex. 2.7C).

In "La fille aux cheveux de lin" the subdominant is prominent in the plagal cadence that closes the first phrase (ex. 2.8), and even more so at the reprise of mm. 28–30 (not illustrated). That the subdominant's pc content lies embedded in the dominant-eleventh chord (as its upper triad) may partially account for Debussy's preference for this more complex form of dominant sonority in the authentic cadences of mm. 9–10, 15–16, and 18–19.[20]

Similar examples of subdominant emphasis abound, especially in the piano music. See, for example, "Doctor Gradus ad Parnassum" (*Children's Corner*), mm. 7–10 (which mixes IV⁷ and iv⁷ in C major; ex. 2.9) and mm. 51–54. "The Little Shepherd" (*Children's Corner*) also makes much of the mixture subdominant triad

Example 2.7. Subdominant emphasis in "Des pas sur la neige"

(iv in A major): the subdominant third, d^2-f^2, is unfolded at the close of the first phrase and the complete (minor) subdominant triad is arpeggiated in mm. 5–7, an octave lower in the bass.

In minor keys, when the subdominant is transformed into a major triad by alteration, its juxtaposition against the tonic produces a Dorian model effect (provided the dominant is absent). The Violin Sonata begins with just such a passage in G minor (mm. 1–7); "La flûte de Pan" contains several (in mm. 2, 5, and 29 in G♯ minor), as does the "Noël des enfants qui n'ont plus de maisons" (where altered and diatonic forms of the subdominant are juxtaposed). Examples such as these may be found throughout Debussy's oeuvre.

Example 2.8. Plagal cadence in "La fille aux cheveux de lin"

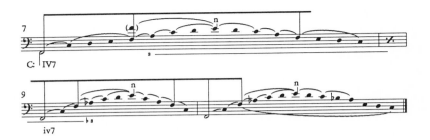

Example 2.9. Subdominant pedal in "Doctor Gradus ad Parnassum"

Neighbor-Note Motion. Upper neighbor-note diminutions of the tonic third and fifth always invoke subdominant chord tones (without necessarily invoking subdominant scale-step function). Such motions abound in the examples cited in chapter 1: in the "Noël des enfants qui n'ont plus de maisons" (ex. 1.6), the subdominant appears prominently in root position in mm. 4–6 (though at a higher structural level it serves mainly to prolong the tonic triad through upper neighbor-note motion). The third of the subdominant appears in both diatonic and mixture forms (degrees 6 and ♯6) evoking the Dorian modal effect. Similar examples may be found in mm. 12–13 and elsewhere.

Modality. Modality is often cited as an important feature of Debussy's music,[21] and certainly one encounters many passages flavored by orderings of diatonic pitch materials that are evocative of Dorian or Phrygian rather than minor, and of Lydian or Mixolydian rather than major.

Modal effects often arise from chromatic alteration, as in some of the examples cited above. A different kind of effect results from emphasis on nontonic scale steps where tonicizing chromaticism is avoided. For major keys, extended subdominant or dominant prolongation without tonicization of these scale degrees alludes, respectively, to Lydian and Mixolydian modes. If "La cathédrale engloutie" (Préludes I) initially sounds Mixolydian, it is due to the emphasis on the fifth scale step at the beginning (even though the stepwise descent in the bass from G to C in mm. 1–14 points clearly to C as tonic, which G serves as dominant). The E pedal throughout mm. 5–13 combines with the emphasis on E and B in the melodic line and doublings to project the sound of the Lydian mode. The scale is E–(F♯)–G♯–A♯–B–C♯–D♯, with E as "final." (The absence of F♯ does not affect the modal color.) The fragility of this kind of modality is apparent in mm. 47–54, where the same melody appears with the same scale, but over a pedal G♯, now clearly the pure minor mode with G♯ functioning as tonic (or, at a higher level, as a tonicized dominant in C♯ minor). The Lydian color is entirely absent.[22]

In minor keys, emphasis on subdominant and dominant scale steps without tonicizing chromaticism creates, respectively, Dorian and Phrygian modal effects. The first six measures of "La danse de Puck" (Préludes I) suggest Dorian mode in their emphasis on F, even though the key signature and the triad unfolded in mm. 2, 4, and 5 point towards C minor.

Two pieces whose dates of composition embrace most of Debussy's mature works illustrate innovative adaptations of variation technique along related lines for which tonal focus plays a crucial role.

In *Prélude à "L'après-midi d'un faune,"* a theme introduced in the opening bars serves as subject for a series of variations. It possesses several characteristics for reference, including pitch (1,7 are referents), timbre (for which flute is referential), register (whose reference is the octave above g^1), harmony (whose constant is a pair of unspecified chords, one each for the descent's boundary pitches), and rhythm (whose constant is a sustained note followed by rapid notes, best seen in the original subject, m. 1). While pitch represents only one among several points of reference, its handling has been singled out for attention because it illustrates another way in which pcs accorded special roles assume structural importance— in this case, as referents contributing to a vital process that unfolds from variant to variant.

In "Pour les sonorités opposées," pc 8 (projected prominently by contextual features such as octave doublings and special register assignments) serves as the only pc constant in a highly fluctuant pc field. The exits and entrances of other pcs throughout the work engender a dynamic aspect that helps to define the composition's formal plan, insofar as changes in pc content tend to coincide with formal partitions effected by other parameters (such as theme and texture), and to remain relatively constant within formal units. Pitch class 8 and its harmonic setting are the subjects of "Pour les sonorités opposées"; changes in setting are its variants.

The subdominant's crucial position in Debussy's tonal relations (exaggerated by the diminished role which he accords to the dominant) is manifest in many ways, including the upper neighbor-note diminutions of tonic third and fifth that permeate his voice leading, and his frequent exploitation of tonic/subdominant-versus-dominant/tonic ambiguity (heightened by modal mixture). Subdominant prolongations devoid of tonicizing chromaticism also account for much of the superficial modality in his music, in particular Dorian and Lydian effects (just as untonicized dominant prolongations account for Phrygian and Mixolydian effects).

If "tonality" means music in which harmony and voice leading pervasively organize and control pitch materials in a matrix of interrelation that embraces a hierarchy of structural levels, then some of Debussy's music is indeed tonal, and most of it, if not all, contains vestiges of tonality (although, stripped of the deeper tonal structure that gives them their meaning, these remnants confound as much as they guide). But considered only from this perspective, even his most conventional diatonic music exhibits an impoverished kind of tonality (compared with the tonal masters whose works are idealized by the Schenkerian model), in which relations are concentrated on the musical surface. Moreover, certain kinds of prolongation are inordinately copious (such as arpeggiation and neighbor-note motion), while others are inordinately scarce (passing diminutions, linear progressions, and bass arpeggiation).

But if "tonal" means music in which some pcs serve as referents for others—with distinctions resting on contextual features (including but not limited to harmony and voice leading) that are capable of projecting certain pcs to prominence while suppressing others, and that are susceptible of organization into hierarchies and structures—then all of Debussy's music is tonal (though not always in the same way), and the range of Debussy's tonality is as rich as it is diverse. In part 2 I will address the ramifications of Debussy's reformulated definition of tonality for other aspects of pitch organization.

PART II
THE PITCH-CLASS SET GENERA

THREE
FOUR GENERA

The topic of part 2 is Debussy's pitch resources. In chapter 3 I identify and describe, one by one, what I call the pitch-class (pc) set genera. My medium is a series of analyses of works chosen for the clarity with which each exposes a given genus. In chapter 4 I will survey compositions throughout Debussy's oeuvre, to see how his rather straightforward handling of these resources in his first mature works gradually evolved into a more intricate technique that reached its full flowering in his late compositions. Instrumental works provide most of the illustrations.[1] Set theory provides efficacious tools for examining intervallic relations that are germane to Debussy, and I assume that the reader is familiar with common set-theoretic terminology and concepts as explicated by standard sources.[2] Appendix 1 provides a reference list of all 220 pc sets.[3] Detailed analyses that focus on different facets of resources and techniques are introduced, as necessary, by brief essays that treat special aspects of pc set relations.

Tonality, the subject of part 1, receives some attention here, especially as it relates to specificity of pc content as a manifestation of general possibilities that inhere in the pc set genera.[4] And although it is more a subsidiary topic than a main one, the path of my argument will intersect with another issue: To what extent may we regard as tonal the pitch materials in all of Debussy's music, and to what extent do they exhibit organization according to principles other than that of tonality?

MOTIVES AND SETS IN "LA FILLE AUX CHEVEUX DE LIN"

Debussy composed many pieces using diatonic materials[5] as primary pc resources, and he accorded them favored status long after he had integrated other pc materials into his vocabulary. "La fille aux cheveux de lin" is just one of many wholly or predominantly diatonic pieces in his oeuvre.[6] Its accessibility and familiarity to most readers facilitates detailed discussion and aural reference, and because it was among the tonal examples cited in part 1, we gain the advantage of insights acquired from opposing perspectives. "La fille aux cheveux de lin" represents a particular type of composition found in Debussy's oeuvre: that which employs a single pc set genus throughout. Such pieces invariably use the diatonic genus.

Since Debussy's handling of intervallic relations seems likely to have issued from motivic considerations, my approach is to identify the motives that serve as resources for the composition's thematic materials, the pc sets that these resources embody, and a processive feature that links them.

"La fille aux cheveux de lin" consists of a series of brief contrasting phrases.[7] Each embodies one or two of five distinct yet interrelated motives. The composition's coherence may be attributed, in part, to its spare thematic inventory, but cohesiveness also arises from intervallic characteristics shared among several conspicuous diatonic pc sets. The relationship between motivic organization and set structure is intimate, since the motives embody the pc sets and the sets are disposed in motives.

Example 3.1 provides a thematic catalog for the prelude, and figure 3.1 presents a formal plan that partitions the piece into phrases. The catalog is arranged in a chronological sequence that shows motives with their rhythms and main harmonies, and identifies important sets. The figure includes a list of sets that appear in each phrase, as well as important cadences and other harmonies. The reader should refer to the example and figure throughout the following discussion.

The First Five Phrases (mm. 1–14)

The first phrase (mm. 1–4) exposes motives A and X. Motive A's essence is its skips, which arpeggiate major and minor triads that combine to unfold a minor-minor seventh-chord. However interpreted, three small pc sets are clearly projected: two inversively equivalent forms of trichord 3–11, and tetrachord 4–26. Earlier I commented about the significance of both the triads and the tetrachord as tonal referents; they also constitute significant pc sets (forms of trichord 3–11, for example, are ubiquitous both as chords and arpeggios). A crucial pentachord, set 5–27, also emerges in this first phrase. Concealed in the conjunction of chord and line, it appears initially in mm. 1–2 and again, in inversion (transposed), in mm. 3–4.[8] Motive X is also exposed here. It consists of four notes descending stepwise. The plagal cadence of mm. 2–3, to which motive X is appended, provides closure for the phrase and establishes a model for others to follow. The function of motive X (set 4–11) will become clearer as we proceed.

Motive B appears in the second phrase. It shares a characteristic anapestic rhythm (exposed in both divisional and subdivisional durations) and an angular contour with motive A, though it changes direction more often. Its pitch content yields set 5–35 (the source set for the pentatonic scale), which serves as a resource for motives yet to come, while the bass voice's counter-theme underscores the significance of tetrachord 4–26 (in its original transposition), from which it is generated. The abundance of major and minor triads in the harmonies of motive B affirms the role of set 3–11 as a crucial pitch construct. (See the alternative

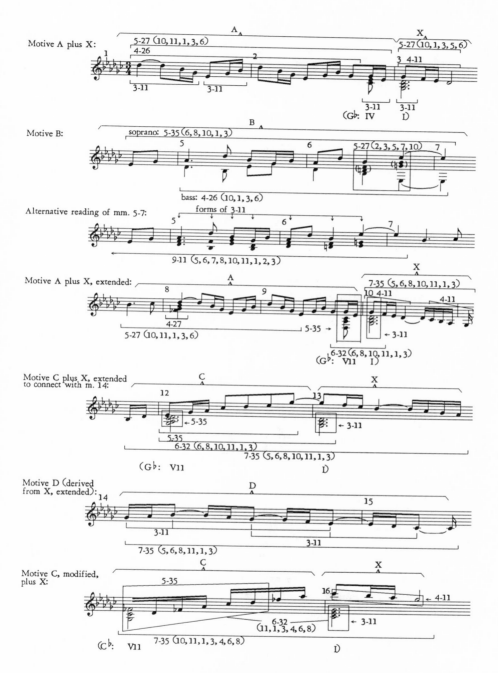

Example 3.1. Motivic catalog for "La fille aux cheveux de lin"

Example 3.1. *Continued*

FIGURE 3.1. Formal plan for "La fille aux cheveux de lin"

Phrase	Measures	Motive	Key	Important sets
1	1	A, X	$G\flat$: IV–I	3–11, 4–26, 5–27, 4–11
2	5	B	$E\flat$: V–I	3–11, 5–35, 7–35, 9–11
3	8	A, X	$G\flat$: V^{11}–I	3–11, 4–26, 5–27, 5–35, 6–32, 4–11, 7–35, (8–22)
4	12	C, X	V^{11}–I	3–11, 5–35, 6–32, 4–11, 7–35
5	14	D	V^{11}–I	3–11, 4–11, 7–35, 5–27
6	15	C, X	$G\flat$: I pedal $C\flat$: V^{11}–I	3–11, 5–35, 6–32, 4–11, 7–35, 5–27
7	17	X	$G\flat$: ii^9–V^9	4–11, 5–27, (5–34), 5–35, 6–32, 7–35
8	19	C	$E\flat$: V^{11}–I	3–11, 5–35, 6–32 (to 4–11 in m. 22)
9	22	X	$A\flat$: V–I	4–11, (3–9), 7–35, 8–23, 9–9
10 (Reprise of pc sets)	24	A (concealed)	$G\flat$: ii^9–V	3–11, 4–26, 5–27, 5–35, 6–32, 7–35
11 (Reprise of theme)	28	A, X	$G\flat$: IV–vi–I	3–11, 4–26, 5–27, 5–35, 6–32, 4–11, 7–35
12	33	D		3–11, 5–27, 5–35, 6–32, (4–11), 7–35
13	35	C	$G\flat$: ii^6_4–I	5–35, 3–11, 6–32
	(39)			

reading of mm. 5–7 in example 3.1). The chromaticism in m. 6 adds two new pcs for a total accumulation of nine; they form set 9–11, complement of 3–11.

Motive A returns in mm. 8–11 with five important modifications: it is harmonized by major-minor seventh-chords;[9] an anacrusis of two notes is added; the appended motive X is extended and encompasses two octaves of descending stepwise motion (which yields set 7–35); the earlier plagal cadence is replaced by an authentic cadence that employs a V^{11} chord; and the phrase's anacrusis adds pc 11 to motive A's tetrachord, which results in another articulation of pentachord 5–27 in the same transposition as mm. 1–2. The cadence at the end of motive A employs pentachord 5–35 as its penultimate chord (the V^{11}), which combines with the tonic chord of resolution to form a new collection: hexachord 6–32.

In the first three phrases, motive A (conjoined to motive X) and motive B are presented and harmonized as so to project prominently the following pc sets: 3–11 and 5–27 (each in two inversely equivalent forms), 4–26 and 5–35 (one form each, no distinct inversions being possible).[10] The extension of motive X in mm. 10–11 adds set 7–35 to the catalog (disposed to project two conjunct transpositions of tetrachord 4–11). The modified cadence (from mm. 2–3) that closes the reprise of motive A projects as a vertical construct (and thereby affirms) pentatonic 5–35 (the V^{11} chord), and the dominant and tonic chords conjoin to form hexachord 6–32.

The pc sets exposed thus far (3–11, 4–11, 4–26, 5–27, 5–35, 6–32, 7–35, 9–11) form a group that are closely connected through inclusion relations—relations that are all the more striking because with only two exceptions[11] the pc content of these sets' initial appearances explicitly exposes the subset-superset interrelations through invariance (see ex. 3.2).

The hexachord formed by the cadence (mm. 9–10) provides a focus for important motivic and subset-superset relations; set 6–32 is formed by the conjunction of 5–35 and 3–11, the chords that harmonize the union of motives A and

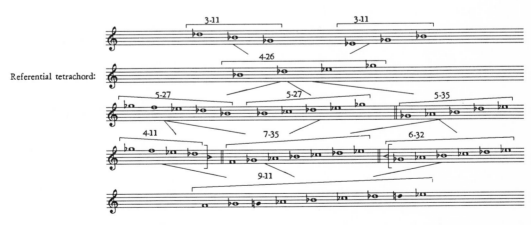

Example 3.2. Matrix of subset-superset relations about 4–26, showing invariance among first forms used

X, and it is a subset of set 7–35 in mm. 11. Sets 5–35, 6–32, and 7–35 are among those very few diatonic sets whose interval vectors (ivs) possess as many instances as possible of ic 5. The significance of this feature (shared among only seven pc sets) will be discussed shortly; for now we may think of hexachord 6–32 as a special set that consists of pentachord 5–35 plus one pc, such that a second form of the pentachord is generated (and can be heard embedded in) the hexachord. Set 7–35 is in a similar relationship with hexachord 6–32 (and contains 5–35 as a subset in three forms).

The phrase of mm. 12–13 presents motive C, to which motive X is appended (with an extension). Motive C shares motive B's characteristic anapestic rhythm and its general contour of steps mixed with skips.[12] The pc content of motives C and X, plus their harmonization, derives from now-familiar sets that culminate in a familiar sequence: (5–35 + 3–11 = 6–32) + 4–11 (superimposed) = 7–35.

Motive D first appears in m. 14. It exhibits close connections with motive X, whose stepwise contour it emulates and whose dactylic rhythm it transforms to iambic. Changes of direction and pauses on longer notes project pcs that form interlocking triads (forms of 3–11) within an overall pc content generated by set 7–35.

So far we have heard "La fille aux cheveux de lin" as a series of contrasting passages that alternate four distinct motives (A through D), to which a fifth (X) is often appended. Each motive is closely associated with crucial pc sets: motive A with trichord 3–11 and superset 7–35; motive X with sets 4–11, 5–27, and 7–35; motives B and C with pc set 5–35; motive D with 3–11, 6–32, and 7–35. A subtle process operates within most of the aforementioned passages, which contain cadences or less idiomatic successions of chords: plagal (mm. 2–3), authentic (V^{11}–I in mm. 6, 9–10, 12–13, 15–16, 18–19, 19–21, 23), half (ii^9–V in mm. 27), IV–vi–I (mm. 28–32), ii_4^6–I (mm. 35–36). Each time, sets 5–35, 3–11, 6–32, and, usually, 4–11 and 7–35 are projected *in sequence:* (5–35 + 3–11 = 6–32) + 4–11 = 7–35. (Sets 5–35 and 3–11 are articulated as chords, 4–11 as a stepwise line.) In spite of changes of key (transposition) and varying harmonic formulae, we hear the same sequence of sets repeated over and over.

Motivic and Set Organization in mm. 15–39

Motives C and X provide the thematic material for each of the three phrases in mm. 15–21, while their pc set content combines with that of the authentic cadences to unfold the sequences 5–35 + 3–11 = 6–32 (extended, in mm. 15–16, to include + 4–11 [superimposed] = 7–35). Motive X is the source of the melodic material for mm. 22–23, harmonized by triads. The chromaticism (C♭, C♮) augments the content to eight pcs that form set 8–23, which is another special diatonic set whose intervallic content is especially rich in ic 5. The sequence of sets recurs here, but with a modification in ordering: (5–35 + 4–11 [juxtaposed, overlapping] = 6–32) + 3–11 (subimposed) = 7–35.

Motive A and tetrachord 4–26 (in its original transposition) serve as sources for the motivic and pc set materials of mm. 24–27. The change of harmony in m.

25 adds pcs 8,11 to form the familiar hexachord 6–32. The half cadence at m. 27 consists of a pentachord on beat 2 (a new transposition of set 5–27) and a triad, which conjoin to form set 7–35. Set 5–27 also appears as the bass line in mm. 24–25 (in its original transposition: 10,11,1,3,6). The pc content of the bass line for mm. 26–27 is derived from set 5–35 (the A♭ in m. 27 adds pc 8 to tetrachord 10,1,3,6). Set 4–11 also appears in m. 27, in its original transposition, concealed in the stepwise thirds of the left hand. Thus are *all* of the important pc sets projected in this passage—3–11, 4–26, 5–27, 5–35, 6–32, 7–35, 4–11—and *all* occur in their original transpositions.[13] Set off sharply from its neighbors by ritardandos and pauses, as well as by a sharp diminuendo and shifts in texture and register, this passage's return to the pc content of the first thirteen measures anticipates the nearly literal thematic reprise at m. 28, as does the rhythmic transition from increasingly active mm. 12–23 to languorous mm. 28–30.

The reprise in mm. 28–32 incorporates four important changes: motive A is placed in a higher register; the C♭ major triad is articulated ahead of the motive and is sustained (with important tonal implications noted in part 1 above); motive X is again extended (to encompass an octave) and its durations are lengthened; and a submediant triad is interpolated between the subdominant and tonic harmonies. The sustained subdominant chord draws attention to the C♭ of set 5–27 (which recurs here in its original transposition); the three chords of mm. 28–32 (IV–vi–I) form 5–27 again (in the same transposition) and demonstrate the importance of pc content and sets, rather than traditional harmonic progressions, as sources of harmonic unity. The passing tone of m. 30 (a♭[1]) adds a sixth pc to the harmonic content of these measures (to form hexachord 6–32) and a fifth pc to that of the melodic line, which it counterpoints (10,1,3,6 + 8 = 5–35). The extension of motive X in mm. 31–32 again yields 7–35, partitioned (as in mm. 10–11) into conjunct forms of tetrachord 4–11.

Measures 33–34 employ motive D in a variant that restricts the line's pc content to hexachord 6–32. Within the stepwise line, tetrachord 4–26 (in its original transposition) is formed by the notes projected through pauses and changes of direction plus the neighbor-note, d♭[1] (in m. 34). It also occurs (in the same transposition) under each appearance of e♭[1] in these bars. The overall pc content of mm. 33–34 yields 7–35 in its original form, and pentachord 5–27 is prominent as the sum of chord and line in m. 33 (in the second transposition from m. 3).

Pentatonic set 5–35 emerges conspicuously in the upper line of m. 35. The last four bars sustain a G♭ major triad, which combines with 5–35 of m. 35 to produce hexachord 6–32 in its original form, thus completing for the last time the sequence: 5–35 + 3–11 = 6–32.

An Early Sketch

As we have seen, the opening bars expose all of the important diatonic sets together with their subset-superset interconnections. Seen in this light, a comparison of mm. 5–7 with an early sketch is instructive.[14] Example 3.3 reproduces

A. Debussy sketchbook (1906–11), p. 104

B. Transcription

Example 3.3. Sketch for "La fille aux cheveux de lin"

the sketch, together with a diplomatic transcription that adds clefs, key, and meter signatures.

The sketch (S) shows chords for mm. 1–2 that combine with the melody to create two inversely equivalent forms of pentachord 5–27. The first of these is identical to the first pentachord of the final version (FV), mm. 1–2 (after adjusting for S's transposition level a M3 higher); S's inversion form (m. 1/beat 3), however, does not correspond to that of FV (m. 3). The first cadence of S differs markedly from FV; S shows a V^{11}–I cadence whose first chord consists of set 5–35 (FV reserves this cadence for the reprise of mm. 8–11). Also, S mm. 4–6 are much more chromatic than FV mm. 5–7; in fact, S mm. 1–6 expose eleven pcs, compared with only nine for FV mm. 1–7.

Among the effects of Debussy's revisions are these: the two inversely equivalent forms of set 5–27 juxtaposed in FV mm. 2–3 both contain the opening theme's tetrachord as a subset; the pc form of 5–35 that appears first in the piece (FV mm. 5–7) also contains the tetrachord as a subset (whereas that of the cadence of FV mm. 9–10 does not); the reduced chromaticism of mm. 5–7 creates a complement relation between the overall pc content of the first seven bars (= 9–11) and the six forms of set 3–11 that provide the major and minor triads for the second phrase. Complement relations are addressed comprehensively in chapter 6; here it may be noted that the presence of six forms of a single set (3–11) in mm. 6–7 is typical, for such multiples usually occur embedded in one or more forms of the complement.

In short, Debussy's revision tightens the pc set relations considerably by rendering subset-superset relations among them explicit rather than implicit and by exposing the sets gradually, in an orderly fashion that permits the listener to compare and discover their interrelations. Yet the sketch shows that all of the crucial sets were present at a very early compositional stage (excepting 9–11, which completes the symmetry of the composition's pc matrix but on a level that is obscure).[15]

Tonal Referents

In my discussion of tonality in "La fille aux cheveux de lin" in chapter 2, pcs 10,1,3,6 of tetrachord 4–26 were designated as tonal referents. Here we may note that changes in pc material from point to point, whether viewed as modulations or merely as alternative transposition and inversion forms of pc sets, tend, ultimately, to emphasize certain pcs: in particular, pc 6 (mm. 1, 10, 24, 32, 36), pc 11 (mm. 16, 21), pc 3 (mm. 6, 19), and pc 8 (mm. 22, 23). Together they form a transposition of set 4–26 (3,6,8,11).

The pc set materials of "La fille aux cheveux de lin" are homogeneous in the extreme; all are diatonic (that is, subsets or supersets of set 7–35, source of the diatonic scale). Conspicuously conjoined throughout are three sets (5–35, 6–32, 7–35) whose interval contents project diatonic characteristics most strongly. As we have seen, these sets (along with 3–11 and 4–11) often form a recurrent sequence used to conclude phrases.

The composition also may be heard as a series of passages that contract and expand in length (within a range of one to six bars). Many combine two gestures—motives A and X, or motives C and X—into graceful arches whose contours contrast skips with steps. This series of reiterated gestures constituted of similar motivic and pc set materials fills the musical surface with constantly varying contours, registers, textures, and temporal spans.

Conventional harmonic progressions and cadences occur throughout, and these encourage an association with tonality; indeed, the prelude's sonorous surface is tonal. But the progressions and cadences are better suited to the realm of pc set relations than to tonality. (They conjoin, for example, to form series of characteristic sets and complement pairs.) As a consequence, they have little currency as traditional harmonic progressions. That is why there is no need for authentic cadences where previous events might lead us to expect them:—at the composition's close or in mm. 30–31. The constituent pc class sets of both the idiomatic and the nonidiomatic progressions accomplish a different type of pitch closure; despite changes of melody and harmony from phrase to phrase, the same small sets (3–11, 4–11, 5–27, 5–35) accrete repeatedly to form the same large sets (6–32, 7–35). While the piece sounds (and is) tonal, tonal focus in the conventional sense is perhaps less important than the intervallic characteristics of shapes and chords within the diatonic constellation of subsets and supersets about 7–35.

THE DIATONIC GENUS OF PC SETS

The large collections of pc materials that serve as abstract and concrete pitch resources for tonal pieces can be (and often are) represented by major and minor scales. These scales function as inventories; they are listed in set-theoretic fashion in table 3.1, notated in concrete transposition forms in example 3.4A. The diatonic genus of pc sets consists of set 7–35, which is source set for the major and pure minor scales, together with all of its subsets and supersets. Set 7–35 is cynosural for this genus; that is, its properties embody the essence of diatonicism and it serves as the primary focal point for interrelations among its family of subsets and supersets.

Diatonic sets are ubiquitous and crucial constituents of Debussy's musical language, significant for their sonorous characteristics quite apart from any tonal role they may (or may not) assume.[16] It is useful, therefore, to separate the issue of tonality—which has to do with special *ways* of using pc materials—from the

TABLE 3.1. Set names, sias, and ivs for major and minor scale collections

Scale	*Set*	*SIA*	*IV*
Major and pure minor[a]	7–35	1–2–2–1–2–2–2	254361
Harmonic minor	7–32	1–2–1–2–2–1–3	335442
Melodic minor, ascending	7–34	1–2–1–2–2–2–2	254442
Melodic minor, ascending, and descending forms combined	9–7	1–1–1–1–1–2–1–2–2	677673

[a]Arranged as a major scale the sia would read 2–2–1–2–2–2–1, a circular permutation of normal order. Similarly, the array for the harmonic minor scale (= pc set 7–32) is 2–1–2–2–1–3–1, and the ascending form of the melodic minor scale (= 7–34) is 2–1–2–2–2–2–1.

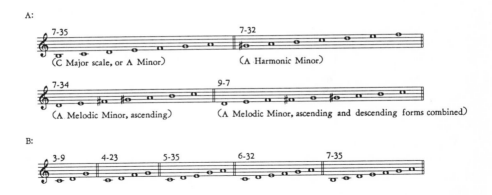

Example 3.4. Sets generated by major and minor scale forms, and characteristic diatonic sets

materials themselves. A literature exists that addresses properties and characteristics of diatonic pc sets.[17] I shall confine my remarks to those features that are especially cogent for Debussy's music.

Diatonic Sets and Their Properties

A complete list of sets for the diatonic genus appears in appendix 2, together with their successive-interval arrays (sias) and interval vectors (ivs.) An important feature is the relatively large number of symmetrical three-to-nine-note sets (identified by asterisks): twenty out of forty-seven.[18] Further investigation reveals that each nonsymmetrical set occurs as cynosural subset or superset in multiple, inversely equivalent forms; as a consequence, any form of any diatonic set bears a concrete connection with some transposition form of cynosural set 7–35; it is not necessary to interpose an abstract operation of inversion, and so inclusion relations among diatonic sets are never abstract. This property's practical ramifications lie in the realm of aural recognition: to associate the sound of a given set with its genus, its contents must map directly onto those of some specific transposition form of the cynosural set—in this case, 7–35. That all diatonic sets meet this requirement contributes to this genus's easy recognition compared with subsets and supersets that cluster about other, asymmetrical seven-note sets. As we shall see, symmetry is a feature exhibited by alternative pc set genera as well.

Characteristic Diatonic Sets

Five characteristic sets form a nucleus for the genus and are shown in table 3.2 and notated in example 3.4B; sets 5–35, 6–32, and 7–35 exhibit especially close connections.[19] The characteristic interval class is 5 (each is a true quartal chord), though among the larger sets ics 2 and 3 are strongly represented as well. Interval vectors confirm the close interconnections, for there is a positive correlation between set size and ic content. The number of entries for ic 2, for example, increases (or decreases) by one whenever the number of pcs increases (or de-

TABLE 3.2. Characteristic sets of the
diatonic genus

Set name	SIA	IV
3–9	2–5–5	010020
4–23	2–3–2–5	021030
5–35	2–2–3–2–3	032140
6–32	2–2–1–2–2–3	143250
7–35	1–2–2–1–2–2–2	254361

creases) by one; the same holds true for ics 3 and 5. Interval classes 1, 4, and 6 exhibit a similar tendency, though the correlation for these noncharacteristic ics is weaker.

Connections among the complete diatonic matrix are not so strong as within this nucleus, but ic 5 still predominates, with ics 2 and 3 well represented. The larger collections (five or more pcs) include a mix of whole and half steps among their sias, with whole steps predominant. The distribution by set size is markedly asymmetrical (owing to the relatively large size of cynosural set 7–35), with far more sets of five pcs or less.

Sets Related to the Diatonic Genus

Four sets are listed parenthetically in appendix 2 (4–Z15, 5–Z36, 6–Z47, and 6–Z48), a convention that identifies them as secondary members of the genus (since although they are not subsets of 7–35, their Z-correspondents are).

Of the four large sets that account for scalar resources used in diatonic-tonal music (see table 3.1 and ex. 3.4A), two are members of the diatonic genus (7–35 and 9–7). The other two (7–32 and 7–34) are not, but they share many diatonic subsets (see table 3.3). As we shall see in the analyses that follow, sets 7–32 and 7–34 appear frequently in Debussy's music, often in close proximity to passages saturated by the diatonic genus. They also occur frequently in near-diatonic passages as supersets of diatonic sets that are projected prominently in the form of motives and chords. Often these septachords (and the passages whose pc contents they bring to account) may be understood to issue from a process of distortion by means of chromaticism applied to diatonic sets (just as harmonic and melodic minor scales may be viewed as tonal distortions through chromatic alteration of the pure minor scale). We may consider this a manifestation of Debussy's post-Romantic tendencies.

THE DIATONIC AND WHOLE-TONE GENERA IN "VOILES"

We turn now to a piece that exploits the differences and interconnections between two contrasting pc set genera. The simplicity of pc materials in "Voiles" well illustrates Debussy's technique of juxtaposing different set genera in order to provide contrast, coherence, form, and vitality. The piece consists of three main

TABLE 3.3. Subset and superset relations among 7–35, 7–32, and 7–34

A. Subsets and supersets of 7–35 shared with 7–32 and 7–34

Set	7–32	7–34	Set	7–32	7–34
2–1	X	X	5–Z12	X	
2–2	X	X	5–20	X	
2–3	X	X	5–23	X	X
2–4	X	X	5–24		X
2–5	X	X	5–25	X	X
2–6	X	X	5–27	X	X
			5–29	X	X
3–2	X	X	5–34		X
3–4	X	X	5–35		X
3–5	X	X			
3–6	X	X	6–Z25	X	
3–7	X	X	6–33		X
3–8	X	X			
3–9	X	X	8–22		X
3–10	X	X	8–26	X	
3–11	X	X			
			9–6		X
4–8	X		9–7	X	X
4–10	X	X	9–9		X
4–11	X	X	9–11	X	X
4–13	X	X			
4–14	X	X	10–2	X	X
4–16	X	X	10–3	X	X
4–20	X		10–4	X	X
4–21		X	10–5	X	X
4–22	X	X			
4–23	X	X			
4–26	X	X			
4–27	X	X			
4–Z29	X	X			

B. Subsets and supersets of 7–35 excluded by 7–32 and 7–34

Set	7–32	7–34	Set	7–32	7–34
4–8		X	6–Z25		X
4–20		X	6–Z26	X	X
4–21	X		6–32	X	X
			6–33	X	
5–Z12		X			
5–20		X	8–22	X	
5–24	X		8–23	X	X
5–27		X	8–26		X
5–34	X				
5–35	X		9–6	X	
			9–9	X	

sections differentiated by their pc materials (see the detailed formal plan in figure 3.2). Pauses or changes of theme define partitions within these sections as noted in the column to the right of the vertical line. The scheme's asymmetrical proportions are as unusual as is its synthesis, in the third section, of elements from the first and second sections (hence the design's representation as A–B–A/B).

A single whole-tone scale (set 6–35) accounts for most of the material in the outer main sections; similarly, a pentatonic scale (set 5–35) is the basis for section 2. As noted earlier, set 5–35 is a characteristic member of the diatonic genus. Set 6–35 represents a different group, the whole-tone genus. The two scales share three invariants (pcs 6,8,10), which form trichord 3–6 (ex. 3.5A), whose significance as tonal referents was noted above.[20] It remains to point out that the composition's main theme (A) begins with a form of trichord 3–6, and that the trichord is projected in other themes as well (several are shown in example 3.5B; note how pcs 8,10,0 of the introductory gesture generate theme A and also appear in theme B).

In m. 31 the whole-tone scale is enriched by two more pcs (1,7). While no doubt their presence contributes to the climax that occurs here, they also interject new possibilities and interrelations. They augment the passage's overall content to eight pcs that form set 8–25, whose complement, 4–25, is prominently projected in this measure by the boundary pitches of the semitonal figures (ex. 3.5C). Set 4–25 is also conspicuous at other points (at mm. 36–37, for instance: see ex. 3.5D). Nine pcs account for the content of the entire piece. They form set 9–8 (as 0,1,2,3,4,6,7,8,10), whose complement, 3–8, is ubiquitous: it is formed at m. 5 by the last M3 of the gesture labeled X plus the first note of the B♭$_1$ pedal (10,0,4); it generates the ostinato in the inner voice at mm. 22–28 (0,2,6); it is formed by the pedal plus the ostinato for mm. 33–37 (10,2,4); it occurs in three transpositions as chords in mm. 56 and 58–61 (8,0,2; 0,4,6; 2,6,8); and it is the last harmony of the piece (0,4,6 in mm. 61–64).

Two features thus forge connections between pc resources, shapes, and harmonies: the concrete manifestation, through its embedding in themes, of invariant subset 3–6, which connects the whole-tone and pentatonic scales; and complement relations represented by prominent trichords (forms of 3–8) and tetrachords (4–25), which pair off either with the composition's total pc content or with that of whole-tone section 1. Contrast is achieved dramatically by the changes of genus at mm. 42 and 48—changes that are form defining, as is the addition of pcs 1,7 at m. 31, which contributes to this moment of maximum intensity thus far.[21]

The way in which pc materials engender a sense of dynamism is as intricate as it is subtle. Compared to the diatonic genus, the whole-tone genus's character is inherently more static due to its members' limited range of ic content, especially when supersets of the whole-tone scale are excluded; there are no m2s, m3s, P4s, or their inversional and compound equivalents. Nor do whole-tone sets evince much variation in the distribution of ics across their ivs. The whole-tone scale itself contains equal numbers of ics 2 and 4 and exactly half as many of ic 6 (6–35 =

FIGURE 3.2. Formal plan for "Voiles"

PC set genus	Measures			Motives, themes
Section 1 (A) Whole-tone genus (6–35 as 10,0,2,4,6,8)	1	(9)[a]		Introductory gesture "X"
	5	(4)		Bass ostinato/pedal begins
	6	(13)		Theme A
	10	(9)		Gesture X superimposed over theme A
	15	(15)		Theme A repeated (with octave doublings) and extended
	22	(11)		Theme B + new ostinato (over B♭$_1$ pedal)
	28	(6)	cédez	
	31	(4)		New ostinato + addition of pcs 1,7
	33	(10)	cédez	Return of theme A (with doublings)
	38	(6)		Variant of theme B
	41	(2)	serrez cédez en animant	
Section 2 (B) Diatonic genus (5–35 as 6,8,10,1,3)	42	(5)		New theme: glissando with turn figure
	44	(1)	emporté	
	45	(6)	cédez, très retenu	Codetta
	47		cédez	
Section 3 (A/B) Whole-tone genus (10,0,2,4,6,8)	48	(4)		
	50	(8)		Theme A over ostinato derived from glissando figure of section 2
	54	(9)		Expansion of ostinato
	58	(8)		Return of gesture X
	62	(3)		
	(65)			

[a]Durations of formal units measured in quarter notes

Example 3.5. Whole-tone sets and motives from "Voiles"

[060603]); hence the extremely uniform sonority throughout sections 1 and 3. In contrast, the pentatonic scale and its subsets exhibit different proportions as well as a broader representation of ics across their ivs (5−35 = [032140]). More intervallic variety is possible, hence a sense of greater intensity. These differences between diatonic and whole-tone genera help to account for the sense of increased activity or acceleration in section 2 compared with sections 1 and 3. Other features that contribute to the effect include copious use of ostinati set against languid themes of limited registral span in the whole-tone sections, in contrast to the pentatonic section's dramatic changes in dynamics coupled with glissandi that span almost four octaves in less than a beat.

Another kinetic feature arises from large-scale rhythmic relations: since, in general, the maintenance of a constant inventory of pcs imparts a static effect, the changes in genera that occur at mm. 42 and 48 (and in pc content at m. 31, where the whole-tone genus is augmented by pcs 1,7) momentarily disrupt the static continuity, until a new inventory of pcs is established. Other parameters contain their own steady states and disruptions; unfolding events in the domains of theme, register, and texture (number of voices and notes articulated per beat) are punctuated by changes of various kinds, and many ritardandos and caesuras disrupt both pulse and meter to impart a sense of motion—of ebb and flow—that is directed by fluctuations in the intervening time spans. The more regular the temporal intervals, the more static the effect; lengthening is heard as deceleration, shortening as acceleration.[22]

Overall, the three sections unfold the acceleration-deceleration cycle. Figure 3.2 calculates the distances (in quarter-note beats) between changes in the domains of theme, tempo, and pc inventory. It shows fluctuation for section 1 between longer and shorter spans up to m. 15 followed by dramatic acceleration to m. 33 and another acceleration through m. 41. Section 2 is partitioned into three units (deceleration follows acceleration), whereas section 3 decelerates throughout (the fermatas of mm. 62–63 can be heard as part of a gradual ritard begun in m. 58).

"Voiles" is a mature work (composed in 1909)[23] that provides a simple archetype of Debussy's technique for employing more than one set genus in a single composition. The composition's enigmatic title has a correlate in the whole-tone genus that provides its main inventory of pcs. This is evident from the divergent views expressed by E. Robert Schmitz, George Perle, and Arnold Whittall.[24] Although the whole-tone genus's symmetrical structure and homogeneous ic content radically restrict the possibilities for tonal relations, there remain other quantitative and contextual means of emphasis that do not depend on unequal scale steps. Among these, invariant relations, in particular, assume a major tonal role. In "Voiles," the rigorous isolation of whole-tone and diatonic genera, with their sharply distinctive characteristics, serve well the imperatives of form, vitality, contrast, and structural coherence.

THE WHOLE-TONE GENUS

The whole-tone genus includes twenty-one pc sets; all are subsets or supersets of nexus set 6–35, the hexachord that generates the whole-tone scale. This perfectly symmetrical genus includes as many supersets as subsets, and together they form ten pairs of complements. The complete list appears in appendix 3.

Five characteristic sets exhibit close correspondences in the distribution of ics for each vector entry (see table 3.4). Each generates a string of adjacent whole steps that connects adjacent pcs, with the exception of set 7–33, formed of the whole-tone scale plus one other pc that partitions one of the whole steps into two semitones.

Characteristic ics include 2, 4, and 6. The rarity of entries for ics 1, 3, and 5 is a striking feature that contributes to the genus's aural distinctiveness (especially compared with the homogeneity of the diatonic genus).

Because its members' ic contents are so distinctive, even relatively inexperi-

TABLE 3.4. Characteristic sets of the
whole-tone genus

Set name	SIA	IV
3–6	2–2–8	020100
4–21	2–2–2–6	030201
5–33	2–2–2–2–4	040402
6–35	2–2–2–2–2–2	060603
7–33	2–2–2–2–2–1–1	262623

enced listeners can identify the sound of the whole-tone genus with ease, and instrumental performers readily recognize whole-tone combinations through the fingering patterns their execution requires.

An intriguing feature of Debussy's juxtaposition of whole-tone and diatonic pc set genera is his manner of transforming pitch materials from one genus to the other by exploiting similarities and differences in each genus's characteristic sias. A common method consists of shifting a portion of a set by a semitone; diatonic tetrachord 4–23, for example, can be transformed into whole-tone tetrachord set 4–21 by transposing one of its dyads by a half-step (ex. 3.6A). Similarly, diatonic (pentatonic) set 5–35 can be transformed into whole-tone pentachord 5–33 by shifting one dyad a semitone (ex. 3.6B), and diatonic hexachord 6–32 can be transformed into whole-tone set 6–35 by a semitonal shift of one of its linear trichords (ex. 3.6C).[25]

It is reasonable to assume that this spatial relationship attracted Debussy's attention because it emerges so easily at the keyboard as a kinesthetic phenomenon, and we may speculate that his pianistic experiments might have led to novel harmonies such as those of the whole-tone genus, as well as others yet to be examined.[26]

Viewed in terms of interval arrays that express semitone and whole-tone

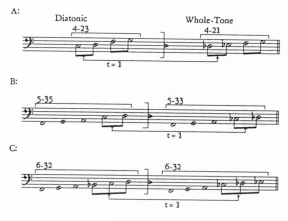

Example 3.6. Transformations of diatonic to whole-tone sets

content, the whole-tone genus represents one extreme (in its concentration of whole tones), the chromatic genus another (in its concentration of semitones). By comparison, the diatonic genus may be considered a middleground that mixes semitones and whole tones. These relationships rest on kinesthetic qualities of the genera vis-à-vis the keyboard and can be seen by comparing sias of sets for each genus. Those of the diatonic genus—4–11, 5–27, and 7–35, for example—mix whole and half steps, while 4–21, 5–33, and 6–35 from the whole-tone genus employ only whole steps.

"JIMBO'S LULLABY"

Composed in 1906–08,[27] the *Children's Corner* antedates slightly the first book of Préludes. "Jimbo's Lullaby," the second of the suite of six pieces, draws from the whole-tone and diatonic genera supplemented by a third group of sets—the chromatic genus. The integration of genera that Whittall finds wanting in "Voiles"[28] occurs in this more typical piece, for Debussy exploits not only the sonorous differences between the whole-tone and diatonic genera, but also the possibilities for ambiguity that arise from the use of shared sets.

A simple principle is the source of contrast and vitality in "Jimbo's Lullaby": the piece proceeds through a series of passages whose pc materials are either diatonic or whole-tone. Some integrate the chromatic genus in the form of chromatic successions that connect pcs of diatonic or whole-tone sets. Diatonic sets mutate to become whole-tone sets, and vice versa, by means of two processes: one or more pcs shift a semitone to create set-counterparts of the other genus; and additional pcs accrete to a small set common to both genera and form a larger set whose generic association is unambiguous.

Form

Formal processes similar to those identified in "Voiles" are also important in "Jimbo's Lullaby." Sudden attenuations of activity (manifest as less frequent changes) in the parameters of register, texture, dynamics, and duration disrupt the musical flow and partition the piece into four large sections of similar but unequal length. The result is a typically Debussyan asymmetrical scheme, which has a parallel in the asymmetrical disposition of thematic material (see fig. 3.3).

The perimeters of sections 1–4 are defined by major points of disjunction at mm. 19, 39, and 63. The boundary between sections 1 and 2 is typical. In mm. 15–18 a marked change of register is accompanied by a thinning of sonorous density, a pronounced diminuendo to pianississimo, a lengthening of the durations between notes struck, and a silent pause. Contrast between the attenuation of activity at the approach of m. 19 and the subsequent quickening creates the point of disjunction, and the abrupt register changes before and after heighten the effect. In similar fashion, mm. 37–38, 59–62, and 74–81 adumbrate the points of disjunction that follow them.

Each section can itself be partitioned into phrases as indicated by the shorter

FIGURE 3.3. Formal plan for "Jimbo's Lullaby"

PC set genus	Measures			Motives, themes
Section 1 (18)[a] Diatonic genus	i	(10)	assez modéré	Theme A
Whole-tone genus	11	(4)		Motive X, theme B
Diatonic + whole-tone	15	(4)		Motive X
Section 2 (20) Diatonic	19	(2)		
Diatonic	21	(8)	un peu en dehors	Theme A
Diatonic	29	(4)		Motive X
Diatonic (and octatonic set 5–31)	33	(4)		Theme C
(Octatonic set 4–12)	37	(2)		
Section 3 (24) Whole-tone	39	(8)	un peu plus mouvementé marqué	Theme B
Chromatic + whole-tone + diatonic	47	(2)		Theme C
Diatonic	49	(5)		
	53	(4)		Theme C
Diatonic + chromatic	57	(2)		Theme C
Diatonic + chromatic				
Diatonic	59	(4)	retenu	Motive X
Section 4 (19) Diatonic	63	(8)	1° tempo	Theme A, theme C
Diatonic + chromatic	70	(4)		Theme C
Diatonic + chromatic	74	(4)	morendo	
Diatonic (+ whole-tone)	78	(4)		Theme B
	(81)			

[a]Durations of formal units measured in bars

horizontal lines. Subdivisions occur whenever a new theme or ostinato is stated (mm. 11, 29, and 33) or an old theme recurs (mm. 19, 39, 47, and 63), but, as we shall see, other features define these points of partition as well. Some phrases overlap (mm. 47–53 with 53–56) and their boundaries are not always clearly defined (mm. 47–53, 57–62, 70–77). Ambiguous partitions are indicated by dotted horizontal lines, overlappings by crossed arrows.

Thematic Material and the PC Set Genera

As in "La fille aux cheveux de lin," the thematic dimension in "Jimbo's Lullaby" is tightly organized. Example 3.7 is a pc reduction that catalogs themes and motives and identifies the pc set genera to which they belong. It employs the following format: sections keyed to the formal plan of figure 3.3 are separated by thick vertical lines; each of the staves on the upper system is assigned to one of four important thematic elements (in order of appearance); the space below catalogs the important pc sets, identifies mutations from one genus to another, and enumerates invariant pcs that link phrases and sections; pcs that serve as the object of tonal focus are notated on the auxiliary staff below, supplied with functional labels where appropriate.

Theme A is lengthy and always associated with the diatonic genus. Theme B is always associated with the whole-tone genus, a feature that is more apparent at its second statement (in m. 38). Theme C is less clearly aligned; it leans toward the diatonic genus but is also associated with chromatic semitonal collections.[29] Motive X—so called because of its brevity and amorphous contour—is flexible in its association: it can be whole-tone or diatonic, or even chromatic when integrated with theme C. Themes A and B and motive X appear immediately in section 1 (in, respectively, mm. 1, 11, and 4). Theme C is not exposed until well into section 2 (m. 33), but its genesis can be traced to the weak-beat eighth notes of motive X, and in this sense it is at least presaged in section 1.

Interrelation of Themes and PC Set Genera

Several processive principles are embodied in the realms of thematic and pc set relations. Each section combines and manipulates thematic materials in a different fashion. The function of section 1 is to expose themes A and B and motive X (which contains within it the seed of theme C). Section 2 cements the association between theme A and the diatonic genus and presents theme C in a diatonic setting in m. 33. Section 3 strengthens the connection between theme B and the whole-tone genus and presents theme C transformed; its linear materials are now chromatic, and its vertical materials mix diatonic and whole-tone chords. Section 3 is the locus of greatest intensity because of the concatenation of diatonic, whole-tone, and chromatic pc set genera with theme C's transformations, the overlapping formal divisions, and the sheer number of pcs used. Section 4 restores a measure of simplicity; all three genera are present, though the diatonic genus predominates. Where section 2 juxtaposed themes A and C, and section 3 jux-

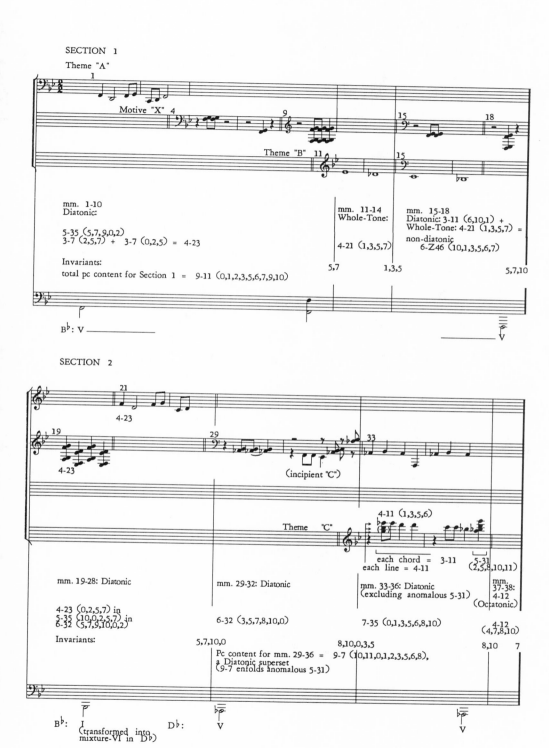

Example 3.7. PC reduction of "Jimbo's Lullaby"

SECTION 3

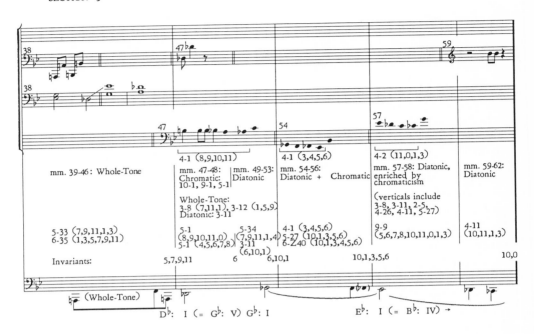

SECTION 4

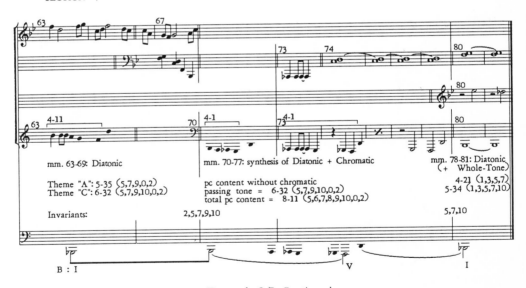

Example 3.7. *Continued*

taposed themes B and C, section 4 superimposes theme A over theme C and alludes to theme B as well.

The interplay of varying associations among the themes and pc set genera creates an elegant rhythmic counterpoint in which each element performs a unique role. The reduction clearly shows the separate evolutionary paths of the themes throughout, in terms of changing conformations and register assignments, and the alternation, opposition, and synthesis of the pc set genera. Theme A maintains a consistent pitch and rhythmic contour and an allegiance to the diatonic genus, while it actively migrates to different registers. Theme B consistently maintains its pitch contour and association with the whole-tone genus, but it undergoes rhythmic modifications as well as register shifts. Theme C is subjected to changes in contour that accommodate its varied diatonic or chromatic settings (or combine elements of both), and it also migrates to different transpositions and octave placements. (Rhythm is its only stable element, and even that undergoes an elongation of durations at the end, mm. 70–78.) Motive X undergoes many transformations in contour, pc content, register, and rhythm, retaining only its functions (rhythmic punctuation and the strong projection of ic 2). A selection of passages will show how the foregoing are manifest.

PC Resources and Processes within Each Section

Section 1. The division of section 1 into subdivisions that present themes A and B also partitions the section into diatonic versus whole-tone passages. Conspicuous in the melodic patterns of mm. 1–10 are diatonic sets 3–7 and 4–23, and the sum of all pcs is diatonic pentachord 5–35. The whole-tone genus is represented in mm. 11–14 by tetrachord 4–21. Since the latter is also a diatonic subset,[30] its association with the whole-tone genus could be equivocal; it is not, however, because the tetrachord is generated by the appearance of pc 1, which is excluded from any form of the diatonic genus that contains the pentatonic set of mm. 1–10.[31] The appearance of pc 1 in m. 12 signals a change in pc content that must mean one of two things: mutation to the whole-tone genus or modulation within the diatonic genus. Since the tetrachord's pc content restricts the possible keys to A♭ major, F minor, and the ascending melodic forms of B♭ minor and A♭ minor[32] (none of which is confirmed by the events of mm. 11–14), the whole-tone genus provides the easiest context for hearing theme B.

Final mm. 15–18 of section 1 intermingle diatonic and whole-tone genera in set 6–Z46, a composite that contains elements of each. The characteristic sets projected by the musical surface are whole-tone tetrachord 4–21 and diatonic major-triad set 3–11. The residue of motive X (pcs 5,7) struck at the end of m. 18 is neutral, having previously occupied positions in both genera. This passage plays on the ambiguity of the potential association of tetrachord 4–21 with either genus. Although previous identification with the whole-tone genus inclines us to retain that association for 4–21, the conditions that conspired against diatonic associations in mm. 11–14 are now contradicted. The presence of pc 10, coupled with the placement of F in the bass, points to one of the diatonic scales to which the tetrachord could belong—namely, F minor—and although hexachord 6–Z46 is not a diatonic set, it is contained in diatonic superset 8–23 (F minor plus G♭), and context treats the G♭ as inferior to the object of its linear focus on F in m. 18.[33]

Section 2. Section 2 opens (mm. 19–20) with an ostinato derived from motive X that serves as an introduction for theme A (mm. 21–28), stated two octaves higher than before. This is followed (in mm. 29–32) by four measures of new material derived from motive X's rhythm and M2s. Example 3.8 traces the transformation of motive X into theme C (through mm. 4, 19, 29, and 33), whose initial statement occurs in a diatonic setting. Diatonic sets 3–11, 4–11, 5–27, 7–35, and 9–7 are all prominently projected in theme C.

A marked change of pc content occurs at the end of section 2. It alerts the listener through the sudden addition of sonorous color and complements features enumerated earlier to adumbrate the important point of subdivision at the end of m. 38. Although section 2 is predominantly diatonic, m. 34 contains set 5–31 and final mm. 37–38 contain tetrachord 4–12. Neither diatonic nor whole-tone, these sets are octatonic.[34] While the octatonic genus is not cogent for this piece, its characteristic sonority contrasts strongly with those of the diatonic genus and provides an external reference to other pieces that employ the octatonic genus.

Section 3. The second subdivision of section 3 (mm. 47–53), which follows an unambiguously whole-tone passage, is devoted to a variant of theme C. It divides into three smaller phrases: mm. 47–48, whose linear elements and overall pc content form sets that are entirely chromatic, while its vertical sets alternate whole-tone and diatonic trichords; mm. 49–52, for which the linear and summary sets are diatonic (4–22 and 5–34 in 8–22), although the chords continue to alternate whole-tone and diatonic trichords; and m. 53,[35] which is diatonic.

Trichord 3–11 is, of course, exclusively diatonic, and, if projected clearly, requires no contextual support to clarify its generic identity. Trichord 3–8 is a member of both whole-tone and diatonic genera: its association with one or the other depends upon its context. Trichord 3–12 is unambiguously whole-tone.[36] Because they follow the whole-tone passage of mm. 39–46, in which their pcs occur, trichords 3–8 and 3–12 in mm. 47–48 easily invoke whole-tone associations that contrast with the form of diatonic set 3–11, which separates them (6,10,1). The pervasive chromaticism of mm. 47–48 promotes neither association.

Example 3.8. Derivation of theme C from motive X

The 3–8 trichords (pcs 7,11,1) of mm. 49–52, however, are more readily interpreted as diatonic because of the inferable diminished-minor seventh-chords (as 1,[4],7,11), whose missing pc 4 is prominent in the treble line. This change of setting for the trichords, from predominantly whole-tone (in mm. 47–48) to predominantly diatonic (in mm. 49–53), results in a subtle change in meaning for the vertical sonorities of those bars. Debussy often exploits ambiguities of this sort.

Measure 53 is linked to those that follow by its sudden shift of content (pcs 1,6 appear in place of pcs 2,7), even while its stress on pc 1 and the diatonic trichord ties it to mm. 49–52: hence the dual formal association for m. 53 indicated on the formal plan (fig. 3.3).

Measures 54–56 restate theme C in a new transposition and octave. As in mm. 47–48, the line is again chromatic, but now the verticals are all diatonic. The chromatic-diatonic dichotomy is reflected in the summary set (hexachord 6–Z40), which belongs to neither genus. (It contains chromatic and diatonic representatives 4–1 and 5–27, which are projected prominently by context.) Measures 57–62 employ a similar mixture of linear chromaticism and vertical diatonicism as a setting for theme C, but in the codetta-like final four bars the quantity of pcs is drastically reduced in favor of diatonic subsets 3–7 and 4–11. Like the attenuation of activity in these measures, this "clarification" of the pc set materials signals the approach of the composition's final section.

Section 4. The return to theme A in section 4 (mm. 63–70), counterpointed by a variant of theme C, is exclusively diatonic. The second, overlapping phrase (mm. 70–77) evokes the chromatic genus through the predominantly semitonal bass line (which forms chromatic set 7–3), while the sustained tones in the upper parts form diatonic set 4–23 and thereby restore the dichotomy posed in section 3.[37] The final bars (mm. 78–81) are diatonic (the summary set is 5–34), but a remnant of whole-tone theme B (in the form of pcs 1,3) refers enigmatically to that genus as well.

Tonality

Throughout the piece tonal focus takes the form of ostinati, pedals, doublings, and linear motions that draw attention to selected pcs which function from passage to passage as scale steps or as pivots to temporary tonics.[38] These include (in order) F, B♭, A♭, D♭, G♭, E♭, and B♭ (identified on the bottom staff of ex. 3.7, together with their scale-step functions). The presence of A♭, D♭, and G♭ (which occur most often in the composition's interior) attests to the prominent role of mixture.

Pitch-class set and tonal relations intersect in invariants that link formal divisions across the composition's fluctuant pc field. Pitch classes 5,10 and, to a lesser extent, pc 7 are common invariants; they appear and are retained more than any other pcs. Pitch classes 5,10 correspond, of course, to primary scale steps (I and V) in the key of B♭ major, and pc 7 corresponds to the submediant.

On balance, considering the absence of any event resembling dominant-tonic closure or linear arrival on B♭, the tonal path through "Jimbo's Lullaby," while easily traced, seems secondary in importance to pc set relations.

"Jimbo's Lullaby" exposes a number of features that are common to much of Debussy's music: the sudden mutations from one pc set genus to another; the exploitation of sharp contrast between the whole-tone and diatonic genera; the use of the chromatic genus only in combination with the other two; and the rhythmic counterpoint that arises from the temporal path of each theme as it intersects with those of the others (along with the possibilities of interaction among the pc set genera to which each belongs).[39] As we shall see, these techniques may operate independently of a tonal framework. An important principle ignored in "Voiles" is the inherent ambiguity of generic association for shared sets, which require context for clarification.[40] In "Jimbo's Lullaby" the dyad, ic 2, is inherently ambiguous, as are trichords 3–6 and 3–8 (since they belong to both the diatonic and whole-tone genera). Debussy exploits their ambiguity in mm. 10–11, where occurs the juncture between diatonic and whole-tone tetrachords 4–23 and 4–21.

Apropos of its pc set genera, "Jimbo's Lullaby" differs from "Voiles" in important ways. In "Voiles," the distinction between whole-tone and diatonic genera focuses on specific pc content. The whole-tone genus is manifest in pcs 0,2,4,6,8,10 (supplemented briefly by pcs 1,7); the diatonic genus is manifest in pcs 6,8,10,1,3. Invariant pcs 6,8,10 provide a unifying link. In "Jimbo's Lullaby," generic distinctions are manifest more in the sets themselves than in specific pc content (though pc specificity sometimes helps to clarify), and unifying links take the form of shared sets.

A final point: in "Jimbo's Lullaby," as in "La fille aux cheveux de lin," *processive* features (principles) take precedence over *static* features (objects) as generators of musical structures and materials.

THE CHROMATIC GENUS

The chromatic genus has no cynosural set; instead, member sets are differentiated by their potential for disposition into semitones. The genus may be defined as follows: *primary* members' pc contents can be disposed entirely in semitones, or in semitones except for one M2; *secondary* members' pc contents can be disposed in semitones except for one interval that is not a M2. Example 3.9 illustrates the distinction: sets 4–1, 4–2, 6–1, and 6–Z4 meet the criteria for primary membership, since their sias are predominantly semitonal (even though whole steps intrude into or attach to either end of sets 4–2 and 6–Z4); sets 4–4, 6–Z6, and 6–Z36 are secondary members owing to the m3s in their otherwise semitonal sias.

The complete catalog is found in appendix 4. Secondary members are listed parenthetically. While there are a total of sixty-four sets, only thirty-four possess primary status, with sets of more than six pcs predominant.

A nucleus of five sets may be considered characteristic of the genus; for each,

A: primary members

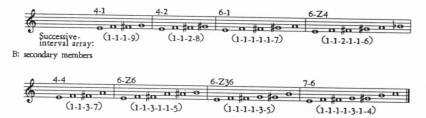

Example 3.9. Representative sets for the chromatic genus

the most numerous ic is 1 (table 3.5). These sets show similar distribution patterns for each entry across their ivs, as well as similar sias.

Like the whole-tone and diatonic genera, the chromatic genus has an important kinesthetic aspect; its pitch combinations are easily formed on the piano keyboard using predominantly semitonal sias. Although the chromatic genus is usually synthesized with another, it occasionally assumes an independent role. In such instances chromatic sets tend to be disposed linearly, not as chords, assigned to registers distinct from the other pc materials.

In mm. 47–48, 54–56, and 70–77 of "Jimbo's Lullaby," chromatic sets appear as lines assigned to the highest or lowest registers and may be heard independently. The chords that result from the interaction of these lines with materials in other registers are associated with the diatonic or whole-tone genera. The chromatic sets are made to fit into the interstices formed by diatonic and whole-tone sets, but the genus does carry an independent role as a sonic resource. This kind of treatment also may be seen in "Pour les degrés chromatiques" (Douze études II), which assigns to the chromatic genus an even greater role as a resource. The etude consistently assigns chromatic sets to a higher register, while the diatonic, whole-tone, and octatonic genera provide the pitch materials for the lower register in alternation.[41] Chromatic sets are nearly always disposed as successions of semitones; if ordered otherwise, they are isolated by register, which facilitates association of elements for easy identification.

Chromatic sets most often occur as manipulators of sets associated with other genera. (They may, for example, generate semitonal successions of triads or

TABLE 3.5. Characteristic sets of the chromatic genus

Set name	SIA	IV
3–1	1–1–10	210000
4–1	1–1–1–9	321000
5–1	1–1–1–1–8	432100
6–1	1–1–1–1–1–7	543210
7–1	1–1–1–1–1–1–6	654321

seventh-chords and thus serve as transposition operators applied to sets from some other genus.) Their more common compositional role differs from those of the other genera in that, as a rule, they do not serve as resources for crucial thematic/harmonic material, but are used, rather, in conjunction with other genera as a source of manipulation and for enrichment through the addition of sonorous color.

The chromatic genus with its dual roles provides a way of understanding Debussy's predilection for chromatic materials.

SHARED SETS AND INTERPLAY AMONG THE PC SET GENERA

Debussy often uses sets shared among two or more genera to conjure up ambiguous associations (or to resolve them) and to effect transitions or forge connections between contrasting passages.

In "Jimbo's Lullaby," we saw how differences between the diatonic, whole-tone, and chromatic genera were exploited to achieve contrast and effect formal partitions. But the genera also evince interconnections through shared sets, a feature that Debussy exploits to facilitate transitions and create form. Sets 3–6, 3–8, and 4–21, for example, belong to both the diatonic and whole-tone genera. Whole-tone set 5–33 and diatonic set 5–34 share tetrachord 4–21 as a subset. Although each pentachord associates readily with its genus (5–33 generates a whole-tone scale minus one note, and 5–34 may be disposed as a V^9 chord), their shared subset 4–21 is inherently neutral and requires the addition of a fifth pc to define its association; its context in a musical setting is therefore crucial. In mm. 11–14 of "Jimbo's Lullaby," association of 4–21 with the whole-tone genus is aided by the fact that one of its pcs, D♭, conflicts with the diatonic pc content embodied in the pentatonic melody of mm. 1–10. If D♭ were consistent with a form of 7–35 that encompassed the pentatonic melody's pcs, there would be every reason to hear the tetrachord as diatonic; indeed, it would be difficult to hear it otherwise. But since D♭ is incompatible with all of them,[42] a change of genus is effected (mutation). The opposite situation obtains in m. 47, where a form of trichord 3–8 (7,11,1) invites association with the whole-tone genus because its pc content is consistent with the unambiguously whole-tone material of mm. 39–46 (where 6–35 = 9,*11,1*,3,5,7). Here a mutation is forestalled, momentarily, until the chromatic lines of mm. 47–48 break the whole-tone hegemony of mm. 39–41. The superset that forms the context of trichord 3–8 two bars later, in mm. 49–52, is *diatonic* pentachord 5–34 (7,9,11,1,4); moreover, the lines in the upper parts form diatonic tetrachord 4–22 (4,7,9,11). As a result, trichord 3–8 now represents (or, more correctly, associates with) the diatonic genus. As discussed previously, in mm. 47–48 a transition from whole-tone to diatonic genus is effected by alternating trichords associated with each genus, while at the same time playing on the ambiguity of shared trichord 3–8. The sudden change to a multiplicity of associations after eight measures of homogeneous pc material also captures the listener's attention in preparation for the important formal event in m. 49: the pronounced point of disjunction caused by the change in genus.

Shared sets and interplay produce another important principle: the juxtaposition of very brief passages whose harmonies clearly belong to different genera but share neutral subsets. Although "Jimbo's Lullaby" does not employ this technique, the piece alludes to it by juxtaposing longer passages that project characteristic sets of contrasting genera, such as 4–23 opposite 4–21 (diatonic versus whole-tone) in mm. 1–9 against mm. 10–14. We will see this technique exploited in "Feuilles mortes" (Préludes II).

Methods of constructing passages that juxtapose, superimpose, or synthesize pc set genera evolved into an intricate and subtle way of composing for which Debussy developed a variety of techniques.

"FEUILLES MORTES"

"Feuilles mortes"[43] makes use of four genera: diatonic, whole-tone, chromatic, and octatonic. The octatonic genus—consisting of the octatonic scale (set 8–28), its subsets, and supersets—is employed in much the same manner as were the diatonic and whole-tone genera in "Jimbo's Lullaby"; its sonorous and sia properties provide resources for distinctive thematic-harmonic materials and serve as a foil to those of the diatonic and whole-tone genera.

In its use of the pc set genera, "Feuilles mortes" exhibits what are by now familiar features. The chromatic genus serves as a secondary pc resource, always conjoined to other genera, superimposed against or integrated into them, and usually associated with transitions that adumbrate important events in the formal scheme. The diatonic, whole-tone, and octatonic genera are used separately as pc resources for passages that contrast sharply with one another, and most often it is mutations that partition the piece into sections and subdivisions. A new feature is the synthesis of diatonic, whole-tone, and octatonic genera to create complex pc surfaces at crucial formal junctures.

Form and the Organization of PC Set Materials

The intricate, bilevel formal scheme of "Feuilles mortes" is typical of Debussy's later works. The piece divides into nine main sections, which subdivide further into smaller units (fig. 3.4). These sections and subdivisions are defined by points of disjunction that result when changes in the domains of theme and pc set materials coincide. (Changes in only one domain do not create partitions on these formal levels.)

Eight themes (labeled A through H) are supplemented by three variants (B$_x$, G$_x$, and G$_y$), and their distribution across the piece appears to be unstructured (example 3.10 provides a catalog). Only theme A followed by transitional theme B is ever repeated. (The pair recurs twice, at mm. 15 and 41.) The highly asymmetrical locations of their reprises across the formal plan (and the disproportionately

FIGURE 3.4. Formal plan for "Feuilles mortes"[a]

Formal unit	Measures			Motives, themes	PC set genus
Section 1/ subdivision 1 (1/1)	1	(9)[b]	lent	Theme A	Octatonic
1/2	4	(5)		Theme B (transition)	Octatonic + diatonic + whole-tone + chromatic
Section 2/3	6	(6)		Theme C	Diatonic + chromatic
2/4	8	(6)		Theme D	Diatonic
2/5	10	(12)			Diatonic (modulation)
Section 3/6	15	(6)		Theme A	Octatonic
3/7	17	(5)		Theme B (transition)	Octatonic + whole-tone + chromatic
Section 4/8	19	(4)	un peu plus allant	Theme B$_x$	Whole-tone + chromatic
4/9	21	(8)		Theme E	Whole-tone
Section 5/10	25	(12)	un peu en dehors	Theme F	Octatonic
Section 6/11	31	(12)	plus lent	Theme G	Synthesis of octatonic + diatonic + whole-tone
Section 7/12	37	(8)		Theme G$_x$	Whole-tone Octatonic Whole-tone Octatonic
Section 8/13	41	(9)	cédez mouvement	Theme A	Octatonic
8/14	44	(7)		Theme B (transition)	Octatonic + whole-tone + diatonic + chromatic
Section 9/15	47	(9)		Themes G$_y$ + H	Octatonic
9–16	50	(9)		Theme H	Diatonic
	(52)				

[a]Subdivisions are numbered consecutively and identified with sections by means of a prefix number; "7/13," for example, is the thirteenth subdivision, which falls within the seventh section.
[b]Durations of formal units measured in quarter notes

Example 3.10. Thematic catalog for "Feuilles mortes"

brief duration each occupies) discourages comparison with rondo-type schemes. Nor does the string of new themes from m. 21 to m. 40 resemble any conventional pattern (though it is a common one for Debussy); indeed, the apparently random distribution appears calculated to defy prediction and convey a sense of improvisational spontaneity. (The abbreviated formal plan in fig. 3.5 more clearly shows the disposition of themes and genera in the piece.)

In contrast, the use and distribution of pc set genera reveal tidier principles (See ex. 3.11. Pertinent sets are displayed on the grand staff, pc set genera below. Sections and subdivisions are labeled above. Thick vertical lines indicate changes in pc set genera [mutations], while thin, broken vertical lines indicate changes *within* genera [modulations]. Invariants that link subdivisions are shown at the bottom of each system.) Each formal unit is associated with one or another genus, among which the octatonic genus serves as referential. Sections 1, 3, 5, and 8 are predominantly or entirely octatonic; sections 2 and 4 are, respectively, diatonic

FIGURE 3.5. Abbreviated formal plan for "Feuilles mortes"

Theme										
		C/D	A followed by B						G$_y$/H	
				E	F	— G —				
Section	1	2	3	4	5	6	7	8	9	
	(14)[b]	(24)	(11)	(12)	(12)	(12)	(8)	(16)	(18)	
Genus[a]	O	D	O	WT	O	O/D/WT	WT/O		O	O/D

[a]O = octatonic; WT = whole-tone; D = diatonic.
[b]Durations of sections measured in quarter notes

and whole-tone; sections 6 and 7 feature vacillation between generic pairs; section 9 is initially octatonic but ends in the diatonic genus.

Octatonicism is strongly associated with theme A. The harmonies of mm. 1–3 are entirely octatonic (forms of 5–31 and 6–27, partitioned by register into 3–10 and 4–27),[44] and establish an essential *sonus*, from which the prelude diverges into diatonic and whole-tone passages, and to which it returns periodically. Transitional theme B passages alternate octatonic, diatonic, and whole-tone sets in configurations that change each time to suit the new goal. In mm. 4–5, for example, theme B is manifest in succession through sets 3–10 (octatonic), 4–24 (whole-tone), and 4–22 (diatonic), to effect a transition from octatonic theme A to diatonic themes C and D. Chromatic sets 3–1 and 4–1, which fill the interstices within and between 4–24 and 4–22, adumbrate the chromatic genus's integration into the pc materials of mm. 6–7 (where they engender semitonal transpositions of diatonic sets). The octatonicism of section 5 is manifest in pentachord 5–10, which generates the middle-voice melody, and in the ostinato, which utilizes the complete octatonic scale collection (set 8–28). The diatonic genus is conspicuous in the harmonies and lines of section 2, with tetrachord 4–22 ascendent among the forms. Similarly, whole-tone tetrachord 4–24 dominates the chords of section 4, while characteristic set 5–33 provides the pc contents of mm. 21–24 (excluding the last note) and forms the combinations of chord and line from beat to beat.

Section 6 alternates between octatonic and diatonic sets (6–Z49 and 5–34, respectively), formed by the pairs of triads that are projected throughout mm. 31–36. The triads themselves—all forms of set 3–11—are members of both genera. The total pc content of the passage forms set 9–12, a whole-tone superset that is foreign to both the diatonic and octatonic genera. In similar fashion, the whole-tone and octatonic genera alternate from one bar to the next throughout section 7 (represented, respectively, by 5–33 and 6–27). In sections 6 and 7, the thematic dimension binds together the pc set materials, for only one thematic shape unfolds in each (and that of section 7 is derived from section 6).

Modulations occur in both octatonic and diatonic passages. Octatonic theme A of section 1 incorporates two modulations: set 5–31 of m. 1 is transposed in m. 2 (the transposition operator [t] = 10) and returns to the original form in m. 3. Similar modulations occur at the reprises of mm. 15 and 41, as shown on the

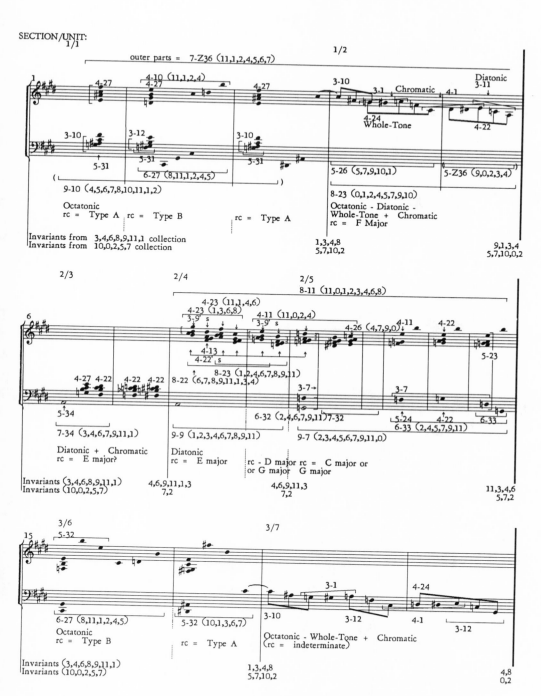

Example 3.11. PC reduction of "Feuilles mortes"

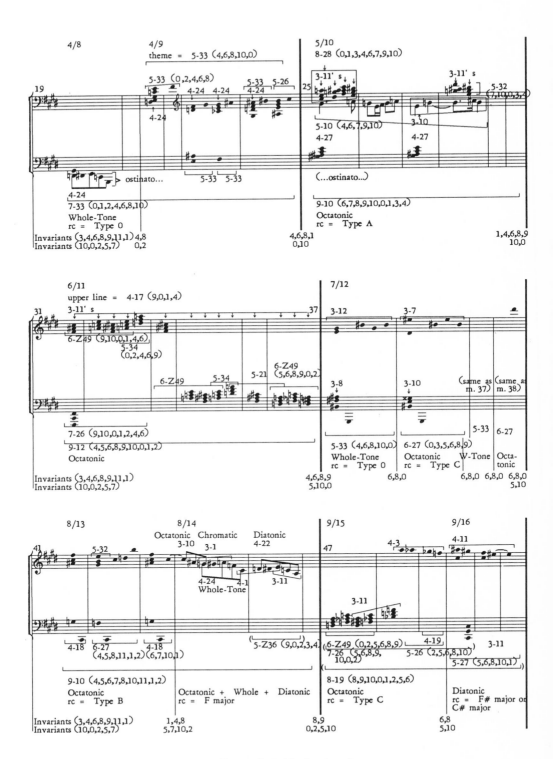

Example 3.11. *Continued*

example.[45] Diatonic modulations occur in section 2 at mm. 9 and 10. Summary sets 7–35 (m. 8), 6–32 (m. 9), and 9–7 (m. 10) are all diatonic, but they represent the different scales shown under the example (labeled "rc" for pc "reference collection").[46] The whole-tone genus undergoes a modulation in mm. 17–18, where trichord 3–12 occurs in two forms related by transposition (t = 1).[47] Most modulations define subdivisions of sections, but there is an exception: an octatonic modulation helps to differentiate a new section at m. 41.

Tonality

"Feuilles mortes" typifies Debussy's treatment of tonality in his later works. The role of harmony and voice leading as tonal determinants is conspicuously weak, and although the key signature implies either E major or C♯ minor, the evidence is insufficient to support a tonic ascription for either. The key signature's broader implications are closer to the mark; they suggest that priority is likely for a selection of pcs encompassed by set 7–35 in its E-major-scale form: pcs 3,4,6,8,9,11,1.

We will proceed from the assumption that the signature points toward the prelude's tonal referents. Table 3.6 examines three aspects of quantitative emphasis—manifest as invariance—that establish priority for some among these seven pcs: the number of subdivisions (out of the total of sixteen) in which each pc occurs (table 3.6A; pcs 1,4,6,8 occur most often); the number of times each pc occurs as an invariant linking adjacent subdivisions (table 3.6B; pcs 4,6,8 occur most often); and pcs invariant across three or more adjacent subdivisions (table 3.6C; pcs 4,8). Pcs that are projected more strongly than others by qualitative means of emphasis—a more dynamic means of asserting priority—are shown in table 3.6D (pcs 1,4,8 predominate). Overall the data reveal a marked emphasis on pcs 1,4,6,8 (especially pcs 4,8), such that these four pcs may be considered tonal referents.

Tables 3.6E and F and the right-hand column of table 3.6D examine invariance relations for the five pcs that are *excluded* from the key signature's implied form of set 7–35, namely, pcs 10,0,2,5,7. They show that pcs 10,2 appear in almost as many subdivisions as pcs 1,4,6,8, and as invariants they link nearly as many adjacent pairs of subdivisions as 4,6,8. Table 3.6D reveals a marked tendency to project pc 5 through qualitative devices (though not as much as referential pcs 1,4,8).

Quantitative and qualitative emphasis of selected pcs in "Feuilles mortes" points to pcs 1,4,8 as tonal referents, but supplemented by pcs 2,5 (and, to a lesser extent, pcs 10,0,6). The composition's tonal referents interconnect with the octatonic, diatonic, and whole-tone genera that serve throughout as pc resources. The three primary tonal referents form diatonic trichord 3–11, which is indeed congruent with the prelude's key signature. The addition of the two strongest secondary referents, pcs 2,5, swells the total of five and forms octatonic pentachord 5–16 (1,2,4,5,8). The remaining supplementary tonal referents accrete to form whole-tone octachord 8–24 (0,1,2,4,5,6,8,10).

TABLE 3.6. Aspects of pc invariance and priority in
"Feuilles mortes"

A. Occurrences, by subdivision, of pcs from diatonic rc = E
    major (set 7–35 as 3,4,6,8,9,11,1)

PC	*Number of subdivisions in which each occurs (16 possible)*
4	14
8	14
6	12
1	12
3	10
9	10
11	6

B. Number of times pcs from diatonic rc = E major occur
    as invariants that link adjacent subdivisions

PC	*Number of times (15 possible)*
4	13
8	11
6	8
1	7
3	6
9	6
11	3

C. Invariants for diatonic rc = E major that appear
    throughout sections

```
3,4,   8,    1  ┐
3,4,6,  9,11    │
3,4             │      mm. 1–36
   4  8         │
   4,6,8,9  ┐┘  │
   4,6,8,9  ┘   │
   4,6,8,9      │      mm. 15–52
   4,  8     ┘
```

Complement Relations

There are many examples of complement pairs in "Feuilles mortes." Two occur in
the first two sections (see ex. 3.11): the octatonic pair, 9–10/3–10, where 9–10
accounts for the total pc content of mm. 1–3, while 3–10 occurs embedded in the
chords and arpeggiated as the first three notes of the second subdivision; and the
pair 7–Z36/5–Z36 formed by the outer parts in mm. 1–3 and the pc content of m.
5. Diatonic 5–34 is embedded in 7–34 at the end of the first transition in m. 6. Two
diatonic pairs appear in mm. 8–14 (3–9 embedded in multiple in 9–9, 3–7 in 9–
7). A diatonic pair also forges a link across the modulation here. (Set 4–11 is the

TABLE 3.6. *Continued*

D. Survey by subdivision of pcs prominently projected (as highest, lowest, first, last, doubled, and accented notes, and as focuses of linear motions)

Subdiv. no.	PCs from rc = E major	Non-E-major pcs
1	4, 11,1	
2	4, 1	
3	4,6,	
4	4, 8,9,11	
5	4, 11,	2,5,7
6	4, 11,1	
7	8, 1	
8	4, 8,	0,2
9	4, 8, 1,	0,2
10	4, 8,9,	7
11	4,6, 9, 1	
12	3, 8,	0, 5
13	4, 11,1	
14	1,	2,5,7
15	9,	0, 5
16	8, 1,	5

E. Occurrences, by subdivision, of non-E-major rc pcs (10,0,2,5,7)

PC	Number of subdivisions (16 possible)
10	13
2	13
5	12
7	8
0	0

F. Number of times non-E-major rc pcs (10,0,2,5,7) occur as invariants that link adjacent subdivisions

PC	Number of times (15 possible)
10	10
2	10
5	9
0	7
7	7

third imbricating melodic tetrachord and is embedded in 8–11, which accounts for the upper line's pcs throughout mm. 8–14.) Whole-tone complements occur in mm. 21–24 (5–33 embedded in multiple in 7–33). Octatonic complements may be found in mm. 25–28 (3–10 embedded in 9–10, and 4–28 embedded in 8–28). Complement pairs occur in each genus excepting the chromatic; they are usually disposed so that the pair's large set embraces the overall pc content of a given formal unit, while the small set is projected conspicuously among chords or lines.

Reference to the 8–17/18/19–Complex Genus

An anomalous group of sets occurs towards the very end: a mixture of octatonic (3–11, 4–3, 4–11, 6–Z49), diatonic (3–11, 4–11, 4–22, 4–27), and unidentified sets (complement pairs 5–26/7–26 and 4–19/8–19) fills the last six measures, which encompass subdivisions 15–16. Although these sets result from a synthesis of the octatonic and diatonic sets of which they are composed, they capture our attention as an independent group, for they have all occurred elsewhere in the piece, and sets 5–26 and 7–26 recur persistently (see mm. 4, 24, and 31–32). These sets belong to another genus that is found more often in Debussy's vocal works and is discussed later. For now it is intriguing to observe that 7–26 also occurs in connection with tonal focus, formed by the referential and nonreferential pcs that occur most often as the invariants linking subdivisions (1,4,6,8 + 2,5,10 = 7–26; see table 3.6B and F).

Debussy's treatment of the pc set genera in "Feuilles mortes" is far more complex than in "Jimbo's Lullaby," since "Feuilles mortes" employs four genera for its sonorous resources (though the chromatic genus has only a minimal role). The octatonic genus provides the main thematic-harmonic materials and serves as a sonorous point of departure and return for the diatonic and whole-tone genera. The prelude's formal scheme embodies a conventional principle—juxtaposition of contrasting passages—but changes in pc content alone (modulation) as well as changes in pc set genera also effect contrast and disrupt sonorous continuity. Hence, formal partitions result as much from mutation and modulation as from changes in the thematic domain. Ambiguity engendered through the use of shared sets among the genera is not greatly exploited, though the subtle changes that occur toward the end of transitional theme B in each of its reappearances always adumbrate the impending change of genus. Ambiguity is embodied in tonal relations manifest through pc content and invariance, and although the thematic-formal scheme appears to be arbitrarily conceived—a hodgepodge of new and recurrent thematic-harmonic units—at a deeper level there is an orderly vacillation between octatonic, diatonic, and whole-tone genera, and between selected referential and nonreferential pcs. Defined as the locus of extremes in most musical parameters, the climax of the piece occurs at mm. 31–40, for the two sections subsumed by these ten bars utilize the widest register span (sixty-seven semitones), highest notes (c#4), densest sonority (thirteen notes sounding simultaneously), loudest dynamic level (mezzo forte followed by crescendo), and longest duration between notes struck (1.75 quarter notes). They also feature the most complex use of pc set genera, for it is here that octatonic, diatonic, and whole-tone materials alternate rapidly to create a complex sonorous surface.

Unlike "La fille aux cheveux de lin" and "Voiles," the role of invariance as a tonal determinant in "Feuilles mortes" is not as simple as sounding a particular group of pcs over and over to the exclusion of others. Here Debussy recycles the aggregate frequently, and although the pcs that are emphasized bear a strong relationship to the key signature, they are not the pcs traditionally construed as primary referents: tonic, dominant, and their triads. Also, the emphasis on pcs associated with the diatonic key signature is countered by giving comparable emphasis to other pcs that are foreign to the signature. Certainly this accounts in part for the recurrent tonal ambiguity vis-à-vis the key signature. Moreover, saturation with pcs from the key signature's form of set 7–35 (pcs 3,4,6,8,9,11,1) fluctuates from one subdivision to the next.[48]

The principle that juxtaposes sets from contrasting genera in single chords or brief passages occupies an important role in "Feuilles mortes," as it structures the pc content of the prelude's most complicated pc fields, in sections 6 and 7. The improvisational effect of the technique (most evident in section 7, mm. 37–40) is characteristic of Debussy's style.

THE OCTATONIC GENUS

The octatonic genus embraces all of the subsets and supersets of set 8–28, which generates the octatonic scale. (A complete list appears in appendix 5.) In size the genus falls between the diatonic and whole-tone genera, with forty-four primary and four secondary sets. The latter include four nonoctatonic hexachords: 6–Z28, 6–Z29, 6–Z42, and 6–Z45 (listed parenthetically in the appendix).

Like the diatonic and whole-tone genera, the octatonic genus includes many symmetrical sets whose sonorous properties make them aurally distinctive and readily identifiable.

The list of characteristic sets in table 3.7 is the longest so far, and its arrangement indicates some unique features. The octatonic genus holds 3 and 6 as its characteristic ics; the interval contents that remain are distributed uniformly across each set's vector. The sets in the right branch of table 3.7 show this most clearly, but those in the left branch exhibit the same trend. An important aspect of the genus (and the scale which gives it its name) is the alternating whole and half steps among many sets' sias; this is especially apparent for sets in the left branch. Sets 5–31 through 8–28 strongly manifest both characteristics; hence the branches merge in them.

Because the sia of octatonic cynosural set 8–28 is highly symmetrical, there are no distinct inversion forms and only three distinct transpositions. The latter appear in table 3.8 labeled types A, B, and C. Each pair of types shares an invariant subset of four pcs that form complementary tetrachord 4–28.

The octatonic genus poses an alternative *mean* to the diatonic genus between the extremes represented by the chromatic and whole-tone genera. Whereas the diatonic genus locates whole and half steps asymmetrically in its sets' sias, the octatonic genus positions them symmetrically.

The octatonic genus shares sets with the diatonic genus, a feature that well suits it to Debussy's techniques of juxtaposition, superimposition, transformation

TABLE 3.7. Characteristic sets for the octatonic genus

Set name	SIA	IV			
3–2	1–2–9	111000			
			3–10	3–3–6	002001
4–3	1–2–1–8	212100			
4–10	2–1–2–7	122010			
			4–28	3–3–3–3	004002
5–10	1–2–1–2–6	223111			

5–31	1–2–3–3–3	114112
6–Z13	1–2–1–2–1–5	324222
6–Z23	2–1–2–1–2–4	234222
6–27	1–2–1–2–3–3	225222
6–30	1–2–3–1–2–3	224223
7–31	2–1–2–1–2–1–3	336333
8–28	1–2–1–2–1–2–1–2	448444

through common elements, and the exploration of ambiguities engendered by shared elements.

The ubiquity of the octatonic scale and its fragments in much early twentieth-century music is common knowledge;[49] that Debussy is among the composers who used it extensively is less well known.[50]

MODULATION IN THE PC SET GENERA

Thus far we have concentrated on properties that arise more from ic content than from pc content. Each genus's cynosural set occurs in any of several distinct pc forms, and any one form determines the pc contents of the rest of that genus's sets. A specific pc form of a cynosural set serves as a *referential collection* (rc) for the subsets and supersets that cluster about it. A mutation from one pc form to another—in other words, from one referential collection to another—extends to the other sets in the genus as well. The cognate for this principle in common-practice tonal music resides in the notion that a distinct scale collection may serve as a reference for one among the twelve major keys.[51] A change from one such scale collection to another is called *modulation*.

Considered in set-theoretic terms, modulation between relative keys is trivial, since referential pc content increases (through chromatic additions) but does not entail replacement of pcs.[52] Modulation to related and distant keys is nontrivial,

TABLE 3.8. Distinct forms of octatonic cynosural set 8–28

Set form (8–28)	Invariant subsets (4–28)	
Type A = 0,1, 3,4, 6,7, 9,10		
Type B = 1,2, 4,5, 7,8, 10,11	1,4,7,10	
Type C = 2,3, 5,6, 8,9, 11,0	2,5,8,11	0,3,6,9

however, because some pcs are *always* replaced by others under the operation of transposition. Assuming no change of mode, the difference in sound between two keys is due to the change in pc content (not ic content); consequently, the greater the change in pc content (the more distant the new key), the greater the sonorous difference. Extremes range from replacement of one pc (as in major scales a P4 or P5 apart) to replacement of five pcs (as in major scales a semitone or tritone apart).

Hereafter, wherever a specific pc content for a genus is identified, it will be labeled rc. In the case of the diatonic genus, rcs will be identified by association with one of twelve major-scale collections whose pc content they encompass. For example, "rc = A major" means an rc of pcs 8,9,11,1,2,4,6. (It does *not* mean "key of A major," though a passage set in this rc may also project A as tonic.) Specific pc forms of octatonic cynosural set 8–28 will be identified by type (A, B, or C), as in "rc = 8–28 type A" (pcs 0,1,3,4,6,7,9,10); pc forms of whole-tone cynosural set 6–35 will be identified as type 0 (pcs 0,2,4,6,8,10) or type 1 (pcs 1,3,5,7,9,11). The whole-tone genus also permits modulation, but between only two transposition forms of set 6–35, its cynosural hexachord; whole-tone rcs will be categorized henceforth as type 0 (for the whole-tone scale that includes pc 0) or type 1.[53] The octatonic genus permits modulation among its three types, A, B, and C, as shown in table 3.8.[54]

For the diatonic genus, it is not always possible to identify an rc with certainty since there may be more than one transposition form of cynosural set 7–35 that contains or is contained in the given diatonic pc field. If a passage's pc content is embodied in set 8–23, for example, there will be two rcs grouped about forms of 7–35: rc = E♭ major or rc = A♭ major (see ex. 4.4A). Similarly, if hexachord 6–32 accounts for the total pc content of a passage, there are two rcs: rc = C major or rc = F major (see ex. 4.4B). In some cases it is possible to identify the rc through implicit association with a tonal-harmonic function. If, for example, in the case of 8–23, pcs 10,0,5,8 are projected prominently as a V[7] sonority, then rc = E♭ major is the more likely choice (though certainly other factors could militate against it). Ambiguous cases must carry identifiers in their ascriptions: a list of multiple rcs is separated by the word *or* (as in rc = A♭ major or E♭ major), unless there is contextual support for one rc over another, in which case that rc is followed by a question mark (rc = A♭ major?).

The whole-tone genus eschews such problems of identification, for any subset or superset can be associated with only one cynosural rc. Octatonic passages rarely resist identification of their referential collections, though some smaller sets point to more than one of the three distinct types. (Any form of tetrachord 4–28, for example, will always fit into two transposition forms of 8–28.)

The concept of modulation has no application to the chromatic genus, which has no cynosural set to transpose. The essence of the chromatic genus resides more in sets of sias rich in semitones than in specific inventories of pcs.

The use of referential collections facilitates sorting of refractory pc fields into appropriate pc set genera and enables distinctions to be drawn between changes of pc content alone (modulation) and changes of pc and ic content (generic mutation). Of the two, change of genus is the more drastic. Debussy availed himself of both means of effecting gross changes in pitch materials, and exploited in various ways the extended range of sonorous contrast they offer.

FOUR

THE PC SET GENERA IN EARLY WORKS

So far as I can determine, Debussy's first pieces to employ the pc set genera appear among the *Cinq poèmes de Charles Baudelaire,* which Lesure dates 1887–89.[1] Two songs, "La mort des amants" and "Le balcon," were completed in December 1887 and January 1888, respectively. Their pitch materials are highly chromatic, tonal, and conform to a style that I would call post-Romantic. A third song, "Harmonie du soir," was completed in January 1889. It, too, is post-Romantic in its use of a diatonic-tonal idiom enriched by copious chromaticism.

The songs that remain—"Le jet d'eau" and "Recueillement"—were completed in March 1889 or later. They do employ the pc set genera. "Recueillement" uses the diatonic, octatonic, and whole-tone genera, which it subjects to the same kinds of treatment found in much later works, including modulations, exploitation of generic ambiguity for shared sets, and juxtaposition of pairs of pentachords from different genera in brief passages where one is transformed into the other by semitonal shifting of a single pc or pc dyad.

There is no trace of the genera in instrumental works until the String Quartet of 1893, though vocal works during that time employ them, such as the first book of *Fêtes galantes* (1891)[2] and the *Proses lyriques* (1892–93).[3] Perhaps the expressive demands of texts drove Debussy to seek more radical pitch combinations for the songs. In any case, the quartet is the first instrumental piece to exploit the genera, and most of his subsequent works incorporate them.[4]

Pitch-class set resources interconnect with nonpitch and extramusical features in several ways, including use of the genera to achieve formal coherence and choice of genus to promote text expression. Complement relations are numerous. They serve to interconnect small sets that are assigned special functions within large collections that provide their local pc fields, and to link together formal units at the level of detail.

"RECUEILLEMENT"

Together with "Le jet d'eau," "Recueillement" marks a break with the early, wholly diatonic-tonal songs.[5] It manifests many features in its pc materials and their relations with nonpitch elements that are typical of Debussy's mature and late works, including: the use of pc set genera as sonorous resources; the principle of mutation between genera through voice leading or kinesthetic shifting (which points to tonal origins for the pc genera); and the use of complement pairs (which are tied to aspects of form). In addition, "Recueillement" shows the composer concerned (as always) with finding efficacious musical materials to aid in text expression.

Form

Baudelaire's poem consists of fourteen lines grouped in four stanzas: four lines in each of the first two and three in each of the last. The phrasing of Debussy's setting follows this form (fig. 4.1). Each line is set in a single phrase except for stanza 3, line 9, which is broken into two phrases. The break reflects that within the line itself; line 9 begins with the end of a sentence ("Loin d'eux") followed by the first clause of the next ("Vois se pencher les défuntes Années"), and is the only line broken in this way. There are, in addition, two introductory phrases. The phrase lengths are similar throughout but highly variable: only five of eighteen span the mean length of about four bars; the rest range from two to nine. Along with other features in the realm of pitch, the fluctuant phrase lengths contribute to an impression of impulsiveness and unpredictability.[6]

PC Sets, Genera, and Referential Collections

It is the appearance of the pc set genera in "Recueillement" that distinguishes it (along with "Le jet d'eau") as a radical advance over earlier works.[7] The diatonic, whole-tone, and octatonic genera (enriched occasionally by the chromatic genus) serve as pc set resources, and the song proceeds through a series of passages, each composed of a particular genus. Mutations or modulations partition the setting into phrases (thus helping to define formal boundaries), but there are also special groups of very brief passages (a measure or less) that vacillate between two genera or between two rcs, and these groups normally cohere to form phrases (thus helping to generate form).

Example 4.1 presents a pc reduction of the song. Its first system displays selected voice-leading motions that connect pairs of genera or rcs; its second system isolates important sets; pc set genera and rcs are identified below.

The diatonic genus is normative for the pc set materials of "Recueillement," and generic mutations use this genus as a point of departure or a goal (fig. 4.1, fourth column). With only one exception at mm. 30–31 (and this for expressive purposes explained below), whole-tone and octatonic passages are always juxtaposed with diatonic passages. Diatonic cynosural set 7–35 is rarely present; it is most often represented by pentachord 5–34, which is one of the composition's characteristic harmonies (along with octatonic 5–31 and whole tone 5–33), and by 6–33, which is a linear subset of 7–35.[8] Since any form of either 5–34 or 6–33 holds only one form of 7–35 as a superset, it is easy to identify rcs for most of the

FIGURE 4.1. Formal plan for "Recueillement"

Phrase	Tempo/meter	Measures		Genus	RC	Stanza/line	Text
(1–3)[a]	4/4—Lento e tranquillo	1	(14)[b]	Diatonic	A major		
(4–6)		4.5	(2)	Octatonic	Type A		
		5	(2)	Diatonic	A major		
		5.5	(6)	Octatonic	Type A		
	Rit. (fermata)						
(7–11)		7	(20)	Modulation	Type C	1/1	Sois sage, ô ma Douleur, et tiens-toi plus tranquille,
(12–14)	(Transition)	12	(4)	Diatonic	D♯ major?	1/2	Tu réclamais le Soir; il descend; le voici:
		13	(4)		G♯ major?		
		14	(4)		C major?		
(15–20)	3/4—A tempo rubato	15	(18)	Diatonic or whole-tone?	F major or type O?	1/3	Une atmosphère obscure enveloppe la ville,
(21–24)		21	(12)	Diatonic	B♭ major	1/4	Aux uns portant la paix, aux autres le souci.

FIGURE 4.1. *Continued*

Phrase	Tempo/meter	Measures	Genus	RC	Stanza/line	Text
(25–28)		25 (3)	Whole-tone	Type 1	2/5	Pendant que des mortels la multitude vile,
		26 (3)	Diatonic	F♯ major		
		27 (3)	Whole-tone	Type 1		
		28 (3)	Diatonic	F♯ major		
(29–31)		29 (2)	Octatonic	Type C	2/6	Sous le fouet du Plaisir, ce bourreau sans merci,
		(1)	Modulation	Type B		
		30 (2)	Modulation	Type C		
		(1)	Modulation	Type B		
		31 (3)	Whole-tone	Type 1		
(32–35)		32 (3)	Diatonic?	F major	2/7	Va cueillir des remords dans la fête servile,
		33 (9)	Modulation	D major		
		34	Modulation	E major		
	Rit.					
(36–39)	4/4—Tempo I°	36 (14)	Diatonic	A major	2/8	Ma Douleur, donne-moi la main; viens par ici,
(39.5–41)	3/4—Stesso tempo	39.5 (2)	Octatonic	Type A	3/9	Loin d'eux.
		40 (7)	Diatonic	A major		
(42–44)		42 (3)	Octatonic	Type B		Vois se pencher les défuntes Années,

Measure	Tempo	Phrase (measures)[a]	Duration[b]		Key/Type	Formal unit	Text
43			(3)	Diatonic	F major		
44			(3)	Octatonic	Type B		
45		(45–48)	(6)	Diatonic	F♯ major	3/10	Sur les balcons du ciel, en robes sur-années;
47			(6)	Modulation	B♭ major		
49		(49–52)	(3)	Octatonic	Type C	3/11	Surgir du fond des eaux le Regret souriant;
50			(3)	Diatonic	E major		
51			(3)	Octatonic/whole-tone?	Type C + type O?		
52			(3)	Diatonic	E major		
53		(53–55)	(2)	Whole-tone	Type 1	4/12	Le Soleil moribond s'endormir sous une arche,
			(1)	Diatonic	B♭ major		
54			(2)	Whole-tone	Type 1		
			(1)	Diatonic	B♭ major		
55			(3)	Whole-tone	Type 1		
56	Rit. Solenne	(56–59)	(9)	Diatonic	F major	4/13	Et, comme un long linceuil traînent à l'Orient,
60	4/4—Molto lento	(60–61)	(8)	Modulation	C♯ major		
62		(62–66)	(2)	Octatonic	Type B	4/14	Entends, ma chère, entends la douce Nuit qui marche.
			(10)	Diatonic	E major		
65			(8)	Modulation	C♯ major		
(66)							

[a] Length of phrase in measures
[b] Durations of formal units in quarter notes

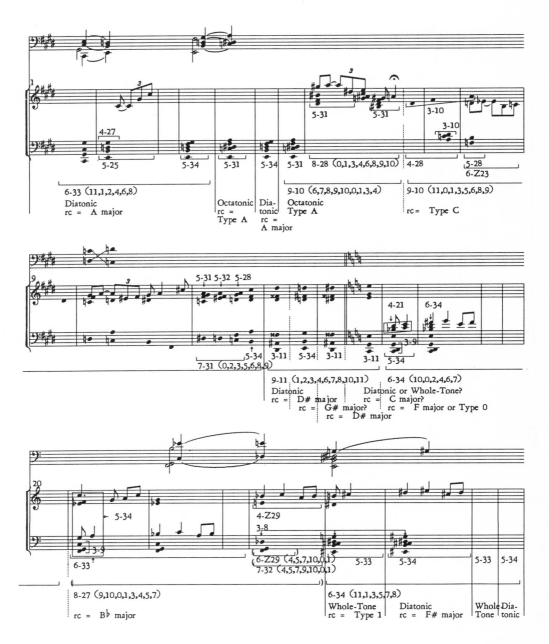

Example 4.1. PC reduction of "Recueillement"

Example 4.1. *Continued*

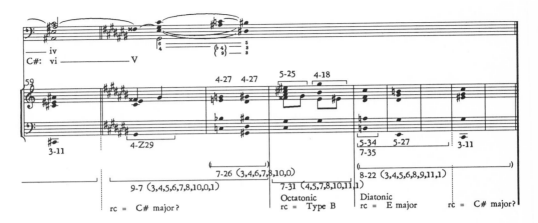

Example 4.1. *Continued*

diatonic passages. Longer diatonic passages include mm. 1–3, 21–24, 56–61, and 62.5–66. Each, save the last, occupies an entire phrase.

A refractory diatonic passage occurs at mm. 12–14, where a dominant-ninth sonority (5–34) is sandwiched between two occurrences of a major triad (3–11). It is refractory because the trichord and pentachord do not belong to the same rc, and because the rc of the former is indeterminate from pc content alone.[9] Here a conventional tonal-harmonic interpretation suggests origins for the chords in a series of enharmonic modulations via German augmented-sixth chords (with added ninths), whose resolutions entail elision (m. 12) and permissible fifths (m. 14). Example 4.2 illustrates this rationale, with conventional resolutions through $^6_4$–$^5_3$ voice leading. The succession of keys proceeds from D♯ major through G♯ major to C major, and encompasses the dominant-ninth sonority (5–34) of m. 11 (an anomalous set at the end of that otherwise octatonic passage). The chromatic-third relationship between the chords of mm. 14–15 requires enharmonic interpretation of the D♯ triad as a mixture mediant (♭III).

The octatonic genus is nowhere more audible than in mm. 5.5–11 (which embody a modulation at the phrase boundary between mm. 6–7).[10] Its characteristic sonority is pentachord 5–31, which appears in inversely equivalent forms in mm. 5.5–6. Other prominent octatonic passages include mm. 29–30 (which incorporates modulations between rc-types C and B) and m. 62/beats 1–2.

The whole-tone genus is most often represented by pentachord 5–33 and tetrachord 4–24. Both are unambiguously whole-tone, since neither occurs in the diatonic or octatonic genera. The genus is conspicuous at mm. 31 and 55; both passages consist of a single form of 4–24 that occupies an entire measure, and both coincide with the ends of lines in the poem.

In contrast to the diatonic genus, the octatonic and whole-tone genera occur mainly in brief passages. (One bar or less is common: see, for example, mm. 4–5, 39.5, and 53–54.) Each is paired with the diatonic genus, where both are represented by pentachords that can be transformed one into the other through

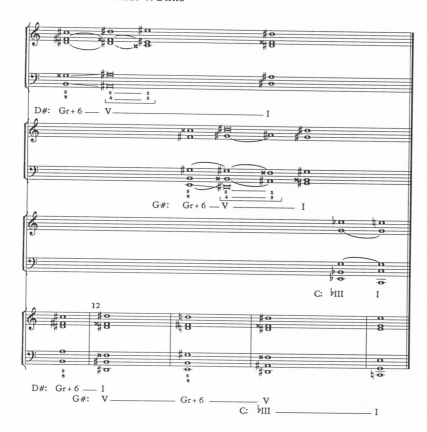

Example 4.2. Harmonic analysis of "Recueillement," mm. 11–15.

semitonal shifts of one or more pcs. The first instance occurs in mm. 4–5, where diatonic 5–34 alternates with octatonic 5–31 in forms that share two invariants (pcs 4,6) and whose remaining elements are related by half steps. The voice leading sketch above m. 4 in example 4.1 shows that octatonic 5–31 results when pcs 2,8,11 move by step to pcs 3,9,0. Of course, construed conventionally, the octatonic harmony results from the neighbor-note motion about the dominant-ninth sonority (5–34), and herein lies a key to the origin of Debussy's pc set genera: his well-established tonal technique, with its emphasis on neighbor-note elaborations, both diatonic and chromatic. Moreover, this particular voice-leading or kinesthetic (semitonal) shift has a precedent in the diatonic sonority of m. 2, where two pcs (2,11) emerge by step from pc 1 of m. 1. There are many similar passages. In mm. 25–28, for example, diatonic 5–34 alternates with whole-tone 5–33 by replacing pc 7 with pc 8,[11] and mm. 42–45 vacillate between diatonic and octatonic pentachords (5–34 versus 5–31) by shifting four pcs around invariant pc 2 (4,7,10,0 replace 5,8,11,1). In all cases there is a diatonic harmony (5–34) that is "distorted" by chromatic stepwise motion to create a nondiatonic sonority. These voice-leading/kinesthetic shifts are all depicted in example 4.1.

In addition, there is one passage in which modulation within the octatonic genus is accomplished by exchanging pcs 3,4,6 around two invariants (mm. 29–30); here, chromatic passing motion rather than neighbor-note motion provides the means for the transformations from rc = type C to type B. The source set for the first rc of each bar is set 6–27, which is a conspicuous hexachord throughout the early twentieth-century atonal repertoire; it is encountered often in Debussy's oeuvre from 1889 on, as a distinct sonority (as in the present example) and not merely as a "coincidence" of voice leading.[12] Passing motion is also crucial in mm. 32–33, where it connects two diatonic rcs. This is one of the few passages where chromatic sets play a distinct role, and they appear in the upper line where they fill the interstices between diatonic pcs (10,0,2,4,5,7).

A special sonority found in "Recueillement" is atonal hexachord 6–34.[13] Though not a member of any of the three genera, it links the pc content of diatonic and whole-tone pairs, as in mm. 25–28, where it results from the pentachords' four invariants plus the dyad of alternating pcs—a typical usage encountered frequently in other works. The hexachord first occurs, however, as the pc content of mm. 16–20, a passage that would be wholly diatonic were it not for a recurrent chromatic neighbor note that embellishes pentachord 5–34 (F♯). In both cases the sonority's origins lie in voice leading.

Examples of formal boundaries in "Recueillement" that are defined either by generic mutation or modulation include the fermata at the end of m. 6, which marks a division between two phrases and is followed by a modulation within the octatonic genus; the boundary at m. 12, which sees a mutation to the diatonic genus (adumbrated at the end of m. 11 by set 5–34, which is anomalous to the octatonic genus but whose pc content is embraced by its superset, 9–10); the modulation at m. 15; another at m. 21; and so forth. There is, in fact, only one phrase boundary that is not supported by generic changes or modulations—that between mm. 3–4. There are, however, numerous mutations and modulations that occur within and cohere to form phrases. Examples include the generic pairs of mm. 4–6, 25–28, 42–44, 49–52, and 53–55, and the modulation pairs of mm. 29–31.

Tonal Focus and Complement Pairs

In spite of the prevalence of nondiatonic harmonies, "Recueillement" is a tonal piece, but its tonality is much closer to that of "Feuilles mortes" than to the "Arabesques" or earliest songs. As the key signature suggests, the pcs associated with E major saturate the piece.

A number of complement pairs occur in strategic locations. Set 9–10 (in two transpositions) accounts for the pc content of mm. 5.5–6 and 7–11; its complement (3–10) appears conspicuously at the juncture of the two, in the vocal line of mm. 7–8 and as the supporting harmony. For Debussy, relations are common and typical between complement pairs and formal features in which the large set accounts for the pc content of a formal unit while the small set is projected prominently at its beginning or end.

Another important pair occurs when the three octatonic harmonies of m. 11 form set 7–31. The first of these is its embedded complement, 5–31, but 5–31 also occurs as the first sonority of the passage (and the one most often articulated) in m. 5. Here the pair frames the octatonic boundaries rather than formal boundaries (since the passage spans more than one formal unit).

A diatonic pair occurs in mm. 12–15, where forms of 3–11 supply three of four harmonies and are embedded in 9–11, which links the pc content of one phrase to the beginning of the next. This striking passage engendered the complicated tonal rationale presented in example 4.2. Another diatonic pair occurs at mm. 56–59 (also complicated tonally), whose first sonority (4–26) complements that of the overall pc content (8–26).

Text Expression

Text expression receives considerable attention in part 3 below. For now I shall draw attention to a few manifestations in "Recueillement."

Only one brief passage in the song embodies real ambiguities in the determination of its genus: mm. 15–20, designated "Diatonic or whole-tone?" in figure 4.1. The ambiguity stems from the presence of nongeneric set 6–34, which is crucial to this phrase. Diatonic sets 3–9, 3–11, and 5–34 are conspicuous aurally in mm. 15, 16, 18, and 20, but the presence of F♯ in mm. 17 and 19 obfuscates by injecting a whole-tone color, especially as a linear extension of the parallel M3s of the bars that precede its appearance. This generic ambiguity matches the words of the poem: "An obscure atmosphere envelops the city."

The phrases that group pairs of genera set the poem's darkest, most intense passages: mm. 25–28 ("While the vile multitude of mortals . . ."); mm. 29–31 ("Under the lash of pleasure, that merciless tormentor . . ."); mm. 42–45 ("See the dead years leaning . . ."); mm. 49–52 ("smiling regret surging from the water's depths . . ."); mm. 53–55 ("The dying sun sleeps beneath an arch . . ."). As we shall see, Debussy developed, for *Pelléas et Mélisande*, a dialectic of text expression through pc genera in which darker emotions are consistently associated with nondiatonic materials and benign emotions linked to the diatonic genus. "Recueillement" does not venture that far, since diatonic and nondiatonic sets are usually paired, but the song does associate its more exotic sonorities with the poem's darker passages and reserves the longer diatonic passages for expression of calmer emotions: mm. 12–15 ("You asked for the evening; it descends, it is here . . ."); mm. 21–24 ("To some it brings peace, to others care . . ."); mm. 60–66 ("Listen, my beloved, listen to the soft night as it steps along . . .").

Of particular interest is a phrase—mm. 53–55—that features whole-tone sets (in alternation with diatonic sets) and hints strongly at death ("dying sun"). As we shall see, in *Pelléas et Mélisande* Debussy consistently associates the whole-tone genus with death and with that which is mysterious, beyond mortal control or comprehension.

A single pairing provides a final illustration: mm. 36–40 feature a truncated, slightly altered reprise of mm. 1–5 to set the sentence "My Sorrow, give me your hand; come over here, / Far from them." The reprise immediately invokes the poem's beginning, as the speaker's attention returns to the companion addressed there.

"LE JET D'EAU"

"Le jet d'eau" shares several features with "Recueillement." It employs the diatonic and whole-tone genera, and its many semitonal fragments augur the chromatic genus, though here (as in "Recueillement") they serve tonal imperatives (filling out linear progressions in mm. 11–12, for example). Particularly striking are the whole-tone passages of mm. 22, 24, and 32, which recur twice more as a group (at mm. 51, 53, 61 and 83, 85, 93). Most of the piece is set in the diatonic genus, enriched by copious chromaticism and frequent modulations. The whole-tone passages coincide with the refrain ("The spring of water that cradles / Its thousand flowers, . . . Falls like a shower / Of huge tears")[14] and seem intended less to set a specific mood or emotion than to frame and draw attention to the refrain. The most overtly erotic portions of the text are set firmly in the diatonic genus, often intensified by descending chromatic lines. (See, for example, mm. 6–11 setting "Rest for a while without opening [your eyes], / In that casual pose / Where you were surprised by pleasure.")[15]

STRING QUARTET

Debussy's first major chamber work, the String Quartet of 1893, is the first instrumental work to employ the pc set genera. The quartet is dominated by the diatonic genus but uses the octatonic and whole-tone genera as well. Example 4.3 presents pc reductions of five of the nondiatonic passages. Each appears within its immediate diatonic context. (Locations of passages are cited above each example counting forward or backward from rehearsal numbers enclosed in brackets; thus, "[1] + 9" means the ninth bar after rehearsal number 1, while "[3] − 1" means one bar before rehearsal number 3.)

In the first passage (ex. 4.3A), the conjunction of 4–25 and 4–27 in octatonic 5–28 evokes that genus (even though each tetrachord belongs to other genera as well).[16] This octatonic passage may be traced to the flatted F (lowered (mixture) third degree in D♭ major), heard as a chromatic distortion of the surrounding diatonicism. Whatever its origin, the sound here is octatonic.

Passages B through E of example 4.3 are whole-tone; they, too, are nestled between diatonic contexts and their pc contents may be heard as arising from chromatic distortion of those of their diatonic neighbors.

All five passages illustrate Debussy's technique of transforming one genus into another by semitonal shifts of selected elements. For passage B, an exchange of pcs 3,5 for 2,4 transforms diatonic hexachord 6–33 into whole-tone 6–35. Pitch classes 6,8 are then exchanged for pcs 7,9 and a seventh pc is added (pc 10), which mutates the whole-tone scale into diatonic set 7–35. In passage C, pcs 0,2 replace

Example 4.3. Nondiatonic passages in the String Quartet, I

Example 4.3. *Continued*

pcs 1,3 with similar effect (the diatonic set is truncated into whole-tone), and in passage D pcs 7,9,11 replace 6,8,10 (diatonic becomes whole-tone). Passage E exchanges pcs 1,3 for 0,2 (diatonic mutates to whole-tone).

Changes in pc set genera create striking sonorous contrasts that are not possible within the diatonic genus alone, and the locations of changes are crucial, for they invariably precede (and thereby capture the listener's attention for) important formal junctures. Passage A occurs precisely at the end of the opening movement's first-theme group and is followed by the initial presentation of the second theme (characterized by marked changes in dynamic level, articulation, figuration, and registral spacing). Passage B's whole-tone materials are bolstered by changes in tempo, dynamic intensity, articulation, texture, and placement in a high tessitura with a relatively wide register span. These features combine with the pc materials to create a moment of unusual intensity just prior to the climax of the development, shortly before the movement's reprise at [5]. Passage C occupies the same position in the recapitulation as passage A in the exposition: it immediately precedes the second theme. Passage D occurs four bars before the first important formal juncture of the third movement's ternary design, at the close of the first section. Passage E, also from the third movement, is one of two whole-tone variants of the diatonic phrases with which they alternate. Together, the three phrases (whole-tone, diatonic, whole-tone) consume fourteen bars beginning at [13]. The climax of this middle section (marked by a more deliberate tempo, forte dynamic level, dense texture, elaborate figuration, and the movement's widest register span) begins at the next bar.

Debussy's use of pc set genera in relatively early works show him developing procedures to establish and interrelate the genera as resources for sonorous contrast and means of coherence through harmonic, thematic, and kinesthetic means. There is also evidence of his concern to integrate these new resources with other musical parameters. In the quartet, the placements of nondiatonic genera are consistently connected with locations of important formal junctures. In the songs, there is evidence of his intent to assist text expression by associating certain general moods or types of emotions with specific genera. These features attest to the pragmatic concerns behind Debussy's flippant remark to his teacher, Ernest Guiraud, as recorded by Maurice Emmanuel: "The tonal scale must be enriched by other scales. . . . There is no theory. You have merely to listen. Pleasure is the law."[17] They also demonstrate concretely Louis Laloy's assertions, of which the following are particularly cogent:

> The invention [of scales] goes back to the ancient Greeks and has lasted until our time. Thus, a sound ceases being a sound in order to become a note, that is to say, a number in a certain order; no particular impression is created by one note or another, but a note is recognized as the first, third, or sixth of a certain scale. . . .
>
> Frequently [Debussy's] melodies use only the notes of the major scale; his chords belong to a specified tonality. Therefore they manifest the classical system, but without any premeditated intention to conform, and only because this disposition is the same as his fantasy. They also manifest other sounds: one seems to hear echos of ancient modes, Gregorian chant, or Greek music, Chinese scales without semitones, or chromatic scales entirely in semitones, whole-tone scales, and still others with accidentals hitherto unknown on the fourth, fifth, and seventh degrees. . . .
>
> There is more: we are arriving at a time when any chord, however built and even if it cannot be broken down into harmonic components, can count as a consonance. A chord no longer needs to be legitimate. It is a sonority which, if properly used, will give the ear full satisfaction. Combinations of sound will contribute to another, overall sound, in the same way that juxtapositions of color will create the impression of another, different color.[18]

The last two paragraphs are compatible with what I have described as the pc set genera. Laloy's reference to "still others [scales] with accidentals hitherto unknown"[19] could describe the octatonic genus (as well as one other that will be discussed below). Since Laloy wrote the only biography approved by Debussy and was in frequent contact with the composer during this period, one may assume that he spoke for Debussy, or at least with Debussy's concurrence. These comments are the closest I have encountered to a specific technical description of Debussy's pitch materials either by the composer himself or by anyone close enough to be considered a spokesperson.

THE 8–17/18/19–COMPLEX GENUS OF PC SETS

Perhaps Debussy's most interesting resource is what I call the 8–17/18/19–complex genus. It occurs throughout his oeuvre and is especially common in vocal and dramatic works. This genus encompasses three octachords (8–17, 8–18, and 8–19), together with their subsets and supersets. The complete list appears in appendix 6 and embraces 152 sets in all: 147 primary sets and 5 secondary hexachordal complements. In this raw form the genus threatens to sow confusion, since it includes many members of the diatonic, whole-tone, and octatonic genera, and, therefore, some passages of limited pc content that would normally be assigned to one of them may be accounted for by this genus as well. This threat is mitigated, however, by the fact that not all sets on the list are prominent in passages identified as 8–17/18/19–complex; in fact, such passages usually feature a much smaller subclass of sets, and a very select group is especially salient. Additional specifications illuminate some unique features and narrow the list to more useful proportions.

The three cynosural octachords share features that link them to one another as well as distinguish them from octachords associated with the other genera. These features reside in their kinesthetic properties, which can be seen in the sias of the octachords' sets, in their basic-interval patterns (bips) as defined by Forte,[20] and in the realm of similarity relations. The sias of 8–17, 8–18, and 8–19, for example, all end in ic 3, whereas those of the diatonic, whole-tone, and octatonic octachords end in ic 2. Moreover, the sias for all of the 8–17/18/19–complex octachords exhibit identical proportions in their mixtures of ics 1,2,3. This is easily seen by examining bips; those for octachords from the other genera are markedly different (table 4.1). Similarity relations among the 8–17/18/19–complex octachords reveal strong interconnections, as do those for octachords within each of the other genera (see table 4.2A). For each genus, the index of similarity for any pair of octachords is no greater than 2.[21] In contrast, a comparison with ivs for octachords of the diatonic, whole-tone, and octatonic genera shows indices of 3, 4, or 5 (see table 4.2B). The strong similarity of intervallic and sia relations *within* the 8–17/18/19–complex genus, and the weakness of such relations *between* the 8–17/18/19–complex octachords and those of the other genera, confirm both the genus's sonorous homogeneity and its distinctiveness.

We may identify three important subgroups within the 8–17/18/19–complex genus. First, fifty-five three-to-nine-note sets are subsets or supersets of all three cynosural octachords (table 4.3). Compared with appendix 6, the sias of sets in

TABLE 4.1. Sias and bips for octachords from the 8–17/18/19–complex, diatonic, whole-tone, and octatonic pc set genera

Genus	Set	SIA	BIP
8–17/18/19–Complex	8–17	1–2–1–1–1–2–1–3	11111223
	8–18	1–1–1–2–1–2–1–3	11111223
	8–19	1–1–2–1–1–2–1–3	11111223
Diatonic	8–22	1–1–1–2–1–2–2–2	11112222
	8–23	1–1–1–2–2–1–2–2	11112222
	8–26	1–1–2–1–2–2–1–2	11112222
Whole-tone	8–21	1–1–1–1–2–2–2–2	11112222
	8–24	1–1–2–1–1–2–2–2	11112222
	8–25	1–1–2–2–1–1–2–2	11112222
Octatonic	8–28	1–2–1–2–1–2–1–2	11112222

TABLE 4.2. Interval-similarity relations for octachords within the 8–17/18/19–Complex genus, and between the 8–17/18/19–Complex genus and the diatonic, whole-tone, and octatonic genera

A. Relations within each genus

8–17/18/19–Complex		Diatonic		Whole-tone	
8–17 [546652]		8–22 [465562]		8–21 [474643]	
8–18 [546553]		8–23 [465472]		8–24 [464743]	
8–19 [545752]		8–26 [456562]		8–25 [464644]	

B. Relations between 8–17/18/19–Complex octachords and other genera

Diatonic	Whole-tone	Octatonic
8–17	8–17	8–17
8–22]3	8–21]4	8–28]4
8–23]4	8–24]4	
8–26]2	8–25]4	
8–18	8–18	8–18
8–22]3	8–21]4	8–28]3
8–23]4	8–24]4	
8–26]2	8–25]4	
8–19	8–19	8–19
8–22]3	8–21]4	8–28]5
8–23]4	8–24]3	
8–26]3	8–25]4	

TABLE 4.3. Subsets and supersets of all three octachords in the 8–17/18/19-complex genus

Set	SIA	BIP	IV	Set	SIA	BIP	IV
3–1*	1–1–10	1110	210000				
3–2	1–2–9	129	111000				
3–3	1–3–8	138	101100	9–3	1–1–1–1–1–1–2–1–3	111111123	767763
3–4	1–4–7	147	100110				
3–5	1–5–6	156	100011				
3–6*	2–2–8	228	020100				
3–7	2–3–7	237	011010				
3–8	2–4–6	246	010101				
3–9*	2–5–5	255	010020				
3–10*	3–3–6	336	002001				
3–11	3–4–5	345	001110	9–11	1–1–1–2–1–1–2–1–2	111111222	667773
3–12*	4–4–4	444	000300				
4–2	1–1–2–8	1128	221100				
4–3*	1–2–1–8	1128	212100				
4–4	1–1–3–7	1137	211110				
4–5	1–1–4–6	1146	210111				
4–7*	1–3–1–4	1134	201210				
4–8*	1–4–1–3	1134	200121				
4–11	1–2–2–7	1227	121110				
4–12	2–1–3–6	1236	112101				
4–14	2–1–4–5	1245	111120				
4–Z15	1–3–2–6	1236	111111				
4–16	1–4–2–5	1245	110121	8–17*	1–2–1–1–1–2–1–3	11111223	546652
4–17*	3–1–3–5	1335	102210	8–18	1–1–1–2–1–2–1–3	11111223	546553
4–18	1–3–3–5	1335	102111	8–19	1–1–2–1–1–2–1–3	11111223	545752
4–19	1–3–4–4	1344	101310				
4–20*	1–4–3–4	1344	101220				
4–22	2–2–3–5	2235	021120				
4–24*	2–2–4–4	2244	020301				
4–26*	3–2–3–4	2334	012120				
4–27	2–3–3–4	2334	012111				
4–Z29	1–2–4–5	1245	111111				
5–10	1–2–1–2–6	11226	223111				
5–13	1–1–2–4–4	11244	221311				
5–16	1–2–1–3–5	11235	213211				
5–Z17*	1–2–1–4–4	11244	212320				
5–Z18	1–3–1–2–5	11235	212221				
5–20	1–2–4–1–4	11244	211231				
5–21	1–3–1–3–4	11334	202420				
5–22*	1–3–3–1–4	11334	202321				
5–26	2–2–1–3–4	12234	122311				
5–27	1–2–2–3–4	12234	122230				
5–30	1–3–2–2–4	12234	121321				
5–32	1–3–2–3–3	12333	113221				
5–Z37*	3–1–1–3–4	11334	212320				
5–Z38	1–1–3–3–4	11334	212221				
6–15	1–1–2–1–3–4	111234	323421				
6–Z19	1–2–1–3–1–4	111234	313431	6–Z44	1–1–3–1–3–3	111333	
6–31	1–2–2–3–1–3	112233	223431				

table 4.3 are significantly more uniform, as is evident especially in the bips of the pentachords. Second, there are forty-four sets that form complement pairs (table 4.4). This list is important because of Debussy's predilection for complements (a subject that will be discussed in chapter 6). It helps to explain the frequent occurrences of sets 7–26 and 7–30 in passages dominated by the 8–17/18/19–complex genus, for although these septachords are not especially strong representatives of the genus (neither appears as a subset of more than one octachord), their pentachordal complements are (both 5–26 and 5–30 are subsets of all three octachords). Third, an exclusive list of nineteen sets includes seventeen that are subsets and supersets of each other, plus two complements (4–18 and 7–21) that are subsets or supersets of most (table 4.5). These nineteen collections may be considered the genus's characteristic sets, both in terms of their sias and their interval contents, and all but three (4–7, 4–20, and 7–21) appear on each of the other lists (in tables 4.3 and 4.4). Conspicuous among their sias are seven trichordal patterns—1–1, 1–2, 1–3, 1–4, 2–2, 3–3, and 3–4—that connect all but two adjacent pairs of successive intervals. The exceptions are set 4–18, which includes 1–5 among its pairs of successive intervals, and 4–19, which includes 4–4 among its pairs.[22] Noticeable among ivs is a relatively large number of entries for ics 3 and 4, and a relatively small number of entries for ics 1 and 6.

The sets listed in tables 4.3, 4.4, and especially 4.5 are those most often encountered in passages dominated by this genus, and ascription of this genus requires the presence of representatives from the list in table 4.5.

Symmetrical Sets

Earlier we noted the prominent place that symmetry holds among the cynosural and characteristic sets of the other genera, a feature that promotes easy associa-

TABLE 4.4. Members of the 8–17/18/19–complex genus that form complement pairs[a]

3–3/9–3	4–17/8–17	5–13/7–13	6–15
3–4/9–4	4–18/8–18	5–16/7–16	6–Z19/6–Z44
3–5/9–5	4–19/8–19	5–Z17/7–Z17	6–31
3–10/9–10		5–Z18/7–Z18	
3–11/9–11		5–21/7–21	
3–12/9–12		5–22/7–22	
		5–26/7–26	
		5–30/7–30	
		5–32/7–32	
		5–Z37/7–Z37	
		5–Z38/7–Z38	

[a]Sets that are subsets or supersets of all three octachords include 3–3/9–3, 3–4, 3–5, 3–10, 3–11/9–11, 3–12, 4–17/8–17, 4–18/8–18, 4–19/8–19, 5–13, 5–16, 5–Z17, 5–Z18, 5–21, 5–22, 5–26, 5–30, 5–32, 5–Z37, 5–Z38, 6–15, 6–Z19/6–Z44, 6–31. Characteristic sets of the 8–17/18/19–complex genus include 3–3/9–3, 3–4, 3–11/9–11, 4–17/8–17, 4–18/8–18, 4–19/8–19, 5–21/7–21, 6–15, 6–Z19/6–Z44, 6–31.

TABLE 4.5. Characteristic sets for the 8–17/18/19–complex genus

Set	SIA	IV				
3–3[a]	1–3–8	101100				
3–4[b]	1–4–7	100110				
3–11[c]	3–4–5	001110				
*4–7	1–3–1–7	201210				
*4–17	3–1–3–5	102210				
			4–18	1–3–3–5		102111
4–19	1–3–4–4	101310				
*4–20	1–4–3–4	101220				
5–21	1–3–1–3–4	202420				
6–15	1–1–2–1–3–4	323421				
6–Z19	1–2–1–3–1–4	313431				
6–31	1–2–2–3–1–3	223431				
6–Z44	1–1–3–1–3–3	313431				
			7–21	1–1–2–1–3–1–3		424641
*8–17	1–2–1–1–1–2–1–3	546652				
8–18	1–1–1–2–1–2–1–3	546553				
8–19	1–1–2–1–1–2–1–3	545752				
9–3	1–1–1–1–1–1–2–1–3	767763				
9–11	1–1–1–2–1–1–2–1–2	667773				

[a]Subset of 4–7, 4–17, 4–19 (but not 4–20)
[b]Subset of 4–7, 4–19, 4–20 (but not 4–17)
[c]Subset of 4–17, 4–19, 4–20 (but not 4–7)

tion of a given set with its genus. The 8–17/18/19–complex evinces no such symmetries among either its octachords or its more exclusive lists of characteristic sets. Of the octachords, only 8–17 is symmetrical, and in appendix 6 the asterisks that denote symmetries are far more sparse than one might expect from such a large list. This feature attests to the richness and complexity of the genus, as well as to its amorphous character compared with the other genera.

The 8–17/18/19–Complex and Octatonic Genera Compared

The 8–17/18/19–complex and octatonic genera share thirty-eight three-to-nine-note sets (listed in table 4.6), including many of the octatonic genus's characteristic sets, such as 4–3, 4–10, 4–28, 5–10, 5–31, 6–27, 6–30, 7–31, and 9–10. Perhaps for Debussy these genera represented two facets of a basic sonus. Rarely are both found in the same piece, and even then they are not played off as foils. When they do appear together (as in "Feuilles mortes"), the 8–17/18/19–complex genus invariably arises from a synthesis of octatonic elements with those from the diatonic or whole-tone genus. At the end of "Feuilles mortes," the theme's descending line mutates from octatonic (4–3 embedded in 5–16) to diatonic (4–11 embedded in 5–27). This transformation accounts for the subtle difference between the overall pc set materials of the anomalous passages set in the 8–17/18/19–complex (mm. 47–52 are accounted for by set 8–19) and for the octatonic passages that occur throughout the composition.

TABLE 4.6. 8–17/18/19–Complex genus sets that are also members of the octatonic genus

Set	SIA	IV	Set	SIA	IV
+[a]3–2	1–2–9	111000			
+3–3	1–3–8	101100			
+3–5	1–5–6	100011			
+3–7	2–3–7	011010			
+3–8	2–4–6	010101			
+3–10*	3–3–6	002001	9–10*	1–1–1–1–2–1–2–1–2	668664
+3–11	3–4–5	001110			
+4–3*	1–2–1–8	212100			
4–9*	1–5–1–5	200022			
4–10*	2–1–2–7	122010			
+4–12	2–1–3–6	112101			
4–13	1–2–3–6	112011			
+4–Z15	1–3–2–6	111111			
+4–17*	3–1–3–5	102210			
+4–18	1–3–3–5	102111			
4–25*	2–4–2–4	020202			
+4–26*	3–2–3–4	012120			
+4–27	2–3–3–4	012111			
4–28*	3–3–3–3	004002	~~8–28*~~ ------ ~~1–2–1–2–1–2–1–2~~ ------		~~448444~~[b]
+4–Z29	1–2–4–5	111111			
5–10	1–2–1–2–6	223111			
+5–16	1–2–1–3–5	213211			
5–19	1–2–3–1–5	212122			
5–25	2–1–2–3–4	123121			
5–28	2–1–3–2–4	122212			
5–31	1–2–3–3–3	114112	7–31	1–2–1–2–1–2–3	336333
+5–32	1–3–2–3–3	113221			
6–Z13*	1–2–1–2–1–5	324222	(6–Z42)*	1–1–1–3–3–3	
6–Z23*	2–1–2–1–2–4	234222	~~(6–Z45)*~~ ---- ~~2–1–1–2–3–3~~ --		
6–27	1–2–1–2–3–3	225222			
(6–Z28)*	1–2–2–1–3–3	224322	6–Z49*	1–2–1–3–2–3	
(6–Z29)*	1–2–3–2–1–3	224232	6–Z50*	1–3–2–1–2–3	
6–30*	1–2–3–1–2–3	224223			

[a]A "+" sign means the set is a subset of all three 8–17/18/19–complex octachords.
[b]Strikethrough means the set is not a member of the 8–17/18/19–complex genus.

Modulation and the 8–17/18/19–Complex Genus

Identifying rcs for passages set in the 8–17/18/19–complex genus poses special problems—first, because each of the three cynosural octachords manifests different pc configurations, and, second, because the octachords' sias are unfamiliar, which makes their pc forms cumbersome to calculate. The fact that two of the octachords are asymmetrical and thus have twenty-four distinct forms each (rather than twelve or less) only compounds the difficulties; it is possible, nevertheless, to identify rcs in much the same manner as for the diatonic genus.

Example 4.4C illustrates the simplest case: it cites an rc for a given form of hexachord 6–22, which is a subset of only one octachord in only one form. Hence,

A. Diatonic genus

B. Diatonic genus

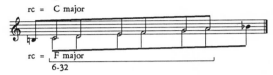

C. 8–17/18/19–Complex genus

D. 8–17/18/19–Complex genus

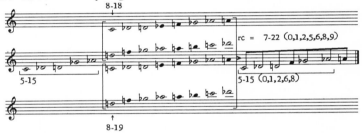

E. 8–17/18/19–Complex genus

Example 4.4. Identification of referential collections (rcs)

rc = 8–19 (0,1,2,4,5,6,8,9). Example 4.4D is more complex: set 5–15 is a subset of two octachords in two forms each; thus, it intersects with four of the cynosural octachord forms. These octachords share seven invariants that form set 7–22, which holds this form of 5–15 as a subset. Here set 7–22 represents as concretely as possible the rc for the 8–17/18/19–complex genus.

Example 4.4E is more complicated (though by no means does it present the most refractory situation). A passage whose pc content is accounted for by means of hexachord 6–Z29 is a subset of one form of octachord 8–17 and two forms of octachord 8–18. There is no common seven-note subset that also contains the hexachord; instead, there are two common seven-note sets, both forms of 7–32, that intersect with 8–17/8–18 pairs (ex. 4.4E). Here the appropriate identifier is "rc = 7–32 (0,3,4,6,7,9,11) or (0,3,4,6,8,9,11)." As with the diatonic genus, contextual features often help to reduce the range of possible rcs for the 8–17/18/19–complex.

Origins and Role of the Genus

An obvious question is: Why did Debussy employ two such similar genera? It is tempting to propose that the 8–17/18/19–complex genus represents Debussy's initial solution in a search for a sonorous alternative to the diatonic and whole-tone genera, and that the octatonic genus was a later refinement. But this is not the case, for we find both genera in early and late works. Despite notable exceptions, however, the 8–17/18/19–complex genus does appear most often in works with texts, whereas the octatonic genus is usually encountered in purely instrumental works.[23] Perhaps Debussy found more flexibility in the diverse set matrix offered by the 8–17/18/19–complex genus and considered it more amenable to his vocal muse and range of expressive possibilities. Octatonic sets may have seemed better suited to instrumental works, more congruent with an absolute conception of musical form. Conjecture aside, Debussy's fondness for the pc materials that constitute the 8–17/18/19–complex genus well suits his aesthetic preoccupation with expressive nuance and ambiguity, and his flexible, nondoctrinaire compositional technique.

FIVE

THE PC SET GENERA IN LATE WORKS

JEUX

The facts surrounding the commission, composition, and production of *Jeux* are well known.[1] Composed in 1912, its premiere on 15 May 1913 garnered a cool reception and was utterly eclipsed by the premiere of Stravinsky's *Sacre du printemps* two weeks later. The public's lack of enthusiasm must have been due in part to the subtlety of *Jeux*, which surely provoked consternation in an audience accustomed to the far more flamboyant spectacle that was the usual fare of the Ballets Russes.

PC Set Genera

Jeux opens with two gestures that contrast sharply: the brief ascending chromatic figure of mm. 1–4, set sparsely in harps, horn, and strings (ex. 5.1A), and the whole-tone material of mm. 5–8, set much more densely in full woodwinds plus strings, horn, and harp (ex. 5.1B). Together they comprise the ballet's "introduction"—in the most profound sense, since they contain within them the stuff of the composition's pitch materials, in terms both of general harmonic resources and of their specific manifestation as motives. These gestures point to the four pc set genera that serve as gross sonorous resources: chromatic, diatonic, 8–17/18/19–complex, and whole-tone. The last is explicitly projected in the second gesture; the others emerge gradually out of the first, whose slow tempo and distinct articulation encourages multiple trichordal and tetrachordal segmentations as well as a linear, tonal interpretation.

The four pc set genera are employed consistently throughout. In addition, the octatonic genus appears very rarely (and always in place of the 8–17/18/19–complex genus).

The chromatic genus is pervasive, integrated with each of the others in ways that are now familiar. Chromatic sets are used as transposition operators to manipulate nonchromatic sets (ex. 5.1C), or else they take the form of chromatic-stepwise lines that constitute motivic shapes used to accompany or counterpoint materials derived from the other genera (ex. 5.1D). Chromatic lines occasionally

Example 5.1. PC set genera in *Jeux*

inundate the musical surface; in such cases the genus predominates (in spite of the nonchromatic sonorities formed by the confluence of those lines; see ex. 5.1E).

The diatonic and 8–17/18/19–complex genera (often conjoined to chromatic sets) serve as the main resources of harmonic and melodic content in *Jeux;* they are also used as foils to provide contrast. Debussy's technique maintains the sonorous integrity of each genus by assigning only one of them at a time (sometimes integrated with the chromatic genus) to each formal unit. This typical construction links together brief passages (ranging from a fraction of a measure to as many as eight or more) into a musical surface that is harmonically fluctuant but sonorously distinct.

The whole-tone genus is rarely used, reserved for strategic moments such as important formal junctures (the whole-tone passage at mm. 43–46, for example, closes the introductory first section, and those at mm. 106 and 114 anticipate the large formal break at m. 138).

An unusual feature of Debussy's use of the 8–17/18/19–complex genus is its representation throughout by the subcomplex of sets about set 8–18. It is remarkable how consistently materials are confined to this subgenus. (Table 5.1 lists the subsets and supersets of 8–18; the ¥ signs indicate the many tetrachords and trichords it shares with the diatonic genus.)

That *Jeux* represents Debussy's most advanced stage of technical mastery is evident in the complexity of its pc resources and their handling. The diatonic, whole-tone, and 8–17/18/19–complex genera, for example, occasionally intersect in multifarious passages that project a different sonus depending on one's aural perspective. Introductory mm. 1–4 illustrate this clearly. The auxiliary staves below example 5.1A show different interpretations of the first gesture: chromatic, diatonic (incorporating a linear tonal motion), and 8–17/18/19–complex. Yet

TABLE 5.1. Subsets and supersets of set 8–18[a]

2–1¥, 2–2¥, 2–3¥, 2–4¥, 2–5¥, 2–6¥
3–1, 3–2¥, 3–3, 3–4¥, 3–5¥, 3–6¥, 3–7¥, 3–8¥, 3–9¥, 3–10¥, 3–11¥, 3–12
4–1, 4–2, 4–3, 4–4, 4–5, 4–6, 4–7, 4–8¥, 4–9, 4–10¥, 4–11¥, 4–12, 4–13¥, 4–14¥, 4–Z15(¥), 4–16¥, 4–17, 4–18, 4–19, 4–20¥, 4–22¥, 4–23, 4–24, 4–25, 4–26¥, 4–27¥, 4–28, 4–Z29¥
5–2, 5–2, 5–3, 5–4, 5–5, 5–6, 5–7, 5–10, 5–Z12¥, 5–13, 5–14, 5–15, 5–16, 5–Z17, 5–Z18, 5–19, 5–20¥, 5–21, 5–22, 5–23¥, 5–25¥, 5–26, 5–27¥, 5–28, 5–29¥, 5–30, 5–31, 5–32, 5–Z36¥, 5–Z37, 5–Z38
6–Z3, 6–5, 6–Z11, 6–Z13, 6–15, 6–Z17, 6–18, 6–Z19, 6–Z23, 6–Z24, 6–Z25¥, 6–27, 6–Z28, 6–Z29, 6–30, 6–31, 6–Z39, 6–Z40, 6–Z41, 6–Z42, 6–Z43, 6–Z44, 6–Z49, 6–Z50
7–16, 7–Z18, 7–19, 7–22, 7–31, 7–32, 7–Z36, 7–Z38
9–3, 9–5, 9–10, 9–11¥
10–1, 10–3¥, 10–4¥, 10–5¥, 10–6

[a]Sets marked "¥" also belong to the diatonic genus.

another example occurs at mm. 146–49 (ex. 5.1F), where the 8–17/18/19–complex genus is represented initially by 4–19 and, overall, by 9–5, but is transformed into the diatonic genus (represented by 8–23) by means of Debussy's technique of semitonal shift, in this case applied to one element of 4–19 (where pc 2 replaces pc 3) to transform it into 4–26 (shown to the right of ex. 5.1F).

Modulation

Modulations occur often within all genera except the chromatic. Example 5.2 shows representative excerpts. The diatonic genus is the source of two, at mm. 159–64 (ex. 5.2A). The rc for mm. 159–60 corresponds to D major (supplemented by pc 5, which originates in the chromatic tetrachord of m. 159). A modulation occurs at m. 161, where pc 8 replaces pc 7 (rc = A major supplemented by pcs 3,7, which originate in the two chromatic dyads), and at m. 164 there is a second modulation where pcs 3,10 replace pcs 2,9 (rc = F♯ major). The first modulation is subtle because the diatonic genus is infiltrated by the chromatic genus in the form of chromatic tetrachords and dyads in mm. 159–62, which expand the overall pc field for these measures, and the rcs of the adjoining passages share many invariants (9,11,1,2,4). As well, the instrumental setting and texture remain constant. The second modulation is more obvious owing to the reduction in the pc field (at m. 164) and the retention of only three invariants (pcs 8,11,1). A distinct change in instrumentation and texture also draws attention to this moment.

A modulation within the whole-tone genus occurs at mm. 213–16 (ex. 5.2B). It is accompanied by marked changes in instrumentation and texture, and since the change in pc content is complete, the modulation is easy to hear. Although one might expect that all whole-tone modulations would be easy to hear, since they involve a shift from one whole-tone scale to the other, this is only true when the genus is manifest through its characteristic subsets rather than supersets. In mm. 220–22, for example, there is a modulation within the whole-tone genus (ex. 5.2C), but here the genus is distorted by an invariant in the form of pc 1 sustained throughout, and by synthesis with the chromatic genus (in the form of tetrachord 4–1 = 7,8,9,10, thrice iterated in m. 221). The result is that whereas one may recognize the whole-tone pentachords embedded within the passage, in spite of the change in pc content at m. 220, the complex relations impede the sorting of referential collections. Indeed, the context of the passage—its immediate proximity to diatonic sets in mm. 217, 218, and 219—conspires with its enigmatic content to impose a reservation on any certain identification of genus. The resultant exotic sound well suits the sense of the moment—the psychological nuances and sexual overtones inferable in the young man's enticement of the girls, the conflict between their attraction towards and fear of him, the shadow cast by his intrusion on their interrelationship, and so forth. Again Debussy's sensitivity to dramatic content is manifest in his handling of pc materials.[2]

Modulations within the 8–17/18/19–complex occur frequently. For examples we may look first at mm. 192–93 (ex. 5.2D), where rc = 7–22 (0,1,2,5,6,8,9) is

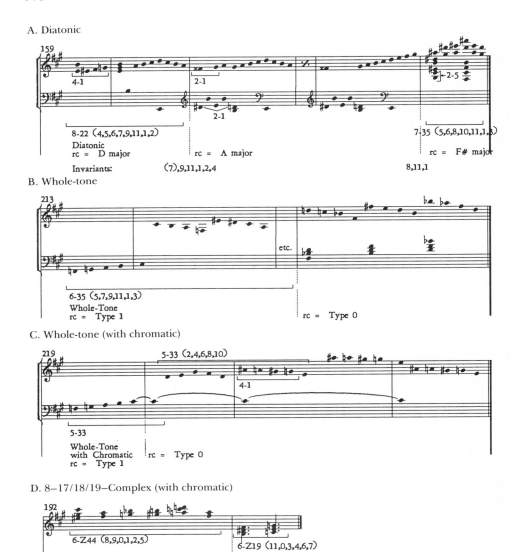

Example 5.2. Modulations in *Jeux*

replaced by rc = 7–22 (3,4,6,7,10,11,0).[3] Only two pcs remain as invariants (0,6), and neither is projected prominently; these features exaggerate the modulation's effect. Modulations also occur at mm. 202–13 (ex. 5.2E). Here the overall pc content of each tiny formal unit yields one of two forms of cynosural set 8–18 (except for m. 205, where the whole-tone genus intrudes briefly). Invariant tetrachords connect the units in pairs, and although they are not projected prominently, these invariant pcs are disposed in close proximity to one another.

E. 8–17/18/19–Complex

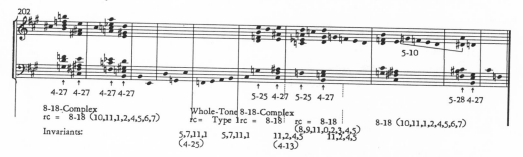

F. 8–17/18/19–Complex

G. Whole-tone

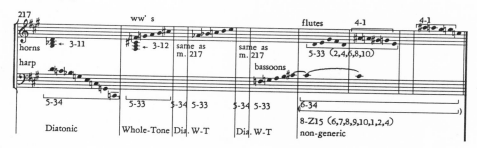

Example 5.2. *Continued*

Again there is a relation to the drama, as the modulations (and this genus) occur just prior to the whole-tone passages mentioned earlier, at a moment where tensions are high owing to the sense of incipient evil that accompanies the arrival of the young man who interrupts the two girls—his intrusion into their preoccupations, the implications of sexual threatening, and so forth.

Yet another example of rapid vacillation between referential collections occurs in mm. 100–105. This passage, where a motive presented earlier is now enriched by harmonies, manifests perhaps the most exotic sonority of the ballet (ex. 5.2F). The upper-voice harmonies are transposed to follow each note of the chromatic line, which causes the referential collections to change quickly. The pc field is further complicated by subtle transformations between subgenera 8–18 and 8–17 caused by their interaction with the bass ostinato. (This is one of the few 8–

17/18/19—complex passages that employs subsets of an octachord other than 8–18.)

Rapid modulations such as these engender an extremely rich pc field. Although there is nothing new in principle about the techniques employed, there is greater subtlety and artifice: the seams show less; the transformations are less predictable (because they involve less literal repetition); the durations of minute formal units are less regular.

Complement Relations

Jeux is replete with complement pairs, which fulfill various roles. The following excerpts are representative:

The piece opens with embedded complements (5–33 is formed by the pc content of the dotted-half-note chord in m. 6, 7–33 by the overall pc content) that interconnect the harp's introduction to the striking whole-tone passage that follows (ex. 5.3A), and thereby unify the two introductory contrasting gestures.

In mm. 9–24, a series of five contrasting passages that draw from the 8–17/18/19—complex (enriched by the chromatic genus) and diatonic genera are linked by set 7–8, with 5–8 embedded within at mm. 9–12 and mm. 19 (ex. 5.3B).

In mm. 150–56, 4–23 appears embedded in 8–23, and 5–35 in 7–35 (ex. 5.3C), linking the woodwinds (plus celeste and harp, which are not shown) to the strings.

A rare octatonic passage (mm. 180–83) finds 3–10 embedded in 9–10, and 4–28 in 8–28 (ex. 5.3D). The pc content of the upper parts yields 8–28 (4–28 as a sonority appears conspicuously within), while the bass ostinato adds pc 3 to form 9–10 (3–10 is projected as an arpeggio in each of mm. 182–83). Here the sonus is especially homogeneous, especially distinctive, since these complement pairs embrace cynosural and characteristic sets, and thereby intensify the ic content associated with the octatonic genus.

The foregoing complements are typical of examples that occur abundantly throughout *Jeux*, where they usually serve one of three purposes: they bind together pc materials of adjacent formal units at the level of detail (as in ex. 5.3B); they intensify a given genus's sonus by saturating its pc field with especially characteristic sets (as in ex. 5.3C–D); or they provide links among apparently disparate pc materials (as in ex. 5.3A). Complement pairs are usually located strategically, the smaller sets placed at the beginning or end of a formal unit, the larger ones embracing all or most of the contiguous pcs of the same formal unit, a feature that is evident at higher formal levels as well, where complement pairs may be found at the beginnings of sections, and at the highest level, where they are conspicuous at both the ballet's opening and closing passages.

Dyads, Trichords, and Motivic Interrelations

The constant reiteration of sonorities embodied in a small number of pc set genera is a structural, unifying device in *Jeux*, but unification of the musical surface is achieved more obviously through myriad thematic and pc set intercon-

Example 5.3. Complement relations in *Jeux*

nections, by which each of the ballet's prominent motives may be related to the opening gesture. The m2s and their synthesis in the opening gesture's motive (m. 1: ex. 5.4A) are subsequently embodied in the *scherzando* theme at m. 9 (ex. 5.4B), and in the eighths and sixteenths of m. 29 (ex. 5.4C). At mm. 34–35 (ex. 5.4D) there is a substantial increase in complexity as multiple forms of sets 2–1 and 3–1

A:

B:

C:

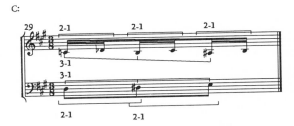

D:

E:

F:

G:

Example 5.4. Sets and motives in *Jeux*

Example 5.4. *Continued*

are compacted densely in both the vertical dimension and the horizontal. The process advances further at mm. 53–54 (ex. 5.4E), when two new motives emerge from the recombination of 2–1 and 3–1, this time conspicuously projecting the latter's boundary interval, ic 3. In turn, ic 3 assumes a prominent role in mm. 57–63, in the accompanying m3s of the bassoons and strings (ex. 5.4F). Other examples of motives traceable to these chromatic cells may be found at mm. 84 and 174 (ex. 5.4G–H).

The whole-tone embedded within the same introductory gesture (expressed melodically *and* harmonically owing to the resonance of the harp; see ex. 5.4I) can be traced similarly; its most immediate offshoot is the whole-tone chords of mm. 5–6, which anticipate other whole-tone passages (such as those of mm. 106–107, and 214–23), but the conjunction of ic 2 with ic 1—also in m. 1—to form set 3–2 points as well to the diatonic genus, and to the many diatonic motives that begin with (or otherwise conspicuously embody) that trichord. (Example 5.4J cites the earliest fully developed diatonic motive of mm. 47–50.)

As these tiny ic motives interconnect the diverse shapes into which they are molded, they contribute a subtle coherence at the most minute level that balances the more generalized interconnections discussed above, such as complement relations and the recurrent use of the four pc set genera.[4]

The foregoing hardly begin to demonstrate the fecundity of invention that characterizes *Jeux* and Debussy at this mature stage of his career. Orledge (*Debussy and the Theatre*, 170–71) cites a letter from Debussy to Gabriel Pierné as testimony to Debussy's keen awareness of the intricate connections among the diverse materials that distinguish the ballet's succession of passages: "The tie that links them [the diverse episodes] together is perhaps subtle, but it exists nevertheless?"[5]

Invariance as a Source of PC Interrelation and Tonal Focus

Jeux offers many examples of the use of invariants as a subtle way to link passages where "contrast" is more apparent than "unity" (passages, for example, that are distinguished by different pc set genera and different motivic material). An example is the link forged by ubiquitous pcs 1,11 throughout the overtly contrasting introductory gestures of mm. 1–4 and 5–8. Thereafter, pc 9 joins with pcs 1,11 to form an invariant trichord that joins the passages which span mm. 5–8 and 8–14. Indeed, it needs no close accounting to confirm that pc 1 (and, to a lesser extent, pcs 9,11) pervade the entire pc fabric of *Jeux* and constitute tonal referents.

Additional Observations Regarding PC Materials

Three remaining observations do not lend themselves well to the above categories:

Modulations and changes in pc genus define form when they create partitions which in turn demarcate passages and groups of passages whose relation and interaction generate formal schemes.[6]

It is rare that Debussy's musical surfaces are as saturated with chromaticism as in mm. 25–34. Here the chromaticism results from a process of accretion (begun in m. 9; see ex. 5.4B), wherein a highly chromatic motive is superimposed over chromatic stepwise lines whose durational values shorten progressively (from dotted quarters in m. 25, to quarters in mm. 26–28, to eighths in mm. 29–35), so that all twelve pcs recycle very quickly. Debussy usually places such an unusual feature in a strategic location where the listener's attention is prepared for an important formal event; this example occurs quite close to the end of the first large section of the ballet, just before the return to the opening whole-tone material in m. 43. Other, comparable passages of chromatic density occur at similar locations relative to higher-level formal junctures: see, for example, mm. 67–69 (ex. 5.4F), which precedes the exact moment when the tennis ball first falls onto the stage.

The pc materials of mm. 217–23 illustrate Debussy's ability to synthesize and integrate contrasting pc set genera. The passage is very complicated (ex. 5.2G, mm. 219–23 were discussed earlier in connection with example 5.2C). The highly chromatic surface allows no one referential set to dominate; instead, the small sets that instrumental timbres and motivic fragments project represent two genera by turns (supplemented by chromatic tetrachord 4–1). They include 3–11 embedded in 5–34 (diatonic) and 3–12 embedded in 5–33 (whole-tone). By the end of the passage (mm. 220–23) the genus is indeterminate, though any (or none) of three can be heard depending on one's aural bias (sets 3–10 and 4–28 representing the 8–18 subgenus emerge in mm. 221–22).

Jeux is a masterpiece that exhibits Debussy's consummate skill in fashioning a contemporary musical art form to complement contemporary ideas about drama and dance in a way that stresses subtle psychological manipulation of the observer as an alternative to a direct appeal to the emotions.

SONATA FOR FLUTE, VIOLA, AND HARP

The Sonata for flute, viola, and harp—composed in 1915, the same year as the *Douze études*—is Debussy's last chamber work. Its economy and intricacy reveal Debussy's exquisite mastery of materials at this late stage of his career. Also remarkable is the grace with which all technical artifices are concealed beneath its delicate and quasi-improvisatory surface.

What is so very striking about the sonata—and distinguishes it from earlier works—is its handling of motivic materials, for here the motives are treated truly as unordered pc sets. The first movement will suffice for purposes of illustration.

Three Motives

As in *Jeux,* the trio's initial gesture (ex. 5.5A) discloses pitch materials crucial to the movement as a whole, including two of three important motives. The first, labeled "X," consists of a pentachord (5–26) that encloses two overlapping tetrachords (4–12 and 4–11); all three sets belong to the 8–17/18/19–complex genus, and the association is especially strong for sets 4–12 and 5–26. Motive X incorporates the sonority of this genus as its signal feature; its contour (intermixed steps and skips in an ascending line across a relatively narrow range) is a secondary and malleable characteristic.

The flute's entrance on the solo harp's fifth note partitions the gesture and exposes a second motive, labeled "Y" (ex. 5.5A). Tetrachord 4–11 is the source set that provides the motive's identity as well as its pc content, for motive Y's contour (of skips and changes of direction), like that of motive X, is only a secondary and highly variable characteristic. Here and elsewhere the tetrachord is embedded securely in the larger sonority of the 8–17/18/19–complex genus (affirmed by the reiterated E♭ at the end of the bar), but in many other occurrences it resides within the diatonic genus. That motive X's pentachord (5–26) overlaps motive Y's tetrachord (4–12) forges a link between these two resources.

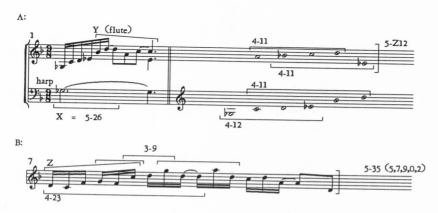

Example 5.5. Germinative motives in the Sonata for flute, viola, and harp, I

A third motive emerges at m. 7 (ex. 5.5B), which draws on the diatonic genus for its sonority and emphasizes characteristic diatonic sets 3–9, 4–23, and 5–35 (supplemented by 3–7)[7] deployed in contours that resemble complex arabesques composed of steps, skips, and numerous local changes of direction. Its diatonic pc materials resemble those associated with motive Y (after the introduction), while its general contour usually resembles that of motive X.

None of the three motives has a fixed contour, but each has a fixed pc set association: motive X with sets 4–12 and 5–26 (and the 8–17/18/19–complex); motive Z with diatonic characteristic sets 3–9, 4–23, and 5–35 (supplemented by trichord 3–7); motive Y with tetrachord 4–11 (and either genus).

Themes and the Formal Plan

The formal plan for the sonata resembles that of *Jeux* in that its structure builds through a series of contrasting passages and is more additive than hierarchic. (Figure 10.16 provides a diagram.) It consists of a series of contrasting passages that may be sorted into three types: those whose nature is essentially thematic (though fragmentary); brief, cadenza-like flourishes; and those that serve a quasi-cadential, terminating function. Many of these passages return, but their reordering suggests a casual and improvisatory impulsiveness. The constant that binds them all together is the inventory of pc sets associated with each of the three motives.

Example 5.6 shows the different passages in reduction—eight thematic, two flourishes, and two terminations—and identifies the motive sets embedded in each passage. Motive Y is pervasive and easiest to trace since it embodies a single set (4–11). Some of the contours into which its tetrachord is disposed include the angular shape of the initial gesture (m. 1); a stepwise, encircling figure (m. 4); the first termination figure (m. 8–9); the second termination figure (m. 13); the broad thematic passage at m. 14 (which is saturated with examples in all three instruments; only two are cited in example 5.6D); the new theme at m. 18; the harp solo at m. 21; and the gigue-like figure of m. 41. As these examples show, though stepwise ordering of the tetrachord is most common, many other arrangements occur.

Motive Z occurs frequently as well, and also in a variety of contours. Like motive Y, it is used both as the basis for passages (the first termination at m. 7; the sustained viola chords at m. 9; the viola-flute imitation of m. 31) and as one of several motives for others (the first portion of the flute line at m. 14; the termination at m. 13; the viola theme at m. 18).

Motive X is used sparingly (which increases its prominence when it does occur), reserved, for example, for the flourishes at mm. 2 and 12 (contour inverted).

The formal plan emphasizes contrast, change, and new material while concealing a subsurface unified by the opening gesture's three motives.

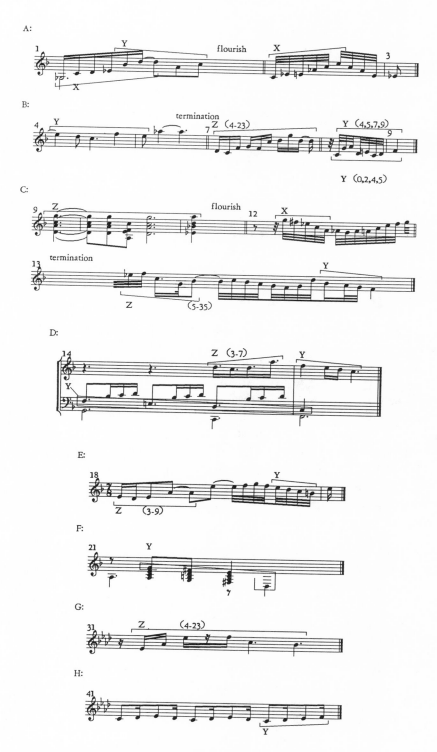

Example 5.6. Themes in the Sonata for flute, viola, and harp, I

The PC Set Genera

This movement makes use of only two pc set genera: the diatonic and the 8–17/18/19–complex. (The whole-tone genus appears in other movements.) Much as we have seen in earlier works, they are employed singly and in alternation, used, along with modulation, to supply the composition's pc content from moment to moment. Example 5.7A presents a pitch reduction of mm. 1–14 that shows several mutations as well as modulations, which occur in both genera.

Of special interest are two passages that feature superimposition of one genus onto another. Both overlay the 8–17/18/19–complex genus (manifest in a flourish assigned to the flute) onto diatonic materials sustained in the viola and harp; the first is reproduced in example 5.7A, enclosed in a rectangle (the other passage is similar and occurs at m. 69).

A few paired passages feature transformations from one genus to another by means of stepwise voice leading. One occurs at mm. 26–27 (ex. 5.7B; the voice leading is shown in parentheses on the auxiliary staff); another transforms the opening gesture from the 8–17/18/19–complex genus to the diatonic genus by "resolving" F♯ to G and E♭ to E (mm. 72–75).

Referential PC Collections and Invariance

Debussy's blatant gestures to tonal convention are a prominent feature of the sonata.[8] Certainly there are numerous conventional tonal cues, such as key signatures, that point to the key and scale of F major as referential for the movement and for the piece as a whole, and there are many examples of voice leading: the g♭ pedal in mm. 1–3 eventually proceeds to F in m. 7 (though the supporting chord is not the tonic triad); the flute's and viola's e^2 in mm. 2–6 adorns F from below (though e^2 does not *lead* conclusively to f^2 until m. 9, and then it is e^1–f^1, not –f^2); and there can be no doubt that the F major (tonic) triad is the goal of voice leading in all parts at mm. 8–9. There is also emphasis on the primary scale step, C (V) and its triad (as at mm. 25–27), and on other scale steps both in and remote from F major.

Conventional tonal referents are supported throughout by quantitative emphasis, a feature that is especially important in the nondiatonic passages where traditional tonal cues are less evident. The composition's pc field is in a constant state of flux owing to modulations and mutations. Table 5.2 surveys this changing pc field and charts invariant relations from one pc inventory to the next. Certain pcs recur as constants, as indicated by their frequent appearance as invariants; they form the F major hexachord (5,7,9,10,0,2).

The foregoing chapters make no pretense of comprehensiveness in their treatment of the pc set genera; they constitute merely an introduction to the topic, which subsequent chapters will pursue as a secondary issue in discussions of other works. Additional examples will help to establish a sense of the pervasiveness of the pc set genera after 1889 and of Debussy's evolving technique.

The pc set genera became an integral part of Debussy's musical language

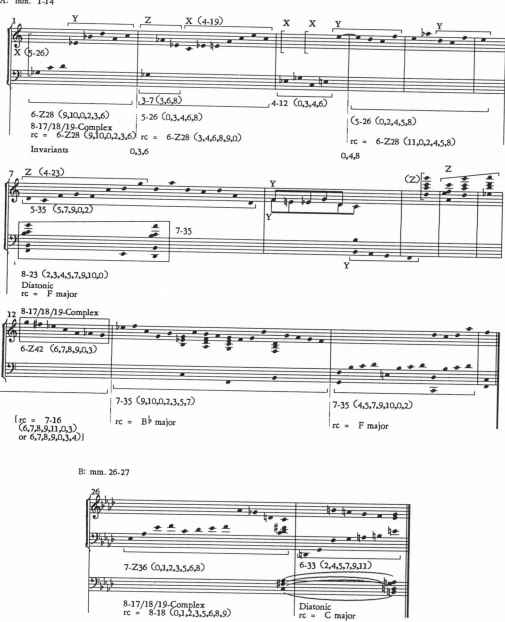

Example 5.7. PC set genera and germinative motives in the Sonata for flute, viola, and harp, I

TABLE 5.2. Pc set genera, rcs, and invariants in the Sonata for flute, viola, and harp, I

Bar nos.	Genus	RC		Invariant PCs
1:	8–17/18/19-complex	6–Z28	(9,10,0,2,3,6)	
2–3:	8–17/18/19-complex	"	(3,4,6,8,9,0)	0, 3, 6
4–6:	8–17/18/19-complex	"	(11,0,2,4,5,8)	0, 4, 8
7–12:	Diatonic	7–35	(F major)	0, 2, 4,5
12:	8–17/18/19-complex	7–16	(6,7,8,9,11,0,3 or 3,4,6,7,8,9,0)	0, 3, 7, 9
13:	Diatonic	7–35	(B♭ major)	0, 3, 5, 7, 9,10
14–17:	Diatonic	7–35	(F major)	0, 2, 5, 7, 9,10
18–20:	Diatonic	7–35	(C major)	0, 2, 4,5, 7, 9
21–25:	Diatonic	7–35	(G major)	0, 2, 4, 7, 9
26–27/beat 2: 8–17/18/19-complex		8–18	(0,1,2,3,5,6,8,9)	0, 2, 6, 9
27/beat 3: Diatonic		7–35	(C major)	2, 5
28–30:	Diatonic	7–35	(A♭ major)	5, 7
31–35:	Diatonic	7–35	(D♭ major)	0,1, 3, 5, 8, 10
36–38:	Diatonic	7–35	(E major)	1, 3, 6
39–49:	Diatonic	7–35	(D♭ major)	1, 3, 6, 9
50–53:	8–17/18/19-complex	8–19	(8,9,10,0,1,2,4,5)	0, 5, 7,8, 10
54–60:	Diatonic	7–35	(F major)	0, 2, 4,5, 7, 10
61:	8–17/18/19-complex	6–Z28	(9,10,0,2,3,6)	0, 2, 10
62:	Diatonic	7–35	(F major)	0, 2, 10
63–64:	Diatonic	7–35	(C major)	0, 2, 4,5, 7, 9
65–68:	Diatonic	7–35	(F major)	0, 2, 4,5, 7, 9
69:	8–17/18/19-complex	7–16	(6,7,8,9,11,0,3 or 3,4,6,7,8,9,0)	0, 7, 9
70–71:	8–17/18/19-complex	7–Z17	(11,0,1,3,4,5,8)	0, 3
72:	8–17/18/19-complex	6–Z28	(9,10,0,2,3,6)	3
73:	Diatonic	7–35	(F major)	0, 2, 10
74:	8–17/18/19-complex	6–Z28	(9,10,0,2,3,6)	0, 2, 9,10
75–83:	Diatonic	7–35	(F major)	0, 2, 6, 10
Most common invariants:				0, 2, 5, 7, 9,10

beginning with the Baudelaire songs of 1889. Thereafter they were absorbed into his sonorous vocabulary. Although each genus maintains its identity through isolation within the successions of small formal units that are a hallmark of his style, certain characteristic sonorities also appear frequently outside of their usual generic contexts: 5–10, 5–26 and 7–26, 5–34 and 7–34, 6–27, 6–34, and 7–32. They often link the pc contents of adjacent brief formal units which are separated by modulations and generic changes, where they themselves are not members of the genus or genera involved. Set 7–34, for example, is often formed by the pc content of adjacent diatonic passages linked by modulation, especially where the passages consist of forms of 5–34; 6–34 often links adjacent whole-tone and diatonic passages as the sum of their pc contents, in particular where the passages pair 5–33 with 5–34. One senses that Debussy included these sonorities alongside other types, even when their particular genus was not invoked, simply because they were an integral part of his sonorous vocabulary in its totality.

The flexibility of Debussy's musical language extends to the list of genera itself, for although the five we have examined constitute the main sonic resources, genera grouped about other cynosural sets also appear from time to time. In "Pour les notes répétées" (Douze études II), for example, a genus about 8–5 and its complement, 4–5, constitutes one of the main sonorous resources, along with the whole-tone and diatonic genera. The evidence does not depict a rigid, highly systematized, unchanging language; it points instead to flexibility within orderliness and consistency, in keeping with Debussy's published remarks.

For some reason there is a gap of several years between the first appearance of the pc set genera and their use in instrumental pieces. As we have seen, the whole-tone and octatonic genera occur alongside the diatonic genus in the String Quartet, four years after their initial appearance in the Baudelaire songs. Perhaps Debussy felt compelled by the expressive demands of texts to explore these new harmonic resources, an impetus not attached to pure instrumental works.

So far as I know, no external evidence exists to suggest that Debussy worked out or contemplated in any systematic fashion the harmonic vocabularies I have called pc set genera. Hundreds of pages of autographs, including sketches, drafts, and fair copies, fail to yield any notes, lists, tables of harmonies, or any other evidence that points in that direction; on the contrary, all of the evidence suggests intuitive and empirical origins. The pieces themselves attest that he was cognizant of their properties and interrelationships, and there is some scant corroboration in Debussy's occasional cryptic comments, such as the letter to Pierné about *Jeux* mentioned above.

SIX

COMPLEMENT RELATIONS

By now so many complement relations have been cited that the reader must sense their ubiquity in Debussy's music. This chapter examines the phenomenon and its ramifications in a variety of works. Although most of the examples involve segmentations that fall within formal units that are defined by a single pc set genus, many of them cross formal boundaries and highlight nongeneric sets. That the latter are susceptible of aural cognition and contribute meaningfully to structure does not contradict the constructional principle in which each formal unit is defined by pc contents associated with a particular genus; it acknowledges, rather, the multifarious nature both of our hearing and of this music's pc materials.

Complement relations occur even in Debussy's early music in the form of pairs indigenous to the diatonic genus, found in his songs from the 1880s. Nothing suggests that their appearance in these works is deliberate; in fact, several features point to coincidence: complement pairs appear infrequently; they entail large sets that hold numerous complement forms as subsets; the subset complements are concealed rather than projected to consciousness and the textures do not draw attention to the superset complements; and the superset complements derive from conventional tonal chromaticism in the form of modal mixture, tonicization, and chromatic-third relations. However, the situation changes in 1889 (at about the same time that the pc set genera emerge) and complement relations begin to assume a structural role.

"Lent"

By the 1890s, complement relations are pervasive on Debussy's musical surfaces in the same contexts that characterize his later works. The first movement of the *Images* (1894)[1] is typical; "Lent" is predominantly diatonic and so most of the complement pairs come from that genus. Two features are especially striking: the piece opens with a clearly projected complement relation, and complement pairs encompass nearly every formal unit. Trichord 3–9 is embedded abundantly in set 9–9 throughout mm. 1–9 (ex. 6.1A; 3–9 is the first set heard in m. 1). Diatonic cynosural set 7–35 accounts for the pc content of mm. 10–13, and complement

Example 6.1. Complement pairs in "Lent"

Example 6.1. *Continued*

5–35 is the source for the final sonority (ex. 6.1B). Bars 18–21 employ the 8–17/18/19–complex genus (and incorporate a modulation); set 9–3 is nested within 10–3 in m. 18, with both complements copiously represented (ex. 6.1C), while 9–5 accounts for the pc content of m. 19 and features its complement in the bass. Measures 21–23, which are saturated by forms of 3–11, are diatonic and yield 9–11 overall (ex. 6.1D). The whole-tone genus appears once, in mm. 40–41, with 3–8 embedded in 9–8 (ex. 6.1E). Other complement relations span mm. 24–26 (4–23 in 8–23), mm. 27–31 (5–35 in 7–35), and mm. 32–35 (4–22 in 8–22: ex. 6.1F). The pc materials for m. 39 issue from the 8–17/18/19–complex genus represented by cynosural superset 10–3[2] (ex. 6.1F). Tetrachord 4–17 appears here, embedded in 8–17, and 4–Z15 is found in nongeneric 8–Z15 (formed by the first two harmonies). There are other complements in "Lent," but those cited involve pairs whose smaller members are easily heard, singled out by their prominence as melodic fragments, harmonies, or combinations of chord and line—in other words, identified by primary segmentations.

"Recueillement" and "Le jet d'eau"

These two Baudelaire songs from 1889 (which provide the earliest clear examples of the pc set genera) contain numerous complement relations, though they are not always projected as clearly as in "Lent."

The opening gesture of "Recueillement" alternates diatonic and octatonic harmonies in mm. 4–5.[3] Each genus is represented by characteristic sets: set 5–34 (diatonic) in opposition to 5–31 (octatonic). Their synthesis yields nongeneric set 8–27, whose complement is conspicuously embedded as the sonority of m. 4 (ex. 6.2A). Pitch class 9 appears in mm. 1–3, which yields set 9–7, whose complement, 3–7, is articulated in the three lowest pcs of mm. 2 and 4 (most easily heard in m. 4).

The next three bars (mm. 6–8) are solidly octatonic. Set 7–31 appears here (complement of 5–31 in mm. 4 and 5); also, the pc content of the two rcs yields set 9–10, whose complement lies embedded within (most prominently in the vocal line of mm. 7–8).

A nonoctatonic pair occurs in mm. 10–11; pentachord 5–Z17 forms the melodic line and is embedded within concealed overlapping forms of Z-complement 7–Z38, while the overall pc content finds expression in octatonic set 9–10, whose complement occurs as the main sonority on beats 3–4 of each bar (ex. 6.2B). The union of sets across the modulation in mm. 15–23 yields set 9–7, whose complement, 3–7, is source for the vocal line of mm. 21–22 (ex. 6.2C).

"Le jet d'eau" also opens (mm. 1–6) with a complement relation: nongeneric 7–34 accounts for the total pc content, with forms of diatonic 5–34 projected conspicuously (ex. 6.2D). Contrasting harmonies are paired in mm. 20–25, where diatonic 5–34 is juxtaposed with whole-tone 5–33 to create two sets of complements: whole-tone 5–33 nested in 7–33 (mm. 20–21) and diatonic 3–9 in 9–9 (mm. 22–25; see ex. 6.2E).

Two other diatonic pairs warrant mention: 5–35 in 7–35 in mm. 18–19 (ex. 6.2F), and, less conspicuously, 3–6 in 9–6 in mm. 6–7 (ex. 6.2G). Finally, the overall pc content of mm. 1–11 forms set 10–2 (it excludes pcs 1,3), complement to the M2 reiterated throughout mm. 1–9: pcs 0,2.

The copious complement pairs in these two songs arise from prominent musical features of the pitch surfaces. They are not, however, as comprehensive in embracing all of the pitch materials as are those in "Lent" and later pieces.

DIATONIC COMPLEMENTS

This section surveys, in detail, complement relations that occur within the diatonic genus. It begins by examining the set pairs themselves and their genesis in the major-minor tonal system.

The diatonic genus encompasses eight important complement pairs: 5–35/7–35, 4–22/8–22, 4–23/8–23, 4–26/8–26, 3–6/9–6, 3–7/9–7, 3–9/9–9, and 3–11/9–11.[4] All are featured prominently in Debussy's works.

A. "Recueillement," mm. 1–8

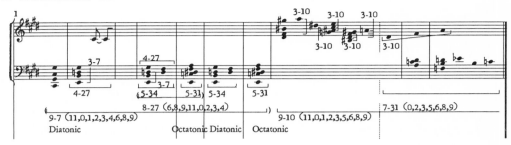

B. "Recueillement," mm. 10–11

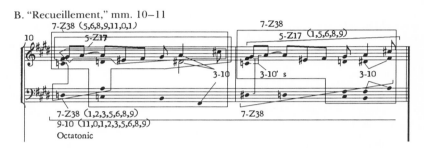

C. "Recueillement," mm. 15–23

D. "Le jet d'eau," mm. 1–6

Example 6.2. Complement pairs in "Recueillement" and "Le jet d'eau"

E. "Le jet d'eau," mm. 20–25

F. "Le jet d'eau," mm. 18–19

G. "Le jet d'eau," mm. 6–7

Example 6.2. *Continued*

Diatonicism and Pentatonicism (7–35/5–35)

The pair that consists of the cynosural set, 7–35, which generates the diatonic scale, and 5–35, which generates the anhematonic pentatonic scale, share a special relationship. Set 7–35 may be formed by adding two pcs to 5–35 such that two new forms of 5–35 are generated in the accretion for a total of three pentachords embedded in the larger set (ex. 6.3). Among the thirty-eight seven-note pc sets, only nine contain 5–35 as a subset, only three (7–23, 7–27, and 7–35) contain it more than once, and only one, 7–35, contains it three times. This embedding and the proportional similarity of distribution of ics across these sets'

Example 6.3. Forms of subset 5–35 in 7–35

ivs couples with the concentration of ic 2s in their sias to create a strong affinity in sound between them. Put differently, 7–35 amplifies the sonorous and kinesthetic characteristics of its complement subset, while 5–35 concentrates those of its complement superset; they are very closely interconnected.

5–35 in PC Form 6,8,10,1,3

The literal complement relation between 7–35 and 5–35 is formed on the piano by the white keys versus the black keys. Throughout Debussy's oeuvre there is a preponderance of diatonic piano works whose pc contents (and key signatures) serve as vehicles for the black-key form of 5–35, embedded in one of its three complementary supersets: the scales of G♭ major (or E♭ minor), D♭ major (or B♭ minor), B major (or G♯ minor), and their enharmonic equivalents. A representative sample of excerpts follows, in which the black-key form of 5–35 is prominent.

From the *Children's Corner:* "Doctor Gradus ad Parnassum," at mm. 37–44, (key signature of five flats), where 5–35 appears as the harmony at m. 38/beats 1–3, within the larger pc context of D♭ major (ex. 6.4A).

From the Préludes I: "Voiles," mm. 42–47, where five flats is a notational cue for pentatonic 5–35, which appears without its complement (ex. 6.4B); "Le vent dans la plaine," mm. 3–4 (and elsewhere), where six flats strongly implies E♭ minor (ex. 6.4C); "Les collines d'Anacapri" (five sharps) initially employs pentatonic 5–35 in the form 4,6,8,11,1 (mm. 1–2), but in mm. 18–20 and elsewhere it

A. "Doctor Gradus ad Parnassum"

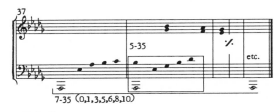

B. "Voiles"

C. "Le vent dans la plaine"

Example 6.4. "Black-key" form of set 5–35

D. "Les collines d'Anacapri"

E. "Hommage à Rameau"

F. "Pour les agréments"

G. "Nuages"

H. "Sirènes"

I. "De l'aube à midi sur la mer"

J. "Eventail"

Example 6.4. *Continued*

appears as 6,8,10,1,3 (ex. 6.4D); "La fille aux cheveux de lin" (six flats, key of G♭ major) uses black-key pentatonic subset 4–26 (10,1,3,6) as its referential sonority.

From the *Images* I: "Hommage à Rameau" (five sharps, key of G♯ minor) conspicuously employs the black-key pentachord in its opening theme, mm. 1–13, decorated once by pc 11 as an appoggiatura (ex. 6.4E).

From the Douze études II: In "Pour les agréments," mm. 9–10 (six flats, plus F♭ notated as an accidental), the pentachord appears as pedal-plus-melody (ex. 6.4F).

Nor is the "black-key" form of 5–35 limited to piano works. It is conspicuous in "Nuages" (*Nocturnes* I), mm. 64–79 (six sharps), formed by the pc material of the bell-like theme (ex. 6.4G); "Sirènes" (*Nocturnes* III), mm. 1–2 (five sharps; ex. 6.4H); and in "De l'aube à midi sur la mer" (*La mer* I), m. 68 (five flats; ex. 6.4I).

It appears in as late a work as "Eventail" (*Trois poèmes de Stéphane Mallarmé*), m. 1, where it is incorporated into the song's initial gesture (ex. 6.4J).

Whether its role is structural or merely subsidiary, the ubiquitous black-key pentatonic scale attests to Debussy's predilection for keys and scales that incorporate these five pcs.

Diatonic Supersets and Chromaticism

A consideration of the eight- and nine-note supersets of set 7–35 will illustrate the nature of 4-to-8 and 3-to-9 pc set complementation within the diatonic genus. The supersets will occur whenever set 7–35 is emended by one or two pcs from among the five that remain in the aggregate. If 7–35 takes the form 11,0,2,4,5,7,9, the pcs that may be added are 6,8,10,1,3.

The eight-note sets formed by the conjunction of 7–35 with each of the complementary pcs are: set 8–22 from pc 1 or 3, whose complement, 4–22, lies embedded within in seven forms (table 6.1A); set 8–23 from pc 6 or 10 (4–23 embedded in five forms; table 6.1B); and set 8–26 from pc 8 (4–26 embedded in three forms; table 6.1C).

The nine-note sets are: set 9–6 from pcs 1,3 (3–6 embedded in seven forms; table 6.1D); 9–7 from pcs 3,6, 6,8, 8,10, or 1,10 (3–7 embedded in eleven forms; table 6.1E); 9–9 from pcs 1,6, 6,10, or 3,10 (3–9 embedded in seven forms; table 6.1F); and 9–11 from pcs 3,8 or 1,8 (3–11 embedded eleven times; table 6.1G).

All of these added pcs can and do occur in tonal music through the chromatic practices of tonicization and modal mixture. Within C major, for example, tonicization often generates the raised first, fourth, and lowered seventh scale degrees (pcs 1,6,10), while modal mixture generates pcs 3,8 as lowered third and sixth scale degrees.

The cynosural supersets occur frequently in the tonal repertoire of the late nineteenth century, so their presence in Debussy's music is not extraordinary per se. Each of the eight-note collections requires merely the addition of a tonicizing or mixture note. Set 9–7 routinely occurs as the natural minor scale enriched by raised sixth and seventh scale degrees. It also results from the addition of tonicizing notes that raise the first degree and lower the seventh (as in vii^{d7} of ii). Set 9–9

TABLE 6.1. Superset forms and subset counts of diatonic complement pairs

Given form of cynosural set 7–35: 11,0,2,4,5,7,9 (= C major scale)	
A. *8–22 (7–35 + pc 1 or 3)*	*4–22 (7 forms)*
(11,0,2,3,4,5,7,9)	(0,2,4,7), (0,3,5,7), (2,5,7,9), (5,7,9,0), (9,0,2,4), (4,7,9,11), (7,9,11,12)
(11,0,1,2,4,5,7,9)	(0,2,4,7), (2,5,7,9), (5,7,9,0), (9,0,2,4), (4,7,9,11), (7,9,11,2), (9,11,1,4)
B. *8–23 (7–35 + pc 6 or 10)*	*4–23 (5 forms)*
(11,0,2,4,5,7,9,10)	(0,2,5,7), (2,4,7,9), (7,9,0,2), (5,7,10,0), (9,11,2,4)
(11,0,2,4,5,6,7,9)	(2,4,7,9), (5,7,0,2), (7,9,0,2), (4,6,9,11), (9,11,2,4)
C. *8–26 (7–35 + pc 8)*	*4–26 (3 forms)*
(11,0,2,4,5,7,8,9)	(4,7,9,0), (9,0,2,4), (11,2,4,7)
D. *9–6 (7–35 + pcs 1,3)*	*3–6 (7 forms)*
(11,0,1,2,3,4,5,7,9)	(0,2,4), (1,3,5), (3,5,7), (5,7,9), (11,1,3), (7,9,11), (9,11,1)
E. *9–7 (7–35 + pcs 3,6, 6,8, 8,10, or 1,10)*	*3–7 (11 forms)*
(11,0,2,4,5,7,8,9,10)	(0,2,5), (2,4,7), (2,5,7), (4,7,9), (7,9,0), (9,0,2), (11,2,4), (5,7,10), (5,8,10), (7,9,10), (9,11,2)
(11,0,1,2,4,5,7,9,10)	(0,2,5), (2,4,7), (2,5,7), (4,7,9), (7,9,0), (9,0,2), (11,1,4), (11,2,4), (5,7,10), (7,10,0), (9,11,2)
(11,0,2,4,5,6,7,8,9)	(0,2,5), (2,4,7), (2,5,7), (4,6,9), (4,7,9), (7,9,0), (9,0,2), (11,2,4), (6,8,11), (6,9,11), (9,11,2)
(11,0,2,3,4,5,6,7,9)	(0,2,5), (0,3,5), (2,4,7), (2,5,7), (4,6,9), (4,7,9), (7,9,0), (9,0,2), (11,2,4), (6,9,11), (9,11,2)
F. *9–9 (7–35 + pcs 1,6, 6,10, or 3,10)*	*3–9 (7 forms)*
(11,0,2,4,5,6,7,9,10)	(0,2,7), (0,5,7), (2,4,9), (2,7,9), (10,0,5), (11,4,6), (9,11,4)
(11,0,2,3,4,5,7,9,10)	(0,2,7), (2,4,9), (5,7,0), (7,9,2), (10,0,5), (3,5,10), (9,11,4)
(11,0,1,2,4,5,6,7,9)	(0,2,7), (2,4,9), (5,7,0), (7,9,2), (11,1,6), (4,6,11), (9,11,4)
G. *9–11 (7–35 + pcs 3,8 or 1,8)*	*3–11 (11 forms)*
(11,0,2,3,4,5,7,8,9)	(0,3,7), (0,4,7), (2,5,9), (5,8,0), (5,9,0), (8,0,3), (9,0,4), (11,2,7), (11,3,8), (4,7,11), (4,8,11)
(11,0,1,2,4,5,7,8,9)	(0,4,7), (1,4,8), (1,5,8), (2,5,9), (5,8,0), (5,9,0), (9,0,4), (9,1,4), (4,7,11), (4,8,11), (7,11,2)

results from mixture in the form of the lowered mediant (♭III), and 9–11 arises from the addition of the lowered submediant (♭VI). Of four nine-note sets, only 9–6 is rare in the tonal music of Debussy's predecessors (though certainly Wagner's style displays an affinity for its chromaticism).

Thus, Debussy's innovation is not the use of the large collections; rather, his conspicuous use of their subset complements is unusual. Although they are found concealed in the tonal repertoire, in general these complements are not projected conspicuously, disposed as melodic fragments and sonorities, as they are in Debussy's music.

The following excerpts demonstrate how Debussy disposes these complement subsets in contexts that render them conspicuous on his musical surfaces.

5–35 in 7–35

As a melodic resource the anhematonic pentatonic scale is ubiquitous in Debussy's music; indeed, pentatonicism is a hallmark of his style.[5] But its source set, 5–35, is even more pervasive than his abundant melodic pentatonicism suggests, for its pc content may also be disposed in ways that attract other appellations. As a sonority it can occur as a V^{11} chord without a third, a common harmony in Debussy's diatonic music (see, for example, "La fille aux cheveux de lin," mm. 9, 12, 15, 18–21); or it may appear as a major triad with added sixth and ninth, as in "Danseuses de Delphes," m. 16/beat 2, m. 17/beat 1 (ex. 6.5A), and in "La cathédrale engloutie" mm. 16–18 (ex. 6.5B); or even as a stack of mixed seconds and thirds, as in "La cathédrale engloutie," mm. 22–27 (ex. 6.5B), and "Sirènes" (*Nocturnes* III), mm. 2–3 and 7, in the voices. These chord types are as foreign to the harmonic vocabularies of Debussy's predecessors as they are common to his.

A. "Danseuses de Delphes"

B. "La cathédrale engloutie"

C. "Reflets dans l'eau"

Example 6.5. Set 5–35 in 7–35

D. "La cathédrale engloutie"

E. "Les collines d'Anacapri"

F. "Pour ce que Plaisance est morte"

G. *Pelléas et Mélisande,* act IV, scene 3, OS p. 310

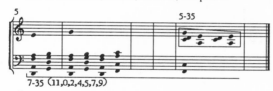

H. *Pelléas et Mélisande,* act IV, scene 3, OS p. 318

I. *Pelléas et Mélisande,* act IV, scene 4, OS p. 360

Example 6.5. *Continued*

Additional examples are found in the following works: "Reflets dans l'eau" (*Images* I), mm. 1–4, the pentachord as a sonority (ex. 6.5C); "La cathédrale engloutie," mm. 1 and 4, the pentachord as a harmonic-melodic complex (ex. 6.5D); "Les collines d'Anacapri," mm. 1–11, 5–35 disposed in its more typical pentatonic-melodic form (ex. 6.5E); and "Pour ce que Plaisance est morte" (*Trois chansons de France*), mm. 2–3, again disposed melodically (ex. 6.5F). *Pelléas et Mélisande* contains all manner of examples, including these three: act IV, scene 3, orchestral score (OS) pp. 310 and 318 (ex. 6.5G–H); and act IV, scene 4, OS p. 360 (ex. 6.5I).

4–22 in 8–22

Tetrachord 4–22 occurs often in Debussy's music, sometimes as an incomplete V⁹ sonority (missing third or fifth), as in "Pour les degrés chromatiques," (Douze études II), mm. 81–82, embedded in its complement (ex. 6.6A). It functions as the source set for an important motive in mm. 11–14, left hand (as 2,5,7,9), that is stated often thereafter.

"Feuilles mortes" (Préludes II), mm. 6–11, employs numerous forms of set 4–22 as chords, and set 8–22 embraces several of them in mm. 8–9 (ex. 6.6B).

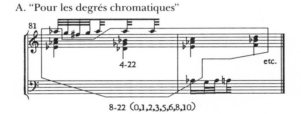

A. "Pour les degrés chromatiques"

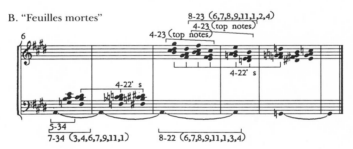

B. "Feuilles mortes"

C. "Danseuses de Delphes"

Example 6.6. Set 4–22 in 8–22

Set 8–22 generates the pc content of "Danseuses de Delphes," m. 3, while set 4–22 is articulated two times in the upper voices (ex. 6.6C).

4–23 in 8–23

Tetrachord 4–23 may take the form of an incomplete V^{11} (third and seventh omitted), a quartal tetrachord, two seconds connected by a third, or a pentatonic-melodic fragment consisting of step-skip-step. The last two permutations are common in Debussy. They are seen, for example, in "Danseuses de Delphes," mm. 11–12, where 4–23 is found embedded in 8–23 in the melody (ex. 6.7A; note set 5–35 embedded in 7–35); and in "Souvenir du Louvre" (*Images*, 1894), at mm. 23–24, where 8–23 embeds tetrachord 4–23, the sole harmony, in two transpositions (ex. 6.7B).

4–26 in 8–26

As a tonal analogue, set 4–26 forms the minor-minor seventh chord (for example, ii^7, iii^7, vi^7). It is a common sonority in Debussy, though it is rarely associated with the aforementioned harmonic functions. "Pour les agréments" is typical: set 4–26 appears in m. 1 as the initial motive (a tonic triad with added sixth) embedded in its complement, 8–26 (ex. 6.8). Note that the raised fourth and second scale

A. "Danseuses de Delphes"

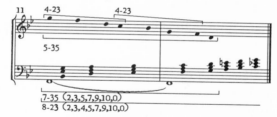

B. "Souvenir du Louvre"

Example 6.7. Set 4–23 in 8–23

"Pour les agréments"

Example 6.8. Set 4–26 in 8–26

degrees of F major create the octachord (B-natural and G♯). Traditional harmonic analysis might posit for the tetrachord a tonic label, decorated by its sixth (or perhaps construe it as a 5–6 change of harmony), followed by major (altered) triads on the second and seventh scale degrees, all disposed over a tonic pedal, thus: I(pedal)—II–VII. Although the function of neighbor-note prolongation is clear here, the chromaticism is certainly atypical of late nineteenth-century harmonic practice.

3–6 in 9–6

The three- and nine-note pairs occur frequently, in contexts that are quite different from the pc environments associated with the tonal repertoire. Furthest removed from nineteenth-century harmonic practice is the pair 3–6/9–6, since it entails both raised first and lowered third degrees. "Pour les agréments" provides an example in m. 4, whose pc content forms set 9–6, while the melodic line, which is quadrupled, forms trichord 3–6 (ex. 6.9A). Another occurs in the opening measure of "Danseuses de Delphes," where the total pc content forms 9–6 under the stepwise soprano line (ex. 6.9B). An earlier example also includes the 3–6/9–6 pair: m. 3 of "Pour ce que Plaisance est morte" (ex. 6.5F).

3–7 in 9–7

Trichord 3–7 is a crucial set in "Danseuses de Delphes," copiously represented throughout as both a melodic figure and a sonority, as in mm. 13–14, where set 9–

A. "Pour les agréments"

B. "Danseuses de Delphes"

Example 6.9. Set 3–6 in 9–6

Example 6.10. Set 3–7 in 9–7

7 appears as the aggregate while trichord 3–7 is prominently embedded in several forms within the pentatonic melody and in the bass (ex. 6.10).[6] Yet another illustration may be found in "Les collines d'Anacapri," the passage cited above (ex. 6.5E): mm. 1–11 yield set 9–7 as their pc content, while 3–7 lies embedded within motives and harmonies.

3–9 in 9–9

This pair occurs in "Souvenir du Louvre," mm. 50–53. Set 9–9 is formed by the pc content of a passage consisting of parallel minor triads. Trichord 3–9 is conspicuously embedded within the melody (ex. 6.11).

3–11 in 9–11

Of all the three- to-nine-note pairs, 3–11/9–11 is the one most likely to appear in the tonal repertoire as a result of mixture—by enhancing the diatonic scale, for example, with the addition of ♭III as in a chromatic third-relation. A striking example cited earlier occurs in mm. 1–7 of "La fille aux cheveux de lin": the pc content forms 9–11 while the complement lies embedded within mm. 5–7 in no less than six forms (ex. 6.12). The chromatic third-relation is present in the modulation from G♭ major to E♭ major.

NONDIATONIC COMPLEMENTS

Complement relations are not limited to diatonic sets, of course. Numerous nondiatonic complements were cited in previous analyses, including those at the

"Souvenir du Louvre"

Example 6.11. Set 3–9 in 9–9

"La fille aux cheveux de lin"

Example 6.12. Set 3–11 in 9–11

beginning of this chapter. Each genus's catalog includes its own stock of complement pairs. Those of the whole-tone genus most often encountered are 5–33/7–33, 4–21/8–21, 4–25/8–25, and 3–8/9–8. The remaining pairs occur far less frequently.[7] Octatonic pairs 5–31/7–31, 4–28/8–28, and 3–10/9–10 are common, but the hexachordal complements are rare.[8] The chromatic genus is replete with complements, among which pairs whose ordinal numbers are 1 or 2 occur most often.[9] The 8–17/18/19–complex genus embraces the largest number of complements, of which the most used are 3–3/9–3, 3–5/9–5, 3–10/9–10, 4–17/8–17, 4–18/8–18, 4–19/8–19, 5–26/7–26, 5–31/7–31, and 5–32/7–32. The remaining pairs, including hexachords, are rare.[10]

Complement relations often involve nongeneric sets. A very common pair, for example, is 5–34/7–34, in which the smaller set is diatonic and the larger nongeneric. Another is 4–27/8–27, where again the smaller set is diatonic and the larger nongeneric. These tonal analogues are integral to Debussy's diatonic music: set 4–27 as the (inversely equivalent) major-minor and diminished-minor seventh-chords; 5–34 as the V^9 sonority.

"Canope"

Complement pairs in "Canope" bind together all of the pc materials within each formal unit. In diatonic mm. 1–6, for example, 5–35 appears as the initial melodic shape, and 7–35 provides the pc content of its melodic-harmonic setting (ex. 6.13A).[11] Tetrachord 4–23 generates the next contour embedded in 8–23, which connects the two tiny formal units defined by these shapes. The pc content of the next fragment (mm. 4–5) is expanded by modulation (between rc = F major and rc = Db major) to encompass ten pcs that form set 10–5, whose complement is represented conspicuously in the low parallel fifths. These introductory bars close with a reference to the opening complement pair in the form of pentatonic 5–35 in the same transposition as mm. 1–3; complements thereby bind together the pc materials of each motivic component within this relatively large formal unit.

The content of mm. 13–16 is diatonic overall, as its largest and smallest collections attest, but modulation and chromaticism engender several nongeneric sets: the pc content of m. 13 forms set 7–28, for example, while mm. 14–16 form 8–27 (ex. 6.13B). Their complements are projected clearly: 5–28 is the initial sonority (pc 9 decorates—and distorts—diatonic 4–27 in m. 13); 4–27 is articulated in several forms in mm. 14–16. Again, motivic components (defined by the modulations) are bound together through complement relations.

Bars 20–23 draw from the whole-tone genus and incorporate two complement pairs: 5–33 in 7–33 (m. 20) and 4–21 in 8–21 (ex. 6.13C).

The 8–17/18/19–complex genus provides the materials for mm. 24–25, though again, chromaticism generates nongeneric collections—this time 8–5 and 8–8—whose complements are formed by conjunct linear segments within each of the two gestures. Generic set 9–5 binds together both measures, and its complement occurs as the final melodic trichord (ex. 6.13D).

A: mm. 1-6

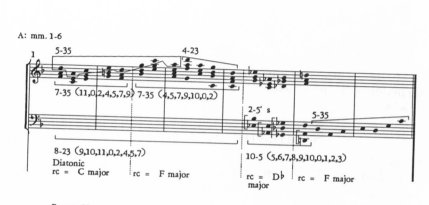

B: mm. 13

C: mm. 20-23

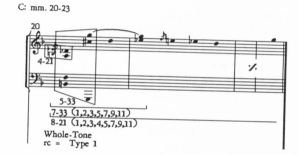

D: mm. 24-25

E: mm. 26-33

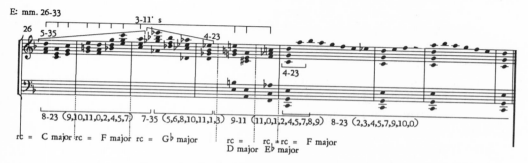

Example 6.13. Complement pairs in "Canope"

The composition's close invokes the diatonic genus with a reprise of the opening material that incorporates complement pairs within and across its surface partitions: 5–35/7–35, 4–23/8–23, 3–11/9–11 (ex. 6.13E).

Sonata for Flute, Viola, and Harp, I

The Sonata for flute, viola, and harp is replete with embedded complement pairs that accomplish all of the functions seen previously, especially that of linking the pc content of an entire formal unit with sets located at its boundaries. The now-familiar first movement contains many complement pairs. The first occurs within mm. 1–6, which comprise the movement's initial formal unit (set in the 8–17/18/19–complex genus). Measure 1 is formed of hexachord 6–Z28 (9,10,0,2,3,6). The two modulations that follow (at mm. 2 and 4) add three pcs to form set 9–8 (2,3,4,5,6,8,9,10,0), whose complement, trichord 3–8, occurs at the very beginning in the first three solo harp notes (0,2,6).

The next diatonic segment is quite long (mm. 7–25), partitioned by several modulations. The first subsection (mm. 7–12; rc = F major) employs eight pcs (set 8–23) whose embedded complement is conspicuous in the first bar (m. 7), in the initiating flourish (4–23 as 0,2,5,7), and also in the first harp chord (5,7,10,0). It appears as well at the close of the segment (m. 12) in the sustained viola chord (10,0,3,5). The termination figure of m. 13 encompasses seven pcs (set 7–35), whose complement is present in the flute lines (5–35, as pcs 3,5,7,10,0).

Many other examples could be cited, but these few must suffice: set 7–35 provides the pc content for the phrase of mm. 14–17, and 5–35 occurs in the harp, m. 14/beat 1 (10,0,2,5,7); mm. 26–27/beat 2 draw from the 8–17/18/19–complex genus represented by set 7–Z36, whose Z-related complement (5–Z12) provides the last five notes of the viola cadenza of m. 26 (to the fermata); set 9–9 is source for mm. 39–49, and complement 3–9 accounts for the harp's bass line (8,10,3).

Whole-tone Genus

Examples of whole-tone complements abound. "Reflets dans l'eau" employs the genus sparingly, but the 5–33/7–33 pair appears, nonetheless, in mm. 44–47, formed by the overall pc content versus that of the melodic fragment that closes the repeated two-measure segment in the bass (ex. 6.14A).

The whole-tone genus is referential for "Cloches à travers les feuilles" (*Images* II). A whole-tone scale in mm. 1–5 is augmented by a seventh pc in m. 6 to form set 7–33, whose complement, 5–33, appears in mm. 1–2 as the pc content of the solo line (ex. 6.14B).

"Pour ce que Plaisance est morte," mm. 18–19, embodies a complement relation in which the large set (7–33) binds together the pc content of juxtaposed pentachords from contrasting genera: whole-tone 5–33 versus diatonic 5–34 (ex. 6.14C).

Whole-tone complements abound in *Pelléas et Mélisande*. Two must suffice, selected from act V: at OS p. 377/(mm.) 5–6, both transposition forms of 6–35

A. "Reflets dans l'eau"

B. "Cloches à travers les feuilles"

C. "Pour ce que Plaisance est morte"

D. Literal complements in *Pelléas et Mélisande,* act V, OS p. 377

E. *Pelléas et Mélisande,* act V, OS p. 397

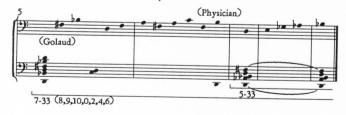

Example 6.14. Whole-tone complement pairs

occur side by side in a rare example of literal complements (ex. 6.14D); at OS p. 397/5–9, 5–33 appears nested within 7–33 as the passage's closing harmony (ex. 6.14E).

Octatonic and 8–17/18/19–Complex Genera

Debussy's use of octatonic and 8–17/18/19–complex complement pairs follows the same pattern as those of other genera. The following examples all come from the Préludes I–II. In "Brouillards," mm. 32–37, the octatonic scale in two transpositions accounts for the overall pc content, but each half of the passage may be partitioned into two forms of 7–31 that project embedded forms of complement pentachord 5–31 (ex. 6.15A). "Les fées sont d'exquises danseuses" also exploits the octatonic genus; a form of 8–28 accounts for the pc content of mm. 70–72, in which 5–31 and 7–31 both appear in close proximity, though somewhat concealed (ex. 6.15B). "Le vent dans la plaine" furnishes an abstruse example of Z-pentachords embedded in their complement or Z-complement; 5–Z17 and 5–Z37 are formed by the middle-register melody with its graces, while 7–Z37 is formed by this material plus the right hand's ostinato (ex. 6.15C).

A. "Brouillards"

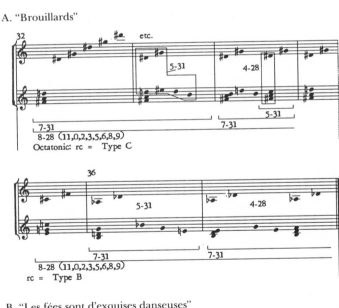

B. "Les fées sont d'exquises danseuses"

Example 6.15. Octatonic and 8–17/18/19–complex complements

C. "Le vent dans la plaine"

D. "Les sons et les parfums tournent dans l'air du soir"

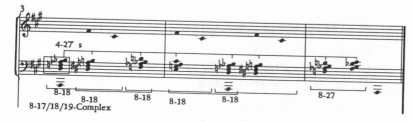

E. "Les sons et les parfums tournent dans l'air du soir"

F. "Les sons et les parfums tournent dans l'air du soir"

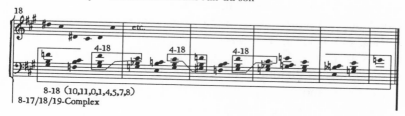

G. "Les sons et les parfums tournent dans l'air du soir"

Example 6.15. *Continued*

The last four examples are all excerpted from "Les sons et les parfums tournent dans l'air du soir" (Préludes I): mm. 3–5 contain many forms of tetrachord 4–27, whose pairs form overlapping forms of 8–18 and, at the end, complement 8–27 (ex. 6.15D). Bar 1 conspicuously projects tetrachord 4–18 (ex. 6.15E); with both 4–18 and 8–18 established thereby at the very beginning of the piece, a striking embedded complement occurs in mm. 18–23, where 4–18 appears several times (in the interaction of chord and line) within the left hand's sonorities, which combine to form octachord 8–18 (ex. 6.15F); at m. 14, 5–31 appears embedded within 7–31 (ex. 6.15E).

Nongeneric Complement Pairs

We have seen several complement pairs for which one member—the larger set—is nongeneric. Two in particular are quite common: 5–34/7–34 and 4–27/8–27. In both cases the smaller set is a tonal analogue that belongs to the diatonic genus.

5–34/7–34. "Pour ce que Plaisance est morte" exposes the 5–34/7–34 pair prominently in mm. 7–8 (ex. 6.16A) and again in mm. 11–12 (where the whole-tone genus represented by 8–21 provides the larger context, with 4–21 embedded within; see example 6.16B). *Pelléas et Mélisande* furnishes many examples, including act IV, scene 4, OS p. 332/7–8 (ex. 6.16C); act V, OS p. 381/6 (ex. 6.16D); and, shortly after, at OS p. 382/4–5, when Golaud hounds Mélisande for the truth about her relationship with Pelléas (ex. 6.16E).

Examples were also cited earlier in connection with the discussion of "Le jet d'eau" (ex. 6.2D) and "Feuilles mortes" (ex. 6.6B).

4–27/8–27. Set 4–27 in its major-minor and diminished-minor seventh-chord forms is a crucial member of Debussy's harmonic vocabulary. A remarkable example of the 4–27/8–27 pair occurs in "Les sons et les parfums tournent dans l'air du soir." Supplemented by 4–18 and 4–Z15, tetrachord 4–27 provides most of the vertical sonorities for this piece, as well as many of the melodic-harmonic combinations. It is first heard at m. 1/beat 3, and its importance is reaffirmed by its iteration at m. 2/beat 3. In mm. 3–5, *all* of the left hand sonorities are forms of 4–27. At first, the composites formed by pairs of tetrachords yield forms of 8–18 (whose complement, 4–18, is a crucial resource), but in m. 5, as subtle changes in pc content and register signal the end of a phrase, the last pair forms 8–27 (see ex. 6.15D). At the end of mm. 7–8 the relation is projected even more prominently (ex. 6.17).

We conclude with two complements that were cited earlier: "Canope," 4–5/8–5 and 4–8/8–8 (ex. 6.13D), and "Lent" (*Images*, 1894), 4–Z15/8–Z15 (ex. 6.1F).

COMPLEMENTS IN INITIAL GESTURES

That many of the excerpts above which served as illustrations were taken from the beginnings of pieces is suggestive; indeed, to open with a complement relation is an integral feature of Debussy's style. Usually the smaller set is embedded in the

A. "Pour ce que Plaisance est morte"

B. "Pour ce que Plaisance est morte"

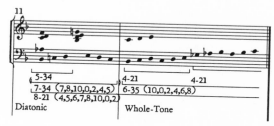

C. *Pelléas et Mélisande*, act IV, scene 4, OS p. 332, mm. 7–8

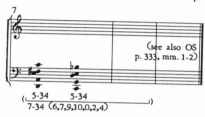

D. *Pelléas et Mélisande*, act V, OS p. 381

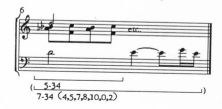

E. *Pelléas et Mélisande*, act V, OS p. 382

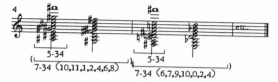

Example 6.16. Nongeneric complement pair 5–34/7–34

"Les sons et les parfums tournent dans l'air du soir"

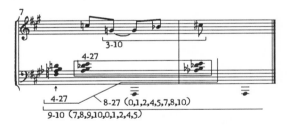

Example 6.17. Nongeneric complement pair 4–27/8–27

larger, though sometimes they occur merely in close proximity. The examples cited below speak to the wide range of possibilities for complement relations in opening gestures. Though they are drawn chiefly from songs and instrumental works (to redress the imbalance perpetrated by the emphasis above on piano works), they illustrate a principle found throughout Debussy's oeuvre after the late 1880s. Among the piano works, for example, nearly every piece in *Estampes*, *Images* (1894 and I–II), *Children's Corner*, Préludes I–II, and Douze études I–II exhibit such relations, and so do most of the songs.

The *Prélude à "L'après-midi d'un faune"* opens with a complement relation: the flute melody's pcs form set 7–1, while 5–1 is embedded prominently within in the sixteenths that descend to pc 7 (ex. 6.18A).[12]

In "La flûte de Pan" (*Trois chansons de Bilitis*), the pc content for m. 1 is 7–35, while the bass of m. 2 contains 5–35 (ex. 6.18B).

"Sirènes" employs set 9–7 as its pc source for the first seven bars (ex. 6.18C), and trichord 3–7 is heard as the bass ostinato plus the horn motive. (Set 3–7 is, of course, well represented as a subset of pentatonic 5–35, which saturates mm. 1–11.)

The prelude music for *Pelléas et Mélisande*, act V, begins with a complement pair: set 8–17 provides the pc content of mm. 1–4, and 4–17 is prominently exposed in the first seven notes (see ex. 7.1). If the passage is extended to encompass the chord of m. 5, with its B♭ (pc 10), the composite forms set 9–3, whose complement, 3–3, occurs conspicuously as the first three notes and many more times throughout these bars in imbrications.

The pc content of *L'isle joyeuse*, mm. 1–2, forms set 9–6, and 3–6 appears embedded within (ex. 6.18D). Also, the last two thirty-second-note groups of mm. 1–2 form whole-tone superset 7–33, while 5–33 is projected in the main descending line of each bar (including the trill note, D♯).

In "De l'aube à midi sur la mer," the pc content of introductory bars mm. 1–5 is too sparse to form a complement relation; mm. 6–11, however, employ set 9–10, while 3–10 appears as the very first sonority of m. 6 and saturates other prominent harmonies (ex. 6.18E). Incidentally, this movement contains several examples of the nongeneric pair, 5–34/7–34, including one in mm. 35–42, where 7–34 accounts for the pc content, with 5–34 embedded in the melody of mm. 38–40.

A. *Prélude à "L'après-midi d'un faune"*

B. "La flûte de Pan"

C. "Sirènes"

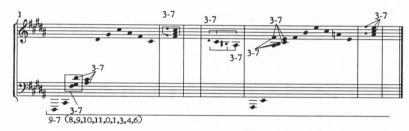

D. *L'isle joyeuse*

E. "De l'aube a midi sur la mer"

F. *Khamma*

Example 6.18. Complements in opening gestures

G. *Jeux*

H. Sonata for flute, viola, and harp

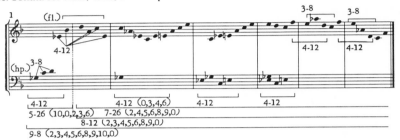

I. Sonata for violin and piano

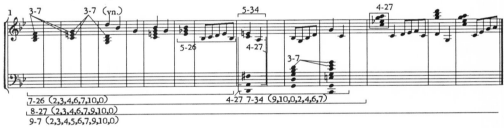

J. "Brouillards"

K. "Les fées sont d'exquises danseuses"

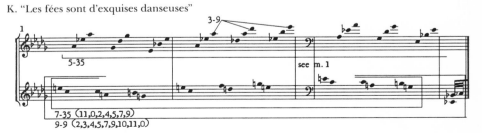

Example 6.18. *Continued*

L. "Bruyères"

M. "Pour les sonorités opposées"

N. "Pour les arpèges composés"

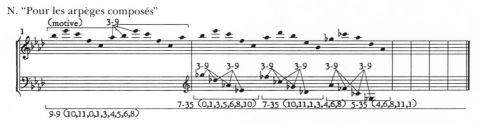

Example 6.18. *Continued*

The movement also closes with a complement relation: the last four bars contain set 8–26, whereas 4–26 occurs as the final sonority.

The ballet *Khamma* (dated 1912)[13] opens with a complement relation drawn from the whole-tone genus; mm. 1–6 employ set 7–33, whereas the bass melody of mm. 3–6, coupled with the incessantly reiterated pc 0, yields 5–33 (ex. 6.18F).

Jeux employs a whole-tone complement pair in mm. 1–8 in a manner similar to *Khamma;* the total pc content yields 7–33, whereas the woodwind chords of mm. 6 and 8 form set 5–33 (ex. 6.18G).

The first movement of the Sonata for flute, viola, and harp provides several examples. Bars 1–6 yield set 9–8 as the pc content; trichord 3–8 is heard in the first three notes of the harp and is also conspicuous in the solo viola, m. 5 (ex. 6.18H). Tetrachord 4–12 is conspicuous throughout the piece. It appears, initially, as the harp's hexachord partitioned into overlapping tetrachords; as the reiterated harp figure of m. 3; and twice in the viola line in mm. 4–5. Its complement, nongeneric 8–12, generates the pc content of mm. 1–6 beginning on the unison D shared by flute and harp in m. 1.

Several complement pairs occur nested within each other at the beginning of the Violin Sonata:[14] the pc content of mm. 1–9 forms set 7–26, and 5–26 occurs in m. 9 as the sum of chord and line (ex. 6.18I); mm. 1–14 yield set 8–27, and although 4–27 is inconspicuous in those bars (embedded in the V^9 sonority of mm. 10–12 as the overlapping upper and lower tetrachords), it is the first harmony heard in m. 15; the pc content of mm. 1–17 forms set 9–7, whose trichordal complement is prominent in the accompaniment's upper line in mm. 10–14 (as 2,4,7). The 5–34/7–34 pair occurs here also: set 5–34 is formed by the union of the two triads in mm. 1–7, and 7–34 follows in the piano's pc content in mm. 10–14.

"Brouillards" (Préludes II) begins with two eighth-note gestures that articulate transpositions of set 7–31, which plays an important structural role vis-à-vis the composition's pc resources; its complement is embedded in the left-hand's white-key chords plus the boundary pitches of the right-hand tetrachords (ex. 6.18J).

"Les fées sont d'exquises danseuses" (Préludes II) opens with a rare literal complement relation: the black-key form of 5–35 in the right hand superimposed above the white-key form of 7–35 (ex. 6.18K). The overall pc content of the left hand for these measures forms set 9–9, whose complement is projected in a prominent motivic fragment of the treble line.

"Bruyères" (Préludes II) provides yet another example of 5–35 in 7–35, the former comprising the unaccompanied antecedent phrase (mm. 1–3), the latter the polyphonic consequent (mm. 4–5) (ex. 6.18L).

Finally, two examples from the Douze études II: mm. 1–6 of "Pour les sonorités opposées" have as their source set 7–32, within which 5–32 may be found partially concealed in m. 5 (ex. 6.18M); "Pour les arpèges composés" unfolds an intricate series of 5–35/7–35 complement pairs in mm. 1–6 (ex. 6.18N), as well as the 3–9/9–9 pair.

Complement relations constitute a structural feature of Debussy's music because they bind together pc materials within and across formal units, and because their presence shapes the larger pitch collections that arise from atomic units in the form of small sets that combine to generate complement members. Complement pairs also contribute to sonorous homogeneity within each genus owing to the effects of amplification, intensification, and compaction wrought by their parallel intervallic tendencies. This is especially evident in the 5–35/7–35 pair, but it is equally true of many others.

The complement relationship provides one rationale for the ubiquitous anhematonic pentatonic scale, since melodic pentatonicism almost invariably occurs within or proximate to diatonic contexts that include cynosural set 7–35.[15] These larger diatonic contexts usually include vertical dispositions of set 5–35 as V^{11} chords (third omitted), or as major triads with added sixth and ninth,[16] a practice that serves to further stress the interplay of complements.

The use of complement relations to open most pieces (beginning with the Baudelaire songs of 1889) correlates with the appearance of such relations in abundance throughout Debussy's works. It is difficult to imagine that he was unaware of complement relations, however he might have rationalized them.

PART III
TEXT EXPRESSION THROUGH PITCH MATERIALS

SEVEN
PELLÉAS ET MÉLISANDE

We have seen how Debussy's manner of handling pitch materials evolved gradually from operations associated with tonal harmony and voice leading towards a system in which intervallic content and its possibilities for relation were exploited for their own values and sonorous characteristics. We traced the modification of his tonal language to accommodate pc set relations, and observed how tonal and nontonal procedures may be understood as different, coexisting aspects of pitch organization, for Debussy neither abandoned one for the other nor merely alternated between them; he devised, instead, a way of working that exploited both at once.

The 1890s were crucial for Debussy's development and center on his composition of *Pelléas et Mélisande,*[1] created during his years of artistic maturation (1893–1902). The pc set genera are conspicuously present, although certain passages resist identification within this model, and not all operations subsequently associated with pc sets are exploited. Nonetheless, the diatonic, whole-tone, 8–17/18/19–complex, and chromatic genera serve throughout as the composition's pc resources.

Although the pitch materials of *Pelléas et Mélisande* are interesting in themselves, the opera especially invites a consideration of their relation to the text, which provides an extramusical imperative in the need to project the drama's meaning and content from moment to moment. Also, the nature of its form differs from instrumental works, where the temporal framework for musical materials can be its own rationale.

A key to the relation between text and music may be found in the myriad points of disjunction that disrupt continuities in the pitch materials, for they are often linked to disruptions in the text and action. When a character's attention shifts significantly the music tends to exhibit some sort of transformation as well, which heightens the effect of the change. Conversely, musical materials sometimes resist modification, which has the effect of minimizing superficial discontinuities in the interest of larger dramatic continuities. One of Debussy's remarkable achievements in *Pelléas et Mélisande* was his discovery of a fundamentally new

163

way to change the character of the pitch materials—mutation—so as to fit them to the ever-shifting sense of the drama; yet his innovations are derived from well-established procedures in use for centuries. Since part 3 of this book is concerned chiefly with the expressive role played by the pc set genera vis-à-vis the psychological content of the drama, a brief digression is warranted to consider the general notion of relation between pitch materials and text expression.

MUSIC AND PSYCHOLOGICAL AFFECT

Most listeners will agree that the manipulation of emotion by musical means, in particular by choice of pitch materials, constitutes a significant aspect of musical experience. Nonetheless, to broach the topic is to tread on the edge of a quagmire, for there are as yet few musical or psychological studies that address this area in a substantive way;[2] for this reason my observations and conclusions are modest.

Let us assume two very general psychological domains that are subject to affect by the manipulation of pc materials.[3] The first is dynamic, and entails the difference between passivity and activity; lassitude and inattention lie at one extreme, alertness and intensity at the other. The second is emotional and embraces the range of mood from what might be described as "dark" to "light"—between extremes, for example, represented by fear and anger on one hand, and by compassion and love on the other. Together, these psychological domains form a field, which may be compared to two dimensions on a plane that represent aspects of emotion and intensity. The dynamic domain encompasses a wide range of emotions, and the emotional domain spans a considerable range of intensity. Table 7.1 conveys something of the possibilities, though I must stress that my conception is relativistic, and the quadrants' boundaries overlap. In opera (as in

TABLE 7.1. Psychological field of intensity and emotion

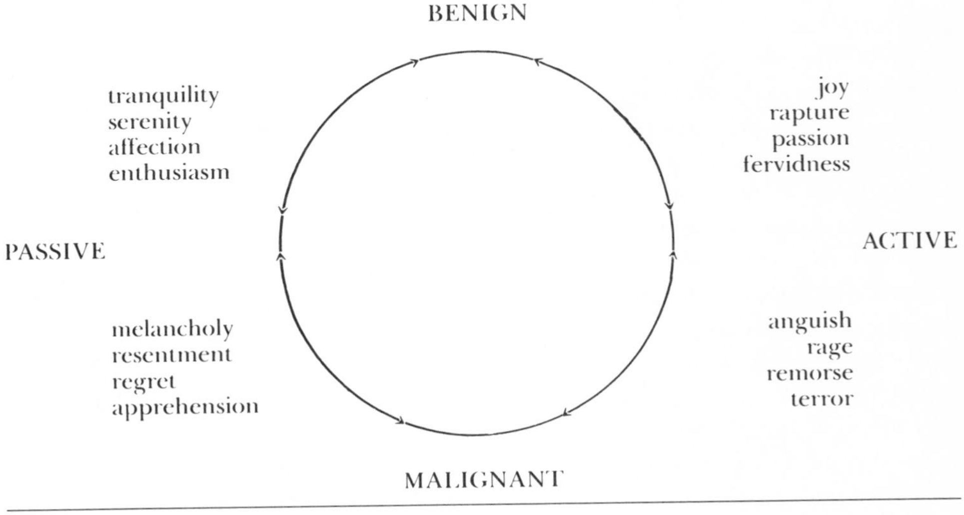

BENIGN

tranquility
serenity
affection
enthusiasm

joy
rapture
passion
fervidness

PASSIVE

ACTIVE

melancholy
resentment
regret
apprehension

anguish
rage
remorse
terror

MALIGNANT

life) a character's position in this field is in constant flux, and a composer's effectiveness in creating and maintaining the auditors' empathy depends on the ability to elicit appropriate changes of mood. Pitch materials furnish a powerful means for manipulating the listener within this psychological framework.[4]

Historically, motivic association, chromaticism, and consonance-dissonance relations have been the means by which pitch materials in Western tonal music are manipulated for expressive purposes. The Baroque concept of *Affektenlehre* and the nineteenth-century leitmotiv share as a common principle the notion that melodic contours and rhythmic patterns can be used to construct associations between pitch materials and objects or ideas.[5] Debussy's use of specific motives attached to characters and events in *Pelléas et Mélisande* has a substantial literature of its own, and writers have no trouble identifying melodic-rhythmic shapes that represent Mélisande, Pelléas, and Golaud.[6] Leitmotivs are certainly important in the opera, but they represent only one source of musical symbolism. The pc set genera are another, pervasively affective source, one that helps to explain the various transformations which occur in the leitmotivs themselves as their contours are modified to conform to those that inhere in each genus.

Chromatic alteration and modulation, through which pc content is enriched or modified, have their own historic antecedents in the form of altered chords and key associations. In Debussy they are embraced by the set-theoretic concepts of pc supersets (enrichment through pc accretions to a given cynosural set such as 7–35), invariance, and the operations of transposition and (by extension) inversion.

Debussy's approach to text expression in *Pelléas et Mélisande* incorporated all of the above means but reformulated them. Instead of limiting himself to the diatonic genus of pc sets (divided into consonant and dissonant combinations, enriched by chromatic alteration, and varied by changes of key or mode), he developed the pc set genera. Each genus has its distinct sonorous properties that issue from the characteristic ics emphasized in its members' ivs, and each has characteristic kinesthetic properties that inhere to its members' sias. Modulation provides additional means for increasing the range of available nuances. Each genus also shares sets with other genera and so each interconnects to some extent with the others. Ambiguity arises from the multiple associations which accrue to shared pc sets, associations that require clarification through context.

Prelude Music to Act V

The brief instrumental prelude that begins act V illustrates, once again, Debussy's use of the pc genera as a source of contrast and continuity, and, as we shall see, as a means of setting an appropriate mood given the psychological associations to which each genus is tied.

The prelude consists of five contrasting passages. A formal plan is provided in figure 7.1, and a pc reduction appears in example 7.1.

The first passage (mm. 1–4), which elides with the next on the chord at the beginning of m. 5 (4–27), projects motives derived from sets 3–3 (represented in multiple), 4–3, and 4–17. The overall pc content is drawn from the 8–17/18/19–

FIGURE 7.1. Formal plan for the instrumental prelude to *Pelléas et Mélisande,*
act V

Section	Measures		PC set genus	Important sets
A	1–4		8–17/18/19-complex	3–3, 4–3, 4–17, 5–16, 9–3
B	5–8		Diatonic	3–11, 4–11, 4–27, 5–35, 6–33, 7–35
A	9–10		8–17/18/19-complex + chromatic	3–3, 4–3, 4–17, 5–16 + 6–1, 7–1
B	11–14		Diatonic	3–9, 3–11, 4–22, 6–32
A	15–16		8–17/18/19-complex	3–3, 3–2, 4–8, 4–19, 7–11

complex and yields set 8–17 within its superset, 9–3 (which includes the B♭ of the
elision chord). The presence of embedded complements (3–3 in 9–3 and 4–17 in
8–17) is, as we have seen, characteristic of Debussy's beginnings. The pc set
materials combine with the instrumental color consisting of muted strings and
harp to produce a mood that is somber, reflective, yet agitated.

Bars 5–8 constitute the next formal unit. Its genus is diatonic, represented by
the parallel thirds, and projects sets 4–11, 4–27, 5–35, 6–33, and 7–35, among
others. Complement relations are prominent in this passage, too, manifest in the
5–35/7–35 pair.

The modulations that occur at half-bar intervals disclose a technique that is
often placed in the service of text expression: rapid changes in pc content (which
draw attention to rapid shifts of focus from one character to another).

The third passage is only two bars long (mm. 9–10). The return of the opening
motive in the flutes, English horn, and harp invokes the 8–17/18/19–complex
genus, though the chromatic genus is also well represented in the clarinets'
hexachord, set 6–1. The diatonic genus provides all of the pitch content for the
fourth formal unit (mm. 11–14), but the pitch materials for the last passage are
derived once more from the 8–17/18/19–complex genus. In its alternation of pc
set genera, the formal plan for the prelude resembles a tiny rondo scheme
(ABABA, where A = 8–17/18/19–complex and B = diatonic).

Expressive Associations for the PC Set Genera

At the level of detail, *Pelléas et Mélisande* is constructed throughout as a series of
brief passages (normally two to six measures). Each employs a particular pc set
genus manifest in a specific referential collection. Mutations or modulations serve
to partition each act and scene into subdivisions and phrases. These changes
achieve contrast, while interrelationships exploited among the genera at the level

Example 7.1. PC reduction of the instrumental prelude to *Pelléas et Mélisande*, act V (mm. 1–16)

of detail promote coherence, as do limitations placed on the number of genera used. Modulations and mutations are keyed to changes in the sense of the drama as it unfolds from moment to moment. In general, mutations reflect marked changes in the sense of the text; modulations align with subtle changes (since modulation is less drastic in its effect). Modulations are most common within the diatonic genus, though they occur in the other genera as well.

Debussy's choice of genus from moment to moment forges consistent connections between the pc set genera and the psychological implications of the characters and their actions. In general, the expressive associations that emerge are as follows (keyed to the psychological field shown in table 7.1):

Diatonic genus = benign, passive hemisphere
8–17/18/19–Complex genus = malignant, active hemisphere
Whole-tone genus = malignant hemisphere (passive or active), but generally reserved for matters of mystery, fate, and especially death
Chromatic genus = neutral, used to intensify or emphasize affect of the genus with which it is conjoined

In *Pelléas et Mélisande,* explicit and implicit psychological content and meaning are disposed throughout on three levels: the first is literal and centers on the actions and reactions of the characters from moment to moment taken at face value; the second consists of the characters' concealed feelings about what is said or done; the third is allegorical and concerns the meaning of characters, objects, and events as symbols and metaphors. Where these levels contradict one another, Debussy tends to lend musical support to the less obvious. The importance of this multileveled structure of objective, subjective, and allegorical meaning cannot be overstressed. It accounts for passages of the most exquisite beauty, where an overly literal approach to understanding the opera is confounded by baffling inconsistencies between dramatic events and the pitch materials that accompany them.

The Characters

There are four main characters in act V: Arkel, King of Allemonde; Mélisande; Prince Golaud, Arkel's grandson; and an anonymous physician. A group of servant women form a ghostly presence late in the act to symbolize powers of clairvoyance beyond comprehension.

The Physician, soothing and calm, is a minor figure whose one-dimensional character serves as an intermediary between Mélisande and the others; he represents the mundane world as it intrudes on their preoccupations. Arkel is kind but incapable of action, unable to influence Golaud or to allay Mélisande's fears. He talks often of man's nature, conflicts, and moral character, but observes everything from a distance.

Mélisande is characterized as isolated and remote, disoriented, uncomprehending, distracted, unable to respond directly to the simplest questions. Yet she is also manipulative and conspiratorial, able to lie and to beguile. To her credit, we must recognize that she is imprisoned in a world (Allemonde) where only men have power and are free to love or brutalize, and so deceit and seduction are among her only weapons. Her posture of innocence, projected throughout, is inherently false, as is proved when she lies to Golaud and encourages Pelléas. Her fear when Pelléas playfully entangles her hair (act III, scene 1) betrays her awareness of the sinister implications of that action. Yet the quality of innocence remains, credible in spite of her culpability, perhaps because she is so passive (she only reacts, never initiates), and we sense that she is not really cognizant of her actions' effect and does not belong to the world she inhabits. In act V we find her disoriented (whether from illness or by design is unclear), dying from a malady as inexplicable as everything else about her.

At all levels of meaning (especially the allegorical), Golaud is the central character, for it is he who engages actively in an unending struggle with his own nature. Preoccupied with right and wrong, good and evil, he anguishes over the ramifications of his and others' actions. Act V finds him consumed with remorse for having murdered his half-brother Pelléas, and by self-pity as he squirms in the trap constructed of the ineluctable consequences of the chain of events of which he is a part, but which fate, rather than he himself, has set in motion. Of all the characterizations, Golaud's is the richest and demands the widest range of treatment in the musical setting.[7]

Pelléas et Mélisande is more than a drama about jealousy, infidelity, and revenge: it is an allegory in which Golaud embodies humanity's struggle to overcome its base qualities; of failure when he succumbs to those qualities; and of the aftermath when he must face the consequences of that failure.

As we shall see, the music for Mélisande, Arkel, and the Physician usually matches their speech and actions taken at face value, because for them there is little conflict between levels of meaning. In contrast, the multiplicity of meanings attached to Golaud's thoughts and actions requires a less direct approach to musical expression.

Act V, mm. 1–120

Figure 7.2 provides a proportional formal plan for mm. 1–120. (Passages are cited by bar numbers counted from the beginning of each page; "p. 378/5" thus refers to the fifth measure of p. 378.)[8] Page/bar numbers keyed to the full score appear in the left column. Mutations define the points of disjunction indicated by horizontal solid lines that section the vertical time-line, while modulations are indicated by horizontal broken lines. Example 7.2 provides a pc reduction organized by formal units. Vertical lines correspond to the partitions of figure 7.2 (they are not bar lines) and carry page/bar numbers keyed to the full score. Crucial pc sets are cited on two staves: the orchestra is assigned to the lower, the vocal parts to the upper.

We shall examine four of five segments into which the events of act V, mm. 1–120 can be divided. In the first, the Physician and Arkel discuss Mélisande's

FIGURE 7.2. Formal plan for *Pelléas et Mélisande,* act V, mm. 1–120

Page/ Mm.ᵃ	Measuresᵇ	PC set genus	Dramatic action
365/1	1	8–17/18/19–Complex	(Instrumental prelude)
365/5	5	Diatonic	
366/4	9	8–17/18/19–Complex + chromatic	
366/6	11	Diatonic	
366/10	15	8–17/18/19–Complex	
367/1	17	Diatonic	Physician comforts Arkel and Golaud
367/9	25	8–17/18/19–Complex	Arkel alludes to Mélisande's grave condition
368/1	28	Diatonic	Arkel affectionately contemplates Mélisande
368/2	29		
368/3	30		
368/4	31		
368/5	32	8–17/18/19–Complex	Golaud's remorse: "I have killed without reason!"
368/7	34	Diatonic	"It is enough to make the stones weep!"
368/9	36		Golaud reflects on innocence of Pelléas and Mélisande
369/2	38	Whole-tone + chromatic	Golaud's mood changes to remorse as he thinks of the murder
(369/4	40)		

FIGURE 7.2. *Continued*

Page/ Mm.ᵃ	Measuresᵇ		PC set genus	Dramatic action
369/4	40		Diatonic	Golaud denies malicious intent
369/6	42			Physician announces that Mélisande is awakening
369/7	43			
369/9	45			Mélisande asks for the window to be opened
370/1	47			Arkel responds with warmth and concern
370/5	51			Mélisande again
370/6	52			
370/7	53			Arkel, Physician, Mélisande
371/1	58			Arkel, Physician, Mélisande
371/1.5	58.5			
371/2	59			
371/2.5	59.5			
371/3	60		Whole-tone	Arkel speaks to Mélisande of death (the setting sun)
371/5	62		Diatonic	Arkel asks Mélisande how she feels
371/7	64		Diatonic + chromatic	Mélisande expresses disorientation
372/3	68		Diatonic	Arkel does not understand
372/4	69		8–17/18/19–Complex	Mélisande is confused, but verges on clarity (knowing that death is imminent)
372/8	73			Mélisande is fretful, worried
373/2	76		Diatonic	Arkel reassures and consoles Mélisande . . .

FIGURE 7.2. *Continued*

Page/ Mm.[a]	Measures[b]		PC set genus	Dramatic action
373/4	78		8–17/18/19–Complex	. . . but is unconvincing
373/5	79			(Modulation underscores fore- boding)
373/6	80		Diatonic	
373/7	81			
378/8	82			
374/2	84			Arkel tells Mélisande of others' presence; mentions the physician
374/4	86		8–17/18/19–Complex	Arkel alludes to Golaud
374/6	88		Diatonic	Arkel reassures Mélisande that Go- laud will not harm her
375/2	92			
375/3	93		8–17/18/19–Complex	Arkel names Golaud; Mélisande asks that Golaud approach her
375/6	96			Golaud drags himself to Mélisande's bed
375/9	99		Diatonic	Mélisande addresses Golaud warm- ly, as though forgetting what he has done
375/10	100			
376/1	101			
376/2	102			
376/3	103			
376/5	105			
376/7	107		8–17/18/19–Complex	Golaud asks to be alone with Méli- sande (he is in torment, anguish)
377/1	109		Diatonic	Golaud assures Arkel and the Physi- cian of his benign intentions, say- ing . . .
377/3	111		8–17/18/19–Complex	. . . he has something on his mind to discuss with Mélisande

FIGURE 7.2. *Continued*

Page/ Mm.[a]	Measures[b]		PC set genus	Dramatic action
377/4	112			
377/5	113		Whole-tone	Asks Arkel and Physician to leave
377/6	114			
377/7	115		8–17/18/19–Complex	Reassures Arkel and Physician; speaks of his misery (to imply harmlessness)
378/1	116		Diatonic	
378/2	117		8–17/18/19–Complex or whole-tone	Golaud alone with Mélisande (it is the chemistry of their relationship that is the mystery here)
(378/5)	(120)			

[a]Orchestra score page number/measure number
[b]Solid horizontal lines indicate changes in pc set genera; broken lines indicate modulations.

condition (mm. 17–41). Mélisande then awakens and speaks with Arkel (mm. 42–59). After a crucial reference to her impending death (mm. 60–61), Mélisande becomes aware of Golaud, who pleads for a moment alone with her (mm. 62–120).

Arkel and the Physician. Act V—the shortest—is unbroken by scenes and derives at least part of its impact from its brevity. The action begins with the Physician, Arkel, and Golaud alone with Mélisande in her room. The pc set materials of p. 367/1–8 are diatonic as the Physician consoles Arkel and Golaud with assurances that Mélisande's wound (inflicted by Golaud) cannot account for her grave condition. The calm and hopeful mood is enhanced by a sympathetic portrayal of Mélisande's helpless innocence. As Arkel brushes hope aside (p. 367/9–11), the pitch materials mutate abruptly to the 8–17/18/19–complex genus, but when his thoughts turn (p. 368/1–4) from despair (he rejects the Physician's optimism) to Mélisande herself (he speaks of her slow breathing and of her soul), the pc set materials mutate once more to the diatonic genus. The two diatonic pentachords that alternate at one-bar intervals in the accompaniment (sets 5–34 and 5–35) represent different rcs (modulations) and effectively suggest Mélisande's breathing. The 8–17/18/19–complex again dominates Golaud's entrance (p. 368/5–6). His words are: "I have killed without reason!"[9] His next thoughts (pp. 368/7–369/1) signal a change of emotional focus accompanied by pc set materials drawn from the diatonic genus: "It is so sad that even the stones weep! They had only embraced as little children do."[10] These two sentences, which convey different (though emotionally similar) thoughts, are separated by a modulation. As the focus of Golaud's attention shifts back to the murder (p.

Example 7.2. PC reduction of *Pelléas et Mélisande*, act V, mm. 17–120

Example 7.2. *Continued*

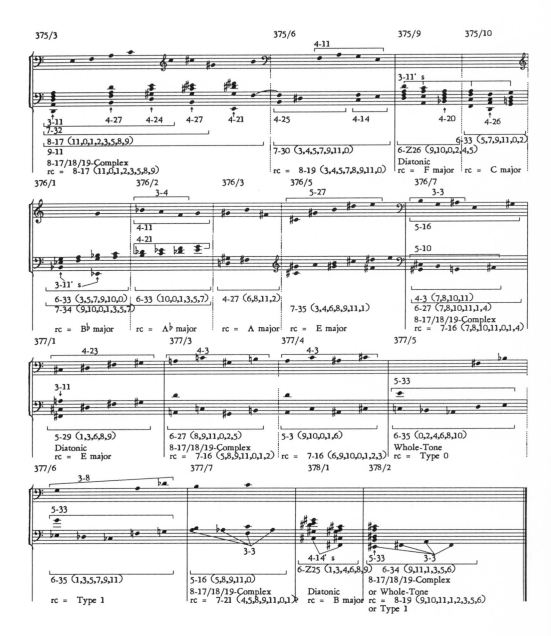

Example 7.2. *Continued*

369/2–3)—"And I, I all of a sudden!"[11]—the pc materials culminate in a whole-tone tetrachord (4–24), which underscores the inexplicability of his own actions and the impetuousness of his violence. Golaud continues (p. 369/4–5) to reassure himself, Arkel, and the Physician that what he did was beyond rational control, contrary to his true intentions and his better nature. Diatonic materials help to portray him sympathetically.

Mélisande Awakens. Bars 42–95 are devoted to the exchange between Arkel and Mélisande that follows her awakening. Of the twenty-eight passages that comprise this section, twenty-two are diatonic, consistent with the benign associations that attach to the characters. The remaining passages employ the 8–17/18/19–complex or whole-tone genus to underscore crucial moments of more ominous portent.

At p. 369/6–8, the Physician warns that Mélisande is awakening. The diatonic genus helps to focus on her. (Here Mélisande equates with "good," "innocence," "helplessness.") Note again the pairing of diatonic rcs represented by, respectively, pentachords 5–34 and 5–35. This modulation (like those at p. 368/1–4) helps to convey the appropriate tentativeness and a slight tension. (Similar diatonic pairings occur elsewhere in comparable dramatic situations; for example, from p. 369/9 to p. 370/4, and at p. 371/1–2.)

From p. 369/9 through p. 371/2, Mélisande, Arkel, and the Physician speak by turns. Diatonic pc sets appropriately support the warmth that they express, with shifts from one character to another underscored by modulations as well as changes in thematic material and character of setting. Even subtle shifts of emphasis within a character's speech are emphasized by modulations, such as Mélisande's second (and more intense) plea for an open window (p. 370/1).

When Mélisande naively inquires whether it is time for the sun to set[12] (note the pair of diatonic modulations at p. 371/1, which underscore her uncertainty), Arkel's affirmative answer—"Yes, it is the sun that sets in the sea; *it is late*" [emphasis mine][13]—ominously invokes the symbolic association between the setting sun and death, a symbolism we sense he understands, but Mélisande does not; hence the whole-tone pc set materials at p. 371/3–4. When, subsequently, Arkel asks Mélisande how she feels (p. 371/5), the set genus is unclear since the diminished triad and tetrachord 4–13 are associated equally with the diatonic and the 8–17/18/19–complex genera. The pitch materials for the instrumental parts at p. 371/7 are drawn from the diatonic genus (oboe and English horn) superimposed over the chromatic genus (flutes and violins), while the vocal line combines elements of both (semitonal voice leading is indicated by slurs). Tetrachord 4–13, inherently ambiguous as a member of both the diatonic and 8–17/18/19–complex genera, is used to set the most ironic line of the passage when Mélisande declares, "I have never been better."[14] Her disorientation and confusion are striking: she remembers nothing; she feels well but is uncertain; she knows something is wrong but cannot recall what. The chromaticism intensifies the anxiety that lurks beneath the placid surface of her remarks; moreover, although their pc contents may be accounted for as constituents of diatonic or chromatic sets in the orchestra parts, the vocal lines form of themselves sets that are unambiguously 8–17/18/19–complex: 6–18 in 8–18. Arkel's gentle question at the end of the passage (p. 372/3)—"What are you saying?"[15]—is set diatonically in trichord 3–11, but as subset of 8–18 it does nothing to mitigate Mélisande's disquieting bewilderment.

Mélisande begins to struggle towards awareness. She complains that she cannot understand all that they say, that she no longer speaks as she wishes, and for seven measures (p. 372/4–373/1) the pc set materials employ the 8–17/18/19–complex genus. A modulation (p. 372/8) correlates to a subtle shift in focus as Mélisande edges closer to awareness; what she says is more focused than her previous musings: "I no longer say what I want."[16] When Arkel declares (p. 373/2), "It makes me very happy to hear you speaking this way,"[17] a clear shift to the diatonic genus (enhanced by the lush string color) expresses the sudden flood of warmth. At p. 373/4 the mood turns dark once more as Arkel expresses his concern for Mélisande, and she asks whether he is alone (reminding us of Golaud's presence). His concern for Mélisande, coupled with anticipation of his task to tell her of Golaud's presence, finds representation in the mixture of small sets, of which 4–27 is diatonic (as well as 8–17/18/19–complex) and 4–24 is whole-tone. Their combination forms set 7–32, which is not diatonic, but belongs to the 8–17/18/19–complex genus.[18] At p. 374/2, when Arkel identifies the Physician—"there is also the physician"[19]—the diatonic genus is invoked. But two bars later, at exactly the point (p. 374/4) where Arkel alludes to Golaud—"And then there is also another"[20]—the 8–17/18/19–complex genus returns. The next four bars strongly project diatonic pc sets (p. 374/6–375/2) coincidental with Arkel's assurance that Mélisande has nothing to fear, and Mélisande's question "Who is it?"[21] engenders a modulation (p. 375/2). The 8–17/18/19–complex returns at p. 375/3 (the small sets are also diatonic, but once again they conjoin in set 7–32), when Arkel finally identifies Golaud—"It is your husband, it is Golaud"[22]—and Mélisande invites him to approach: "Golaud is here? Why doesn't he come nearer?"[23] The 8–17/18/19–complex helps to underscore the threat that Golaud represents, his intentions notwithstanding, and also the ominous issue of Mélisande's relation to Pelléas, which he intends to revive.

Mélisande and Golaud. That the pc sets which accompany the moment when Golaud drags himself to the bed and calls Mélisande by name (p. 375/6–8) include shared whole-tone 4–24 as well as other sets that are emphatically 8–17/18/19–complex is consistent with the (death) threat that he represents to Mélisande. Her assertion that she hardly recognizes him (p. 375/9–10) brings a shift to the diatonic genus (with a modulation between her question "Is it you, Golaud?"[24] and her remark "I barely recognized you."[25] Her next comment (p. 376/1–2)—"It is because I have the evening sun in my eyes"[26]—is accompanied by a pair of diatonic rcs that conjoin to form nondiatonic set 7–34,[27] whose presence supports the tension conveyed by Mélisande's (unwittingly symbolic) allusion to her ap-

proaching death through reference to the setting sun. Her remarks to Golaud—
"Why do you look at the walls? Oh, how old and thin you have become"[28]—
remind us of his torment and awareness of her condition.

Golaud now asks to be alone with Mélisande as he wishes to say something to
her. His request is initially set in the 8–17/18/19–complex genus (p. 376/7–8), but
when he promises to leave the door open (for reassurance), the pitch materials are
drawn from the diatonic genus (p. 377/1–2). His comment (p. 377/3–4) that "I
wanted to say something to her"[29] is set once again in the 8–17/18/19–complex
genus—and appropriately so, since this remark alludes to his intended confrontation with Mélisande. The sudden shift to whole-tone sets in p. 377/5–6 (high-
lighted by an acceleration) projects Golaud's lack of self-control (which his apparent composure seeks to mask) and warns that he will not be able to keep his
promises, for this will end badly, as he allows Mélisande's maddening vagueness to
provoke his volatile temper. The 8–17/18/19–complex genus returns, followed
by the diatonic genus (p. 377/7–378/1), coincidental with his appeal to Arkel's and
the Physician's sympathies (and ours as well). He declares, "I am a miserable
man."[30] The rapid vacillation between genera supports the complex mixture of
emotions implied in his anguished declaration. Whole-tone set 5–33 dominates
the four-bar interlude heard as Arkel and the Physician leave, but it is set within
8–17/18/19–complex hexachord 6–34, to which the strings' trichordal motive
(3–3) belongs as well. The passage evinces sonorities of both genera which are
distinguishable by their differing timbral and textural dispositions. Golaud's composure, maintained with difficulty, is for the benefit of Arkel and the Physician.
The vacillation among diatonic, 8–17/18/19–complex, and whole-tone genera
during these nineteen bars (p. 376/7–378/10) helps to draw attention to the
contrast between Golaud's calm surface and his inner turmoil.

The first 120 bars manifest two types of relations between pc materials and the
drama: those (the majority) where the affective association of the chosen genus
supports the literal sense of the drama, and those for which the genus contradicts
the literal sense in support of subsurface meaning. In the case of the former, the
cooperation between music and drama simply enhances the listener's empathy
with the characters and their experiences. In the case of the latter, the music helps
the listener to see the deeper realities disguised by surface appearances. Arkel's
reply about the sunset is a case in point: harmless on the face of it, the sunset's
morbid symbolism is efficiently conveyed by the use of the whole-tone genus, and
the contrast between the benign question and the malignant answer allows each
character's unconscious to speak directly to our own, informing us instantly of
their different states of awareness (and arousing our apprehension), yet without
distracting us from the dramatic surface.

Golaud's plea for Arkel and the Physician to leave him alone with Mélisande
provides another illustration of conflict between psychological levels. When
Golaud first asks them to leave (p. 376/7), the 8–17/18/19–complex genus reveals
his inner turmoil, but when he assures them of his benign intentions (p. 377/1) the
diatonic genus helps project his desire to garner their sympathy and persuade

them of his sincerity. When he says he has something to tell Mélisande (p. 377/3) the pc sets betray him by mutating to the 8–17/18/19–complex genus, which warns of his jealousy and instability. The change to the whole-tone genus as he again asks to be left alone with Mélisande (p. 377/5) emphasizes his lack of self-control and warns that the threat he represents is deadly. The return of the diatonic genus (p. 378/1), which accompanies his final plea, demands our sympathy once more. Lest such rapid vacillations among genera of opposing associations appear to negate the principle that the pc set genera support the expression of a character or an event, we must recall that Golaud's character is rife with psychological conflict and contrary impulses. Debussy's settings ingeniously reflect this and reveal his ability to create powerful and subtle musical resources that generate rich emotional nuances.

Selected Passages from Acts I, IV, and V

We will turn now to other passages that demonstrate four features: the use of the whole-tone genus; the early linkage (in act I, scene 1) of the pc set genera with psychological states; additional instances of psychological conflict or ambiguity; and expressive links with pitch materials and the use and psychological function of the pc set genera in purely instrumental passages.

More Examples of the Whole-tone Genus. Towards the end of act V (p. 396/8–397/4), the servant women of the royal household quietly line the walls of Mélisande's room as a signal that death is near. The pitch materials are drawn from the 8–17/18/19–complex genus (the low strings carry the first motive from act V's instrumental prelude) and underscore the moment's tension. Asked by Golaud and Arkel why the women have come, the Physician denies knowledge of their purpose, but the symbolism is obvious and at this point (p. 397/5–9) the pc sets align with the whole-tone genus (represented by complement pair 5–33/7–33). The eerie effect is most apt.

The moment of Mélisande's death (p. 405/11) is set in the whole-tone genus (represented by tetrachord 4–21). The diatonic genus dominates the music beginning soon after (p. 406/14) and the remainder of act V, consistent with the notion that her soul's release through death brings Mélisande peace and repose just as it restores calm to the house and to the inhabitants of Allemonde.

Throughout the opera, death as mystery and the suspension of the rational are consistently associated with the whole-tone genus. Act I, scene 1 (beginning at p. 5/6) finds Golaud lost in the forest after having wounded a wild boar. As he wanders, seeking his way, whole-tone sets underscore his disorientation and the sense of having stepped out of the ordinary world into a place where man's rules have little currency. The whole-tone genus emerges again with his reference to the boar's blood (p. 6/6), and it returns to dominate most of the scene's end as Golaud admits to Mélisande that, like her, he is lost.

The psychological implications of the symbolism of scene 1 warrant an extended essay. I shall resist the temptation, but I will propose a brief interpretation of the allegory that resides beneath the surface. The forest represents forces that work upon us in the world, unseen and beyond our control. The beast, which Golaud has wounded (but not destroyed), represents the dark side of his own nature. In the chase through the forest, as in his encounter with Mélisande (with whom he is immediately smitten), he loses his way. The chase and the forest are metaphors for losing one's way in the world; Golaud drifts off of his correct path and falls into the trap of material distraction at the expense of his larger purpose. One can lose oneself as easily through obsessive concern with self-reform (chasing the wild boar) as by succumbing to one's nature (through infatuation with Mélisande). At the close of the scene, Golaud, having failed to kill the beast, has set in motion catastrophic processes; as he seeks his way out of the forest with Mélisande, he has changed his life's path.

Orledge observes that a comparison of Debussy's libretto with Maeterlinck's drama reveals a tendency to remove passages that clarify matters involving a character's motivations.[31] Yet that is precisely the function of the material which occurs near the beginning of act I, scene 2, as Geneviève and Arkel discuss Golaud's original mission to consummate a political marriage with the princess Ursule (see p. 30/1–39/11 and, especially, p. 35/5–8). These plans represent Golaud's designated worldly path from which, instead, he has strayed by taking Mélisande as his wife. Had Debussy excised this passage as he did others, he could have left unaddressed and mysterious the mundane details that clarify why Golaud strayed so far from Allemonde. Perhaps he retained it because this material is essential to the allegory since it discloses Golaud's fundamental flaw; his sudden infatuation with Mélisande is not merely impulsiveness, it is weakness in the face of duty. The feelings of unease and apprehension aroused by the whole-tone materials at the end of scene 1 are appropriate, for Golaud has made a crucial and terrible decision. Evidently a part of Golaud knew what he had wrought, for it is a recognition of forces unleashed and destinies forged at this moment to which Golaud refers in act V (p. 379/8) when he tells Mélisande, "I cannot tell you of the wrong I have done, but I can see it all very clearly today, *from the very first day*" [emphasis mine].[32]

The 8–17/18/19–Complex Genus. Just as the whole-tone genus's association with things beyond our control is forged very early in the opera, so also are the associations of the other pc set genera established at an early stage. The 8–17/18/19–complex genus first appears (in the form of hexachord 6–27) when Golaud encounters Mélisande weeping at the well (p. 7/9.5), and thereafter whenever she expresses fear or anguish. The large sets that most often represent the genus in act I, scene 1 are 7–32 and 6–27, and both are prominent throughout the opera (act V included). Hexachord 6–27 is conspicuous in act IV, scene 3, where Yniold complains that his arm is not long enough to free the ball (p. 309/10), and later, when he declares that the sheep are afraid of the dark (p. 313/1). In both cases, Yniold's psychological state is one of extreme anxiety.

The Diatonic Genus. The association of the diatonic genus with that which is propitious and benign is established in act I, scene 1, when Golaud approaches

Mélisande for the first time (p. 8/9), and shortly thereafter (p. 9/5), where lush string chords set his words "Oh! You are beautiful,"[33] cementing the affective possibilities of the genus to positive emotions. Another emphatically diatonic passage occurs at p. 11/3 (again set in lush string sonorities), where Golaud comforts Mélisande: "Come, no more tears."[34]

The instrumental prelude to act I, scene 1, opens with diatonic pc sets (p. 1/1–4 and p. 2/1–4), whose genus is referential for the opera's first twenty-seven bars, alternating by turns with the whole-tone and 8–17/18/19–complex genera. Whereas Golaud's first words are set in the whole-tone genus (he declares he is lost), the passage in which he first speaks of the wounded boar is set in the diatonic genus (p. 6/1–4). In the face of his plight we may question the tranquil setting, but it appropriately reflects his unawareness of the ramifications that accompany his abandonment of a known path in favor of another whose destination is unknown.

More Conflicts between Surface Explication and Subsurface Implication

Act V. In the midst of a diatonic passage of act V where Mélisande warmly addresses Golaud (p. 375/9–376/6), there is a moment (p. 376/2) where she refers obliquely to her impending death through the symbolism of the setting sun: "It is because I have the setting sun in my eyes."[35] The vocal line conspicuously projects diatonic trichord 3–4, but whole-tone tetrachord 4–21 is embedded in the instrumental line of the violins and flutes. Perhaps because the reference to death is oblique, the predominantly diatonic color of the overall setting is only slightly distorted, and only for a moment.

A complicated passage in act V (p. 379/3–384/7) occurs in the midst of Golaud's lengthy speech, where he acknowledges to Mélisande the injury he has inflicted. Although the speech is dominated by the 8–17/18/19–complex genus represented by sets 5–9, 5–30, and 7–30, other sets appear whose association is ambiguous since they belong also to the diatonic genus (4–Z29, 5–20, and 5–24, as well as trichord 3–11, which is conspicuous in the vocal line).[36] The ambiguity of pc set association parallels Golaud's ambivalence as he attempts to excuse his misdeeds through lack of intention.[37] In the next passage (p. 380/1) the pc set materials shed their ambiguity (in favor of the 8–17/18/19–complex genus) at Golaud's crucial words "But I can see it all very clearly today, from the very first day." At this moment he acknowledges the inevitable and disastrous consequences brought about by the conjunction of his destiny with Mélisande's, owing to the conflict between his volatile, rigid nature and her placidity and shallow innocence. His complex emotional reaction upon at once apprehending the extent to which he is blameworthy and at the same time a victim of his own nature is expressed through the use of pc sets drawn from the 8–17/18/19–complex genus, diluted by sets shared with the diatonic and whole-tone genera. Thereafter, as Golaud speaks of his love for Mélisande, radiating warmth and affection, the pc set materials become entirely and conspicuously diatonic.

The passage that sets the end of Golaud's speech (p. 382/4) is diatonic harmonically, whole-tone melodically, and almost diatonic overall. His fervent plea for the truth from Mélisande employs diatonic chords (several transpositions each of 4–27 and 5–34). The moment's anguish demands a whole-tone or 8–17/18/19–complex setting, however, and the melodic dimension projects a striking refinement: the parallel descending woodwind lines inscribe four transpositions of whole-tone tetrachord 4–21. Moreover, the diatonic pc set content is distorted, since the prominent septachord is 7–34 and not diatonic cynosural set 7–35. Since "truth" is an idea associated with the diatonic genus, Debussy's choice of diatonic harmonies is consistent; at the same time, intense anguish is reflected in the distortion of the diatonic genus by the use of 7–34 (rather than 7–35) engendered by the whole-tone lines, and by other features of the musical surface.[38]

Act IV, Scene 3. Psychological conflict and references to death both occur in the ostensibly charming, yet foreboding scene with Yniold and the sheep (act IV, scene 3), which opens (p. 307/1) at the well outside the castle, set to diatonic pitch materials that support the image of a boy at play—he is struggling to free his golden ball, caught under a rock. The placidity of the musical surface is disturbed, momentarily, by the intrusion of 8–17/18/19–complex hexachord 6–27 (p. 309/10), which emerges when Yniold voices his frustration and anguish: "My little arm isn't long enough, and this stone will not be raised."[39] The diatonic genus returns for six more bars (p. 310/5–10, where tetrachord 4–23 serves both genera as a connecting link), but the intrusion of the 8–17/18/19–complex hexachord has warned us that the scene's pastoral tranquility belies sinister undertones.

Whole-tone materials appear[40] as Yniold notices a flock of bleating sheep, which he thinks are weeping (p. 311/3)—"I hear the sheep crying"[41]—and he notices that the sun is setting (p. 311/7): "There is no more sun."[42] As he continues to observe the approaching sheep, the diatonic genus returns (p. 312/1), but when he senses their fear (p. 313/1)—"They are afraid of the night. They huddle together! They are weeping and fleeing!"[43]—the 8–17/18/19–complex genus dominates.[44]

When the shepherd responds (in a striking monotone) to Yniold's questions that the sheep are not on the path to the stable, the boy wonders where they will spend the night. This section (p. 315/1–318/11) is relatively calm and predominantly diatonic. There are, however, allusions to the 8–17/18/19–complex genus (represented by set 5–28: p. 317/11–13).

The scene is replete with allegorical symbolism that the pc set materials help to underscore. The rock that holds Yniold's ball symbolizes the immutability of worldly events set in motion, while the golden ball itself represents (the boy's, or anyone's) human capacities and possibilities for progress, which are constrained by such events. Yniold's futile attempt to free his ball is a metaphor for the struggle of the characters—Pelléas, Mélisande, and Golaud—against their respective destinies, which are pointed clearly towards disaster. Debussy's use of the 8–17/18/19–complex to set Yniold's lament on the shortness of his arm exaggerates the frustration of a boy who is merely engaged in play, but it does not exaggerate if we understand that his arm represents his will, which is insufficient to thwart the forces that shape his destiny.

The arrival of the sheep, which distracts Yniold from his distress over the ball (hence the transformation back to the diatonic genus), distracts us as well. But as their fear is transmitted to him (and to us), the 8–17/18/19–complex genus returns. So it goes throughout the scene; mutations facilitate empathy with Yniold's emotional vacillations. Aided by whole-tone pc sets, Yniold's remark that the sun is fading (a reference to death), juxtaposed with his declaration that the sheep are weeping, augurs Pelléas's death, and Mélisande's as well. The metaphor is reinforced as the sheep pass by and we discover (by inference) that they are being led to slaughter. The pc set associations profoundly support this sublime mixture of anecdote and symbolism, and when the metaphoric aspect is taken into account, nothing is overdone.

This scene was omitted from the initial performance of the opera, and although some accounts blamed the cut on dramatic weaknesses (suggesting that the pastoral scene inhibited the momentum towards the opera's climax in scene 4), Orledge maintains that problems with Blondin, the first singer of Yniold's role, were behind the decision rather than any perceived musical or dramatic fault.[45] Certainly the scene's symbolism is crucial since it presages events that occur in the remainder of the opera, and, perceived allegorically, there is no attenuation of the tension accumulated in scene 2.

The Expressive Role of the PC Set Genera in Instrumental Passages

The brief instrumental prelude to act V effectively establishes the right mood and state of anticipation for the drama's dénouement. Because of associations established previously, the prelude music's vacillation between the diatonic and 8–17/18/19–complex genera expedites, for the auditor, the establishment of a psychological posture that combines apprehension (in the aftermath of the murder in act IV, scene 4) with somber resignation (as the tragedy's remaining threads are taken up and the characters' destinies fulfilled—in particular, as Mélisande recedes, through death, from a world to which she does not belong and in which she cannot actively participate).

The prelude to act I functions similarly, alternating diatonic passages with those derived from the whole-tone or 8–17/18/19–complex genera. As the first heard and most recurrent, the diatonic genus serves as referent for these twenty-seven bars, from which the nondiatonic passages depart and to which they return. This music presents to the listener the sonorous inventories that will be used throughout the opera (along with prominent leitmotivs), and in this regard it is a typically Debussyan "introduction." Apropos of the genera's psychological associations, the prelude music's adoption of the diatonic genus as referent takes an inert emotional posture as its point of departure, and uses the other genera to stimulate the listener's sense of proximity to malignancy and mystery.

The foregoing psychological interpretation rests on an important assumption—namely, that the listener knows from the outset the appropriate associations that attach to each of the genera. Yet could this be true for listeners who are unfamiliar with the opera, who have not been indoctrinated into the dramatic meaning of its harmonic language? Do the pc set genera possess intrinsic affective powers along the lines specified throughout this chapter? These are difficult (and important) issues, and they engender others: If associations between the set genera and specific psychological states have not yet been activated by bringing together word and music, is the act I prelude music merely decorative? Does it serve only to attract the audience's attention (at least for the first-time listener)? Or is it possible that the pc set genera are affective even in the absence of dramatic support to lend specificity, and that the associative ties occur naturally? Further, if the associative ties do not arise spontaneously for listeners in general, is it possible that the genera embodied specific associations for Debussy at least, so that when he was contemplating a text, particular psychological implications consistently suggested settings within a particular genus? The answers to most of these questions must await systematic study. As for the last, although external evidence in the form of statements from the composer is unavailable (and nonexistent, so far as I know), internal evidence uncovered through a survey of other vocal works is suggestive and informs the next chapter.

The interaction of pc set materials as an evocative symbolic language with the languages of word and gesture provides a window into Debussy's conceptions of the characters. Consider the moment, in act V (p. 380/1), when Golaud (speaking to Mélisande) realizes that conflicts between and within their respective characters doomed them from the moment of their first encounter. In its delicate alternation between diatonic (4–22) and whole-tone (4–24) tetrachords, the musical setting impugns the notion that Golaud is simply a brute, or that Mélisande is simply naive, for here as elsewhere the harmonic complexities belie such simplistic characterizations. Her posture of innocence is betrayed by a sense that it derives from a lack of cognitive focus that is perhaps contrived. His brutality seems engendered more by his impulsiveness than by a character that is essentially evil. These facets of their natures suggest subtler, more human personalities, consistent with the subtle musical setting.

Other parameters interact with pitch and affect expression in their own ways. Low register and close spacing of chords are generally associated with darker psychological states. Just as chromaticism (which increases pc content) is used to intensify psychological states induced by other types of pitch materials, increased activity in the form of rapid-note figurations, thicker textures, and scoring for larger numbers of instruments effects intensification in the domain of rhythm. The resetting of familiar material in richer sonorities (through additional doublings, wider spacings, or other changes in orchestration) also intensifies feeling. Compare, for example, the prelude music to act I, p. 1/5–6 and p. 2/5–6, with p. 7/1–2 and 3–4. The horn color in the latter two passages generates more intensity than the initial settings in the woodwinds. These parameters may have less expressive power than pitch,[46] but they are potent resources nonetheless. Sometimes they serve to lessen or counter affect from within the domain of pitch. The prelude music to act I, scene 1 begins with diatonic pitch materials (p. 1/1–4 and p. 5/2–5), but low register and dark instrumental color combine with subdued dynamics to exert a far more somber affect than one might expect. In the same prelude (p. 2/5–6 and p. 7/1–3), pc set materials derived from the sinister 8–17/18/19–complex genus are counterbalanced by close spacing in middle registers, thin texture, quiet dynamics, and lush instrumental color that are more evocative of a bright and cheerful demeanor. Such musical dichotomies provide yet another means of addressing contradictions between surface appearances and underlying realities, of simultaneously setting both sides of an issue.

The general psychological states that are either explicitly evoked by the sense of the libretto or implicit in the drama's subtler shadings are tied, by proximity, to the various set genera. Often the associations are obvious: Golaud speaks of Mélisande's beauty and the pc set materials are diatonic; he refers, with remorse, to having murdered Pelléas and the pc set materials are drawn from the 8–17/18/19–complex genus; references to death (Mélisande's in act V; the allegorical sheep in act IV, scene 3) are coupled with whole-tone materials; chromatic materials superimposed on or integrated into other genera coincide with intensifications of emotional states. Where the psychological implications are complex and embody conflict between outer appearances and inner feelings, the musical setting tends to affirm the least obvious. When Yniold abandons his ball (the object of play) to regard the sheep as they are led to slaughter (a serious matter), the pitch materials shift from the malevolent 8–17/18/19–complex genus to the benign diatonic genus. The apparent contradiction does not exist, in fact, because Yniold's golden ball is a metaphor for something much more profound (the human soul); his distress is underscored by the acerbic 8–17/18/19–complex genus, whereas the sheep at first pose a distraction from his distress, and the diatonic setting helps to express his momentary relief. (That the sheep also serve as a harbinger of doom is reflected in the pitch materials a few bars later.) The associations of pc set genera with emotional and dynamic psychological states are not merely based on naive correspondences of symbols to characters or actions. Although Debussy does employ leitmotivs in this fashion (Mélisande's motive, for example, invariably accompanies her appearance or references to her), his use of the pc set genera is much more sophisticated and permits the music to assist in the expression of multileveled, wide-ranging, and subtle shadings of meaning. The result is characterizations that are more human and less like caricature. If we consider language and gesture to be vocabularies of aural and visual symbols by which the drama's psychological states can be communicated (in other words, expressed), then Debussy's achievement in the pc set genera was to devise a new vocabulary of musical symbols.

EIGHT

A SURVEY OF TEXT EXPRESSION IN EARLY, MIDDLE, AND LATE WORKS

EARLY WORKS: "NUIT D'ÉTOILES"

Debussy's earliest published song, "Nuit d'étoiles," exhibits his traditional approach to text expression through pc enrichment, substitution, and rotation, along with certain tendencies that characterize later works such as *Pelléas et Mélisande*—in particular, his attention to nuance and detail in his handling of texts.

Although there is disagreement regarding its exact date,[1] "Nuit d'étoiles" was probably completed during the composer's conservatory years. The poem, by Théodore de Banville, consists of four stanzas, of which Debussy sets stanzas 1, 2, and 4 (hereafter referred to as stanzas 1, 2, and 3). Debussy alters stanza 1, which is used as a refrain, by repeating its last line. The music for stanzas 2 and 3 is similar and contrasts with that of the refrain. Table 8.1 shows the rondo-like scheme.

Banville's poem proceeds from a contemplative state of mind focused on the present (stanza 1) to an agitated state, in which the poet's feelings about a past love are revealed (stanzas 2–3: presumably the lover has died). The refrain, however, interrupts the linear course by twice returning to the original contemplative state. Table 8.1 provides a literal translation of the text (the French syntax is crucial).

The musical setting reflects the poem's psychological shifts. The relatively stable pc content of mm. 1–24, and the reprises in mm. 38–56 and 72–91, help to communicate the appropriate sense of quiet contemplation. (Table 8.2 traces invariants and changes in pc content from phrase to phrase.) Bars 25–37 set stanza 2 in which the poet plunges into the past, recalling, with intensity, facets of the lost lover. The profound shift in mood is complemented by dramatic changes in pc content through modulations to the keys of B♭, D, and F♯ major. The rapidity of changes reflects the psychological and physiological acceleration of a sudden turn of thought and change of emotion (agitation, rush of adrenaline, racing heartbeat). The *animato*'s acceleration of the musical pulse (m. 25) intensifies the pacing of mood changes. Bars 57–71 function similarly to mm. 25–37, which they resemble; they set stanza 3 and reassert the more active mood of stanza

TABLE 8.1. Literal translation of "Nuit d'étoiles," identifying key words

Stanza	Line	Text	Translation
1	1	Nuit d'étoiles,	Night of stars,
(Refrain)	2	Sous tes voiles,	Under your veils,
	3	Sous ta brise et tes parfums,	Under your breezes and your scents
	4	*Triste lyre*	*Sad lyre*
	5	Qui soupire,	That sighs
	6	Je *rêve* aux *amours* défunts.	I *dream* of *lovers* gone (deceased).
		[Je *rêve* aux *amours* défunts.]	[I dream of lovers gone.]
2	7	La *sereine* mélancolie	The *serene* melancholy
	8	Vient éclore au fond de mon coeur,	Comes bursting from the bottom of my heart
	9	Et *j'entends* l'âme de ma mie	And *I hear* the soul of my lover
	10	Tressaillir dans le bois *rêveur.*	Throbbing in the wood (that) *dreams.*
(Refrain)	1	Nuit d'étoiles, etc.	Night of stars, etc.
3	11	Je *revois* à notre fontaine	I *see again,* in our well
	12	Tes *regards* bleus comme les cieux;	Your *glances* blue as the skies
	13	Cette *rose,* c'est ton haleine,	This *rose,* it is your breath
	14	Et ces étoiles sont tes yeux.	And these stars are your eyes.
(Refrain)	1	Nuit d'étoiles, etc.	Night of stars, etc.

2. This passage traverses two keys in only thirteen bars, and the accelerated change of pc content is intensified by an animato.

Debussy's setting responds to minute shifts in the poem's meaning at the level of detail. Crucial words (italicized in table 8.1) that signal new associations and changes of mood coincide with changes in pc content. In stanza 1, line 4, for example, the words *triste lyre* coincide with such a change (pcs 1,4 replace 2,3)[2] and suggest a shift in mood from serenity to something darker. The sixth line (emphasized by repetition) intensifies the new mood even as it illuminates the reason for the sudden somber emotion; in mm. 17–22 the poet speaks of *dreaming* of *lovers gone,* and pcs 11,2,3 replace pcs 0,1,4. This change restores most of the original pc content and by association helps the listener return to the original passive psychological state consistent with the sense—at the quieter repetition of the words *amours défunts*—of turning one's attention away, towards a more congenial line of thought. The word *revois* (m. 57) coincides with a drastic change in the pc content (pcs 9,0 replace pcs 8,10,11,2). This word wrenches one's attention back towards the past lover and away from contemplation of the pleasant evening. The word *regards* coincides with the next change in pc content (m. 60) and brings focus to the source of the change of mood of m. 57. (The noun renders specific the new source of the poet's attention, signaled by the word *revois.*) The last change of pc content in this section occurs at the word *rose,* whose association with *haleine* focuses even more intimately on the remembered lover. Certainly the listener's mood is not affected by pc materials alone, for changes in other parameters such as tempo,

TABLE 8.2. Keys, pc content, and invariants in "Nuit d'étoiles"

Section	Measures	Key	PC content	Invariants
A (refrain)	1–12	E♭ major	7–35 (2,3,5,7,8,10,0)	
				5,7,8,10,0
	13–16	F harmonic minor	7–32 (4,5,7,8,10,0,1)	
				5,7,8,10,0
	17–24	E♭ major	8–26 (3,5,7,8,10,11,0,2)	
				10,0,2,3,5,7
B	25–28	B♭ major	7–35 (9,10,0,2,3,5,7)	
				7,9,2
	29–32	D major (plus ♯4th degree)	6–Z40 (6,7,8,9,11,2)	
				6,8,11
	33–37	F♯ major	6–32 (6,8,10,11,1,3)	
				8,10,3
A Refrain (see mm. 1–24)	38–56			
				3,5,7,10
B (varied)	57–59	B♭ major	5–34 (3,5,7,9,0)	
				7,9
	60–61	D major	5–35 (7,9,11,2,4)	
				7,9,11,2,4
	62–69	D major	7–35 (1,2,4,6,7,9,11)	
				7,9,2
(transition to reprise)	70–71	D minor (plus ♭5th degree)	6–Z40 (2,5,7,8,9,10)	
				2,5,7,8,10
A Refrain (see mm. 1–24)	72–91			

register, and dynamics also exert their influences, but changes in pc content do capture the listener's attention with astonishing immediacy.

In Banville's poem, lines 4–6 initiate a shift towards the darker psychological state embodied in the second stanza. (When stanza 1 recurs as a refrain, these same lines gain potency since the focus of recollection has acquired specificity in stanza 2.) Debussy acknowledges their importance by interjecting a change of pc content that is radical compared with previous lines (especially the exchange of pc 11 for pc 0) and by repeating the last line.

Throughout the song, changes in pc content correlate with the psychological sense of the text and combine with changes in other parameters[3] to heighten effects as well as achieve the gradations of nuance required by the shadings in mood.

As shown in table 8.2, each passage's pc content usually forms a diatonic collection, but sometimes not: sets 7–32 and 6–Z40 are foreign. However, even the nondiatonic sets can be explained in tonal terms, resulting from common alterations to diatonic major- and minor-scale degrees.[4] Changes in pc content always leave invariants and the invariant subsets are always diatonic. The invariant pcs most used are, in order of precedence: pc 7 (eight times), pc 2 (five times), and pcs 3,5,8,10,0 (four times each). They combine to form 2,3,5,7,8,10,0 (= 7–35), corresponding to the E♭ major scale.

In "Nuit d'étoiles" Debussy reacts with both subtlety and skill to the shifts of psychological state that he perceived in the poet's text using means available to him within the tonal system, in which he was so thoroughly trained: chromatic alteration, enrichment, and modulation. Changes in the musical setting conspire with psychological changes in the text to manipulate the listener within this tonal framework.[5] The formal symmetry in "Nuit d'étoiles" is characteristic of Debussy's early works in general, and betrays his naivete. His penchant for it during this period probably attracted him to Banville's poem, with its symmetrical construction. His attempts to respond comprehensively to the text's nuances, however, look forward to mature works.

SONGS CONTEMPORANEOUS WITH *PELLÉAS ET MÉLISANDE*

Songs that date from the period during which Debussy composed *Pelléas et Mélisande* treat pc set materials in much the same way as the opera: brief passages consisting of no more (and often less) than a few measures alternate pc set materials drawn from the diatonic, whole-tone, and 8–17/18/19–complex genera.

"La flûte de Pan"

The diatonic genus is the source for most of "La flûte de Pan" (*Trois chansons de Bilitis* I). Of its seven sections, all but one strongly project characteristic diatonic trichords, tetrachords, and pentachords.[6] The exception is section 5 (mm. 17–21). Although its summary set is a member of the diatonic genus (9–11, whose embedded complement is the G major triad of m. 21), nondiatonic set 7–31 and its complement are also prominent: set 5–31 forms the sonority of m. 18/beat 2 (and m. 20/beat 2), while set 7–31 accounts for the total pc content of mm. 17–20. The sonority of this complement pair strongly colors these bars and invokes the 8–17/18/19–complex genus (to which 9–11 and 3–11 also belong). The passage sets the words "It is late; here is the song of the green frogs that begins at night-fall,"[7] whose sense contrasts sharply with the preceding lines because they signal (for the girl who is narrating) the startling intrusion of the mundane world, abruptly ending her erotic sojourn with Pan. The choice of the 8–17/18/19–complex genus is consistent with its use elsewhere; it reflects her alarm at the thought that her long absence will make her mother suspicious. The diatonic genus appropriately sets the rest of the poem's languid eroticism.

Fêtes galantes II and *Trois chansons de France* were composed shortly after *Pelléas et Mélisande*.[8] Their construction is familiar: series of brief, discrete passages that project sets drawn from one or another genus, whose associations with psychological states are consistent with those established in *Pelléas et Mélisande*.

Fêtes galantes II

The 8–17/18/19–complex is source for the sets used to set the first three lines of "Les ingénus" (*Fêtes galantes* II), mm. 1–13: "High heels struggled with long skirts / So that, depending on the terrain and the wind, / Occasionally a lower leg gleamed, . . ."[9] It is easy to see the good-humored connection between the text's voyeuristic imagery and the 8–17/18/19–complex genus used, in *Pelléas et Méli-sande*, to support intense emotions generated by more serious foci. The next line (mm. 14–15)—". . . too often intercepted!"[10]—is set in the diatonic genus, consistent both with its implications of attenuated intensity (as the watcher self-consciously withdraws on discovering that he himself is watched) and its effect of abrupt contrast through materials used to underscore the sudden change of poetic mood. Whole-tone passages in "Les ingénus" are used to set portions of the text that evoke a sort of madness and excitement—for example, "and we loved that duplicitous game. / Sometimes also the sting of a jealous insect / Disturbed the collars of the girls under the branches" (mm. 16–26).[11] "Les ingénus" is tongue-in-cheek, with a strong sense of self-satire, for which an exaggerated musical expression is appropriate.

Given its consistent alignment with references to death, the whole-tone genus is an obvious choice for "Colloque sentimental" (*Fêtes galantes* II); its subject is an exchange between two ghosts who once were lovers.

"Pour ce que Plaisance est morte"

The predominantly diatonic setting of Charles d'Orléan's *rondel* "Pour ce que Plaisance est morte" (*Trois chansons de France*) employs three genera in its brief twenty-three bars: diatonic, whole-tone, and 8–17/18/19–complex. Figure 8.1 presents a literal translation of the fifteenth-century poem aligned to the setting's mutations and modulations, and example 8.1 is a pc reduction that shows the

FIGURE 8.1. Formal plan for "Pour ce que Plaisance est morte"

Line	Measures	Genus	Text
1	1	Diatonic	Because
	3	Diatonic + chromatic	
	4	Whole-tone	Pleasure is dead
2	5	Diatonic	This May, I dress in black;
3	7	(Whole-tone and	It is a great pity to see
	7.5	nongeneric sets)	
4	8		My heart discomforted like this.
	8.5		
5	9		I dress myself in a way
6	10	8–17/18/19-complex + chromatic	Which is suitable, out of duty;
7	11	Diatonic	Because
	12	Whole-tone	Pleasure is dead
8	13	Diatonic	This May, I dress in black.
9	15	8–17/18/19-complex	The weather brings this news
10	16	Diatonic	Which wants (tolerates) no diversion;
11	17		But because of the rain was the way
12	18	Whole-tone	(to the countryside) closed,
		Diatonic	
			Because
13	19	Whole-tone	Pleasure is dead.
	20	Diatonic	(Piano alone)
	23		

Example 8.1. PC reduction of "Pour ce que Plaisance est morte"

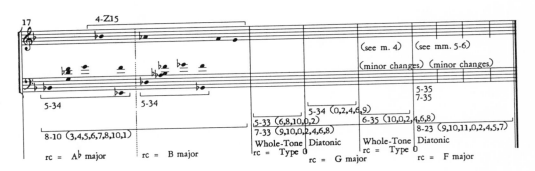

Example 8.1. *Continued*

segmentation. References to death are always tied to the whole-tone genus, but associations for the other genera are less consistent. In "Pour ce que Plaisance est morte," the pc set genera function less to affect momentary transformations correlated to each word than to create a fluctuant state of bittersweetness that well expresses the poem's underlying angst.

The phrase "is dead"[12] is invariably set in whole-tone sets (it occurs three times, in mm. 4, 12, and 18–19). The 8–17/18/19–complex genus appears twice, setting line 6 (m. 10), "Which is suitable, out of duty"[13] (chromatic sets underscore the word *duty,* towards which the line's intensity is directed) and line 9 (m. 15), "The weather brings this news. . . ."[14] Both phrases imply bitterness. Two passages pair diatonic modulations that conjoin to form exotic harmonies which lie outside the genus: the first (mm. 7–8), sets lines 3–4 with two transpositions of diatonic set 5–34 that combine to form (nondiatonic) complement 7–34. (Meanwhile, the right hand strongly projects whole-tone pentachord 5–33 across the modulation.) Bar 11 also projects the 5–34/7–34 complement pair.

The points of disjunction created by mutations and modulations partition the piece into segments that correspond to the poem's lines, or natural breaks of thought within lines (such as "Because . . . Pleasure is dead"). In addition, frequent modulations and mutations within phrases at mm. 7–12 contribute to the sense of agitation implicit in lines 3–6. Debussy's responsiveness to even minute changes in the text's mood or focus of attention, manifest in the frequent and wide-ranging changes in pc materials, has its roots in the early, wholly diatonic songs, but his tools here are both more sophisticated and more powerful.

LATER WORKS

Le martyre de Saint-Sébastien

The most extensive vocal work after *Pelléas et Mélisande* is *Le martyre de Saint-Sébastien,* which was composed in 1911.[15] Compared with *Pelléas et Mélisande,* a striking difference is the tendency for a given genus to dominate for many bars at a time, in contrast to the short spans that separate mutations and modulations in the opera. Virtually the entire prelude to "La cour des Lys" (part 1) is diatonic and it encompasses fifty-nine bars. It is often repetitious, alternating sustained chords with sparse diatonic melodies accompanied by a few harmonies widely spaced. This contrasts sharply with the very dense score of *Pelléas et Mélisande*, a contrast that may be explained in part by the haste with which *Le martyre de Saint-Sébastien* was composed. It occupied Debussy for two months (February–March 1911), compared with twenty-two months for the first draft of *Pelléas et Mélisande*,[16] a difference disproportionate to the works' lengths. A more economical approach could have accommodated its rapid composition; those passages in *Pelléas et Mélisande* that were added hurriedly during the first production's final rehearsals are also repetitious and exhibit a similar terseness in thematic and harmonic resources and sparseness of texture.[17]

All of the pc set genera are used in *Le martyre de Saint-Sébastien*. The whole-tone genus is encountered frequently wherever the text deals with matters relating to death or mystery; the 8–17/18/19–complex genus is used to set piquant emotions, grief, anguish, and the experience of physical pain especially, while the diatonic genus most often occurs in proximity to references involving beauty or virtue, and for the expression of the work's overt religiosity.

"Le concile des faux dieux." "Le concile des faux dieux" (part 2, no. 7) is typical of the range and use of pitch materials throughout *Le martyre de Saint-Sébastien*. Its thirty-four bars fall into thirteen formal units defined by pauses (fermatas), mutations, or both. Figure 8.2 presents a formal plan, enumerates crucial pc sets, and summarizes the text in translation.[18] Formal units range in length from one-half to six bars. The pc set genera align with the text as follows: sections 1–4 (mm. 1–16) employ the whole-tone genus enriched by the chromatic genus (death is central to the sense of the texts); section 7 (mm. 23–26) is whole-tone as well (its text, beginning "Lower now the torches,"[19] is also a symbolic reference to death); sections 5 (m. 17) and 6 (mm. 17–22) employ the 8–17/18/19–complex genus (the latter sets the anguished declaration "He descends towards the dark Portals! All things that are beautiful, dismal Hades carries off");[20] sections 8–12 are very brief and vacillate between the diatonic and 8–17/18/19–complex genera (they set the words "Eros! Weep ye!"[21] and a sigh); they effectively attenuate the emotional fervor as part 3 draws to a close.

Most of the sets identified with the 8–17/18/19–complex genus are also members of the octatonic genus, but hexachord 6–Z43, which comprises the pc content of the last section (mm. 29.5–34), is not. Since all of the sets, including 6–Z43, belong to the 8–17/18/19–complex genus, and in the absence of the octatonic scale itself, there is no reason to invoke the octatonic genus. True octatonicism occurs so rarely in *Le martyre de Saint-Sébastien* that the octatonic genus may be discounted as a significant resource for this work. When used, however, it functions for expressive purposes in the same way as the 8–17/18/19–complex genus.[22]

In sum, *Le martyre de Saint-Sébastien* employs the same pc set genera, exhibits the same approach to formal construction, and assigns the same expressive asso-

FIGURE 8.2. Formal plan for "Le concile des faux dieux"

Section	Measures	Genus	Text
1	1	Chromatic, whole-tone	He is dead . . .
2	7	Whole-tone, chromatic	He dieth, the lovely Adonis!
3	11	Whole-tone, chromatic	He is dead . . . Weep ye!
4	15	Whole-tone, chromatic	(Instrumental interlude)
5	17	8–17/18/19–Complex and diatonic	(Instrumental interlude)
6	19	8–17/18/19–Complex	He descends towards (Hell) . . .
7	23	Whole-tone	Lower now the torches,
8	27	Diatonic	Eros! Weep ye!
9		8–17/18/19–Complex	
10	28	Diatonic	
11		8–17/18/19–Complex	
12	29	Diatonic	
13		8–17/18/19–Complex	
	(34)		

ciations as *Pelléas et Mélisande,* except that the formal units defined by changes in pc set materials tend to be much longer. Besides the practical compositional expedient this change in technique offers, the markedly slower rate of changes is also consistent with the drama's languid tone.

"Eventail"

Composed in 1913,[23] "Eventail" (*Trois poèmes de Stéphane Mallarmé*) is an advanced composition that looks ahead to Debussy's last works in its intricate treatment of pc

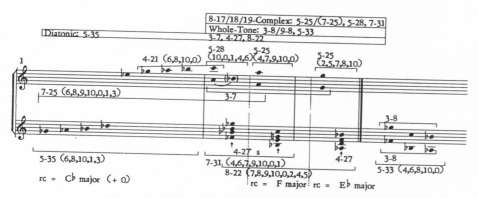

Example 8.2. PC reduction of "Eventail," mm. 1–3

relationships. The first three bars are a microcosm of both the set resources and their manner of treatment throughout the work. The diatonic genus is well represented: m. 1 opens with a pentatonic/diatonic glissando followed by three diatonic chords that punctuate offbeats in mm. 2–3 (forms of tetrachord 4–27; see ex. 8.2); the pc content of the last two sonorities combines to form diatonic set 8–22; the quarter notes in the right hand form diatonic trichord 3–7. It is also possible to hear other genera through alternative segmentations. The tetrachords in mm. 2–3, for example, combine to generate forms of whole-tone trichord 3–8 for each "voice"; the outer parts combine to form whole-tone set 5–33 (which is conspicuous throughout the song), while the tetrachords' overall pc content forms whole-tone set 9–8. An auditor who focuses on the total sonority of each beat in mm. 2–3 will hear the 8–17/18/19–complex genus through its pentachordal representatives 5–25 and 5–28, plus 7–31 formed by the pc content of m. 2. This multifariousness arises from diatonic modulations between three different rcs (namely, Cb major, F major, and Eb major), which account for all of the pc materials (the first modulation engenders the nondiatonic complement that opens the passage: 5–25/7–25). The diversity achieved by integration of pc set genera is not characteristic of Debussy's earlier works, but it is an integral feature of his late compositions, as we have seen already in *Jeux* and the Sonata for flute, viola, and harp.

The variegated musical surfaces of "Eventail" extend multifariousness to the song's ever-changing thematic content, in which return and reprise are rare. "Eventail" incorporates eleven distinct thematic entities distributed among fifteen formal units (see fig. 8.3). Theme A returns twice (at m. 12 where it is subjected to extension, and at m. 46, where it is expanded by pre-extension). Theme E, which first occurs at m. 27 and combines whole-tone and chromatic sets, recurs immediately at m. 34 (but purged of chromatic sets). Theme I first appears at m. 50 and recurs (with modifications) at m. 54. The remaining themes (B, C, D, E, G, H, J, and K) occur once each. These eleven themes may be reduced, however, to the three contrasting pc set genera (enriched by the chromatic genus) from which their pc materials are derived. As in *Jeux*, Debussy combines the opposing principles of growth through constant transformation and reuse of a limited group of

FIGURE 8.3. Formal plan for "Evantail"

Section	Measures	Theme	Set genus	Text
1	1	A	Diatonic, whole-tone, 8–17/18/19–complex	(Piano solo)
2	4	B	8–17/18/19–complex	Oh dreamer, that I may dive into pathless delight, know, by a subtle lie, to protect my wing in your hand.
3	12	A	Diatonic, whole-tone, 8–17/18/19–complex	A freshness of dusk comes to you with each beating . . .
4	19	C	Whole-tone transforming into 8–17/18/19-complex	. . . whose imprisoned stroke delicately pushes back the horizon.
5	25	D	Chromatic, transforming into diatonic	Vertigo!
6	27	E	Whole-tone, chromatic	See how Space shudders like a great kiss that, frantic at being born for no one,
7	34		Whole-tone, chromatic (less than section 6)	cannot spurt forth, nor sub-
8	36	F	8–17/18/19–complex, chromatic	side. Do you sense the savage paradise . . .
9	40	G	Diatonic	. . . like a laughter enshrouded, creeping from the corner of your mouth . . .
10	44	H	Diatonic, 8–17/18/19–complex	. . . into the center of the unanimous undulation!
11	46	A	Diatonic, whole-tone, 8–17/18/19–complex	(piano solo)
12	50	I	Whole-tone	This domination of shores (that are) . . .
13	53	J	Diatonic	. . . pink
14	54	I	Whole-tone	. . . stagnating on golden evenings,
15	59	K	8–17/18/19–complex	. . . it is this, this closed white wing that you place against a fiery bracelet.
	65			

pc set resources. In addition, his synthesis of the genera in mm. 1–3, where the pitch materials for the whole work are adumbrated in a single stroke, is echoed in his synthesis of the nonchromatic genera in sections 4 (m. 19), 5 (m. 25), and 10 (m. 44).

Apropos of text expression, "Eventail" follows the model of *Pelléas et Mélisande* less than that of "Pour ce que Plaisance est morte," for it uses the pc genera to support its overall mood rather than to pinpoint psychological states from moment to moment. Modulations and mutations contribute to the sense of extreme agitation, of extravagant sensitivity appropriate to this strange, exquisitely exotic text. The numerous mutations are tied, in general, to the poem's formal boundaries of lines and phrases; modulations are even more frequent and contribute to a sonic image of incredible concentration made up of minute units, each distinguishable by its specific pc content and genus.[24] Certainly this is congruent with the text, in which every word is vivid and rich with association.

Here it is appropriate to recall three works discussed in part 2, for which text expression is germane: "Recueillement" and "Le jet d'eau" (both from *Cinq poèmes de Baudelaire*), and *Jeux*.

The Baudelaire songs, which predate *Pelléas et Mélisande*, tie the pc set genera to the same general psychological associations that are found in the opera. "Recueillement" consistently aligns octatonic materials with text that expresses deep melancholy and sorrow, while the whole-tone genus is associated with references to mystery and to death in particular, as well as with intense darker emotions such as remorse (in which it functions interchangeably with the octatonic genus). The diatonic genus is reserved for calmer emotions and for eroticism (the latter especially in "Le jet d'eau").

Both exotic and erotic imagery permeate *Jeux*, which is nearly contemporaneous with *Le martyre de Saint-Sébastien*. Debussy's use in *Jeux* of the 8–17/18/19–complex genus as generic referent is appropriate to the drama's consistently dark undertones, and in this the expressive power of the pc set genera functions in a way that resembles "Pour ce que Plaisance est morte," where a single genus assigned a predominant role signals a basic mood or attitude towards the subject in general. The copious use of the 8–17/18/19–complex and whole-tone genera contributes an exotic sonus that suits an exotic subject well. There are also many moments that exploit a genus's affective association to support specific dramatic features. Two illustrations are: the use of the 8–17/18/19–complex genus to accompany the arrival of the young man (with its sinister implications for the two girls), and the use of the diatonic genus (rc = F♯ major) to set the climactic triple-kiss (mm. 677–88). These and similar examples adhere consistently to associations between genus and psychological-emotional states established in *Pelléas et Mélisande* and affirmed in other works.

In Debussy's earliest works, text expression through pitch materials is accomplished chiefly by tying changes in pc content to changes in the sense of the text, with the further refinement that intensity and darker emotions are reflected in more radical and frequent changes in pc content. *Pelléas et Mélisande* embodies a significant advance—presaged in the Baudelaire songs of 1889—through its use of the pc set genera and a system of relation that links them to psychological meaning in the drama. The expressive power and range of the opera are astonishing: its words and gestures answer the emotional questions raised by the music and vice versa, transcending mere musical rhetoric (in which a thing is naively assigned a sound). *Pelléas et Mélisande* presents us with a language, possessed of a language's subtlety and power of expression.

"Nuit d'étoiles" shows nothing radical or innovative in Debussy's initial approach to text expression. At that time his resources were still those of the traditional major-minor system with its diatonic scales and chords. Even during his conservatory years, however, he was sensitive to the psychological nuances of his texts, reflected in both form and pitch materials. His subsequent development of the pc set genera provided him with a greatly expanded vocabulary of expressive resources.

The vocal works composed while he was at work on *Pelléas et Mélisande* exhibit much the same expressive approach as his later works. The whole-tone genus, in particular, seems almost always to be associated with death and mystery, though sometimes it is used interchangeably with the 8–17/18/19–complex genus, which (together with the octatonic genus) is associated with more piquant emotions such as physical pain and anguish. The diatonic genus is reserved for the expression of calmer and pleasanter states: virtue, religiosity, and eroticism. The chromatic genus still appears in combination with the others, having no associative domain of its own.

The late works, represented by *Trois poèmes de Stéphane Mallarmé,* exhibit the same highly sophisticated approach to the synthesis of the set genera and the same tendency towards construction of complex pitch matrices susceptible of multiple interpretations (depending on the listener's aural focus during a given hearing) that we saw in the late instrumental works.

PART IV

ASPECTS OF FORM

NINE

FORM AND PROPORTION

Form in Debussy has always been a refractory issue.[1] Perhaps this is because formal analysis usually consists of identifying schemes according to a taxonomy developed for music of the tonal and pretonal eras, one that is only marginally operative in most of Debussy's music.[2] Such terms as *phrase, period,* and *cadence* engender difficulties in music where the defining characteristics long associated with them are either incomplete or lacking altogether.

This chapter dwells in some detail on the analytical approach that underlies all of the formal schemes provided in previous chapters. It considers the importance of architectonic hierarchy in Debussy's designs and its nature in instrumental and vocal works to show how Debussy's schemes evolved from naive designs of charming regularity to those of remarkable fluidity and astonishing complexity. It proceeds from a concept of musical form as dichotomous, in its opposing aspects of *morphological* and *kinetic* form. Morphological form conceives the disposition of events in time in terms of spatial metaphors: balance versus imbalance, regularity versus irregularity, symmetry versus asymmetry, contrast versus return. Kinetic form addresses the sense of vitality that we perceive in music, and it treats the disposition of musical events as metaphors for *motion:* acceleration versus deceleration, ebb versus flow, building towards versus receding from.

FORMAL PARTITIONING AND ARCHITECTONIC LEVELS

Traditional tonal period-forms emphasize internal content over external context. They tend to define architectonic levels automatically since phrases, by definition, occur at the level of detail, while periods comprise the next level and conjoin to form larger formal units at a higher level still. Because each level consists of groups of formal units from the one immediately below, levels are tied to the relative durations of the units they encompass, with the briefest units consigned to the level of detail. Thus, in music that exploits traditional phrase and period-forms, the length of a given formal unit holds the key to its place in the formal hierarchy.

Debussy's avoidance of traditional phrase and period construction poses acute problems for the analyst, for most of his works do not easily reveal their architectonic levels. He subordinates the customary role of continuity as a means of grouping like events into coherent entities to that of discontinuity as a means of separating disparate events; discontinuities define formal units from without, by determining their boundaries. Moreover, lengths of units on any level can vary across a wide range, so length is unreliable as an indicator of architectonic level. Discontinuities create partitions and entail all musical parameters including meter, tempo, successive-attack activity, sonorous density, harmonic and thematic pitch materials, texture, instrumental color, register, and loudness.

I assume three broad levels of formal structure: the level of detail, closest to the musical surface; the highest, most remote level, consisting of a composition's main sections; and an intermediate level that encompasses coherent subdivisions of the main sections. Intermediate levels consist of partitions whose discontinuities are more drastic than those assigned to lower levels and milder than those of higher levels. Sometimes it is necessary to identify "subunits" at the level of detail where such units constitute distinct formal entities; these tend to be intermittent rather than continuous, and as a rule their constituent formal units are strongly interdependent. For most longer works, clarity requires a division of the intermediate stratum into two or more strata, while shorter works often benefit from consolidation that eliminates the middle level altogether. Thus, the three-tiered conceptual model is often manifest, in practice, in formal plans with as few as two or as many as four (or more) architectonic levels.

As a model for form, the three categories of lowest, intermediate, and highest levels are typical of reductive theories, including Schenker's concept of tonal structure, in which a "middleground" mediates between "foreground" and "background." My view differs, however, insofar as I focus more on the partitions that create formal boundaries than on the content that separates them. The chief criterion for assigning a partition to a particular architectonic level (and, therefore, the formal unit it defines) is the degree of disruption; more drastic discontinuities associate with higher levels, milder discontinuities with the level of detail. Disruptions are rare that involve all or most parameters, and they define formal units at the highest architectonic level; more common are those that entail modest changes in a few parameters and merely partition the musical surface. This conception is receptive to the possibility that some higher-level formal units could be very brief and might not consist of groups of lower-level formal units;[3] this is, in fact, a common feature in Debussy's later works. A corollary is the possibility that a lower formal level may be discontinuous; that is, the lowest architectonic formal level may occasionally give way to an intermediate level, which would replace it for a time.

Below are enumerated eleven form-defining parameters to consider when evaluating discontinuities. It is easy to enumerate changes, more difficult to identify their extent (there is as yet no means of quantification) and balance a change in one parameter against one in another; even so, gradations are taken into account in the following explanations, which include as many references to degree as to kinds of changes.

Form-Defining Parameters

Meter. Here meter refers simply to notated bar-line meter.[4] A change in the number of beats for the metric group (for example, from 4/4 to 2/4 or vice versa) is less drastic in effect than a change in the type of subdivision (duple to triple or vice versa, as from 2/4 to 6/8) because the latter entails a change in tempo at the level of the lowest common denominator as well as a change in the frequency of metric accents.

Tempo. Slight changes in tempo (indicated by phrases such as *en animant* and *en retenant*) are less drastic in effect than marked changes (for example, *plus mouvementé*), since the former may be classified as types of rubato, which are usually countered in performance by compensatory opposite changes.[5]

Successive-Attack Activity. Successive-attack activity refers to the number of notes articulated in succession for a given durational unit. A shift from quarter notes to sixteenths (without a change of meter or tempo) constitutes an increase in activity, and vice versa. Fluctuations in the number of successive notes struck within a given duration often combine with changes in other parameters to effect partitions. It usually suffices to compare the number of successive attacks for several bars on either side of a partition, taking into account marked changes of tempo. Differences within a range of one-half to twice as many attacks are common and minimally disruptive; differences beyond one-fourth or four times as many attacks are dramatic and far more rare.

Sonorous Density. Sonorous density refers to the number of voices, parts, or instruments that sound simultaneously, and complements the parameter of successive-attack activity. Differences of one-half to twice as many events are common and disrupt only slightly; differences beyond one-fourth to four times are rare and extreme.

Harmonic Resources. The genus that accounts for a passage's overall harmonic sonority is its harmonic resource, and the rc is its specific pc inventory. A modulation is less drastic than a change of genus since the latter involves change of sonority *and* pc content, whereas modulation involves only pc content.

Thematic/Motivic Resources. Here the terms *theme* and *motive* are construed broadly (and interchangeably) as referents to any distinctive melodic-harmonic entity such as a pitch contour, a group of sonorities, or their combination. The appearance of a new theme or motive, an ostinato, or a distinctive subsidiary supporting element is commonplace, though initial statements of crucial themes are often marked in ways that identify them as more important (and thus more disruptive) events. Changes in thematic-motivic material are pervasive on Debussy's musical surfaces; indeed, partitions that omit them are rare. That this feature reflects Debussy's traditional training is attested by his early works where initiation and completion of melodic contours determine phrase and period structure. In later works, his reformulation of the principle permits abrupt changes that thwart pattern completion, supported by changes in other parameters less methodically exploited in early works. The practice becomes a prevalent stylistic idiosyncrasy.

Repetition/Recurrence. Repetition and recurrence entail "starting over" in some sense and are always disruptive since they imply closure (or at least cessation) of the preceding material. Immediate repetition is least disruptive; more disruptive is a return of content that follows intervening material (especially when it involves the return of a crucial theme) because it entails change as well as the punctuation of closure.[6]

Quality of Texture. The most common textures are homophonic, monorhythmic, heterophonic, and contrapuntal-imitative. Changes from one to another usually are subtle and only moderately disruptive.

Orchestration. Changes in orchestration are often difficult to rank. They may affect texture (for example, change from solo to soli or tutti), or instrumental color (brass to woodwind, or strings, or percussion), or both (solo flute with strings to trumpet and English horn with strings, or tutti brass to solo violin with strings and harp). Changes range from slight to marked.[7]

Register. Register entails both the range employed within a given passage (the span, in semitones, between the outer parts) and the placement (the mean pitch between the upper and lower extremes).[8] Only gross changes are noted. Shifts of an octave in placement, or of additions or subtractions in span, are moderately disruptive; changes that involve as many as four octaves are extreme.

Loudness. Debussy tends to utilize low levels as his norm, with high levels reserved for occasional brief moments. Subtle changes in loudness are common.

Table 9.1 summarizes the eleven parameters and serves as an implicit reference for the analyses in the next and previous chapters, and as an explicit reference for chapter 11, where the issue of formal definition is especially refractory.

PROPORTION, SYMMETRY, ASYMMETRY, GOLDEN SECTION

Although symmetry, asymmetry, and proportion are essentially spatial concepts, we often apply them to music's temporal relationships. Perhaps this reflects the fact that we represent temporality in a score through the medium of length, or, conversely, we may represent time's passing through the medium of length because we conceive of music's (and time's) passing as a cognate of spatial distance.[9] Either way, musicians do frequently describe the passage of musical time with the aid of spatial metaphors, as though it were a sort of distance.

TABLE 9.1. Form-defining parameters

1. Change of bar-line meter
   a. change of division (e.g., 4/4 to 2/4)
   b. change of subdivision (e.g., 4/4 to 12/8)
2. Change of tempo (slight or marked)
3. Change of successive-attack activity (successive attack points measured as the average of adjacent bars)
4. Change in sonorous density
5. Change in harmonic resources
   a. modulation
   b. change of genus
6. Change in thematic/motivic resources
   a. new ostinato, new subsidiary or supporting parts, new theme
   b. first statement of a crucial theme
7. Repetition/recurrence
   a. immediate repetition
   b. return of previous material
   c. return of crucial theme
8. Change in quality of texture (e.g., from imitative to monorhythmic, heterophonic, or homophonic)
9. Change in orchestration
   a. change in texture (e.g., from solo to soli or tutti)
   b. change of instrumental color
10. Change of register
    a. shift from low to high, or vice versa
    b. expansion or compression of registral space
11. Change of loudness
    a. change of level (e.g., piano to mezzo piano)
    b. momentary peaks of loudness

Proportions Based on Equal Divisions

Proportions based on equal divisions partition a work into lengths of similar duration, or balance spans of similar size on either side of an axis. A thirty-six-measure segment could be partitioned variously into equal divisions, including two sections of eighteen measures each, three of twelve, or four of nine. Divisions that encompass architectonic levels are also possible: two sections of eighteen measures, for example, could subdivide into 6 + 6 + 6 bars each; yet another possibility places two equal sections on either side of a third that is different, such as a pair of ten-measure sections flanking one of sixteen bars.

An early song, "Beau soir" (ca. 1880),[10] illustrates an equal division for its central thirty bars (ignoring, for the moment, the four-bar introduction and the seven-bar coda) into two large sections of fifteen measures each (fig. 9.1). The layout of the figure is as follows: the topmost horizontal scheme displays the song's phrase structure as a series of arches measured in bars; antecedents and consequents are shown by longer arches that span two or more phrases and are also measured in bars; proportional schemes that arise are labeled and shown on auxiliary horizontal axes below the main axis.

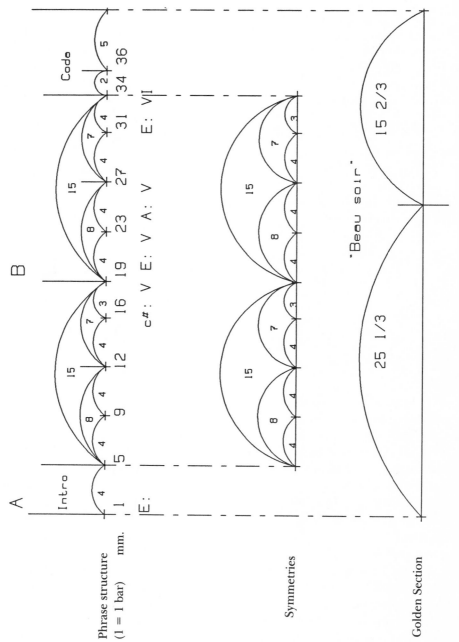

Figure 9.1. "Beau soir"

Although few of Debussy's compositions employ them overall, equal divisions often control proportions at intermediate and surface levels.

Proportions Based on Arithmetic Series

In Debussy's music, consecutive surface-level formal units often employ spans whose durations correspond to arithmetic series based on terms ordered consecutively. The terms may appear unordered. "Beau soir," for example, juxtaposes phrases of four and three bars, and closes with four phrases consisting, respectively, of four, three, two, and five bars.

Proportions Based on the Golden Section

Although his interest in esotericism is well known,[11] Debussy's awareness of the Golden Section (also known as the Golden Mean and the Golden Proportion) is more obscure.[12] Given his affinity for natural phenomena, where Golden Section relationships abound,[13] it should not surprise us to find Debussy incorporating the Golden Section into his own work.

The Golden Section occurs when a line is bisected such that the ratio formed by the proportions of the shorter segment to the longer is equal to that of the longer to the whole. The relationship may be expressed in the formula

$$b : a = a : a + b$$

where a = the longer segment and b = the shorter. The relationship of the shorter segment to the longer is .618034 . . . or approximately 61.8 percent. In "Beau soir," the Golden Section falls after beat 1 of m. 26, coincidental with the song's climax on its highest, loudest, and longest note. Howat has demonstrated that Debussy applied the ratio to linear temporal relationships that arise from partitionings, where the relation of successive adjacent passages forms the Golden Section ratio, as well as among nested partitionings.[14]

Summation Series and the Golden Section Ratio

A summation series is a number series in which each successive term equals the sum of the two previous terms—for example: 25, 30, 55, 85, 140, 225, 365, 590, and so on. For all such series, no matter what the ratios of the original pair of terms, those of adjacent terms soon begin to approach the Golden Section. In the series above, the ratio of 25:30 = .833 (rounded off) is remote from the Golden Section ratio of .618, nor is 35:55 much better at .545, but 55:85 = .647 and 85:140 = .607 are much closer, and three terms later the ratio is very close indeed (365:590 = .618644).

It is possible to plot the length of a composition in measures or beats, and then section it according to a proportional scheme based on the Golden Section. But this is unnecessarily complicated, since summation series can easily be used to build up proportional schemes one formal unit at a time.

Certain summation series are widely known, and it appears likely that Debussy was aware of at least two of them—the Fibonacci and Lucas series—since they often appear embedded in his morphological formal schemes.[15] Also common are two related nontraditional series, which I have identified as "N" and "N$_v$".

The Fibonacci series is named after the thirteenth-century Italian monk credited with its discovery, Leonardo da Pisa, commonly known as Fibonacci. It is: 1, 1, 2, 3, 5, 8, 13, 21, 34, 55, 89, 144, 233, 377, 610, . . .

The Lucas series takes its name from Edouard Lucas, a nineteenth-century mathematician. It is: 1, 3, 4, 7, 11, 18, 29, 47, 76, 123, 199, 322, 521, 843, . . . Beginning with the number 4, each of its terms can be subdivided symmetrically into three terms that form segments from the Fibonacci series; for example: $4 = 1 + 2 + 1, 7 = 2 + 3 + 2, 11 = 3 + 5 + 3, 18 = 5 + 8 + 5, 29 = 8 + 13 + 8, 47 = 13 + 21 + 13$.

The N and N$_v$ series are frequently found in Debussy's early works. The N series is: 5, 4, 9, 13, 22, 35, 57, . . . Its second term is smaller than the first, though otherwise it is a normal summation series. The N$_v$ series is a variant that reverses the first two terms: 4, 5, 9, 14, 23, 37, 60, . . .

TEN
MORPHOLOGICAL FORMS AND PROPORTION

Debussy's morphological forms divide roughly into two categories: those that employ traditional symmetrical and cyclical schemes at the highest level and neoclassic period-forms at the lowest; and other paradigms that transform in novel ways the essential features of the traditional form types. The first category predominates in his earliest works, the second emerges later and typifies his mature style, but both types are found throughout his oeuvre.

TRADITIONAL FORM TYPES AND PROPORTION

ABA and related schemes are common in Debussy's songs and piano pieces from the 1870s and 1880s. The boundaries of large sections are often marked by key signature changes combined with contrasts in the general character of thematic material and its setting, as well as changes in the parameters of tempo, meter, register, successive-attack activity, and loudness. Phrases and periods usually are defined by initiation and completion of melodic contours, which harmonic cadences sometimes support (though cadences become increasingly rare as Debussy's style matures). Melodic closure is usually effected by a pause, either in the form of a final note of longer duration, or of a rest (see example 10.1A–C, which excerpt phrases from three songs). Alternatively, repetition and recurrence may signal the initiation of a new phrase and, by implication, completion of the previous one. In example 10.1D, the second phrase restates the motive in a higher register; in initiating a new phrase, it also marks off the end of the preceding phrase.

At the level of detail, Debussy's period-forms include phrases, periods, and phrase groups. The standard four-bar length is often modified by pre-, inter-, and post-extensions. Phrases also may be truncated or elided. The result is a predominantly regular musical surface for which four-bar phrases are the norm, but rendered flexible and unpredictable by the liberal use of extension, truncation, and elision. Four relatively early compositions will serve to illustrate these features.

211

Example 10.1. Phrase closure through internal features

"Nuit d'étoiles"

"Nuit d'étoiles" (ca. 1880) employs a simple rondo scheme whose symmetrical proportions are nearly perfect (fig. 10.1): four bars of introduction and the one-bar discrepancy between the lengths of the B sections are the only anomalies. Each A section consists of a period and a phrase group, each B section of a phrase group. Imperfect authentic cadences close the periods, while pauses or recurrences that complete or initiate melodic patterns bring about internal partitions. The overall rondo-like design supports the poem's scheme of alternation between new material and reprises. The B section's two irregularities that disrupt the normal phrasing occur in m. 33 (extension coupled with elision) and mm. 70–71 (the extension-transition before the last reprise).

Whether Debussy deliberately imposed a scheme other than the symmetrical rondo to control overall proportion is a matter for conjecture, though we must note the coincidence of the song's Golden Section after m. 56/beat 2, just before the juncture of the second A and B sections (see fig. 10.1).

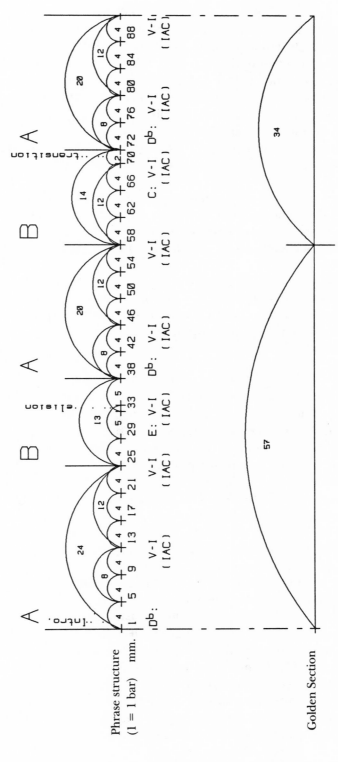

Figure 10.1. "Nuit d'étoiles"

"Mandoline"

Composed at least two years after "Nuit d'étoiles," "Mandoline" (1882)[1] exhibits a similar cyclic tendency in its ternary scheme—though its symmetry is flawed by the length of the reprise, which considerably exceeds that of its correlate owing to its long winding-down (fig. 10.2). Many of its phrases are distorted by extension (at mm. 8, 22, 28, 66), insertion (m. 43), truncation (mm. 15, 33), and elision (m. 50), and even the three-bar introduction is irregular; indeed, as many phrases contradict as conform to the four-bar norm. Cadences are rarer in "Mandoline" than in "Nuit d'étoiles" and most are half-cadences (though closure is clearly audible, accomplished by pauses at the ends of phrases, and implied by the initiation of recurrences).

A high-level partition suggests premeditation in its interaction with the song's sole metric idiosyncrasy: the boundaries of the first and second sections occur at the end of the anomalous 3/8 measure (m. 27) and coincide with the negative Golden Section.[2] This precise bisection would be inexact were m. 27 a "normal" 6/8 bar.[3]

But even more suggestive is the extensive proportional scheme based on the Lucas series that spans most of the song (mm. 1–61) and springs directly from the irregularities of phrasing. The scheme possesses an exquisite internal balance between symmetry and asymmetry, and accounts for *all* of the irregular phrases save the last.

First "Arabesque"

The conservative idiom of Debussy's earliest published piano piece, the first "Arabesque" (1888), extends to its formal construction: a symmetrically proportioned ternary scheme subdivided pervasively into four-bar phrases (especially in the B section; see fig. 10.3). There are, however, numerous irregularities in the form of pre-extensions (of phrases that begin at mm. 21, 95), post-extensions (mm. 1, 26, 71, 80, 91), and insertions (m. 103). There is also an elision (m. 95) that immediately follows the sole metric anomaly—a bar of 2/4 in the otherwise consistent 4/4.

The Golden Section does not coincide with important partitions in the ternary scheme, but several summation series appear at the level of detail generated by the phrasing irregularities. Two involve the Lucas series and are shown on the lower schemata of figure 10.3: the first is embedded in the principal theme of the A section (mm. 6–16); the second spans the entire B section and extends across the reprise as well, up to m. 95, the bar that is conspicuous as the site of the composition's only meter change and its only elision. The A sections are proportioned by Fibonacci ratios (ignore introductory mm. 1–5 and 71–75); the first is inaccurate by one measure, the reprise by one beat (the counts exclude the last bar, which is empty after beat 1). The difference is the 2/4 bar in the reprise (m. 94), which shortens sufficiently the overall span so that the proportions, measured in quarter notes, are more precise. If these schemes were imposed deliberately, then the inaccuracies and adjustments suggest a quality of experimentation. That

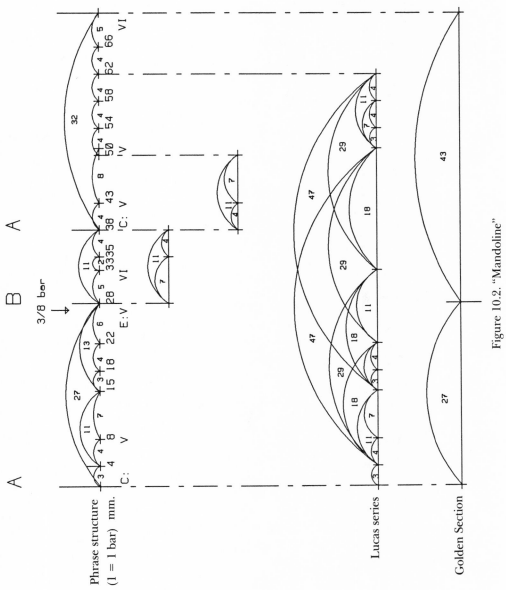

Figure 10.2. "Mandoline"

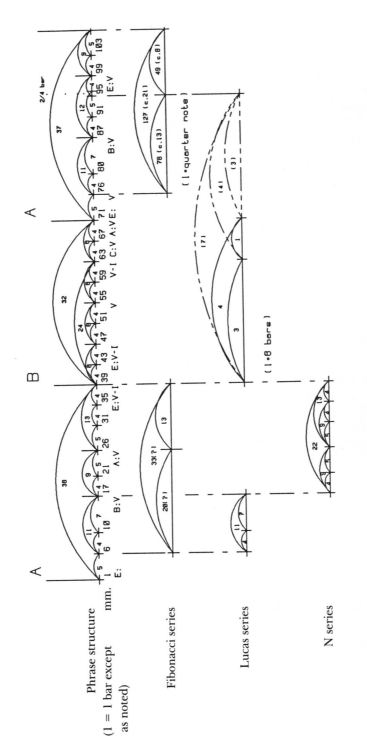

Figure 10.3. First "Arabesque"

impression is reinforced by the presence of a scheme based on the N series, 5, 4, 9, 13, 22, . . . , which spans the reprise *within* the first A section. As we shall see, this series is prominent in other works as well.

Second "Arabesque"

The second "Arabesque" resembles the first in its harmonic and formal conservatism. It employs a rondo scheme (ABABA) whose typically cyclic scheme contrasts with the asymmetrical proportions of its five sections (fig. 10.4). Four bars is the normal length for phrases, but many are distorted by post-extensions and insertions that engender, in turn, the proportional schemes shown.

Each section has its own scheme: the first A section employs the N_v series; the first B section, a symmetrical scheme; the second A section, another N_v series that overlaps its surrounding B sections; the second B section, a Fibonacci series; and the last A section, a Lucas series. Various local schemes are found within sections. The overlapping N_v scheme used to interconnect two or more sections prefigures Debussy's practice in later works.

String Quartet I

Architectonic control of the String Quartet's 194-bar-long first movement poses a far greater challenge than shorter pieces. Compared with the Baudelaire songs, which precede it by several years, the quartet's harmonic idiom is still relatively conservative, as is its form, which nevertheless provides fertile soil for new techniques.

Overall, the first movement conforms to the general contours of a sonata design that emphasizes a ternary principle of exposition-development-reprise (see fig. 10.5). The exposition divides into first and second theme-areas plus a codetta-transition (mm. 1–38, 39–60, 61–74). The development subjects the exposition's themes to transformations and the reprise eschews faithful parallelism in favor of a freer reuse of material; both procedures are consistent with French Romanticism. The three large sections exhibit well-balanced proportions, though the trend from one to the next is towards compression.

Phrase construction favors four bars as the norm, though post-extensions are common, particularly in the development, and there are three examples of truncation (phrases at mm. 61, 67, 161). The result is an essentially conventional phrase structure that generates numerous asymmetrical proportional schemes. Phrase extensions invariably precede—and signal thereby—higher-level divisions. The only exceptions occur in mm. 120–37, where three successive extended phrases adumbrate the recapitulation that follows in m. 138.

The movement's phrasing generates three Lucas series: at the second theme area of the exposition; at the beginning of the recapitulation; and at the second theme's return. The N series generates a complicated scheme that spans the first and second theme areas of the exposition (but not the reprise), though its alignment is not precise until the beginning of the contrasting middle portion (m. 13).

Most striking is the symmetrical nesting of Golden Section ratios across the

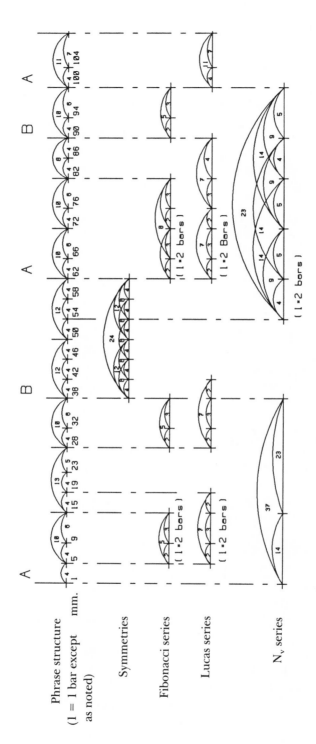

Figure 10.4. Second "Arabesque"

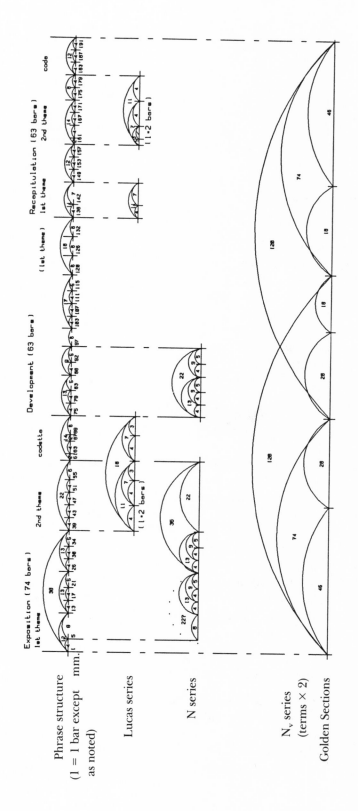

Figure 10.5. String Quartet, I

movement as a whole: the negative Golden Section coincides with the beginning of the development (after m. 74); the positive Golden Section coincides with the first of three six-bar statements of the principal theme at the end of the development (which serve as a transition to the recapitulation); lower-level Golden Section partitions after mm. 46, 102, and 148 coincide with divisions at the phrase and period level.[4] This large scheme yields a summation series whose terms, when divided by 2, correspond to those of the N series: 18, 28, 46, 74, 120 ($\div 2 = 9, 14, 23, 37, 60$).

A trend towards compression is evident in the proportional schemes of medium and small scale, at least up to m. 103, and mimics the tendency of the sonata scheme as a whole. An opposite trend toward expansion emerges at the approach of the movement's end. One result is to impart a sense of acceleration overall, as partitions occur at more frequent intervals, followed by deceleration as the durations that separate them gradually increase. We shall examine such tendencies more thoroughly later on.

Symmetrical, cyclical forms and neoclassic four-bar phrase construction are found in a few of Debussy's mature works. Examples include "Des pas sur la neige" (Préludes I), "Noël des enfants qui n'ont plus de maisons," and the first movement of the Violin Sonata. In these works, however, irregularities are more striking than in those we have examined, and just as Debussy's resolutely diatonic music absorbs some of the influences of his more adventurous style, so also do his conservative formal schemes in late works reflect his increasingly multidimensional approach to form. As a consequence, mature works that hew to early formal principles sound more flexible and more complex than their earlier prototypes.

"Noël des enfants qui n'ont plus de maisons"

As we saw in part 1, the "Noël des enfants qui n'ont plus de maisons" (1915) is a diatonic piece that adheres to neoclassic phrase construction set within a large, symmetrical ternary plan. There are many distortions through extensions, but more striking are truncated phrases of two and three bars (mm. 1, 3, 20, 40, 42, 52, 60; see fig. 10.6). These irregularities generate numerous Lucas and Fibonacci summation series. Especially important are the Fibonacci schemes that span two of the largest sections. The B section's series embodies many symmetries. (Nonseries symmetries are also found in the A sections and throughout the piece.) Note that the two-bar introduction is excluded from all but the overall symmetrical scheme.

NONTRADITIONAL FORM TYPES AND PROPORTION

Ternary design and strophic variations, which share the principle of reprise but employ it in quite different ways, provide the basis for morphological forms that imaginatively transform Debussy's early traditional form types into new models.

Ternary design is the source for three paradigms plus a variant. Most common is the archetype whose opening material is modified to generate new but related

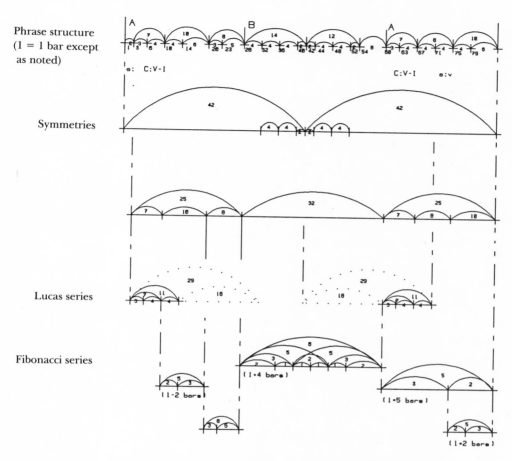

Figure 10.6. "Noël des enfants qui n'ont plus de maisons"

material, which in turn becomes the basis for more new material. The process is repeated over and over—Eimert has characterized it as "developing variation" and "endless variation"[5]—until an advanced stage is reached, followed by a brief and rather literal reprise (fig. 10.7A). The pronounced asymmetry of its truncated reprise and the absence of a readily identifiable B section obscure its ternary roots. Compositions in all genres follow this archetype, though it is generally reserved for those of modest proportions (about forty to one hundred measures). Examples include "Danseuses de Delphes" (Préludes I), reprise at m. 25 (fig. 10.7B); "La fille aux cheveux de lin" (Préludes I), thematic reprise at m. 28, though the original *pc* content returns at m. 24 (fig. 10.7C);[6] "Eventail" (*Trois poèmes de Stéphane Mallarmé*), reprise at m. 47 (fig. 10.7D); and *Jeux*, whose reprise at m. 702 and close eight bars later carry the principle to its logical extreme (fig. 10.7E). The Préludes I–II contain many more examples: "Le vent dans la plaine" (reprise in m. 44), "La cathédrale engloutie" (m. 84), "Minstrels" (m. 78), "Feuilles mortes" (m. 41), "Les fées sont d'exquises danseuses" (m. 101), "Bruyères" (m. 44), and

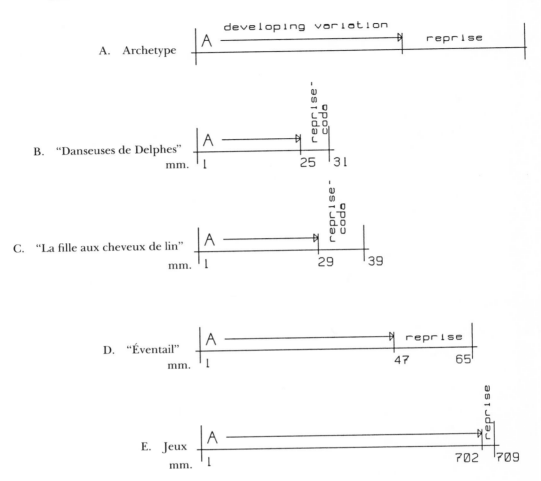

Figure 10.7. Ternary-derived morphological plans

"Feux d'artifice" (m. 88). A rondo-like variant is one in which the reprise recurs twice or more (fig. 10.8A). Examples include "Brouillards" (fig. 10.8B, reprises at mm. 20 and 41) and "La danse de Puck" (fig. 10.8C, mm. 71, 87)—both from the Préludes—and "La flûte de Pan" (*Chansons de Bilitis;* fig. 10.8D, mm. 12, 27).

Another ternary-derived archetype is the tripartite design shown in figure 10.9A, whose last section synthesizes characteristic features of the first two. Examples include "Voiles" (Préludes I; fig. 10.9B), "Canope" (Préludes II; fig. 10.9C), and "Pour les arpèges composés" (Douze études II; fig. 10.9D). In "Voiles," the third section (mm. 48–64) utilizes the ascending glissandi of the brief middle section, but set within the whole-tone genus that provides the pc materials for the first section. The last section of "Canope" contains a reference to the B section within its reprise of A. The third section of "Pour les arpèges composés" also juxtaposes brief passages of thematic-motivic material taken from its first and second sections. "Et la lune descend sur le temple qui fut" (*Images* II) provides

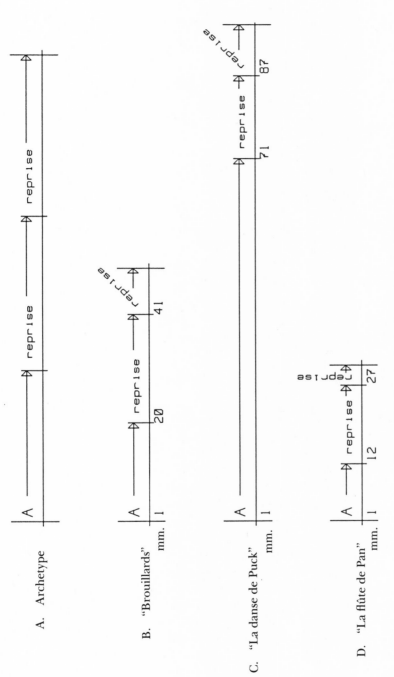

Figure 10.8. Rondo-derived morphological plans

Figure 10.9. Tripartite morphological plan

another example, which synthesizes materials in a much more intricate fashion. It accumulates a succession of new harmonic-melodic motives during mm. 1–38, which are then superimposed in various ways in mm. 39–57.

Yet another ternary-rondo-derived paradigm is the arch form (fig. 10.10A). The first large section of "De l'aube à midi sur la mer" (*La mer* I) utilizes a nearly perfect palindrome based on this model (fig. 10.10B). The fourth and tenth etudes, "Pour les sixtes" (Douze études I) and "Pour les sonorités opposées" (Douze études II), also illustrate this type (fig. 10.10C–D): the proportions of sections in "Pour les sixtes" are markedly asymmetrical; the incomplete arch form of "Pour les sonorités opposées" lacks a final A section.

Forms derived from a synthesis of strophic variations with the first ternary archetype's principle of continuous development interrupted by reprise may be found in a number of pieces (fig. 10.11A). Examples include "Des pas sur la neige" (Préludes I; fig. 10.11B) and "Pour les notes répétées" (Douze études II; fig. 10.11C). The latter consists of three presentations of A–B pairs. The *Prélude à "L'après-midi d'un faune"* may be heard as a succession of eight rather free variations (the third and fourth are the most abstract), of which each takes the opening flute solo as its point of departure (fig. 10.11D).[7] Another example is "Pour les

A.   Archetype

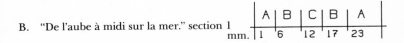

B.   "De l'aube à midi sur la mer." section 1

C.   "Pour les sixtes"

D.   "Pour les sonorités opposées"

Figure 10.10. Arch forms

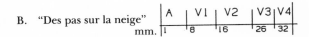

A.   Archetype

B.   "Des pas sur la neige"

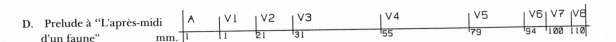

C.   "Pour les notes répétées"

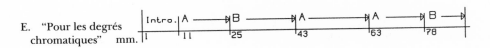

D.   Prelude à "L'après-midi d'un faune"

E.   "Pour les degrés chromatiques"

Figure 10.11 Morphological forms derived from strophic variations

degrés chromatiques" (Douze études II), whose two themes alternate to initiate each of five sections (after an introduction), followed by free development.

Debussy also composed pieces whose forms are wholly linear (fig. 10.12A). Examples include the overall plan for "De l'aube à midi sur la mer" (*La mer* I), whose five large sections avoid any clear reprise (fig. 10.12B).[8] Likewise, the first etude, "Pour les cinq doigts" (Douze études I) forgoes any conspicuous recurrence in its six sections in favor of material that constantly evolves (fig. 10.12C). "Pour les quartes" (Douze études I) provides yet another example with its three non-replicative sections; its initial material is transformed to generate ever-new harmonies and motives. One might expect that Debussy's songs would furnish an ideal hunting ground for this archetype, since the concept seems especially well suited for setting texts whose sense and associations are constantly evolving, but in fact they are rare. An exception is "Soupir" (*Trois poèmes de Stéphane Mallarmé*), whose four sections avoid any reprise (fig. 10.12D).

Together these six paradigms account for most of Debussy's music that employs the pc set genera as well as some of the wholly diatonic music. No doubt he abandoned neoclassic phrase construction in favor of rapidly and constantly changing musical surfaces because to cling to the former would subvert the effects so carefully cultivated in his pitch materials.

MORE EXAMPLES OF PROPORTIONAL MORPHOLOGICAL FORMS

Howat argues persuasively that symmetrical and asymmetrical proportions based on summation series account for many aspects of form in Debussy's music.[9] His study largely excludes very early and late works, however, which he contends do not exhibit schemes structured by the Golden Section. We have already noted the incorporation of Golden Section and summation series in the formal schemes of very early works. The examples below explore their use in late works, and in a passage from *Pelléas et Mélisande* discussed previously.

Pelléas et Mélisande, Act V, mm. 1–16

The brief instrumental prelude that opens *Pelléas et Mélisande*, act V, combines symmetrical and asymmetrical schemes. Mutations divide its sixteen bars into five formal units disposed symmetrically on two architectonic levels (fig. 10.13): two highest-level divisions comprise four durations each (where 1 = two bars). The lower level subdivides the first large section into two two-duration spans while the second section is trisected into equal, outer subdivisions that flank a longer unit. In addition, the durations reveal a comprehensive asymmetrical scheme based on a Fibonacci series.[10]

Fanfare Preceding "Le concile des faux dieux," mm. 1–32

The fanfare that precedes "Le concile des faux dieux" (*Le martyre de Saint-Sébastien* III) is extensively partitioned at the level of detail by pauses, changes in instrumentation, motivic contrast, and recurrence. Its pc materials section the piece into

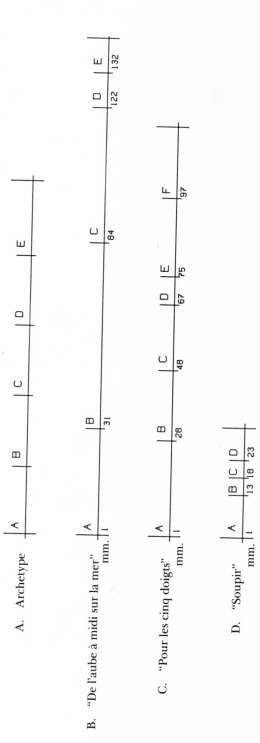

A. Archetype

B. "De l'aube à midi sur la mer"

C. "Pour les cinq doigts"

D. "Soupir"

Figure 10.12. Forms that avoid reprise

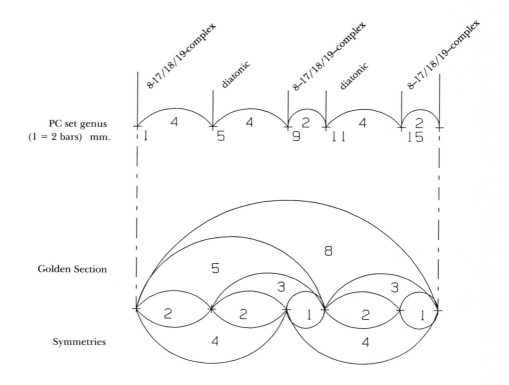

Figure 10.13. Instrumental prelude to *Pelléas et Mélisande,* act V

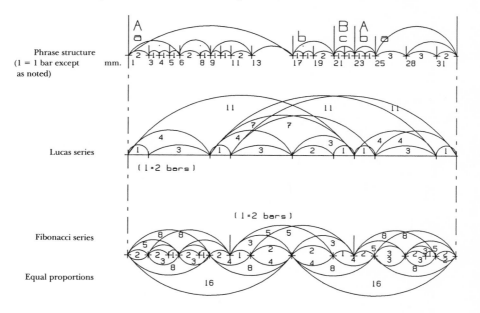

Figure 10.14. Fanfare preceding "Le concile des faux dieux"

a large arch form nested within a ternary form (abcba in ABA where A = ab and B = c). Both schemes contain many asymmetrical subdivisions (fig. 10.14). Two sets of highly symmetrical schemes based on summation series occur on the surface: a Lucas series incorporates a prominent asymmetry at the level of its largest term, 11, and spans the entire piece; and two Fibonacci series of different scales trisect the piece. These schemes are remarkable for their density, and they encompass all of the fanfare's major partitions. An intricate scheme based on ᵉᵞ˙ıal proportions embodies many of the same partitions.

"Le concile des faux dieux"

The main partitions of "Le concile des faux dieux" are defined by changes in pc materials and pauses (fig. 10.15), and many lesser partitions are created by motivic contrast and recurrence, as well as through changes in vocal and instrumental color, register, and loudness. There are a total of thirty-four bars, an auspicious number that points to the Fibonacci series; the partitions do not incorporate a series whose largest term is 34, however, nor does any series span the entire

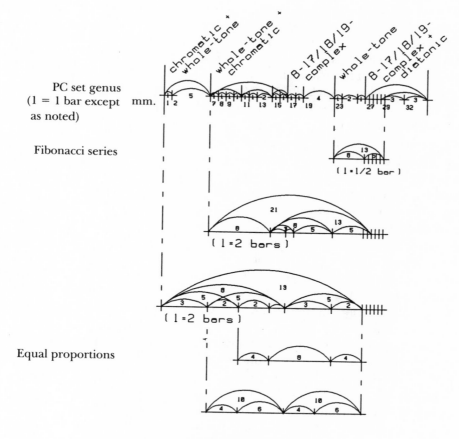

Figure 10.15. "Le concile des faux dieux"

movement. Instead, several symmetrical and asymmetrical schemes based on summation series arise from partitions each of which accounts for large overlapping segments of the piece.

Sonata for Flute, Viola, and Harp, I

Figure 10.16 presents a comprehensive formal plan that identifies thematic passages (with upper-case letters), flourishes ("fl"), terminations ("t"), and transitions ("*") drawn to proportion; the unit of measure is the eighth note in the original tempo.[11] Local proportional schemes are shown on separate axes below the main axis. The durational unit of measure for each proportional scheme varies from one section to the next.

Local proportional schemes support a division of the sonata's first movement into six sections as shown. Sections 2 and 5 do not exhibit clear-cut proportional schemes; they are defined, instead, by the boundaries of neighboring sections 1, 3, 4, and 6, which do manifest such schemes.

The boundaries for the six sections all coincide with crucial events: an *animando*, a marked change of character, and a striking new theme at m. 18, (juncture of sections 1 and 2); the *vif et joyeux* at m. 26 (juncture of sections 2 and 3); a *I° tempo* at m. 48 (juncture of sections 3 and 4); the reprise of the *tempo animando* at m. 63 (juncture of sections 4 and 5); and a flourish at m. 69 (juncture of sections 5 and 6). The opening gesture's reprise at m. 72 coincides with the symmetrical portion of section 6. Many of these main partitions are also supported by tutti pauses or rests of at least an eighth note's duration (for example, mm. 18, 48, 72).

The partitions of section 1 reveal an arithmetic series, 6,5,4,3,2,1 (1 bar = 1), in which some durations are nested within others (though adjacent terms are always contiguous). The subdivisions of section 2 approximate the ratio 1:3 (the latter divided into 1:2), but the proportions are not exact. Section 3 employs the series 1,2,3,4,5. It proceeds in segments of 5 durations each (1 = one bar) in which each segment is composed alternately of 2 + 3 and 4 + 1 durations. The first three segments subdivide symmetrically into (2 + 3), (4 + 1), and (3 + 2); the overall asymmetry is achieved by appending an extra segment (2 durations) at the end of the fourth segment of 5 durations. Section 4 exhibits the nested series 1 + 2 = 3 on several levels. It is seen as 1,2,3, and 2,4,6 (where 1 = one bar). Section 5 presents an incomplete series: 2,[ ],4,5,6 (3 does not appear). Section 6 begins with a nested series, 1,2,3 as 2 + 1 = 3 (1 = one bar), which is immediately replicated in an expanded version (durations quadrupled) that features symmetrical pairs: 8 + 4 = 12 (manifest as 4,2,2,4 = 6,6, or 4,8 overlapping 8,4).

There is an overall bipartite partition of the movement at m. 48 (marked by the return to *I° tempo*), whose second division is symmetrically tripartitioned into 135 + 43 + 135 durations (where 1 = one eighth note in the original tempo).

In this movement, there are no overall partitions at points of the Golden Section nor local schemes based on summation series; non–Golden Section arithmetic series and symmetrical schemes seen in earlier pieces are evident, however,

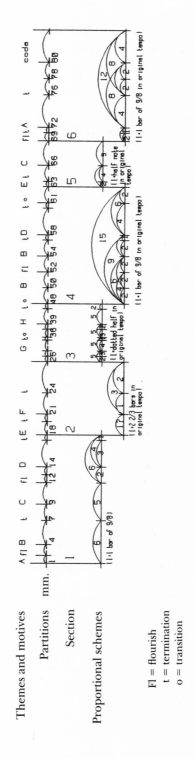

Figure 10.16. Sonata for flute, viola, and harp, I

and they reveal a systematic, yet flexible, means of controlling the composition's pacing that belies its impulsive, improvisatory effect.

Debussy's earliest constructional formal principles are consistent with those of the late nineteenth-century French Romantic tradition that characterized the Conservatoire's milieu. His subsequent innovations entail formal principles compatible with his innovations in the realm of pitch materials. As compositional resources, mutation and modulation point directly towards the exploitation of contrasts between and interconnections among sonorities and kinesthetic patterns and expose the latter's essential paradox of unity within variety. Debussy explores this dichotomy over and over in a continuing testament to its rich potential. Since a distinctive sonorous type can be established very quickly (and contrasted with another type that it replaces), a technique that juxtaposes very brief formal units, each differing in sonority or pc content, is an efficacious way to project and compare those special properties and relations. Dramatic fluctuations in the lengths of formal units and, therefore, in the rapidity of changes, provide a temporal analogue to the range of fluctuation in sonority inherent in modulation and mutation; together they widen the listener's range of experience. Since Debussy's practice of employing a wide range of temporal spans is especially appropriate for those works that employ several pc set genera, it should not surprise us that his wholly diatonic pieces, such as the late "Noël des enfants qui n'ont plus de maisons," tend to conform to earlier formal principles, while those that use the pc set genera tend to avoid them.

About the role of proportion in Debussy's evolving style, Howat observes that the late works "carry the process of subverting proportional systems to its full conclusion . . . [and] largely [avoid] the types of proportional system found in earlier works. . . . The forms of the sonatas and etudes are less dependent on them than earlier works have been seen to be."[12] This is wholly consistent both with Debussy's growing technical mastery and with his penchant to avoid repeating himself. The early works like "Mandoline" and the "Arabesques" tentatively explore the use of symmetrical and asymmetrical schemes based on number series that encompass the main materials (though not necessarily *all* materials) to control proportions within individual sections at the highest level of formal structure. In more mature works such as the String Quartet he inclines towards schemes that interconnect all levels of a composition and even imposes relationships across movements within a large work.[13] Having explored the possibilities of proportional schemes in such detail, it seems reasonable that he would abandon them to pursue other principles.

ELEVEN

KINETIC FORMS

Kinetic form arises from the organization of discontinuities and imparts the sense of motion that is such an important aspect of musical experience. In morphological form, stability engenders continuity; in kinetic form, changes engender continuity. For each, continuity derives from consistency, but embodied in different characteristic features. The broad range of events that may cohere into a morphological formal unit include (but are not limited to) a theme, instrumentation, texture, spacing, tempo, meter, key, genus, rc, or (usually) a combination of these.[1] Kinetic form derives coherence from a consistent pattern of *changes* of a particular type: a series of entrances separated by ever-shorter durations; of ever-expanding register extremes across a fluctuant register-field; or of ever contracting formal units (which would themselves be morphological formal units); of coordinated series of any type, even embracing several parameters at once. Kinetic formal units are defined by the boundaries of tendencies of increase or decrease in any musical parameter and may be perceived as a sense of motion towards or receding from these boundaries. A kinetic tendency may interact with other organizing features to capture the listener's attention and induce a sense of activity which has, as its object, a goal or goals; it may help, for example, to draw attention to a main boundary in a composition's morphological formal plan. Its means are the manipulation of musical features in ways that alternately excite or suppress listeners' expectations and thereby arouse and direct their attention; its medium is rhythm in its aspect of the structural pacing of events in time.

Most essays that treat kinetic form proceed by identifying a composition's climactic points,[2] a legitimate posture which nonetheless reflects a bias towards the boundary that lies at a tendency's zenith at the expense of the boundary that marks a tendency's nadir. (One may speculate that this is because the zenith of a processive event compels attention whereas its nadir repels it.) Both boundaries are equally important, however, insofar as together they define a tendency's limits, and an approach to formal segmentation that identifies both is less arbitrary and addresses kinetic form directly rather than through its effect.

Kinetic form and morphological form represent opposite manifestations of

233

music's temporal organization, its nature, and effect. Whereas morphological form entails a spatial conception of form as a fixed and static disposition of musical elements, kinetic form evokes a locomotive conception of form as fluid and actively changing during a composition's course. Kinetic form is perhaps inherently more musical since it confronts temporality directly, while morphological form owes its comprehensibility to our experience with spatial relationships and its cognition requires the medium of metaphor.

Kinetic form is most easily described in terms of tendencies, trends, and their effect. If a composition's major sections, for example, occupy successively shorter time spans, the listener may perceive an acceleration—all other things being equal.[3] All other things are rarely equal, however, and tendencies in one parameter frequently contradict those in another.[4]

Kinetic form is a potent organizing force in Debussy's music. The five analyses of mature works that follow explore kinetic form and compare it to morphological form. In them, the issue of formal boundaries is often refractory, and so the discussions invoke the criteria enumerated in chapter 9 and summarized in Table 9.1.

"DE L'AUBE À MIDI SUR LA MER"

Apropos of sources for "De l'aube à midi sur la mer" (*La mer* I): my remarks derive from study of a reprint based on the 1909 Durand edition[5] and Lucien Garban's two-hand piano transcription[6] (after adding the 1909 revisions).

The pitch materials of *La mer* exhibit characteristics that place it among Debussy's advanced compositions; it is complex and multifaceted, and its pc resources are not so easily compartmentalized as in earlier works such as *Pelléas et Mélisande*.

Debussy employs four genera in this movement: diatonic, whole-tone, 8–17/18/19–complex, and chromatic; the last is either integrated into or juxtaposed with the other genera. (See, for example, mm. 61 and 62, where chromatic lines connect members of diatonic and whole-tone chords, respectively; and m. 90, where chromatic lines are sub-imposed against a diatonic melodic line.) The diatonic, whole-tone, and 8–17/18/19–complex genera are utilized as in works examined earlier; the piece proceeds as a succession of brief passages (of from one to sixteen quarter notes' duration) which mutate among the three genera.[7]

Modulation provides another means of contrast and is used within each genus. (See, for example, mm. 66–84, which are diatonic but employ various rcs, and mm. 115–21, which are whole-tone but employ both rc types.) Sometimes this complicates pc content sufficiently to render generic identification difficult. An example is mm. 64–65, which are motivically homogeneous (their summary collection is nongeneric 8–27) and employ sets associated with the 8–17/18/19–complex genus (including 4–27, 4–28, 5–31, 6–Z28, and 7–31). Each bar is partitioned by modulations.

Morphological Form

I have partitioned "De l'aube à midi sur la mer" into five large sections that constitute the highest of four architectonic levels.[8] Figure 11.1 shows the resultant formal plan; each section is displayed on a separate horizontal axis, and the heights and styles of intersecting vertical lines distinguish levels as follows: highest vertical lines indicate the highest hierarchic level; intermediate solid lines indicate the intermediate level; short solid and dotted lines indicate the lowest levels. Durations are measured by means of a basic unit, which corresponds to different note values depending on tempo.[9] Each partition is defined by disjunctions within any of the eleven parameters from table 9.1 (indicated by entries below the horizontal axis, which are keyed to table 9.1 on the left border of the figure). Partitions on level 4—the lowest, least disruptive level—exhibit changes in 1–5 parameters; those on level 3 involve 4–7 parameters; on level 2, 6–10 parameters; and on level 1 (the five sections), 9–11 parameters. The norm, at each level, falls near the middle of the range.

Changes in meter and tempo strongly contribute to partitioning at the highest level and are seldom involved at the lowest, whereas changes in pc set genera, rcs, orchestration, thematic contrast, and recurrence most often contribute to partitioning at middle and lowest levels. There is, throughout, a positive correlation between the number and quality of changes and the structural level to which each partition is assigned.

Of the five large sections, the first (as Howat notes)[10] is an arch form in both its proportions (15–12–10–12–16 units) and its alternation of material (A-B-C-B-A). The other sections are organized in linear rather than cyclical fashion and juxtapose new and recurrent materials in a succession of brief passages without forming any clear patterns.

Kinetic Form

Six kinetic tendencies emerge from the fluctuating spans of the movement's formal units at each architectonic level: a tendency towards expansion followed by compression in the overall lengths of the five sections; cycles of compression-expansion or expansion-compression in the fluctuating durations that separate level 2 partitions; other distinct tendencies of fluctuation within each section; shifts, from section to section, in parameters that manifest changes (with implications for morphological form); a rhythmic counterpoint created by the interaction of contradictory tendencies between one architectonic level and another; and the maintenance of constants to counter the effects of changes (that is, to "hide the seams") that form the boundaries of formal units.

The general tendency towards expansion followed by compression is easily seen by comparing the lengths of the five sections. Sections 2 and 3 are significantly longer than the others. Similar and contrary tendencies may be seen within sections by examining the lengths of formal units at the level of detail. In section 1, the level 2 partitions at mm. 6, 12, 17, and 23 form a compression-expansion cycle

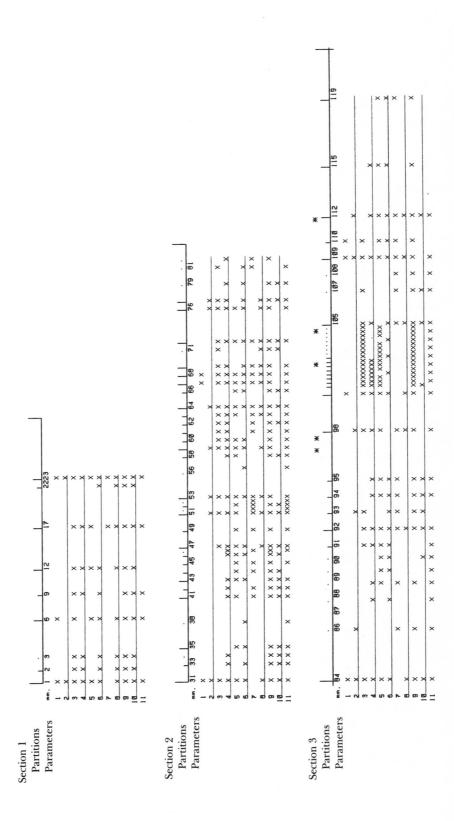

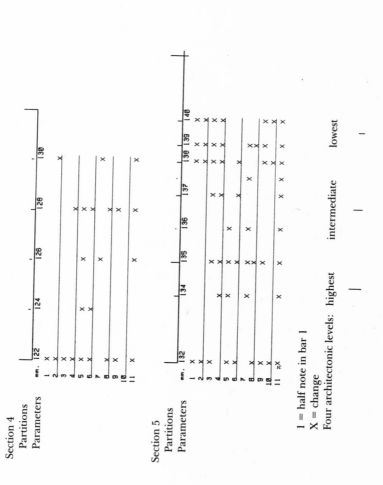

Figure 11.1. "De l'aube à midi sur la mer"

through the near-palindromic series of lengths: 15–12–10–12–16. Level 2 partitions in section 2 replicate the tendency of level 1 partitions with four-and-one-half overlapping series of expansions-compressions: 8–12–4–8–8–4–12–10–6–3–2–6–8–2–14. Section 3 mimics the tendency of section 2 with three overlapping cycles of its own: 12–24–24–9–17–16–10–12–16–12. Sections 4 and 5 each contain only one marked partition, but these conjoin to form a single cycle of compression-expansion: 36–24/24–50.

In contrast to the prevailing tendency, partitions at levels 3 and 4 exhibit a gross tendency towards compression followed by expansion (evident in a visual sweep of the five sections), which reveals, when scrutinized closely, a series of cyclic undulations that both mimic and counter those of higher levels. In section 2, for example, lower-level partitions occur much more frequently than in section 1, where twenty-four of thirty-nine passages span two durations or less (three level 4 partitions are each only one duration long), whereas in section 1, only one of nine partitions is as short as two durations, and most span at least six. This trend extends to section 3, where nineteen of thirty-six passages span two durations or less. Especially striking are mm. 101–04, which encompass fifteen one-duration partitions; these bars are the locus of many disruptions and are followed by a marked lengthening coupled with a striking statement of the horns' motto-theme at m. 105. Surely it is not accidental that these four bars of high activity, which command the listener's attention in preparation for the dramatic horn fanfare, occur at the center of section 3 and culminate at the mean (m. 104/beat 2) between the center point of the movement (m. 97/beat 3) and its Golden Section (m. 111/beat 4)—in other words, at the locus of crucial points in two important proportional schemes.[11]

Locus of Changes

The locus of changes that create partitions varies widely from section to section, though there are constants in the parameters of thematic resources and recurrence (changes occur frequently), and meter and tempo (changes seldom occur). The most active parameters in section 1 (besides thematic resources and recurrence) are orchestration and register. In section 2, loudness and sonorous density join orchestration as parameters in which changes occur frequently, while quality of texture joins tempo and meter as least active parameters. In section 3, successive-attack activity and harmonic resources replace sonorous density alongside orchestration and loudness as active parameters. In section 4, harmonic resources and loudness remain active in contrast to successive-attack activity and register, which become relatively inactive. In section 5, successive-attack activity, sonorous density, and loudness are most active, while quality of texture and register are least.

What should be clear from the foregoing (and will be clearer as we proceed to other works) is that Debussy does indeed manipulate orchestration and loudness, as well as register, density, and successive-attack activity, in ways that are form defining. Although in "De l'aube à midi sur la mer" there is no emerging pattern of use in the domain of, say, orchestration that corresponds to a motive or harmonic progression in the domain of pitch, there are trends and patterns of *change* in this and other domains that correspond to trends and patterns of change in the domain of pitch, and these contribute to continuities and discontinuities, which in turn give rise to formal schemes. This is evident in the way trends are "assigned" to formal sections and thereby contribute to the latter's distinctiveness. The strikingly regular and relatively long level 3 and 4 partitions of section 4 (twelve durations each), for example, compared with the erratic lengths of those in section 3 (one to sixteen durations each), the more regular but rapid spans of section 2, the symmetrical pattern of section 1, the irregular and relatively slow spans of section 5—all evoke different sensations, of stasis, of impulsive starting and stopping, or of marked acceleration.

Contradictory tendencies from one level of partitioning to another, in particular of compression versus expansion, generates a kind of rhythmic counterpoint that is evident in the sense that things are "slowing down" on one level (in the level 1 partitions, for example, where section 2 is longer than section 1, and section 3 is longer still) at the same time that they are "speeding up" on another (level 3 and 4 partitions occur at ever more frequent intervals across these three sections).

Other notable features include Debussy's use of constants to form continuities that subtly mitigate the contrasts between formal units—at the level of detail, especially, but at higher levels also. These may take the form of a theme that crosses one or more lower-level partitions (section 4, mm. 122–31, English horn) or a pc dyad (pcs 8,10 held invariant throughout mm. 110–13 of section 3), an ostinato (section 2, mm. 32–42), an instrumental color (section 1, mm. 9–16, English horn and trumpet), or simply the focus on particular parameters (the prominence of orchestration and loudness as active parameters in both sections 2 and 3).

Debussy often alerts (and thereby prepares) the listener prior to higher-level partitions. The relatively strong partition at m. 23, for example, anticipates the change of section at m. 31; moreover, mm. 23–30 function as transition, and their relatively minor changes in the parameters of attack activity, harmonic resources, and quality of texture reflect the continuity that spans the boundary between sections 1 and 2 (and partially offset radical changes in meter, tempo, theme, and orchestration that characterize the beginning of the new section).

Each large section is unique in its locus of changes and the fluctuation in lengths of its formal units. A consistent trait is the mutability of all parameters: those which are emphasized vary, the degree and nature of changes within each vary, and their combination and interaction vary. The overall effect is a variegated and undulating musical surface that draws the listener's attention from one parameter to another among diverse effects achieved through novel combinations. The differing emphases between sections constitute an important formal principle that reflects, on the large scale, the constantly changing musical surface, and the impression is truly kaleidoscopic. Each section begins with a concentration of disruptions and contains one or more secondary concentrations that coincide with lower-level points of partition: m. 17 of section 1 is the site of a secondary concentration (the entire section builds in stages towards this point); secondary points in section 2 at mm. 35 (changes in five parameters), 43 (in six), 51 (in nine), and 53 (nine) occur ever more rapidly and build in intensity before falling off, only to build again at mm. 64 and 76; secondary concentrations occur in section 3 at mm. 86, 98, and 105, falling off gradually after m. 112. Sections 2 and 3 are turbulent, but in different ways: section 2 is less violent, less extreme in its changes, and the length of durations fluctuates less drastically; section 4, which is unusual for its five regular twelve-duration level 3 and level 4 partitions, is bounded by partitions that embody relatively weak values for such high-level partitions (nine changes each). Section 4 is a calm passage that offers a respite from the turbulence of section 3. Section 5 is also relatively calm (though more restless than section 4), as is section 1. These dynamics feed the movement's vitality in two ways: variations in weights of partitions form series of increasing and attenuating concentrations of changes, which are mimicked by smaller, similar series nested within the large ones; variations in durations that separate partitions on each structural level form series of time spans that expand and contract, or vice versa, and trends within one level generally differ from (and contradict) those within another.

Nothing is ever regular for long; no pattern or tendency is truly uniform. In its proportions and means of partitioning, the musical surface resembles and emulates natural surfaces—such as the sea, with its myriad disturbances of magnitude both great and small.

PRÉLUDE À "L'APRÈS-MIDI D'UN FAUNE"

A relatively early mature work, *Prélude à "L'après-midi d'un faune"* is predominantly diatonic, though the 8–17/18/19–complex, whole-tone, and chromatic genera are also used. The opening flute theme is blatantly chromatic, but it also contains the seeds of the other genera. The overall pc content forms chromatic set 7–1, and the pauses on the first and fourth notes project chromatic sets 6–2, 5–1, and 4–2 (ex. 11.1A). Whole-tone and diatonic sets may also be heard, however, as shown in example 11.1B, as well as characteristic 8–17/18/19–complex set 5–10 (ex. 11.1C).[12] The chromatic genus integrates with other genera in two ways: in its many reappearances, the chromatic flute theme is supported by diatonic chords (mm. 21, 94) or by 8–17/18/19–complex chords (m. 100); also, diatonic melodies are sometimes counterpointed by chromatic countermelodies (mm. 13–14, 24–25). The synthesis of diatonic and chromatic genera accounts for most of the composition's harmonic resources: see mm. 37–99, for example.

Most modulations occur within the diatonic genus. Diatonic mm. 21–30 expose four different rcs, and there are sixteen modulations in mm. 37–99. Modulations also occur within the 8–17/18/19–complex genus (mm. 100–105). Modulations and mutations occur at frequent intervals—in every bar, for example, of mm. 44–46.

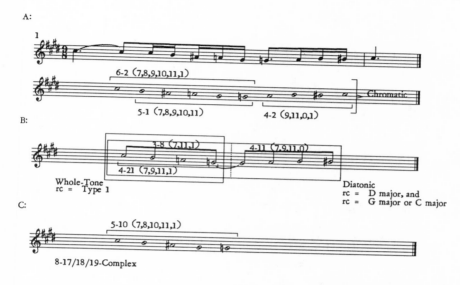

Example 11.1. Generic content of flute solo, *Prélude à "L'après-midi d'un faune"*

Kinetic Form and Parameters Other than Pitch

Figure 11.2 catalogs the partitions wrought by changes in various parameters; its partitions encompass those of Howat's proportional scheme[13] and include many others. The consistent rapidity of changes is striking: significant changes occur at extremely brief intervals, often every measure. The most active dimensions are those of theme, orchestration, register, and loudness, but all parameters are subject to frequent modification; tempo and meter are the most stable.

Taken as a whole, the changes exhibit this tendency: formal units at the level of detail become progressively shorter towards the composition's midpoint (m. 55) and progressively longer thereafter. This trend is contradicted at the intermediate architectonic level, whose spans exhibit four cycles of increase-decrease that align with the main sections' boundaries. The highest architectonic level replicates the lowest level's cycle; the lengths of the four sections are shortest for the interior pair and longest for the outer pair.

The piece's climax, characterized by its largest instrumentation, widest register span, thickest texture, loudest dynamic level, and greatest number of successive attacks per durational unit, occurs in mm. 55–71 (especially in mm. 61–70), which follow the composition's midpoint. The sense of quickening momentum induced by the progressively shorter durations at lowest and highest formal levels (as mm. 55 approaches), and the subsequent attenuation through generally longer durations, contribute to the sense that the music is moving towards and receding from the climactic passage of mm. 55–71.

Just as the change in the rate of fluctuation from the first half of the piece to the second helps to draw attention to the composition's midpoint, so also do similar tendencies in the pacing of surface-level changes (which precede and

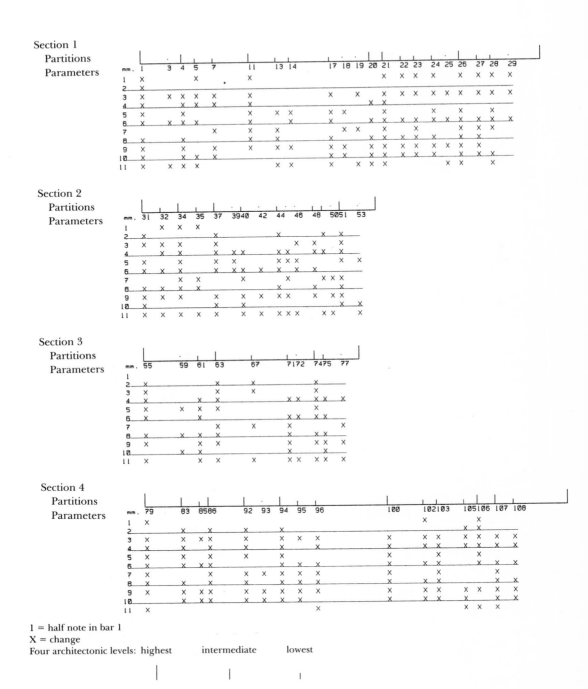

Figure 11.2. *Prélude à "L'après-midi d'un faune"*

follow middle-level partitions) help to highlight those partitions. To the extent that discernible patterns arise (in the pacing of changes) at lower levels that enable the listener to predict (or at least anticipate) important partitions at higher levels, the dynamism of partition pacing is form defining.

Several other features distinctive to this work include the rapidity and variety of gross and minute changes, which engender a musical surface in constant flux, and the distribution of changes across so many parameters. Later works tend to reserve rapid changes for a few crucial moments and tie changes within particular parameters to specific sections. Orchestration, for example, might garner the listener's attention for one passage or section, only to be replaced by register or sonorous density in the next. Highest-level partitions are prominently marked by singular events: m. 31 is preceded by a virtual cessation, in m. 30, of the intense activity that accumulates throughout mm. 21–29; m. 55 introduces an important new theme that employs, for the first time, a genuinely homophonic accompaniment; m. 79 reduces the strings to the lowest level of activity since mm. 8–9 and features the harp in an extended solo role against the flute. To be sure, these points are also marked by strong disruptions in continuity, but they are not always stronger than others that define lower-level partitions (such as m. 21). This is quite unlike Debussy's later style, represented by "De l'aube à midi sur la mer," where the highest-level partitions are consistently marked by the strongest disjunctions.

Besides its form-defining role, the dynamics of partition pacing and fluctuation among parameters contributes to a sense of an ever-changing temporal medium that complements the ever-changing sonorous surface. The rich mixture of temporal, timbral, and sonorous contexts for the reiterated (though always varied) motivic-thematic resources yields an extravagantly diverse yet coherent experience.

"NUAGES"

Composed during the years 1897–99,[14] the three *Nocturnes* represent a significant evolutionary step beyond both the earlier *Prélude à "L'après-midi d'un faune"* and *Pelléas et Mélisande*, which was still undergoing revisions. "Nuages" anticipates refinements of Debussy's later style that we associate with works like *La mer* and *Jeux.*

Three prominent themes alternate throughout. The first opens the piece and occurs in two forms, one diatonic, the other 8–17/18/19–complex (ex. 11.2A). It reappears at mm. 11, 57, and 94. The second, set within the 8–17/18/19–complex genus, is the motto-theme associated with the English horn (ex. 11.2B). It first occurs at m. 5 and recurs at mm. 21, 42, and 80. The third theme (ex. 11.2C) is pentatonic (diatonic) and does not emerge until m. 64. It recurs only once, in m. 98, but it dominates mm. 64–79.

Each section alternates restatements of these three themes with development based on their transformations; for example, the "new" material of mm. 13–14

Example 11.2. Thematic catalog for "Nuages"

grows out of theme 1 (ex. 11.2D), whose most extreme transformation occurs in mm. 33–41 (in its 8–17/18/19–complex variant).

"Nuages" illustrates Debussy's technique of fabricating form from a limited number of themes that are presented by turns and for which new material is generated through transformation. The varied lengths of each theme presentation evoke an improvisatory impression that emulates nature's unpredictability in the flow of events from a complicated source (as with the changing appearance of clouds moving slowly across the sky at a constant speed, in which certain shapes may reappear, but in an unpredictable, seemingly random fashion).

Harmonic Resources

Pitch class resources include the diatonic, 8–17/18/19–complex, whole-tone, and chromatic genera. Three genera are embodied in mm. 1–10 and are explicit or concealed even in mm. 1–2. Set in octachord 8–22, mm. 1–2 are diatonic (rc = A major), but the lower line is chromatic and adjacent dyads combine to form 8–17/18/19–complex tetrachords (4–18, 4–19). The chromatic counterpoint set against a predominantly diatonic line is characteristic of the chromatic genus's use throughout "Nuages."

The opening material's subtly modified continuation in mm. 3–8 is marked by an overt shift to the 8–17/18/19–complex through superset 9–10, which accounts for the pc content in those bars. The opening gesture's diatonic tetrachord 4–11 is transformed into 8–17/18/19–complex pentachord 5–10 in mm. 3–4, and an inversion form of the same set then provides the pc content of the English horn motto-theme in mm. 5–8. In mm. 9–10, pc 8 replaces pc 7 to form ic 3 with pc 11 (in the bass tremolo). While ic 3 is characteristic for the 8–17/18/19–complex genus, it is also well represented in the diatonic genus, and so this change both draws attention to and smooths the way for the return to the diatonic genus in mm. 11–12 through a reprise (of mm. 1–2, with modifications in register and doublings).

Modulations are common; seven occur within the diatonic genus between mm. 11 and 32, at mm. 13, 14, 17, 19, 21, 29, and 31.[15]

In mm. 21–28, the diatonic genus (in the form of an ostinato based on pentachord 5–34) is superimposed onto the 8–17/18/19–complex genus embodied in the English horn motto-theme. The two genera are distinguishable by their assignments of register, instrumental color, texture, and successive-attack activity as well as by function (as shown in table 11.1). The overall pc content forms nongeneric set 7–34, complement of the ostinato pentachord 5–34. The juxtaposition of genera and the use of a nongeneric complement to link them are typical of Debussy's mature works.

In mm. 29–30 the 8–17/18/19–complex genus is replaced by the diatonic genus. In mm. 33–36 and 39–42, the interaction between the chromatic half-note line and the diatonic quarter-note line forms harmonic blocks from the 8–17/18/19–complex genus represented by a succession of rcs. Prominent sets include 6–22, 6–Z24, and 7–26. The apparently diatonic sonorities of m. 42 are misleading: all belong to the 8–17/18/19–complex as well, and the larger groups formed by adjacent harmonies are unequivocally 8–17/18/19–complex (and nondiatonic). Modulations occur at mm. 35, 39, 40, and 43.[16]

A splendid example of transition may be seen in m. 95, whose thematic content connects with m. 96. Bar 95 is diatonic (6–33), while m. 96 is 8–17/18/19–complex. The change is effected when pc 9 is replaced by pc 10; A♯ signals the change of genus, and the invariant residue forms set 5–25, common to both genera. In m. 95 set 5–25 is submerged in diatonic 6–33; in mm. 96–97 it is eclipsed by 8–17/18/19–complex set 5–10 embedded in set 9–3.

TABLE 11.1. Distinguishing contextual characteristics for the diatonic genus versus the 8–17/18/19–complex genus in "Nuages," mm. 21–30

Parameter	Diatonic genus	8–17/18/19–Complex genus
Register:	Low, upper-middle, and high	Lower-middle
Timbre:[a]	Strings	English horn
Texture:	Chordal, monorhythmic	Solo line
Successive-attack activity:	About 6 notes struck per bar	About 3 notes struck per bar
Function:	Ostinato	Theme

[a]The horns in mm. 23–27 link the genera by means of invariant pcs (both genera share pcs 5,11) dispersed across each genus's register (low and low-middle).

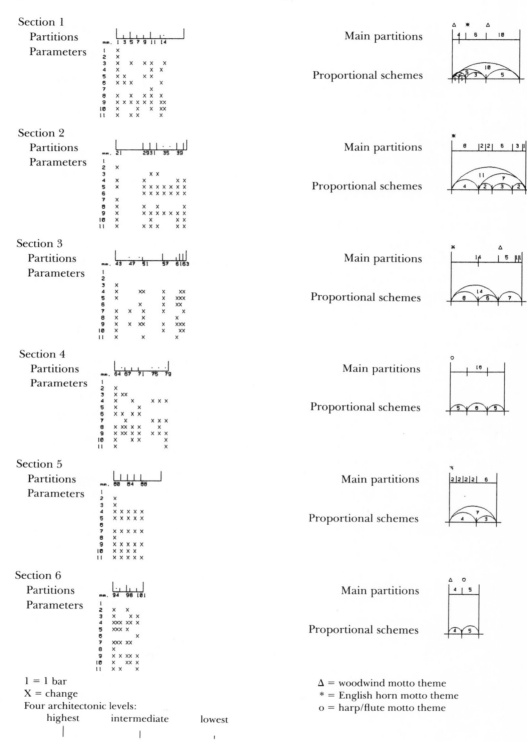

Figure 11.3. "Nuages"

Proportion and Morphological Form

Proportional schemes arise from formal units at the highest and intermediate levels in "Nuages." The piece divides readily into six large sections (fig. 11.3B). Its Golden Section follows the movement's sole whole-tone passage (m. 62), which signals the end of section 3 and precedes the composition's strongest partition. The beginning of section 4 coincides with the initial statement of the crucial third theme (ex. 11.2C). Overall symmetry is emphasized by the alignment of the end of the English horn solo in section 3 with the midpoint of the piece (following m. 51).

Equal divisions and summation series (sometimes in combination) provide proportional schemes for four of the six sections: 1, 2, 3, and 5 (as shown in fig. 11.3B and summarized in table 11.2). Sections 4 and 6 segment themselves into proportions based upon superparticular ratios, as does section 3, whose compound segment of fourteen durations relates to the remaining seven as 2:1. Other superparticular ratios found among adjacent composites include ratios 1:2 and 2:3, which bind together the first three segments of section 1; ratios 6:5 and 2:3, which occur among adjacent segments or pairs of segments in section 2; and the ratio 4:3, which relates the segments of section 5.

Kinetic Form

There are countertendencies among the three main architectonic levels defined in the formal plan of figure 11.3A. At the highest level, the lengths of sections tend towards compression (acceleration). Within sections 1, 5, and 6, the lengths of intermediate formal units exhibit expansion (deceleration), in contrast with sections 2 and 3, which tend towards compression (acceleration), and section 4, which exhibits a cycle of expansion-compression. At the level of detail, passages in which themes are stated tend to be longer than others, in particular those passages devoted to the English horn's motto-theme (this is most easily seen in fig. 11.3B).[17] Compressions immediately precede (and thus signal) the beginnings of sections 3–5. Given the ever-changing spans of surface-level formal units, the unvarying tempo and bar-line meter is striking.

Overall, the constantly fluctuant spans between partitions in "Nuages" evoke

TABLE 11.2. Sources of proportional control in "Nuages"

Section	Controlled by	Groupings (in measures)
1	Summation series (Fibonacci) and equal division	$(1 + 1) = 2 + 3 = 5; 5 + 5$
2	Summation series (Lucas/Fibonacci)	$4 + 7$ (subdivided as $2 + 3 + 2$) $= 11$
3	Summation series (Lucas) and superparticular ratios	$4 + 3 = 7$ (all terms times 2) $= 14 + 7$ $(= 2:1)$
4	Symmetry by superparticular ratios	$5:6:5$
5	Summation series (Lucas)	$3 + 4 = 7$
6	Superparticular ratios	$4:5$

the kaleidoscopic effect observed in "De l'aube à midi sur la mer," an effect that is heightened by the incessantly regular microrhythm of quarter notes. These features, coupled with the superimposition of contrasting genera in section 2 and the concealed embedding of chromatic and 8–17/18/19–complex genera in diatonic mm. 1–2 (adumbrating their subsequent importance), look away from the initial compositions of Debussy's mature period towards later works such as *La mer*, the Préludes, and Douze études.

Despite its innovations, Debussy's treatment of thematic-motivic material in "Nuages" is still conventional insofar as it proceeds through a series of formal units devoted to statements of themes that alternate with formal units which fragment and develop them.[18] The second *Nocturne*, "Fêtes," is even more conventional in this regard, with its clear ternary design and well-defined themes. The march that comprises the center section even employs period-forms. But "Sirènes," third of the trilogy, takes a resolute step along a new path, for it has no real melody or theme. It consists, rather, of a series of ostinati whose unusual sound colors result from superimposed layers of reiterated pc and rhythmic patterns, and sonorities assigned to various combinations of instruments and female voices.

"SIRÈNES"

As in "Nuages" and "Fêtes," the diatonic genus predominates; the 8–17/18/19– complex and whole-tone genera appear as well, however, and all three integrate occasionally with the chromatic genus.

Of special interest in "Sirènes" are the many passages whose cynosural sets do not belong to any of the above genera, but result, instead, from distortions. There is a tendency throughout to distort diatonic materials, which serve as a sort of referential sonus, in ways that transform them to resemble other genera. At mm. 12–13, for example, the diatonic genus supplies the parallel chords (forms of set 5–34), but their transpositions are guided by multiple forms of trichord 3–10, which takes the overall pc content out of the realm of the diatonic genus and closer to that of the 8–17/18/19–complex genus (ex. 11.3A). In mm. 14–16 the process is extended, and although diatonic sets are prominent (for example, 4– 23, 5–34, 6–33), so is 8–17/18/19–complex subset 7–Z17. The tendency of pc materials to mutate from diatonic to 8–17/18/19–complex genus culminates in mm. 20–25, where set 8–19 emerges as the summary set (ex. 11.3B).

Measures 89–118 contain a series of modulating passages in which diatonic pc materials undergo distortion that produces sets which evoke the sound of the whole-tone genus. The crucial sets are 5–34, 6–34, and 7–34, three sets that share close subset-superset relations; ic 2—central to both genera—is especially well represented in their ivs and sias.[19] Sets 5–34 and 7–34 form a common non-generic complement pair; set 6–34 belongs to the 8–17/18/19–complex genus, but its high quotient of ic 2s alludes more strongly to the diatonic and whole-tone genera, especially here, in its essentially diatonic context. The prominence of 6–

A:

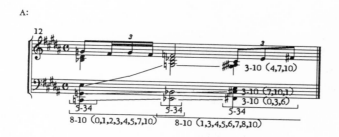

B:

C:

Example 11.3. Excerpts from "Sirènes"

34 and 7–34 in passages that refer to the whole-tone genus within a predominantly diatonic context contributes generic ambiguity. Measures 107–88 are similar, with 7–34 again a crucial nondiatonic set.

As in "Nuages," Debussy is parsimonious in his use of whole-tone sets; mm. 119–20 are the only truly whole-tone bars, and they fulfill the mutative tendency of diatonic distortion towards whole-tone from mm. 89–118. An opposite tendency towards diatonicism may be seen in mm. 121–26, where 6–34 results from a distortion of the preceding whole-tone hexachord 6–35 (from mm. 119–20). These opposing tendencies achieve parity at mm. 127–28, where diatonic 5–34 is juxtaposed with whole-tone 5–33. Measures 128–29 synthesize both pentachords and, by implication, both genera in set 7–34, and they provide a key to the earlier mutative tendencies, which serve to explore (in set 7–34) a common but external connection between the diatonic and whole-tone genera.

Modulations occur in diatonic, 8–17/18/19–complex, and mutated genera. Examples may be found in mm. 20–37 (8–17/18/19–complex genus), mm. 38–78 (diatonic genus), and mm. 93–100 (genus about 7–34).

Morphological Form and Kinetic Form

"Sirènes" divides into three large sections: mm. 1–55, in which the undulating theme A and the transitional motive X predominate; mm. 56–100, where theme B is introduced and developed, punctuated by trumpet-motive Y; and mm. 101–46, marked by a return to theme A followed by a reprise of all motivic-thematic materials (see ex. 11.3C and fig. 11.4). Strong partitions occur at mm. 46, 56, 72, 101, 121, and 131, but only those at mm. 56 and 101 define main formal boundaries.

Overall the partitions vary considerably in weight and engender four levels of hierarchy; any impression of structural formal levels is tempered, however, by the sense of building in stages—alternately approaching, receding, and reapproaching (through partitions of gradually increasing weight) the composition's most conspicuous disruption, which occurs in m. 101, after which the strength of partitions attenuates in a similar cyclic fashion.

Each new main formal division (mm. 58, 101, and the movement's conclusion) is prepared by a series of increasingly stronger partitions that occur at ever more frequent intervals. Disruptions often precede immediately rather than coincide with important partitions. They effect transitions as well as smooth discontinuities. An increase in sonorous density at m. 82, for example, signals (and helps prepare) the partition at m. 83; a decrease in loudness in m. 22 prepares the partition at m. 26; a shift to lower register in mm. 52–55 anticipates the partition at m. 56, and the changes in m. 56 anticipate the entrance of the new theme in m. 58.

Debussy's technique of immediate repetition (literal or with minute modifications) is nowhere more evident than in "Sirènes." See, for example, mm. 28–37, where two-bar units are subdivided throughout into half-bar units. Also striking is the regular length over long spans of formal units defined by thematic-motivic changes (as in mm. 26–58), which contrasts markedly with the fluctuant distance between partitions engendered by changes in other parameters.

The most active parameters in "Sirènes" are thematic-motivic resources and orchestration. Sonorous density and successive-attack activity are also very active in the first half of the piece, but not in the second. Tempo and meter are inactive, and register is unusually stable throughout.

The two prominent motives carry formal functions: motive X is introduced by English horn (the "motto instrument" for *Nocturnes*) and serves to signal impending events of various kinds. In m. 12, it augurs the end of introductory material and the approach of theme A. The trumpet-motive Y is used similarly: in mm.

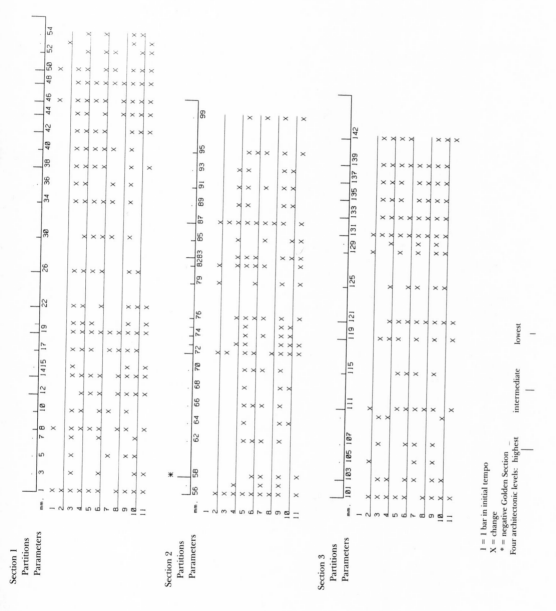

Figure 11.4. "Sirènes"

83–86 it prepares the return of theme B (in m. 87); in mm. 115–16 it signals the composition's dénouement (in m. 121).

Changes in orchestration occur very frequently, often at regular intervals: mm. 34–50, for example, and mm. 87–107 (changes every two bars). Consequently, changes that occur at irregular intervals attract attention, as at mm. 72 and 129–30, where accelerations signal, respectively, the approach of the composition's midpoint (at m. 74) and conclusion. In the domain of register, changes vacillate between fluctuant (mm. 1–22, 42–54, 72–75, 129–42) and stable (mm. 26–41, 54–64). The biggest changes occur at mm. 44–46, 101, and 121; of these, m. 101 is climactic and m. 121 signals the approach of the conclusion. Frequent changes in loudness point towards the strong partitions, with increases in the number of changes before and decreases after. Formal pacing on the surface of "Sirènes" is unusually regular and two-bar units constitute the norm, but there are also cycles of fluctuation in which stable periods alternate with irregular ones.

One of the most unusual features of "Sirènes" is the interaction and synthesis of diatonic characteristics with those of the whole-tone and 8–17/18/19–complex genera. We have seen this feature of Debussy's late works in "Feuilles mortes" and "Eventail," but not in compositions from the period around 1900.

The long spans during which a single genus predominates are striking and recall *Le martyre de Saint-Sébastien* as well as the hastily written late additions to *Pelléas et Mélisande*. Notable also is the movement's fabrication through series of ostinati assembled from superimposed layers of reiterated pc and rhythmic patterns distributed among various combinations of instruments and female voices.

Only the negative Golden Section correlates with a major partition and sectional boundary in "Sirènes"; it marks the juncture of sections 1 and 2, and coincides with the first occurrence of the movement's second prominent motive (theme A at m. 58). The positive Golden Section falls at m. 90, which has no partition. Nor do equal divisions play much of a role in the formal plan; it is, instead, m. 101 that stands out as the focal point of the dynamic processes that operate in the realms of form and pc materials. Measure 101 marks the dividing point before which partitions gradually increase in weight and after which partitions decrease in weight; it marks the culmination of a series of increases in sonorous density and loudness in the longest sustained forte and tutti; and it follows the heaviest point of disjunction brought about by the largest number and greatest magnitude of changes in all parameters. In short, m. 101, located just after the movement's two-thirds point, is the moment towards which all activity converges and from which all recedes. The one-third point (m. 50, rehearsal number 5) follows a moderately strong partition but is otherwise undistinguished. In "Sirènes," proportion is a less important source of control than the dynamism seen in the purposeful fluctuation of changes evident within various musical parameters, in the prominence accorded to each, and in their coordination to a common arrival point.

Nocturnes reveals Debussy testing new means of control as he steps securely and resolutely towards his later style. Certainly "Sirènes" and "Nuages" are wholly as interesting, as meticulously constructed, as exquisite as any of Debussy's orchestral works.

JEUX

In *Jeux* the link between pc materials and form is very close indeed. Mutations, for example, invariably partition the piece. To be sure, they are always supported by changes in other active parameters such as tempo, meter, orchestration, loudness, successive-attack activity, and register—as well as by changes in thematic resources (itself an aspect of pc materials).

The form-defining role of pitch and its relation to other parameters may be seen in the first substantial section (mm. 1–46), which encompasses the two contrasting (but related) introductory gestures (mm. 1–4 and 5–8), the *scherzando* passage of mm. 9–42, and the return of the second introductory gesture in mm. 43–46 (fig. 11.5).

The Scherzando's internal partitions reveal the close coordination of changes among parameters. The partition at the beginning of m. 25, for example, is caused by change of genus (8–17/18/19–complex to diatonic, both supplemented by the chromatic genus) accompanied by increases in successive-attack activity (the string tremolos), changes in orchestration (horns enter, lower strings exit), and the introduction of new motivic material (harmonic seconds in the clarinets and violins). Comparable partitions occur at mm. 15, 17, 19, 29, 35, and 39; all but one are distinguished by changes in genera (at m. 19 there is a modulation). The continuities between these partitions are disturbed by still-lower-level disjunctions caused by modulations (for example, at mm. 31, 32, and 34), and changes in motivic material (mm. 10, 11, 13, 18, and 23).

The nature of changes in the realm of harmonic resources plays a role in establishing formal hierarchies wherein changes of genus correlate with the highest levels while modulations coincide with intermediate and lower levels. Since the extent and impact of motivic changes varies, so do the hierarchic levels at which they contribute, depending on whether the change is subtle or drastic. A prominent new motive set off by a special timbre contributes to a more marked (higherlevel) partition than does an immediate repetition of a brief motive or an inconspicuous change in supportive material.

There are also superficial discontinuities that occur frequently throughout the Scherzando, caused mainly by subtle changes in orchestration, register, and loudness. At this lowest level the role of pitch is largely secondary.

The interaction of form, pitch, and other parameters is thus active and determinant of both pattern and hierarchy. In addition, there are trends that contribute to kinetic form.

In the Scherzando, rapid though subtle changes in orchestration, loudness, and aphoristic motivic material evoke a sense of constant movement and tension that contrasts sharply with the relatively static nature of the framing subdivisions, where changes of any sort are sparse (mm. 1–8 and 43–46). Moreover, the sudden

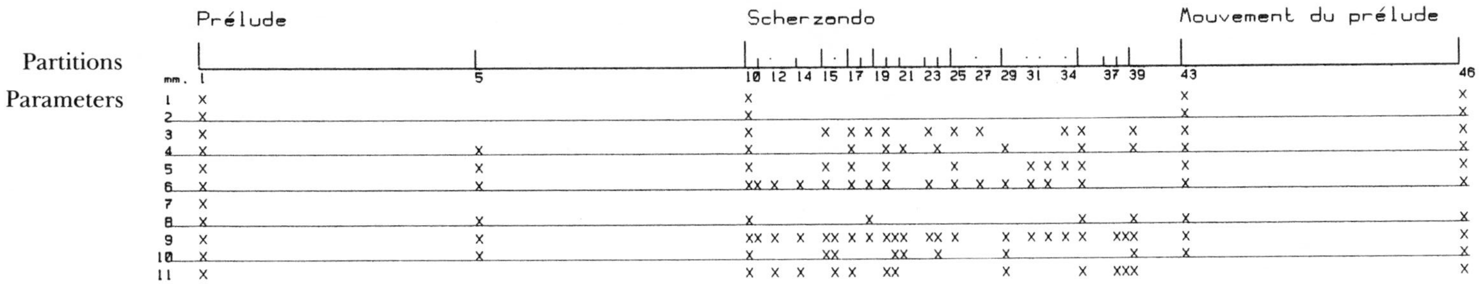

Prélude
Scherzando
Mouvement du prélude
Partitions
Parameters
mm.
1
5
10 12 14 15 17 19 21 23 25 27 29 31 34 37 39
43
46
1
2
3
4
5
6
7
8
9
10
11

2 = quarter note, 3 = dotted quarter note of the scherzando
X = change
Four architectonic levels: highest intermediate lowest

Figure 11.5. *Jeux*

reduction of changes in mm. 35–38, exaggerated in mm. 39–42, redoubles the listener's alertness in preparation for the impending change of character in mm. 43–46 and even anticipates the nature of that more static material.

The sense of ebb and flow embodied in this first large section characterizes the work as a whole. Similarly, the formal hierarchy is a microcosm of the whole, and is intimately tied to the expressive content of the drama.

Throughout the rest of *Jeux,* and in contrast to the section just cited, most major points of partition are preceded by rapid changes, either mutations or modulations. Such changes occur at one-half-measure intervals in mm. 205–08 and 217–19, for example, just before the major partition at m. 224.

The surface of *Jeux* is ever changing. As in "De l'aube à midi sur la mer," even the rate of pacing of changes varies from one moment and section to the next. Thus, the fourth large section of the overall plan (mm. 138–223) is very active compared with the first (mm. 1–46), which is relatively stable. We can trace this in the pc materials by noting relative distances between mutations and modulations.

Other large-scale trends are manifest within the pc domain. For example, from sections 2 (mm. 47–83) to 3 (mm. 84–137) to 4 (mm. 138–223), there is an acceleration in the number and frequency of changes, whereas section 5 (mm. 224–63) decelerates once again.

The fluctuant musical surface is well suited to the dramatic structure, in which events succeed one another in a progressive and cumulative fashion, each building on what has preceded until the action halts and in a sense returns to the original state in m. 702. But even the "reprise" is substantively modified from the opening (by its greater density of pc materials and orchestration—the whole-tone genus overlaid with chromaticism), consistent with the notion that the return is to passivity (a cessation of action) but not to the original state of mind, because the characters' actions since the beginning have altered them irrevocably.

PART V
ASPECTS OF STRUCTURE IN ORCHESTRATION, METER, AND REGISTER

TWELVE
ORCHESTRATION, INSTRUMENTAL EFFECT, AND STRUCTURE

The structural role of timbre or "color," achieved through orchestration and special effects, is manifest through several principles and techniques.[1] Changes in instrumentation can call attention to important events in other parameters: they may coincide with the introduction of a crucial theme, for example, or a mutation; they can underscore crucial dramatic events in songs and stage works, or occur in concert with changes in other parameters to create partitions and define formal boundaries; they can presage important events in other parameters and aid comprehension of form by capturing the listener's attention prior to crucial moments. A particular timbre may occupy a special, signaling role through its consistent association with a particular type of event in another musical parameter. (An example would be the reservation of a particular instrumental timbre to mark main sectional divisions.) The orderly disposition of timbres may generate patterns independent of those in other parameters, and thus engender their own morphological forms. A timbre that persists throughout a section or composition may serve as a stable background against which other, fluctuant timbres are made to project more prominently. The manipulation of timbres is not confined to contrasting instrumental colors, but embraces subtleties of effect within a single instrument or family; hence, works for piano solo also employ timbre as a dimension of structure.

These features are illustrated in the seven analyses that follow. The fanfare from *Le martyre de Saint-Sébastien* provides a relatively uncomplicated analytical model. *Jeux* offers an opportunity to explore the issues in a large, complex, and mature composition and broaches the question of the relationship between orchestration and extramusical elements, which is explored further in *Pelléas et Mélisande*. *Prélude à "L'après-midi d'un faune,"* "Sirènes," and the Sonata for flute, viola, and harp provide an evolutionary view of orchestration, and the sonata offers an opportunity to consider Debussy's use of timbre in chamber music. "Pour les arpèges composés" (Douze études II) illustrates the use of special effects as a cognate for orchestration in a composition for solo instrument.

FANFARE FROM *LE MARTYRE DE SAINT-SÉBASTIEN*

The brief brass-choir fanfare that precedes "Le concile des faux dieux" (*Le martyre de Saint-Sébastien* III) exhibits many features of Debussy's later treatment of orchestration.[2] The palindromic scheme of its morphological form (abcba) contrasts with its asymmetrical proportions (16 + 4 + 2 + 2 + 8 bars), as shown in figures 2.2 and 10.14.

The instrumentation divides into four groups: horns, trumpets, trombone-plus-tuba, and timpani. Their deployment is shown in figure 12.1. Of fifteen possible combinations, only six are utilized, and only two of them occur more than once (tutti, and soli trumpets). In addition, changes from one group to another coincide with formal partitions at all hierarchic formal levels (including surface partitions such as m. 3, marked by a repetition). Changes occur very frequently—far more often than in other parameters, such as pitch. Continuities in instrumentation bridge partitions and link formal units to soften the effect of discontinuities in other parameters. (At m. 3, for example, the trombone's repetition of the opening motive sustains that timbre across the partition between mm. 1–2 and mm. 3–5, and, similarly, the continuation of trumpets at mm. 9 and 23 links adjacent formal units.) Although there are no special effects or unorthodox techniques, nor any exotic instruments, the demands made (and effects obtained)

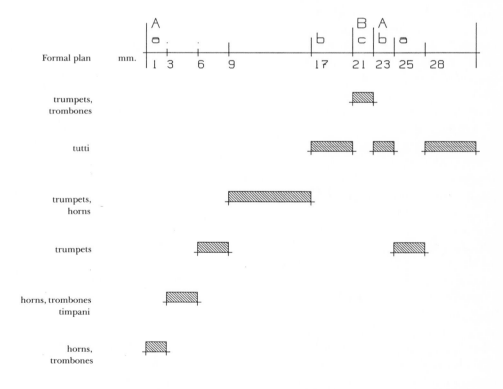

Figure 12.1. Instrumentation in the fanfare preceding "Le concile des faux dieux"

are unusual nonetheless. Close overlapping of parts, for example, produces striking timbre mixtures in rapid succession (as at mm. 23–24 and 28–30), and contradictory rhythmic patterns are superimposed to produce complex effects of articulation (m. 31). The ranges of loudness and articulation are very wide also, and fluctuate rapidly. Bars 4–5 cover a range of loudness from pianississimo to fortissimo, and mm. 21–23 embody a spread of articulation that encompasses legato, staccato, accent, and bell-like attacks.

On a timbre-scale that ranges from euphonious to strident, horns and trumpets represent the extremes, with trombones and timpani in the middle. The fanfare's moment of greatest intensity occurs in mm. 21–22; here the harmonic resources reach their maximum (9 pcs), the registral span is widest, and the sonority is loudest. Orchestration supports the climax by withholding its most strident timbre for these bars (full instrumentation, trumpets predominant), which it approaches, by degrees, from the euphonious end of the scale. The fanfare begins with horns plus trombones and timpani, and when trumpets enter they are alone and in unison.

Although the instrumentation augments only slightly the late nineteenth-century symphony orchestra brass section, the composition's effect is unique in the repertoire, owing in part to features enumerated above coupled with the essentially aphoristic nature of the motivic and harmonic resources, but also to the novel (though not unidiomatic) demands made of the performers. None of the requirements specified for trumpets at m. 6 is difficult of itself—forte, staccato, rapid notes, contours that incorporate wide skips in the upper-middle register (where partials are more closely spaced)—but their combination in loud, short, rapid figures that skip produces passages which are hard to execute cleanly and hence avoided. Such passages are typical of Debussy's late style, however.[3]

JEUX

In *Jeux*, each family of instruments plays a different functional role.[4] The strings provide the background timbre (somewhat analogous to a background color in a painting)—an ideal choice given their timbral homogeneity across a wide register span. They are heard constantly throughout and provide unobtrusive support for or readily mix with other timbres. The four woodwind types, whose sonorities are inherently more heterogeneous, furnish a resource of subtle contrasts. Like the strings, the woodwinds are used pervasively, but frequent changes in their number and mix create a variegated sonorous surface. Because the timbre of each is quite distinct, the woodwinds provide a variety of instrumental colors; they also stand out clearly against the strings' background timbre. The brass instruments appear sporadically: horns are most common, usually combined with harps (with or without celeste); trumpets are used sparingly (about half as often), trombones even less. Trumpets and trombones rarely appear without horns. The richer, striking brass timbres add bright spots of instrumental color to the woodwinds' variegated but more muted tones. The percussion battery—especially instruments that produce metallic sounds, such as cymbals—assume the special role of providing rare moments of exotic timbres. Among the five instrumental families, ubiquity versus rarity in deployment is correlated directly to the degree of distinctiveness each timbre possesses: the more mundane the sound, the more it is used; the more exotic, the more rare.

The variegated and kaleidoscopic timbral surface produces an astonishing variety of mixtures both striking and subtle, limited only by the consistent background sonus of the ubiquitous strings and woodwinds. Full tutti passages *never* occur, though there are near-tuttis that combine representatives from all instrument families (see, for example, mm. 43–46, 461–74, 521–22, and 535–50).

Orchestration and Form

Timbre is form defining in the sense that the general mix of instruments remains relatively constant within, yet changes between, intermediate-level or foreground-level formal units. Within section 1, for example, the second intermediate-level division (mm. 5–8) adds woodwinds to the preceding division's horns, harps, and strings (refer to fig. 11.5); the next series of intermediate-level formal units (mm. 9–42) is marked by a change in the *character* of changes in instrumentation (instruments enter and exit at frequent intervals compared with mm. 1–8), as well as by the addition of percussion (and deletion of harp and celeste); mm. 43–46 see a return to the stable instrumentation of mm. 1–8, and this is one of the few passages in the ballet that features all five instrument families at once. Overall, the ternary form that is characterized by the treatment of thematic and harmonic materials in section 1 is manifest in orchestration in precisely the same fashion through the morphological-formal pattern of presentation-contrast-reprise and the kinetic-formal cycle of stable-fluctuant-stable.

The instrumentation of section 2 (mm. 47–84)—and of those that follow—exhibits the character of the Scherzando of section 1 (mm. 9–42) in its rapid fluctuations among instrumentations. Section 2 also employs the Scherzando's instrument families (woodwinds, horns, percussion against strings as background). The section's intermediate-level partitions (mm. 47–52, 53–60, 61–69, 70–83) are each marked by the deletion or addition of instruments or families. Section 3 (mm. 84–137) reintroduces harp and adds trumpets (for the first time). Divisions within section 3 are marked by deletions or additions of instruments used for drastic changes (at or near mm. $91\frac{2}{3}$, 92, 98, 116, 124, 126, 128) or striking spots of color (at mm. 106, 108, 111, 113 [entrance or exit of harp], and 118 [entrance of percussion]).

But although changes in the nature and number of instruments help to partition the piece into its main and subsidiary formal divisions, orchestration also softens partitions in two ways: by maintaining instrumental timbres across partitions and by introducing new timbres just before partitions. See, for example, mm. 17–18, which straddle a partition caused by mutation plus changes in successive-attack activity, sonorous density, new motivic-supportive material, and loudness (as well as by adding violins to violas); the horns carry the main thematic material throughout both bars and mitigate slightly the effect of the changes. Similar examples occur at mm. 124 (percussion bridges the partition) and 128 (flute). At m. 138, the juncture of sections 3 and 4 (caused by pronounced changes in tempo, loudness, and motivic material), the strings, woodwinds, and brass *all* cross the partition. Examples of timbres introduced just prior to partitions include the bassoon entrance just before m. 47, flute before m. 53, harp before m. 84, and trumpet before m. 126; each time, the change of timbre alerts the listener to the impending partition.

Coherence in the realm of orchestration is served by consistent maintenance of instrumentation over lengthy spans (harps, for example, play almost continuously throughout mm. 226–61, as do horns and harps in mm. 530–610) and by association of certain instruments and mixtures with specific thematic resources (high soli strings at mm. 174–78, for example, and their motive's transformations at mm. 224–25, 245–46, 270–71, 276–78, 290–92, 523–26, 635–38). Yet repeated assignment of exact instrumental mixes to motives is extremely rare. Exceptions that prove the rule include mm. 619–26, which repeat *almost* exactly the pc material of mm. 611–18 with *exactly* the same instrumentation (the second passage transposes the first where t = 3), and mm. 245–54, which repeat *exactly* the material of mm. 224–33 with *almost* exactly the same instrumentation. The second passage accords more prominence to the harps and makes other subtle adjustments, such as adding celeste and assigning trills to the horns.

Thus, formal patterns are shaped by the assignment of instrumental timbres to various locales, formal units are defined by changes in orchestration, the cause of coherence is aided by consistency in the disposition of timbres and by association of timbres with motivic-thematic entities, and Debussy's abhorrence of literal reuse ensures that a given combination of instruments with other parameters never recurs exactly.

There is, finally, a general correlation between orchestral timbre and the drama, in which choice of instrumentation (which emphasizes exotic combinations and subtle effects) and the tendency towards rapid changes of widely varied degree reflect the exotic and ever-shifting character of the story with its aberrant mix of fear, sensuality, evil, innocence, and whimsy.

PRÉLUDE À "L'APRÈS-MIDI D'UN FAUNE"

In *Prélude à "L'après-midi d'un faune,"* as in *Jeux*, changes in orchestration usually coincide with important events in other parameters. (Refer to figure 11.2, which defines three architectonic levels plus an intermittent level at the surface.) See, for example, m. 4, which is the site of an intermediate-level partition; here changes of orchestration include texture (solo to tutti) and timbre (exit flute; enter oboes, clarinets, horns, harp). See also m. 11, another intermediate-level partition, where changes include texture and timbre (from soli horns to tutti and solo flute, clarinets, and strings). At m. 31, a high-level partition (juncture of sections 1 and 2), there are changes in texture (from tutti to accompanied solo) and timbre (enter solo clarinet and harp; exit flute and upper strings). Another high-level partition (at m. 55) is marked similarly by changes in texture (from soli flute-oboe-clarinet-violins and horns to tutti woodwinds and strings) and timbre (enter full strings and English horn; flute shifts from supporting role to solo).

As in *Jeux,* orchestration is the focus of constant changes that occur in virtually every bar and often several times within a measure (see mm. 31–36, for example, where as many as four changes of timbre or instrumental effects occur per bar).

The motto-theme numbers the flute timbre among its salient features. Other primary characteristics include its overall contour (a protracted descent followed by a more rapid ascent), texture (homophonic), and the use of two chords to set the theme's boundary tones. The presence or absence of chromatic coloration is among its variables (chromaticism is conspicuous in the original theme, but some variants, such as that at m. 55, are diatonic), as are the boundary interval formed by the initial and lowest notes of the descent and the fluctuant harmonic setting. The motto-theme undergoes a series of transformations. Many produce simple variants through transposition, compression of the boundary interval, and slight rhythmic modifications such as the duration of the initial note (mm. 1, 11, 21, 23, 26, 79, 86, 94, 100). Only one among these assigns the motto-theme to an instrument other than flute (oboe at m. 86). Other transformations are more drastic and entail modification of even the primary characteristics, though the connection with the motto-theme itself is always evident. Bar 31 begins a series of transformations that culminates in the lyrical theme of m. 55. At m. 31, the motto-theme's durations are modified to produce a regular duple subdivision in rapid-note values, the theme is transposed, the boundary interval is compressed, and the timbre is reassigned to clarinet (example 12.1, B compared with A). Bar 37 excises the chromaticism in favor of a diatonic contour, extends the rhythmic modifications to emphasize the duple subdivision, reassigns the timbre to oboe, stretches the boundary interval (to a P5), and extends the contour (ex. 12.1C). The next transformation produces the contrasting theme at m. 55 that features slow, simple triple meter, transposed initial note (to pc 8), expanded boundary interval (to a m10), and an abruptly compressed contour (ex. 12.1D). The timbre returns initially to flute, but the repetition (m. 63) adds violins.

Two more transformations produce subsidiary materials late in the piece. The first occurs at m. 83 and is reiterated at m. 90: the theme's long initial note is transposed and broken into syncopated diminutions; the timbre is assigned to oboe (English horn at m. 90; see ex. 12.1E). The last (m. 107) closes the piece: the initial note is transposed (to pc 8); the boundary interval is compressed; the durations of the descending and ascending notes are lengthened; the timbre is reassigned to the horns in a striking three-voice setting (ex. 12.1F).

These three series of transformations account for all of the prominent thematic materials in the composition: the first consists of the simple transformations dispersed throughout the piece; the second consists of transformations that culminate in the broad theme of mm. 55, repeated in m. 63; the third begins in m. 83 and culminates in the concluding three-voice setting. The first series employs

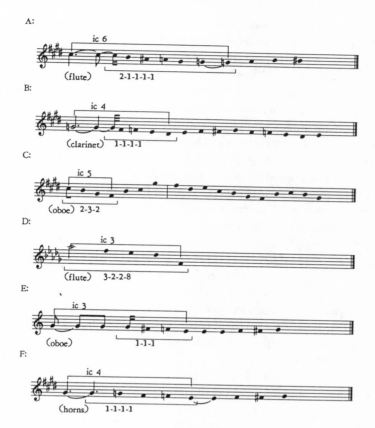

Example 12.1. Motto-theme transformations in *Prélude à "L'après-midi d'un faune"*

flute with one exception (m. 86); the second consistently avoids flute with one exception (m. 55) and transforms the motto-theme more radically than the third.

There is no background timbre in *Prélude à "L'après-midi d'un faune."* Indeed, this would impede the intricate relations between timbre and the motto-theme. But as in *Jeux*, the strings generally remain in the background, the woodwinds (whose heterogeneity results in constant if subdued fluctuations) are always prominent in the foreground, the horns and harps provide sharp moments of instrumental color, and the percussion—antique cymbals—are withheld until the final measures, where they provide an exotic and extravagantly subtle addition to the sonority.

Full tuttis are rare, though they do exist (notably in mm. 61–70); but as in *Jeux*, the emphasis throughout is on sparse instrumentation for the sake of timbral variety, rather than on complexity or volume of sound.

Advanced instrumental techniques are not to be found among the special effects in *Prélude à "L'après-midi d'un faune,"* but there are many unordinary instrumental combinations and ensemble demands. These include dovetailed instrumental entrances over exits (such as flute to oboe at m. 14); use of unisons or octave doublings for new timbres to set immediate repetitions (as at m. 105, where flute is added to oboe); and changes of instrument for immediate repetitions, as at mm. 32–33 and 35–36 (where flute and clarinet exchange passages), 44–45 (woodwinds versus strings), 46–47 (same), and 48–50 (horns to flute and harp).

There are innovations in the choice of instrumentation: a full complement of woodwinds (plus horns) and strings is augmented by two harps and the antique cymbals, but conspicuously absent are standard instruments like trumpets, trombones, timpani, and other percussion. Debussy chooses instruments that combine readily to produce subtle mixtures, and avoids the more strident brass and percussion. His lifelong fondness for woodwinds, horns, and harps is revealed here, as is his tendency to relegate strings to an essential but unobtrusive supportive role. His fascination with exotic instruments emerges in his use of the antique cymbals, an interest he indulges in other works (with the oboe d'amore in "Rondes de Printemps," for example).

Orchestration and Form

Although in *Prélude à "L'après-midi d'un faune"* (unlike *Jeux*) orchestration does not contribute to pattern formation, nor to hierarchic distinctions by consigning instrumental combinations to formal units of a particular architectonic level, many other features do adumbrate Debussy's treatment of instrumental color in the ballet. Changes in orchestration usually coincide with formal partitions; thus, orchestration is form defining in a very general way, just as it is in *Jeux*. Orchestration is also used to mitigate the effect of partitions, as at m. 4, where the retention of flute for two eighth-notes provides a timbral link across this intermediate-level partition. Another, vivid example may be seen at m. 14 (a surface-level partition), where the flute is held for four eighth notes following a partition and dovetails (via its diminuendo) with the new oboe timbre. Yet another example occurs at the intermediate-level partition in m. 20 (caused by drastic reductions in forces, successive-attack activity, and loudness), which adumbrates the high-level partition at m. 21; the prominent (and only) timbre is solo clarinet, a color already incorporated into the preceding tutti's sonority. A series of passages bounded by mm. 31–36 is tied together by the consistent use of harp across their partitions (at mm. 32, 34, and 35). The introduction of a new timbre just before partitions often helps to capture the listener's attention. Examples include m. 50 (the addition of flute and harp anticipates the partition at m. 51) and m. 105 (flute is added to the instrumentation of m. 104, just prior to the intermediate-level partition of m. 106). Materials that are repeated literally receive new instrumentation (compare mm. 63–66 with mm. 55–58, where strings accompanied by woodwinds replace woodwinds accompanied by strings—the repetition also adds figuration), while pc materials that vary on repetition employ similar instrumentation (compare mm. 90–92 with mm. 83–85, where the repetition is transposed down a semitone). High-level formal partitions (at mm. 21 and 55) are marked by pronounced changes in instrumentation and effect, but there is no comparable correlation at lower levels since intermediate- to surface-level partitions may exhibit slight changes (for example, mm. 22, 23, 24, and 26, the last an intermediate-level partition) or drastic ones (mm. 40, 44, 50, which are surface-level partitions, and mm. 11, 20, and 31, which are intermediate-level partitions). Orchestration contributes variety through its constantly changing instrumental timbres, and coherence through the fact that these changes are restricted to the limited instrumentation.

"SIRÈNES"

Motivic relations interconnect the three *Nocturnes*.[5] The trumpet's prominent motto-theme in "Sirènes" (mm. 83–84) is a variant of the English horn's motto-theme from "Nuages" (mm. 5–8),[6] which also appears transformed in "Fêtes" as the prominent "cortège" theme (mm. 125–28; see ex. 12.2A–C). Other recurring motives in the three movements include the undulating motive in "Sirènes" (ex.

Example 12.2. Cyclic themes in *Nocturnes*

12.2D) associated with the women's chorus (mm. 26–27), first heard in "Nuages" (m. 1) and prominent in "Fêtes" as the brass-fanfare motive (m. 6) used to punctuate the ends of phrases and sections (ex. 12.2D–F). Instrument assignments vary considerably to match the transformed character of the materials; the undulating motive's loud and strident variant is given to trumpets in "Fêtes," whereas the restrained version in "Nuages" is assigned to clarinets and bassoons. In all of these examples (and others could be cited), orchestration plays a key role in the process of transformation.

'Sirènes" incorporates all of the features of orchestration observed in *Jeux* and *Prélude à "L'après-midi d'un faune,"* but with innovations that show, as always, the fluidity of Debussy's evolving compositional technique. "Sirènes" employs repetition to a degree that is unusual even for Debussy: nearly every statement of material is repeated at least once, many are reused over and over, and ostinato is pervasive. Though there are exceptions, in general Debussy orchestrates repetitions just as in the other works I have discussed: literal repetition of pc materials features changes of orchestration (compare m. 2 to m. 1, and m. 16 to m. 15), while repetitions that vary pc materials (by transposition, for example) tend to retain the same orchestration (compare mm. 5–7 to mm. 1–3, and mm. 20–21 to mm. 15–16).

The instrumentation of "Sirènes" is similar to that of *Prélude à "L'après-midi d'un faune"*: a full complement of woodwinds and strings, horns, and two harps. Trumpets are an addition (but they are used very sparingly), as is the women's chorus (which occupies a central role); percussion is omitted altogether. Debussy's predilections for certain solo and mixture timbres—flute, oboe, English horn, clarinets-plus-bassoons, horns-plus-harps, soli strings (including divisi)—are much in evidence, as is his use of dovetailing (for example, mm. 56–57, horns to clarinets) and doubling (mm. 15–16 and 38–39, which synthesize woodwinds and strings into complex mixtures) to transform timbres gradually and to create new ones.

A few special effects demonstrate Debussy's growing inventiveness. Most obvious is the use of women's chorus for purely timbral effect. Except for its lack of text, the choral writing demands nothing unusual or difficult, but the overlapped unisons that permit a continuous line free of breaths are effective (mm. 58–72), as is the change of timbre at m. 101, where the chorus is instructed to sing with mouths closed. The vocal overlap has an instrumental counterpart throughout mm. 101–10, where overlapping entrances within flutes, horns, harps, and low strings enable breaths, attacks, and subtle shadings without breaks in sound. This layering of timbres requires the use of most of the instrumentation (no trumpets or contrabasses), yet subdued dynamics, short note values, and overlapping achieve a quiet transparency.

Special effects in other movements also bear mention: in "Nuages" there are subtle doublings (unison oboes in mm. 3–4, flute and harp in mm. 64–69—even more subtle when the harp plays harmonics in mm. 77–78); and in "Fêtes" the combination of harps and muted trumpets (mm. 116–39) is most unusual, as is the doleful tuba solo at mm. 252–56.

A particular connection between harmonic resources and solo timbres merits attention. The chief sonority for "Sirènes" is provided by the diatonic genus; there are, however, some important passages that employ either the 8–17/18/19–complex genus or the whole-tone genus. The first lengthy passage based on the 8–17/18/19–complex genus contains the initial statement of the undulating theme, at mm. 20–37, just after statements of the English horn's motto-theme of mm. 12–13 and mm. 17–18 (see ex. 12.2G; the motto-theme adumbrates the undulating theme in its underlying vacillation between G and F). The second substantial 8–17/18/19–complex passage occurs at mm. 101–06 and marks the beginning of section 2, preceded by the first statement of the trumpet's motto-theme at mm. 83–84 (see ex. 12.2A). Two passages that employ the whole-tone genus occur at mm. 119–20 and 121–28,[7] following four more statements of the trumpet's motto-theme (in mm. 111–12, 113–14, 115–16, and 117–18; the third is assigned to the English horn). The composition's closing bars prominently feature whole-tone (mm. 131–32 and 135–36) and 8–17/18/19–complex materials (mm. 139–41); both motto-themes appear here as well, and the second alternates English horn with trumpet. Each time, the combination of timbre and theme signals mutation to a nondiatonic genus: the first theme's pc content strongly alludes to the 8–17/18/19–complex genus (ex. 12.2G); the second motto-theme points towards the whole-tone genus (especially given its larger context in m. 83, in which pc 8, supplied only by the motive, distorts the otherwise diatonic pc content).[8] After four statements, four "unsuccessful attempts" at transforming diatonic into whole-tone materials, the conversion succeeds (mm. 119–20). The genus is unstable, however, for the hexachord that supplies pc materials for mm. 121–28 contains a semitone (6–34).

PELLÉAS ET MÉLISANDE: ORCHESTRATION AND TEXT EXPRESSION

The direct association of specific instrumental timbres with dramatic events, characters, and ideas is a large topic that warrants a far more comprehensive study than this book can accommodate.[9] Certain principles explicated in part 3, however, have applications in the realm of orchestration.

First, the selection of voice-types is tied to the natures of the characters. On one hand, the Physician, Arkel, and Geneviève are figures who observe and comment but do not really participate, and they are represented by the mellifluous lower male and female voice ranges (bass and contralto). Pelléas and Mélisande, on the other hand, serve not only as focuses of action throughout, as those whose fates concern us, but also as protagonists in the sense that they are positive and active, whereas the Physician, Arkel, and Geneviève are passive and negative.[10] Yniold, who represents the innocent and benign side of human nature, is resolutely positive and active. Also, his role as intermediary in the allegory of act IV, scene 3, associates his persona strongly with those of Pelléas and Mélisande. All three are represented by higher male and female voice ranges. As for Golaud, his complex character embodies conflict as its essence. In his struggle to master his destiny, Golaud is active and impotent, positive and negative, good and evil. His baritone voice ranges both high and low, demanding a wider registral span than any of the other parts.

Debussy treats orchestration in much the same manner as pc set materials: he narrows the possibilities to a few general categories of timbres and effects which he associates with various psychological-emotional elements of the drama according to their placement on a dynamic and emotional psychological field (whose dynamic axis ranges from passive to active and whose emotional axis ranges from malignant to benign).

Table 12.1 provides a chart of representative timbre associations. The strings' associations are the most diverse, and vary according to register disposition, spacing, and dynamic level. When unobtrusive, as in accompanying voices, they are neutral; when prominent, upper strings spaced closely are often tied to the benign, passive hemisphere, while lower strings (especially contrabasses at loud dynamic levels, often paired with bassoons) represent the malignant, active hemisphere. The upper woodwinds (flutes, clarinets, oboes) in middle and higher registers represent benign passivity (especially when closely spaced with staccato articulations), while the bassoons' lower register (especially when the instruments are paired in thirds) is tied to the malignant hemisphere (often combined with contrabasses and low horns or trombones). Trombones, tuba, and timpani are generally associated with active malignancy, while harps tend towards the benign, passive hemisphere alongside upper strings and woodwinds.

A few instruments and combinations are reserved for signal roles. The horns are generally tied to dramatic elements that involve mystery, fate, and especially death; they often appear in whole-tone passages and are frequently associated with Golaud (who least controls his destiny). The solo trumpet functions similarly,

TABLE 12.1. Expressive associations for orchestration (keyed to table 7.1)

Woodwinds in middle and higher registers, closely spaced (especially flutes, oboes, clarinets) Strings in middle and higher registers, closely spaced (especially violins and violas) Harps	= benign, passive hemisphere
Strings in lower register (especially contrabasses) Trombones in low register, tuba Bassoons in low register (especially when paired in thirds) Timpani Louder dynamic levels	= malignant, active hemisphere
Horns (all dynamic levels)	= mystery, fate, death
Trumpets (all dynamic levels, but especially solo trumpet, *piano*)	= same, but more benign, in particular the soul
Full strings, *forte*, widely spaced	= affection, love, passion
Strings (accompanying voices with quiet, sustained notes or repetitive, unobtrusive figurations)	= neutral

but in a more specialized role: it is used where attention centers on the soul—the departure of Mélisande, for example, in act V. Affection, love, and passion are usually underscored by the full complement of strings, closely or widely spaced but centered in the middle register, mezzo forte to forte, sometimes mixed with woodwinds but always predominant.

Many of the categories listed in table 12.1 allow for a variety of modes of expression through orchestration, and this permits considerable flexibility. In general, wherever levels of meaning (explicit, implicit, allegorical) conflict, Debussy's orchestral setting favors the more obvious. This contradicts the principle that associations tied to the pc set genera usually favor the more obscure. A technical complication is the necessity for the orchestra to avoid covering the voices, which requires that low dynamic levels be maintained or that the instruments avoid the vocal registers. Much of the singing is accompanied by strings and woodwinds at low dynamic levels; where expression demands louder timbres, Debussy often places the required timbre just ahead of the singer's entrance. For these reasons attempts to assign specific dramatic-expressive functions to specific instruments and combinations invariably suffer from oversimplification, just as motivic associations tied to dramatic-expressive functions oversimplify in spite of the principle's general validity.

The following examples help to illustrate the foregoing points:

Act I, Scene I
Golaud first encounters Mélisande. His aside "Oh! you are beautiful"[11] (OS p. 9/5) is set with lush strings in the middle register.

Act I, Scene 3
At the moment of Pelléas's encounter with Geneviève and Mélisande, his affection for them both (and relief at his release from confrontation with Golaud) is underscored by the sudden prominence of violas and violins (p. 52/2).

Act IV, Scene 3
The opening instrumental passage anticipates the orchestration used throughout the scene, which stresses woodwinds and upper strings, soft dynamics, and repetitious figurations that project energy without heaviness, used consistently to project Yniold's benign and innocent character. In contrast, the pc set materials alternate between the diatonic and 8–17/18/19–complex genera consistent with the shifts in meaning within the psychological field of the allegory this scene conceals, which Yniold serves as intermediary. Often orchestration and pc set genera conflict, as do the mundane and allegorical aspects of the drama, for Yniold is only dimly aware of its sinister elements. But when the shepherd delivers his ominous, monotonic reply to Yniold's persistent questions about the sheep (p. 316/11), which thrusts the portentive allegory into the drama's foreground, the horns enter, so that orchestration and pc materials are in associative agreement, for a few bars at least.

Act V

In many passages the prominent use of full strings is associated with kindness, love, and passion, as in Arkel's exclamation "I am so happy to hear you speak thus" (p. 373/2)[12] or Mélisande's reply to Golaud's plea "Yes, yes, I forgive you" (p. 378/11).[13]

Act III, Scene 4

This scene's tone is sinister throughout, and it is not surprising to find emphasis in the orchestration on the bassoons (frequently assigned low thirds), cellos, and basses. But there are light moments, too—as Golaud, for example, tries to calm a frightened Yniold with a promise to give him a quiver full of arrows (p. 225/1). The orchestration changes abruptly to quiet pizzicati in upper strings coupled with muted horn, not at the moment when Golaud speaks of the gift—"I will give you something tomorrow. . . . A quiver and arrows"[14]—but just after, when Yniold's distraction becomes evident in his enthusiastic reply "With long arrows?"[15] The orchestration helps to give a momentary respite from the scene's pervasive tension.

Act IV, Scene 4

When Mélisande hears Golaud in the trees (p. 352/5), the trombones sustain a low M3 (G♭-B♭), after which they exit for four bars while Pelléas dismisses her fears as imaginary and the characters resume their self-absorption. When Mélisande sees Golaud (p. 355/5), the trombones reappear.

Act V

Golaud's initial passage in act V (p. 368/6) incorporates subtle shifts in mood as he recalls with dismay the events at the close of act IV, where he murdered Pelléas and chased and wounded Mélisande. His anguished declaration "I have killed without reason! It is enough to make the stones weep!"[16] is set very sparsely in the middle and lower registers of horns and cellos. His emotion shifts to tenderness as he asserts that "they embraced like little children. They were brother and sister."[17] It is accompanied by quiet strings, closely spaced in the middle register (with pc materials drawn from the diatonic genus [rc = A major]). But at his anguished outburst "And I, I all of a sudden!"[18]—referring to his murder of Pelléas (p. 369/2–3)—the upper strings exit and the accompaniment shifts to the low register of the bassoon, cello, and bass. These changes are congruent with changes in pc set materials (from 8–17/18/19–complex genus to diatonic to chromatic), and together they conspire to project Golaud's torment and inner conflict.

Act III, Scene 2

Immediately following Golaud's admonition for Pelléas to avoid Mélisande, the whole-tone genus helps to convey the magnitude of Golaud's implicit threat—of death—should Pelléas ignore his warning. Golaud's jealousy is also underscored by the horns entrance (p. 216/1–2). The threatening reference lasts only a brief two bars before it is replaced by the diatonic genus (rc = D major) and the horn timbre is diluted by woodwinds. Other brief whole-tone passages occur in the instrumental interlude that precedes scene 4 and are also conjoined to the horns.

Act V

The pianissimo trumpet solo appears as Mélisande approaches death and helps to signify the departure of her soul (p. 403/6). The association is also active at the end of act IV, where trumpets join the orchestral tutti at the moment of Pelléas's murder (p. 361/5 and in the act's four closing bars).[19]

Throughout the opera, Debussy's handling of orchestration exhibits the characteristic features we have observed in other works. The strings furnish an unobtrusive and pervasive background timbre for the ubiquitous woodwinds, which contribute a subtle and variegated musical surface through their ever-changing mixtures. The harps are most often heard in combination with woodwinds and horns. Among the brasses, horns are used the most, with trumpets and trombones reserved for special moments. As in other works, *Pelléas et Mélisande* has strings, woodwinds, horns, and harps as its basic sonority to which trumpets, trombones, tuba, and timpani are added from time to time. Subdued dynamic levels are the norm, though there is no shortage of forte passages. Unlike *Jeux* (but more like *La mer*), whose use of trumpets exploits only the soft timbres (muted and unmuted), *Pelléas et Mélisande* uses the trumpets' and low brass's formidable upward range of intensity to good advantage for rare moments of fortissimo. Two such passages occur at the end of act IV, scene 4, where the tragedy's violent culmination is underscored with extraordinary efficacy by the addition of trumpets and low brass to orchestral tuttis towards the ends of powerful crescendos (pp. 361/5 and 364/4).

Changes in instrumentation are more numerous than changes in other parameters and invariably coincide with formal partitions of large and small dimension. Overlapping of exits and entrances, retention of timbres across formal partitions, and foreshadowing-changes that immediately precede formal partitions are all features to be found in abundance. Specific instrumental forces vary somewhat from one large-scale formal unit to the next (the omission of harps from act I, for example, and of trombones from act V), but this is not overtly form defining as in *La mer* or *Jeux;* it results, rather, from other considerations that determine which instruments are needed and which are to be withheld.

CHAMBER MUSIC: SONATA FOR FLUTE, VIOLA, AND HARP

The three instruments of the Sonata for flute, viola, and harp yield seven timbre combinations: three solo timbres, three pairs, and tutti. The predominant timbre combination is tutti, followed by viola and harp. (Table 12.2 summarizes counts of instrumental combinations by formal units based on figure 10.16.) Together they account for well over half of the composition, and thus may be considered the movement's background color (a feature that applies to the remaining movements

TABLE 12.2. Timbre combinations
and their use in the Sonata for flute,
viola, and harp, I

Timbre combination	No. of occurrences	No. of durations[a]
Solo flute	4	9
Solo viola	9	63
Solo harp	14	41
Flute and viola	12	64
Flute and harp	12	62
Viola and harp	17	87
Tutti	38	133
(Silence)	(5)	(11)
Total possible:	111	570

[a]Where 1 = 1 eighth note in the original tempo

as well). Solo timbres are uncommon; solo flute is especially rare, reserved for termination passages so that when we hear the flute we know that a section is about to close. Solo viola passages occur less often than solo harp but consume far more durations; this is because while solo harp is usually reserved for beginnings of formal subdivisions (introductory or transitional fragments), solo viola is used most often to expose thematic material. Solo timbres thus carry formal roles: the flute signals closure, the harp signals initiation, the viola signals expository passages. Pairs assume the role occupied in the orchestral scores by soli and tutti woodwinds plus horns and harps: they occur frequently, but since they embody a range of contrasts, they contribute to a sound-surface that changes constantly.

Most of the six sections exhibit stability at their beginnings (few changes in instrumentation) and instability at their endings (many changes); sections 3 and 5 are exceptions whose beginnings feature numerous changes.

The successive juxtaposition of timbre combinations creates distinct timbre patterns. Some recur in similar relative locations within various sections: for example, the timbre pattern found towards the end of section 1 (viola-harp alternates with tutti, the flute rests frequently) recurs towards the ends of sections 3 (mm. 27–47) and 4 (mm. 57–60), in spite of the quite different thematic-motivic material of section 3 and the somewhat different material of section 4. This same timbre pattern recurs so frequently that it provides a unifying device for the movement after the manner of a recurrent motive. Each section's last timbre pattern includes the harp and so the harp's timbre becomes associated with closure.

Pacing

Main partitions are often marked by a change in the rate of change of timbre combinations. This usually correlates directly to changes in tempo; that is, a change to a faster tempo also sees a shift to more rapid changes in timbre. See, for example, mm. 26–30 (more rapid changes coupled with a shift to rapid tempo), mm. 48–51 (slower changes/slower tempo), and mm. 63–66 (rapid changes/rapid tempo). Measures 69–70 exhibit a countertendency (rapid changes/slower tempo), an anomaly that signals the movement's most prominent reprise, the return of the opening gesture in m. 72.

Rapid changes in timbre (especially in slow-tempo sections) invariably precede and signal important formal junctures; see, for example, mm. 45–47 (which precede section 4: 1–2 changes per bar), mm. 64–66 (2–6 changes per bar) and 69–71 (2–7 changes; both passages precede the reprise), and mm. 79–81, which precede the movement's close at m. 83 (2–8 changes).

The pacing of changes in timbre combination fluctuates over two cycles of decrease-followed-by-increase. (Table 12.3 lists the mean number of combinations within each large section as defined by the formal plan of figure 10.16.) The number of changes rises dramatically by section 3, drops in section 4, and the cycle repeats in sections 5 and 6. These tendencies join with those in the realms of theme and pc set genera to convey a sense of heightened activity as the composition's interior is approached, with section 4 (mm. 48–62) the site of a temporary lull and the reprise of the opening gesture (m. 72) a signal for the decisive final shift to deceleration.

Though Debussy's use of instruments is hardly radical, he does produce unique timbres by innovative pairings, such as the flute/viola unisons and octaves.[20] The pc materials are disposed throughout in figurations carefully tailored to the instrumental assignments, so that substitutions are not feasible either for realization of a passage's figuration or for its interaction with other instruments. (This piece does not transcribe well.)

As we have seen earlier, instrumental timbres are sometimes used to project subtleties in the realm of pitch: for instance, the entrance of the flute in m. 1

TABLE 12.3. Mean tallies of timbre combinations, lower-level formal units, and pc fields within each major section of the Sonata for flute, viola, and harp, I

Section	Timbre combinations	MD^a	Formal units	MD	PC fields	MD
1	20	7.7	9	17.0	6	25.5
2	5	7.6	4	9.5	3	12.7
3	18	3.7	8	8.3	8	8.3
4	21	6.4	8	16.9	6	22.5
5	13	3.3	3	14.3	3	14.3
6a	11	2.5	2	13.5	2	13.5
6b	23	5.1	4	29.5	4	29.5
Totals	111	5.2	38	15.0	32	17.8

[a]MD denotes "mean duration," where 1 = 1 eighth note in the original tempo.

midway through the harp's gesture, which overtly exposes tetrachord 4–11 (motive B) for the first time.

SOLO PIANO MUSIC

Debussy's solo piano compositions are generally regarded as highly idiomatic. His idiom, however, transcends mere exploitation of pianistic techniques, for he exploits the structural implications that reside in the piano's timbral possibilities by disposing pc materials into specific, idiomatic figurations. Evidence of structure may be seen in the use of recurrent timbral effects that function like motives. Like harmonic and motivic resources, the organization of pianistic effects into patterns and tendencies provides another dimension of structure, as does the interaction of pianistic effects with other parameters (helping, for example, to define formal partitions).

"Pour les arpèges composés"

In spite of their value as models for explication, pc reductions invariably diminish their objects, but in the case of "Pour les arpèges composés," a reduction that eliminates the composition's figuration strips it of virtually all its meaning. To be sure, there are motives (whose rhythmic contours are their chief characteristic) and rcs (most of them diatonic), but as resources they are woefully incomplete without the figurations into which they are disposed.

Example 12.3 presents a catalog of the etude's most important pc resources for mm. 1–25. Where possible the lower staff reduces the figuration to harmonies. Although motives may be discerned, they share a sameness and flatness of character in their use of alternating long and short durations that belies the rich surface which characterizes this piece. The chief distinction among the first three examples is found in the differing shapes of the figurations: example 12.3A consists of a circling arabesque figure (set in measured sixteenth-note sextuplets); example 12.3B traces an arc; and example 12.3C consists of a long, descending run (B and C are measured but more nearly resemble glissandi). The motive of example 12.3D associates with example 12.3C because in both instances the figurations share the same shape; example 12.3E associates with example 12.3B for the same reason; example 12.3F introduces a new shape that is inversely related to example 12.3C–D. Throughout the etude it is the rapid figurations that provide each formal unit with its identity. The form-defining role of the figurations rests on the fact that they effectively partition the piece into formal units in the same way that motives and themes normally do. The formal plan thus arises directly from the figurations themselves.

The Préludes I–II furnish many more illustrations. In "Voiles" the first and second sections are distinguished chiefly by their respective genera, but figuration also plays a prominent role in the identity of section 2, since its glissandi are an integral part of its pc materials (ex. 12.3G). The synthesis of sections 1 and 2 in section 3 combines the whole-tone genus and motives of section 1 with the

A. "Pour les arpèges composés"

B. "Pour les arpèges composés"

C. "Pour les arpèges composés"

D. "Pour les arpèges composés"

E. "Pour les arpèges composés"

F. "Pour les arpèges composés"

Example 12.3. Piano figurations

G. "Voiles"

H. "Voiles"

I. "Le vent dans la plaine"

J. "Brouillards"

K. "Et la lune descend sur le temple qui fut"

Example 12.3. *Continued*

figurative glissandi of section 2 (ex. 12.3H). "Le vent dans la plaine" employs a
striking figuration in mm. 28–34 (ex. 12.3I). This passage occurs near the piece's
midpoint and constitutes the C section of an approximately symmetrical rondo-
like design. The first six bars of "Ce qu'a vu le vent d'Ouest" are inconceivable
without the piano. Many of the motives in "La danse de Puck" are highly orna-
mented with idiomatic figurations (for example, m. 8). "Minstrels" is also highly
figured (mm. 1–8). "Feux d'artifice" resembles "Pour les arpèges composés" in
the way its figurations are wholly integrated into its pc materials.

Among the piano's special features is its ability to sustain sounds by means of the damper pedal while articulating new sounds.[21] In "Brouillards" (Préludes II), for example, the damper pedal permits each of the two initial eighth-note gestures to be heard as forms of the seven-note sonority that is seminal for the prelude's octatonic pc materials (set 7–31; see ex. 12.3J). "Et la lune descend sur le temple qui fut" (*Images* II) also depends on the damper pedal for projection of its complex and exotic sonorities (ex. 12.3K), as do "Pour les sonorités opposées" and "Pour les agréments" (both from Douze études II).

The piano works manifest their own form of structure through sonority. In orchestral works a precise balance in intensity between low and high registers and among families of instruments is absolutely necessary to render the complex sonorities perceptible. Similarly, careful attention to pedaling is essential to the piano music. The principal difficulty in transcription is that any loss of effect obtained through figuration means far more than a mere loss of detail; it means the loss of deeper relation as well.

A mature though relatively early work, *Prélude à "L'après-midi d'un faune"* does not exhibit the special instrumental effects and intricate interconnections with form that one finds in such late works as *La mer* and *Jeux*. Nonetheless, many traits are already in place, including enormous variety of instrumental mixtures and an instrumental texture in constant flux; prominent use of woodwinds that exploits their internal heterogeneity to produce many subtle timbres; relegation of the ubiquitous strings to an inconspicuous, supportive role; coordination of changes in orchestration to partitions in the formal plan; the use of timbral links across partitions to mitigate the effect of partitions; the introduction of new timbres just prior to partitions as means of signaling their approach; orchestration as a concomitant feature of repetition, where literal repetition is offset by changes in instrumentation while varied repetition is softened by consistent instrumentation; a predilection for the exotic and subtle (manifest in the use of antique cymbals and in the propensity for low dynamic levels); and the forging of intricate relations between orchestration and other parameters (manifest in the linkage between the flute, the motto-theme, and its transformations).

Later works show trends in handling timbre and orchestration similar to those in pitch materials and form. Debussy's technique increases in subtlety, imagination, and complexity as he continues to explore possibilities posed in early works, and integration increases among all compositional aspects. Orchestration serves expressive purposes in stage works such as *Pelléas et Mélisande*, *Le martyre de Saint-Sébastien*, and *Jeux*, and features of orchestration find cognates in the late chamber works.

THIRTEEN

METER

Meter is a refractory topic. It is popularly regarded as concerned with grouping beats into bars, subdividing beats into duple versus triple units, and identifying such features by means of bar lines and meter signatures. Meter does embrace these things, but they are merely obvious, external manifestations of something that is far more complex. This chapter deals with meter in its less obvious aspect, in particular its role as a medium for music's temporal structure.[1] We shall begin with some definitions.

RHYTHM

Musical events generate durations that span the distances between their beginnings. Rhythm refers to relations among these durations, and rhythms are the patterns formed by such relations. The rhythm of a motive, for example, is the pattern formed by the series of durations that span the intervals between the beginnings of the notes. Similarly, the rhythm of a bass line, clarinet part, chord changes in a harmonic progression, points of closure, instrument exits and entrances, or a collection of phrases—in short, of any series of events that conjoin to form a group—is the pattern of durations that span the beginnings of successive-adjacent pairs of those events.

The notions of duration, class, successive-adjacent, group, and pattern are all crucial to the concept of rhythm.

Durations are time spans. Though they may be represented in other ways, durations are expressed conventionally by symbols attached to notes and rests keyed to meter signatures and tempo indications. The frame of reference that gives meaning to durations is the temporal field[2] bounded by a composition's beginning and end.

Class refers to events of the same type (where "type" is whatever one declares it to be so long as its events generate durations). The notes that comprise a given theme, for example, constitute a class whose "type" is notes; similarly, the notes and rests of that theme constitute a class of events whose "type" is notes and rests. The rhythms of these two classes would be different.

Contiguous elements of a progressive series generate ordered relations that are successive and adjacent. For a series of notes ("a,b,c,d, . . ."), *successive-adjacent* refers to the ordered durations that arise from "a,b" followed by "b,c" and "c,d." It excludes durations that arise from "a,c" followed by "b,d" and "a,d" (since not all events in each pair are adjacent) and those formed by, respectively, "b,c," "b,a," and "c,d" (because although they arise from adjacencies, their order is not successive).

A *group* is a set of events of the same class. A *pattern* is the particular form manifest in the ordered durations of a group.

Two examples will illustrate: for the rhythm of a theme, the class consists of notes, the group includes the notes that make up the theme, the durations arise from the spans that separate the beginnings of both notes in each successive-adjacent pair of notes, and the pattern is the ordered series of durations; for the rhythm of orchestration, the class consists of changes in orchestration, the group is all such changes that occur within given boundaries, the durations are the spans that separate the initial moments of each successive-adjacent pair of changes, and the pattern is the ordered series these durations produce. Because all musical parameters consist of events disposed in time, all parameters generate rhythms. Even the partitions of formal plans engender higher-level rhythmical schemes.

METER

Meter is a special kind of rhythm whose durations are grouped by *accents* and whose events incorporate *pulse* as a class attribute. Pulse—a series of equal durations—can change often or infrequently (to establish a pulse requires a minimum of two durations) and can be explicit (embodied in a series of identical durations articulated in some way), implicit (concealed in a series of different durations, none of which serves as common denominator for the rest), or both by turns.

Metric Accents, Metric Groups

Accent imposes emphasis or stress upon an event that differentiates it from proximate and otherwise similar events. Accent occurs when one of two or more events is singled out in some way—"marked for consciousness," to use Cooper's and Meyer's phrase.[3] It is achieved by the attachment of a prominent feature to an event that its neighbors (of the same class) lack.

Accents are conventionally classified into three types: dynamic, agogic, and tonic. Any musical parameter may serve as a medium for emphasis. Examples include timbre (stress achieved by means of a special instrumental color or effect), density of texture (stress through an increase in the number of concurrent sonic events), articulation (emphasis effected by an increase in the number of concurrent notes struck), or tonal prolongation (emphasis accorded one pitch because of its superior structural role vis-à-vis other, proximate pitches). In other words, any feature that serves to intensify a particular musical event may impart accent. Construed as extensions of the three conventional categories, timbre, density of texture, and articulation are forms of dynamic accent, while tonal prolongation is a subtle form of agogic accent that relies on perception and cognition of one event's relation to other, subordinate events which substitute for it and, by implication, extend its duration to encompass theirs as well.

Compound accents combine several types of emphasis at once. All types of accents use mechanisms of differentiation that draw attention to one among a field of moments by marking it as somehow more significant. Repetition and reprise (literal or varied) aid differentiation by enlisting the listener's power of recall, which recognizes an accent that resembles one heard previously.

Accents may occur as moments (analogous to points on a line), or they may require duration (analogous to portions of a line); agogic accents require duration, as do compound accents.

Since we cannot tell whether an accent has occurred until we have compared it to surrounding, unaccented events, we may assume that most accents are identified only in retrospect. An exception would be accents that occur within repetitions; repetition allows us to predict such accents since association of one event with a previous event includes a recognition of all its characteristics, including its accents.

To be metric, events must cluster about successive-adjacent accents of comparable class. Metric accents define metric units, one accent per unit.

A metric accent may occur at the beginning, middle, or end of a metric unit, depending upon whether the unit begins with an anacrusis and whether the anacrusis consumes all or only a portion of the unaccented durations.[4] Beginning-accented (that is, nonanacrustic) units have their initiating boundaries defined explicitly by the moment of accent; their closing boundaries are defined implicitly since a new unit cannot commence unless the previous unit has concluded. For interior-accented (short-anacrustic) and end-accented (long-anacrustic) units, both boundaries are implicit, and each must occur at the moment that immediately precedes the next anacrusis.

Metric units may overlap if at least one of them is familiar (that is, a reiterated metric unit whose accent and boundaries resemble a similar unit heard previously). Overlap occurs where the familiar unit appears first and the next unit's accent or anacrusis occurs prior to the first unit's expected conclusion; overlap can also result if the familiar unit appears second and its accent or anacrusis (defined by association with a similar unit heard previously) coincides with that of a prior, anacrustic unit.

Metric Hierarchy and Other Aspects of Meter

Metric units are usually disposed across a hierarchy of levels. A single unit on one level may consist of a group of lower-level units, and it may combine with other units on its own level to form a higher-level unit. Hierarchic metric levels are tied partly (but only partly) to relative durations (lower levels usually consist of shorter metric units, higher levels usually consist of longer units), but the relative weight of metric accents is the chief criterion: units grouped about stronger accents are assigned to higher levels; weaker accents are assigned to lower levels.[5]

A *metric group* is a conjunct series of two or more metric units whose accents are of comparable class (except that the first accent may belong to a higher metric level). Metric groups are bounded by metric units whose accents belong to higher or lower metric levels, or by a composition's beginning or end. A metric group on one level may constitute a metric unit at a higher level.

A *metric level* consists of at least one metric group. A metric group, for example, whose units are characterized by accents of a particular type may form a unit within a particular metric level. Weaker accents (therefore of a different class) may subdivide that metric unit into lower-level units. Verification of meters and metric levels requires clear comparability of units whose accents constitute a class. Many of the explanatory notes that accompany the analytical examples below address features of comparability that bind together units within a given metric level.

Among the three fundamental types of accent, relative strength correlates with immediacy and ease of perception. Dynamic accents tend to be stronger than other types because their perception derives directly from sensation, with a minimum of reflection and comparison. This is because duration is not a salient characteristic of dynamic accent, and so the event itself requires no time period for its experience. Also, we need only compare dynamic accents to the events immediately adjacent in order to evaluate them. Agogic accents are less readily perceptible, therefore weaker, because they require time and a comparison with surrounding events (of briefer duration) for perception and verification; thus, they rely for their apprehension as much or more on cognition as on sensation. Tonic accents are weaker still, since they require not only duration and comparison with adjacent events, but also reference to the disposition of pitches (which entails considerations external to the notion of accent itself).

In some instances, other features may upset this list of priorities. Chief among them is the fact that each type of accent may range from mild to strong; a strong agogic accent, for example, may outweigh a mild dynamic accent: assigning accents to hierarchic levels entails making judgments.

In general, tonic accents denote lower hierarchic levels, dynamic accents denote higher levels, and agogic accents denote intermediate levels. Within a given type, mild accents are assigned to lower levels. Compound accents are assigned to levels according to each type's degree of strength, the number of types, and the types themselves.

A given metric level may contain nonmetric accents. The analyses that follow ignore nonmetric accents.

Meter is fluctuant, in that the durations of metric units can (and usually do) change during the course of a composition.

In common-practice tonal music, bar lines usually correlate with metric units on at least one hierarchic level and provide clues for the determination of meter; nonetheless, bar lines do not in themselves constitute or define metric units. Likewise, metric units both transcend and partition bars, motives, themes, and their rhythms. In posttonal music, bar lines and metric units are more likely to conflict. In meter as in other things, Debussy stands with one foot in each era: metric units and bar lines often exhibit a high degree of relation (especially in the early diatonic works), but in later pieces that employ the pc set genera, meter's less predictable manifestations are reflected in more flexible barring and more frequent changes in meter signatures.

Metric analysis entails identification of metric units and assignment of their accents to appropriate hierarchic levels. On any level, conjunct series of metric units group themselves within the boundaries defined by metric accents of the next-higher level. The figures below note the duration of each metric unit using integers where the duration of the smallest metric unit = 1. The graphs display the resultant metric levels and their interaction.

Not all rhythms are metric (since not all rhythmic groups are defined by accent), but all meters are rhythmic (since they consist of groups of durations in the form of successive-adjacent metric units that contain accents of comparable class). Most rhythmic groups incorporate or occur within metric schemes.

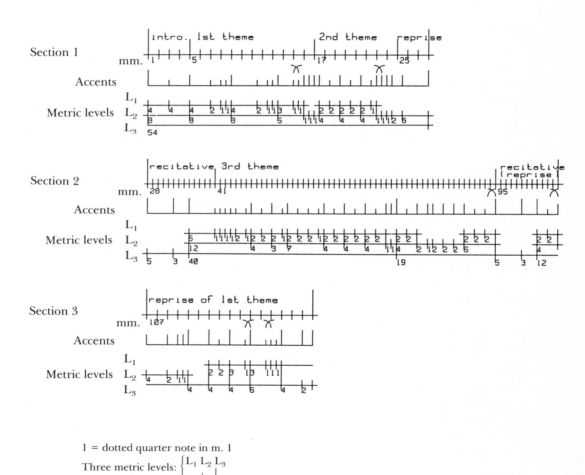

Figure 13.1. Metric groups and hierarchy in the String quartet, III

METRIC STRUCTURE IN SELECTED WORKS

The first two pieces illustrate aspects of meter in some detail; the remaining brief examples are drawn from a number of works throughout Debussy's oeuvre.[6]

String Quartet, III

The third movement of the quartet employs a conventional ternary design with asymmetrical proportions (figure 13.1 displays the formal plan section by section), and both features are replicated at a lower level in the tripartite subdivisions of sections 1 and 2. The movement lends itself readily to more detailed formal analysis disclosing phrases, periods, episodes, and transitions—as does the entire quartet, which is the last of Debussy's works to subscribe so blatantly to conventional formal principles.

Several partitions coincide with the Golden Section. To cite but two: the overall Golden Section occurs at m. 76, coincidental with the movement's point of maximum intensity achieved through successive-attack activity (within the rapid figuration), loudness, sonorous density, and placement of the theme in the extreme upper register. This is marked by the return to the diatonic genus following the movement's only whole-tone passage. At a lower level, the Golden Section of section 1 coincides with the beginning of the second theme (m. 17).

The metric scheme encompasses three clear levels of hierarchy. Level 1 (L_1), closest to the surface, is made up of units whose compound accents consist of agogic stress and increased sonorous density. These are light accents, noticeable nonetheless in the context of surrounding events. The first occurs at m. 2, where agogic stress is reinforced by thicker texture (ex. 13.1A). This metric unit is anacrustic (since the accent occurs after seven eighth notes).

Example 13.1. Classes of metric accent in the String Quartet, III

The intermediate metric level (L_2) comprises units whose stronger accents combine agogic stress with dynamic accent in the form of simultaneous articulations. The first L_2 accent occurs at m. 5/beat 1: three (of four) voices feature attacks; also, second violin mixes a range of durations in mm. 5–8 of which the first is by far the longest (ex. 13.1B).

Metric accents at the highest level (L_3) combine exaggerated agogic emphasis with greatly increased sonorous density (ex. 13.1C; this example is dramatic both for its extended anacrusis of four bars and for its drastic increase in sonorous weight). A sample of L_1 accents includes those of m. 7/beat 4 (weak compared to m. 5 because of diminished agogic stress), m. 8/beat 2, m. 8/beat 5, m. 11/beat 1, m. 12/beat 1, m. 12/beat 4, and, in section 2, m. 41/beat 3.5, m. 42/beat 3.5, m. 43/beat 1, m. 44/beat 1, m. 45/beat 1, and m. 47/beat 1.[7] Intermediate (L_2) accents may be found at m. 9/beat 1 (four simultaneous articulations plus agogic stress in the second violin and cello), m. 13/beat 1, m. 15/beat 5, m. 16/beat 2, m. 16/beat 5, m. 17/beat 1, and, in section 2, m. 48/beat 1, m. 53/beat 1, m. 55/beat 1, and m. 62/beat 1, to cite but a few.[8] L_3 accents are sparse, but they define several metric units such as those that begin at mm. 28, 33, and 36 (all anacrustic), and mm. 76 and 95 (anacrustic).[9]

Durations of metric units are indicated in figure 13.1 using integers (dotted quarter note = 1). Each metric level is assigned its own horizontal axis and is labeled L_1, L_2, or L_3. Vertical lines that intersect two or more metric levels indicate metric groups. In general, factors of two relate the durations both within and between levels, though there are numerous exceptions (such as the units of 3, 5, 7, and 19 durations found at mm. 13, 22, 28, 41, 52, 55, 76, 95, 100, 115 and 117). Most anomalies result from overlapping, at mm. 14–15, 22, 91, 105, 116, and 118.

An important feature is the tendency towards shorter durations over the course of a given metric group; L_1 groups 2 through 4, for example, exhibit durations (4–2–1–1) and (3–1–1). This tendency is manifest at all metric levels and in almost all metric groups, often complicated by bifurcation, wherein the tendency is thwarted momentarily by a longer duration, after which the tendency towards shorter durations resumes. See, for example, the second L_2 metric group whose durations are (12–4–3–7–4–4–4–4–1–1), and the highest-level succession (54–5–3–*40*–19–5–3–*12*–4–4–4–6–4–2).

There are two exceptions to the trend towards shorter durations: the initial and third L_2 series (8–8–8–5–1–1–1–4–4–3–1–1–*1*–2–6 and 4–2–*1*–2–2–2–6) manifest an opposite tendency. Soon I will suggest a reason for these anomalies.

The L_1 metric units are longer in the outer portions of the movement than in the middle, a trait that is reflected in the meter signature change to 6/8 for mm. 28–106, and contributes on the musical surface to a sense of acceleration towards the movement's interior. This feature is not found at the L_2 and L_3 levels, however, since it would prevent them—especially L_3—from manifesting the prevailing tendency towards shorter durations.

Metric relations interact with formal organization in ways that are mutually supportive. The boundaries of metric groups often coincide with important partitions in the formal plan (though there is not always a direct correlation between hierarchic levels of form and meter). There are also places where it appears that one parameter has influenced another: the reprise at m. 25, for example, coincides with one of those anomalous countertendency metric series of increased durations (. . . $1-1-1-2-6$ in L_2); the reprise in section 2 (m. 95) is preceded by another ($4-2-1-2-2-2-6$). Yet another anomalous series appears at mm. 41–47 ($1-1-1-1-2-1$); this passage serves as an introduction to the third theme, which actually enters at m. 48. At mm. 103–06 there is an unusual overlap of a higher-level metric boundary with a main formal partition, which softens the effect of both junctures and contributes a degree of ambiguity to their definition.

There are two instances where the shortening of L_2 metric durations is especially drastic: m. 16, where durations are reduced from 8 to 5 to 1; and m. 74, where the reduction is from 7 to 4 to 1. Both occur just prior to the points of Golden Section mentioned above.

Metric durations in the quartet convey definite effects of stability, acceleration, or deceleration, which in turn draw our attention to other features, such as form.

"Les ingénus" (*Fêtes galantes* II)

Composed before the end of June 1904,[10] the second series of *Fêtes galantes* features three poems of Paul Verlaine that share nostalgic humor as a common trait, which is emphasized in Debussy's settings. Girl watching, the tongue-in-cheek subject of "Les ingénus," is recalled by an unnamed speaker (by implication from a vantage point some years' distant).

The poem's three stanzas each contain four lines; the second stanza expresses the most active mood and is the focus towards which the first converges and from which the third recedes. The form of the musical setting is tied closely to that of the poem: major partitions separate each pair of stanzas, which are surrounded by introductions and codettas; phrases set each line (though the lengths vary considerably). A general formal plan keyed to the disposition of stanzas and lines appears in figure 13.2.

Like the quartet movement, the song's metric organization reveals three classes of accent disposed across three hierarchic levels: L_1 consists chiefly of light tonic accents (ex. 13.2A); L_2 relies more on dynamic accent (though low dynamic levels are the norm) achieved by the addition of voices and doublings (normally five or six notes are struck at once; see ex. 13.2B); L_3 accents (there are only three) combine tonic or agogic stress with dynamic accent (ex. 13.2C). L_1 and L_2 accents are sometimes anacrustic but more often not; L_3 accents are always anacrustic.

The metric units of "Les ingénus" feature durations that alternate factors of three and two; the former predominate (they open and close the song), while the latter are confined to a portion of the song's interior, except for mm. 42–45 (to which we will return).

Metric units defined by L_1 accents dominate the musical surface of the song's first half but give way to L_2 accents in the second. Up to m. 35, the durations of metric units tend to be stable; as a consequence, deviations are quite noticeable.

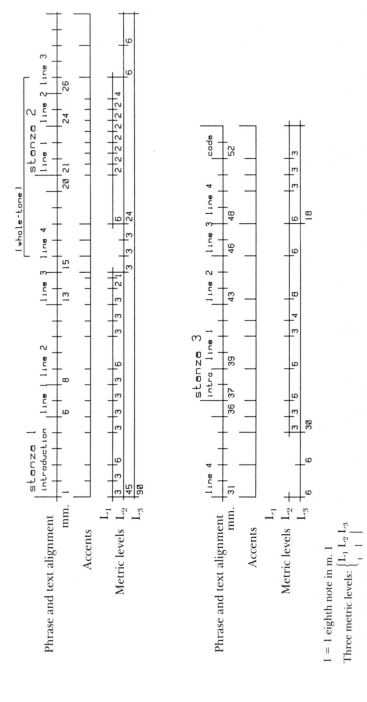

Figure 13.2. "Les ingénus"

Example 13.2. Classes of metric accent in "Les ingénus"

For examples, see mm. 14 and 21 (which feature changes from factors of 3 to 2) and m. 27 (where the durations closest to the surface—first L_2 and then L_3—are suddenly longer). The tendency within metric groups towards shorter durations is evident, but here also it is not always manifest in a consistent progression. It emerges, instead, in series of cycles that proceed from longer durations to shorter ones, and in the tendency, on all three metric levels, for longer durations to appear closer to the beginning of the song rather than towards the end.

Throughout "Les ingénus" there is a strong correlation among metric organization, the poem's content, and its form in Debussy's setting. The speaker's mood and train of thought point to the second stanza as a psychological climax and turning point. The first two stanzas pursue a single idea as the speaker recalls (with growing excitement) his idle voyeurism, while the third stanza denotes a shift of attention as he recalls strolling with the girls who were the object of his glances. The third stanza recedes from the tension that builds throughout the first two.

The poem's most dramatic moment (stanza 2, line 4) is manifest in a curve of increasing musical intensity that peaks at mm. 31–36 (which combine extremes of register, sonorous density, successive-attack activity, and maximum loudness). This is also the location of three (of four) L_3 metric accents. The moment is prepared by a shift in metric durations, coincidental with the beginning of stanza 2, from factors of 3 to 2 and back again towards the end—a shift that conveys a sense of acceleration congruent with the sense of mounting excitement in this stanza.[11]

The crucial word in the last line of stanza 1—"Caught!" (in the act of staring)[12]—is marked, at m. 16, in the pc set materials by the song's only whole-tone passage, perhaps used here (in view of the whole-tone genus's consistent association with mystery and death in other works) to exaggerate the sense of excitement over the "forbidden pleasure" of voyeurism.[13] It is prepared in the preceding metric group by a series of progressively shorter durations (6–3–3–3–2–1—the only occurrence of a metric unit whose duration = 1) and is marked by the first L_2 accent at m. 16.

The dramatically longer durations of metric units in mm. 27–30 (spans of 6 compared to spans of 2 in mm. 21–25) coincide with the speaker's last, risqué recollection: "And there were sudden flashes of white necks."[14] Those of mm. 42–44 (4 and 8) underscore the subject of the second line of stanza 3 (which serves as the focus towards which stanzas 1 and 2 point): "*These beauties*, leaning dreamily on our arms . . ."[15] [emphasis mine].

There are many correspondences among metric grouping, formal partitions, and text. In general, the boundaries of stanzas and lines correlate to those of formal units defined by phrases, mutations, modulations, and so forth. The same points usually serve as boundaries of metric groups and as junctures for changes in the durations of metric units.

Overall, metric fluctuations are more fluid and less predictable than in the quartet movement. In part this reflects Debussy's maturity and experience by 1904 compared with 1893, but it also reflects his concern for the demands of expression imposed by the text and his conviction that music must support the text unobtrusively.

Together the quartet movement and the song illustrate the range of metric treatment in Debussy's music, in which songs and stage works evince more flexibility in the service of extramusical features, while absolute music reveals clearer schemes of pattern and tendency that may be experienced for their own sake.

The following excerpts taken from the beginnings of a number of later works provide opportunities to explore other aspects of metric organization. They include the first five Préludes from Book I, the *Images pour orchestre* and the Sonata for flute, viola, and harp. Refer to example 13.3 and figure 13.3, which illustrate accents for the excerpts and display their metric schemes. Accent classes are identified in example 13.3 as follows: sites of metric accents are marked with accents; single accent signs represent lowest-level accents, double-accent signs (stacked vertically) represent the next-higher level, and so forth.

"Danseuses de Delphes," mm. 1–5

Two levels of metric hierarchy characterize mm. 1–5 (ex. 13.3A, fig. 13.3A): L_1 embraces metric units whose dynamic accents consist of simultaneous attacks, usually coupled with agogic emphasis on initial notes (for example, mm. 1–2, inner voice, and mm. 3–4, upper voice); L_2 adds tonic accents to the dynamic accents of L_1 (those in mm. 1–4/beat 2 are anacrustic).

The nonanacrustic accent of m. 4/beat 2.5 causes an overlap that coincides with a conflict between acceleration in the pacing of L_1 units (towards shorter

A. "Danseuses de Delphes"

B. "Voiles"

C. "Le vent dans la plaine"

D. "Les sons et les parfums tournent dans l'air du soir"

Example 13.3. Metric accents in selected examples

E. "Les collines d'Anacapri"

F. "Gigues"

G. "Ibéria"

Example 13.3. *Continued*

H. "Rondes de printemps"

I. Sonata for flute, viola, and harp, I

Example 13.3. *Continued*

A. "Danseuses de Delphes"

B. "Voiles"

C. "Le vent dans la plaine"

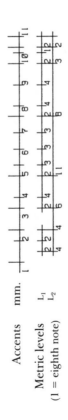

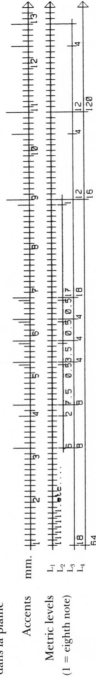

Figure 13.3. Metric groups in selected instrumental pieces

D. "Les sons et les parfums tournent dans l'air du soir"

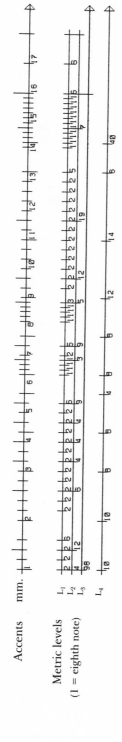

E. "Les collines d'Anacapri"

F. "Gigues"

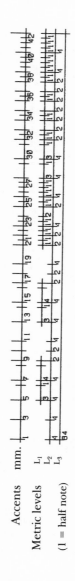

G. "Par les rues et par les chemins"

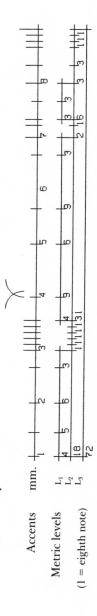

H. "Rondes de printemps"

I. Sonata for flute, viola, and harp

durations) and the deceleration within L_2 units (towards longer durations). It is this deeper metric scheme, and not the surface rhythms, that conveys a sense both of acceleration and rhythmic disjunction at m. 4, and accounts for the bar of 4/4.

"Voiles," mm. 1–10

Of the two levels defined here, the accents of L_1 are agogic (eighth notes or longer), while the accents of L_2 add tonic stress to agogic (ex. 13.3B, fig. 13.3B). An important effect is the "layering" of thematic-motivic materials, which appear in separate registers without a fixed vertical alignment (that is, their alignment changes in subsequent presentations). The fluctuations of durations across metric units in both levels are carefully calculated and contribute much to the overall effect of objects floating slowly by at slightly different speeds.

"Le vent dans la plaine," mm. 1–12

These twelve bars reveal four metric levels (ex. 13.3C, fig. 13.3C): the very weak accents of L_1 consist of mild dynamic accent accorded $b\flat^1$ in the ostinato (L_1 accents are implicit wherever the sextuplet ostinato occurs—throughout mm. 1–8, for example, but not in mm. 9–12); the accents of L_2 (m. 4) are also weak, but add tonic emphasis to the dynamic of L_1; the dynamic accents of L_3 are stronger (at the peaks of crescendos that terminate in $d\flat^1$); the accents of L_4 (m. 9) add tonic emphasis to the dynamic accent effected by increased sonorous density.

The lowest metric level is monotonously stable and serves as a measure of metric relations at higher levels. L_2 consistently alternates long and short durations and is sometimes absent (it first enters at m. 3 and exits at m. 9, where it yields to L_3 accents).[16] L_3 groups exhibit a tendency towards shortening, seen in the durations of the first three groups (*18–8–8–4–4–4–(18), 12–4, 12–4*). L_4 accents are sparse and widely separated. Most metric activity takes place within the first three levels.

"Le vent dans la plaine" derives its metric complexity from its multiplicity of levels whose tendencies contradict one another, and from the frequent exits and entrances of lower levels.

"Les sons et les parfums tournent dans l'air du soir," mm. 1–18

These eighteen bars encompass four levels of metric accent (ex. 13.3D, and fig. 13.3D): three are linked by a common hierarchy (L_1, L_2, L_3); one is independent (labeled L_4). L_1 consists of weak dynamic accents achieved by simultaneous attacks. L_2 adds tonic accent to the dynamic accents of L_1 (sometimes reinforced by agogic, as in the $c\sharp^3$ in m. 2). Only one L_3 accent occurs in this passage (at m. 16), and it is achieved by the addition of marked agogic stress to the tonic and dynamic emphasis associated with levels L_1 and L_2. The distinctions between L_1, L_2 and L_3 accents are differences of accretion. L_4 does not participate in this hierarchy but constitutes a separate, independent metric stream that is confined to its own, low register; its accents are dynamic and consist of the reiterated A_2's in the bass.

Metric durations are fluctuant at all levels within both streams, and they follow increase-decrease cycles of durations. The L_1 cycles are replicated on L_2, as may be seen by comparing the durations for each level, which change in close proximity to each other; that is, a change to longer durations in L_1 usually coincides approximately with a similar change in L_2. (In mm. 1–3, for example, L_1 exhibits the series 2–2, 2–6–2–2, 2–2–2, 2–2, while L_2 unfolds the cycle 4–12–6–4.) The durations of L_4 exhibit similar cycles, though they are not aligned with those of L_1 and L_2. The discrepancy between L_4 and the other metric levels—they align only once during the first seventeen bars, at m. 13/beat 2, and then only L_4 and L_1 are involved—creates a complex rhythmic counterpoint whose overall effect is fluid and irregular.

"Les collines d'Anacapri," mm. 1–11

This excerpt's L_1 metric units (ex. 13.3E, fig. 13.3E) consist, variously, of anacrustic tonic accents (as in mm. 5 and 11) or weak dynamic accents (as on beats 1 and 2 of mm. 8–9). That these accents involve different classes of events raises the question of their assignment to the same metric level. In fact, the lowest metric level that is consistently present in this passage (and throughout the piece) is that designated L_2. It is more appropriate to consider L_1 a sublevel which subdivides the units of L_2.[17] As such, the L_1 accents of mm. 5 and 8–9 are of comparable weight but do not belong to the same continuum of metric groups. The accents of L_2 consist of stronger tonic accents supported by dynamic accents that result from simultaneous attacks (as in mm. 3, and in the offbeats of mm. 6–10), while the accents of L_3 add agogic stress to a more marked dynamic emphasis. This excerpt's sole L_4 accent (m. 10) is anacrustic and embraces the agogic-dynamic stress of the bass register's half notes, as well as the tonic-dynamic emphasis that falls on the second eighth of beat 1.

This piece abounds in anacrustic accents: all L_3 accents are anacrustic (with especially long anacruses in mm. 1 and 6), as is the lone L_4 accent; some L_2 accents are also anacrustic (see m. 3). The series of anacrustic accents of progressively higher metric levels—the L_1 accent of m. 5, the accent of m. 6, the L_4 accent of m. 10—imparts a sense of vitality comparable to (though different from) that wrought by acceleration in the pacing of events.

The foreground metric groups of L_2 exhibit a tendency towards shorter durations throughout this excerpt,[18] and all metric levels feature marked changes in durations that convey a sense of impulsive fluctuation between acceleration and deceleration.

The foregoing examples reveal three general categories of metric structures: highly fluctuant schemes, which exhibit changes in both durations of metric units, and exits and entrances of metric levels; schemes that consistently maintain a regular series of durations on at least one level and whose metric levels remain more or less continuously present; and schemes that incorporate a separate metric stream which is independent of the composition's metric hierarchy and establishes a metric counterpoint to the other, unified levels. Superimposition of metric streams and overlapping of metric units frequently complicate metric structures.

Excerpts from the *Images pour orchestre*

Completed in 1912,[19] the *Images pour orchestre* is Debussy's last purely orchestral work. The stylistic path begun with *Prélude à "L'après-midi d'un faune"* was advanced in *Nocturnes* and explored further in *La mer,* three works united by a continuity imposed through an evolving technique based on several important compositional principles (including use of the pc set genera, nontraditional morphological form types that use Golden Section proportions, and ever-larger instrumentations chosen less for sonorous weight than for diversity of timbres). Each work applies these with increased skill, subtlety, and complexity. By comparison, the orchestral *Images* takes a turn onto a new path: its formal boundaries are obvious (in contrast to the seamlessness of *La mer*); it is more tuneful, its themes and motives less fragmentary, more clear-cut, and possessed of rhythmic patterns more sharply distinct than those of the *Nocturnes* or *La mer;* and the orchestra is frequently used to produce programmatic effects, especially in *Ibéria.* In other important ways *Images* further explores paradigms already established. It employs the pc set genera, for example, and its orchestration uses strings as background and woodwinds as a source of constant diversity within their relatively narrow range of timbres. Although the brass (especially trumpets and trombones) are exploited more in *Images* than in previous works, they are still used primarily for bright spots of color against a timbral field comprised of strings and woodwinds.

In its metric structures the *Images* reveals techniques that are not seen in other works. We shall briefly examine excerpts taken from the beginnings of each of the three pieces that comprise the set, "Gigues," "Ibéria," and "Rondes de printemps."

"Gigues," mm. 1–42. This passage comprises the entire introduction (ex. 13.3F, fig. 13.3F). There are three metric levels: L_2 is distinguished by mild dynamic accents (the attacks, for example, at the beginnings of mm. 1, 3, and 5); L_1 is a sublevel whose light accents combine dynamic stress (mm. 6 and 8—attacks in one or two voices only) with agogic emphasis (the markedly longer durations, as in mm. 21ff); the sole L_3 accent in these bars (m. 43) is dynamic and immediately follows the partition between the introduction and the first large section. Tonal prolongations sometimes reinforce L_2 accents, as at mm. 21–38 (prolongations for those measures shown on the subimposed auxiliary treble staff).

Metric overlaps at mm. 28, 32, and 39 coincide with phrase elisions and heighten the disruptive effect of dramatic changes in the character of thematic-motivic material.

Factors of two predominate, especially among the durations of L_2. Within each level the effect of changes in durations is to project a sense of a lethargic beginning that accelerates gradually to the main, brisk tempo of m. 43. Fluctuations in the durations of metric units at lowest and intermediate levels align with formal partitions at the level of phrases and motives.

Meter in this excerpt differs from the Préludes excerpts in the long delay of the first L_3 accent (the entire introduction actively engages only two metric levels), a delay that is due perhaps to the large scale of the piece, which accommodates a slower pacing of high-level events.

"Ibéria" I: "Par les rues et par les chemins," mm. 1–15. This excerpt from the first main section of "Ibéria" begins with an L_3 accent (ex. 13.3G, fig. 13.3G), followed quickly by another at m. 3. The next L_3 accent occurs after eleven bars, followed by another after only two bars. These heavy, erratically spaced accents constitute an unusual beginning; it is far more common to commence with lower-level accents that build towards higher levels.

Durations of metric units are fluctuant in both L_2 and L_3 and tend to increase in length. In contrast, the durations of L_1 metric units are monotonously regular; their stability provides a bland metric background that heightens the drama of changes in higher metric levels.

L_1 metric units group themselves about weak dynamic accents caused by unison attacks in a few voices; L_2 accents add agogic stress (seen in the bass, not illustrated) to slightly heavier dynamic stress (more voices); L_3 accents combine heavy dynamic with strong tonic emphasis.

"Rondes de printemps," mm. 1–21. This excerpt, which encompasses the movement's introduction, reveals three metric levels (ex. 13.3H, fig. 13.3H). As in "Gigues," L_2 constitutes the true metric foreground for which L_1 serves as a sublevel that exits and re-enters periodically. L_2 consists primarily of dynamic accents (simultaneous attacks), reinforced by tonic emphasis (see mm. 1 and 9), L_1 of weak dynamic accents (simultaneous attacks in a few voice). The accents of L_3 are dynamic, achieved by increases in sonorous density often intensified by agogic stress (see mm. 10 and 17). The first two L_3 accents (mm. 10 and 12) are conspicuously anacrustic, a feature replicated by several L_1 accents as well (see mm. 14 and 21).

The severe regularity of durations within lower metric levels during the movement's initial bars contrasts sharply with the fluctuant durations that follow at m. 10. Similarly, the movement's remainder contrasts stable and fluctuant passages.

Sonata for Flute, Viola, and Harp, I, mm. 1–8. These first eight bars encompass the movement's first large section (ex. 13.3I, fig. 13.3I). They expose a rich metric content on three levels, which L_2 serves as the metric foreground (L_1, which exits occasionally, is merely a sublevel). L_1 units are defined by weak tonic accents, usually anacrustic, L_2 units by slightly stronger dynamic accents, usually nonanacrustic, and L_3 accents by markedly stronger dynamic accents reinforced by agogic emphasis, usually anacrustic. Bar 4 is the site of a metric overlap caused by the dichotomous e^2, whose duration serves as terminus for the L_2 unit that begins on the sixth eighth note of m. 3, and also as initial note of the anacrustic L_1 unit whose accent occurs on the seventh eighth note of m. 4. The timbre addition that occurs with the viola's entrance on e^2 highlights the metric overlap through its own overlap with the flute.

The metric structure poses difficulties for performers who do not understand it, owing chiefly to the complex effect of anacrustic versus nonanacrustic accents disposed on different metric levels. The accents both partition and serve as goals, and they hold the key to a convincing performance, which will convey a sense of hesitation—of stopping and starting—throughout this movement due to the constantly varying durations of its metric units at all levels and to the conflict between nonanacrustic (initiating) and anacrustic (terminating) accents.

The extent to which the treatment of meter resembles that of other parameters attests to the composer's instinctive concern to create comprehensive structural contexts suited to the expression of his musical ideas.

Debussy's attention to detail in his notation, everywhere remarkable, is no less so with regard to metric accents. In "Le vent dans la plaine," for example, the opening ostinato consists of sixteenth-note sextuplets whose initial notes are double-stemmed as unison eighths and sixteenths. This notation directs the performer to impose upon the doubled notes a very subtle dynamic emphasis.

Debussy's superimposition of separate metric streams unlinked by a common hierarchy is analogous, in practice and effect, to his layering of contrasting pc set genera. In both cases, the medium of separation is register, which allows the listener to readily distinguish either stream and to experience the effect of their conflicting interaction as it occurs, not as a *point* in time, but as a *segment,* a kind of experience that yields a rich harvest of conflict, resolution and contrapuntal interaction.

The relegation to a background role of one metric level (usually the lowest) by assigning equal durations to its units has an analogy in the domain of orchestration, where the constant presence of a given instrument or family (usually strings) consigns that timbre to a background role.

Metric organization exhibits both pattern and dynamism, and thereby adds its contribution to morphological and kinetic form. In general, its patterns and tendencies reinforce those in other domains, but sometimes they do not; when they conflict, they produce a complex counterpoint comparable to that discussed in connection with similar phenomena involving other parameters.

A considerable range and variety of metric organization characterizes Debussy's music, as does a tendency throughout his oeuvre towards greater subtlety of effect and flexibility (in shifting durations and the use of hierarchic levels which may freely exit and re-enter). These trends surface first in vocal and dramatic works.

Those pieces that exhibit regularity and stability in durations on lower metric levels (in particular the Spanish-style works like "Ibéria") usually reveal complexities at higher metric levels, including impulsive exits and entrances of hierarchic levels, dramatic changes in higher-level durations, and metric overlaps.

Tendencies observed in the pacing of changes for other parameters are found in the realm of meter as well. For example, the outer portions of pieces are likely to be paced moderately, in terms of the durations of metric units, while the interior is often faster paced. There are, of course, exceptions, such as "Pour les octaves" (Douze études II), whose outer sections are quite rapidly paced while the interior is much slower moving, but they usually occur in ternary designs where the contrasting middle section is sharply partitioned off from the outer sections.

FOURTEEN
REGISTER

Despite general acknowledgment of its importance in Debussy's compositional process, register as a source of structure has received little attention in the literature.[1] This chapter focuses on register as a parameter that is both distinct from and complementary to pitch class. It proceeds from the assumption that register does serve as a source of structure in Debussy's music, both independent of and in conjunction with other elements. It concentrates on five features: a tendency to fix themes in specific transpositions and octave registers, and then move them to other registers for special effects; a progressive tendency towards expansion of register compasses, which often is manifest on several hierarchic levels at once; the interaction of register with other aspects of structure; the manipulation of register for expressive purposes in music with texts; and the use of register to separate disparate elements that belong to other domains.

We will consider two aspects of register: the variable distance ("register span" or "register compass") between highest and lowest sounding pitches, and the variable placement of pitch content ("mean placement") about a pitch axis that lies equidistant from both extremities of the register span. On the examples, register spans in semitones are identified under the lower notes by integers placed in brackets. Mean placements are identified by pitches notated as filled noteheads enclosed in parentheses; for example, given highest and lowest pitches, respectively, of c^2 and c, the register span is [24] and the mean placement is c^1.

THEMES FIXED IN SPECIFIC TRANSPOSITIONS AND REGISTERS

Debussy tends to fix themes in specific transpositions and octave registers for subsequent reassignment elsewhere (often to fulfill formal imperatives). The practice is especially prevalent in his solo piano compositions, perhaps because this genre offers less in the way of sonorous contrast than do chamber and orchestral music, and because manipulation of a motive's register assignment provides a compensation. The Préludes I and II offer numerous examples.

The most common treatment fixes and maintains a theme or motive in a given transposition or octave register until its last presentation, near the end of the piece, where it is reassigned to a register one or two octaves higher. "Des pas sur la neige" (Préludes I) illustrates this type (ex. 14.1A). Its ostinato appears at four locations, including mm. 1, 8, 16, and 26, always in the original transposition and octave register; the fifth and final appearance (m. 32) sounds two octaves higher.

"La fille aux cheveux de lin" (Préludes I) places its opening theme on d♭2, restates it in the same register at m. 8, but sets its reprise (m. 28) an octave higher, on d♭3 (see ex. 14.1B).[2] The reprise's C♭ major chord is spread across a much wider register compass and sounds an octave lower than in m. 2.[3] We shall return to this feature.

"Voiles" (Préludes I) embodies a slightly different principle (ex. 14.1C). Instead of establishing a single transposition or octave register, its ascending step-

Example 14.1. Register assignments for motives and themes in selected examples

E. "Feuilles mortes"

[23]   [27]   [35]

F. "Les sons et les parfums tournent dans l'air du soir"

[43]   [27]

G. "Le vent dans la plaine"

[13]   [14]   7

[14]   [13]

[14]   [13]   [22]

H. First "Arabesque"

[36]   [48]

Example 14.1. *Continued*

I. "Pour les arpèges composés"

J. String Quartet, III

K. "Pour ce que Plaisance est morte"

Example 14.1. *Continued*

wise gesture of m. 7 is raised an octave in an interim reappearance at m. 15, and in its last appearance at m. 50 it is placed higher by one more octave.

"La danse de Puck" (Préludes I) exposes yet another variant. Of its initial theme's four statements, the first and third occur in the same register (f^1 at mm. 1 and 71), whereas the second and last are set an octave higher (f^2 at mm. 64 and 87; see ex. 14.1D).

"Feuilles mortes" (Préludes II) immediately repeats (and thereby fixes) the first bar of its opening gesture whose initial note is $f\sharp^2$ (ex. 14.1E). Its reappearance at m. 15 is truncated and occurs one octave lower; the final reprise at m. 41 is set on $f\sharp^3$, one octave above the original register.

What links all of these examples is the higher register assignment of a prominent motive's final appearance—usually one octave higher. Often the original assignment is preserved until the last appearance, though it is not unusual for the theme to migrate within the piece.

Octave adjustments are not the only kinds of register reassignments; sometimes themes are transposed by other intervals. In "Les sons et les parfums tournent dans l'air du soir" (Préludes I), the initial and recurrent gesture of m. 1 is rearticulated many times with e^2 as the initial pitch, but the last time, at m. 44, it sounds a M6 higher (ex. 14.1F).

Some pieces exhibit alternative principles for handling register assignments. "Le vent dans la plaine" (Préludes I) fixes its register only approximately (ex. 14.1G). It first recurs (at the same transposition) in m. 15 and is transposed up progressively in mm. 19 and 36, after which it gradually returns (at mm. 40 and 44) to its original assignment before *descending* in m. 46 to a lower octave. Although this motive's specific pitch level is not fixed, all but one of the transpositions occur within a narrow tessitura that ranges from $e\flat^1$ to $C\sharp^1$ for the starting pitch; consequently, the final reassignment to lower-octave $d\flat$ has the effect of a more radical change, comparable to other pieces whose fixed registers are abandoned for their theme's final appearances.

Pieces that use more than one recurrent motive may mix techniques. "La cathédrale engloutie" (Préludes I), for example, contains three prominent motives (found initially in mm. 1, 7, and 28, respectively): the first retains its original register assignment throughout, including its last appearance in m. 84 (where added doublings thicken the sonorous density); the second recurs at m. 47, placed two octaves lower (though by m. 54 it has regained its original register); the third migrates one octave lower in its second and final appearance at m. 72.

A few pieces disregard fixed register assignments altogether. The *vif* motive from "Les collines d'Anacapri" (Préludes I) migrates both up and down from its original register ($f\sharp^3$), including placements on $c\sharp^4$ and $f\sharp$ before its final placement on $f\sharp^1$.

Debussy's tendency to fix themes in specific registers and to reassign them near the end appears quite early. In the first "Arabesque," the theme that follows the brief introduction (m. 6) reappears for the last time (m. 99) one octave higher (ex. 14.1H). The second "Arabesque" treats its initial theme similarly.

Later works show the principle well entrenched. "Reflets dans l'eau" (*Images* I), for example, repeatedly states a three-note motive that is first exposed in mm. 1–2. Its penultimate statement (m. 74) occurs one octave above its original placement and is followed by the final statement (mm. 83–84) yet another octave higher.

A late example, "Pour les arpèges composés" (Douze études II) frequently exposes its opening gesture in the original register (ex. 14.1I), but it is twice transposed two octaves lower: at m. 48, where it adumbrates the final reprise and at m. 62, where it signals the etude's close.

Instrumental Works and Songs

Although fixing themes in particular registers is not especially evident in chamber and orchestral works, there are some examples. The third movement of the String Quartet fixes its first theme (m. 5) in the middle register (on f^1), where it remains in all subsequent statements (mm. 9, 13, 25, 107) except for the last (m. 111), which occurs on f^2 (ex. 14.1J).

The transformations of the opening theme of the *Prélude à "L'après-midi d'un faune"* include various transpositions, though most remain close in register to the original pitch level (whose initial pitch is $c\#^2$), including the last two statements in the flutes (at mm. 94 and 100); consequently, the transposition a P4 lower for the last transformation is striking. It conspires, along with changes in timbre and texture (horns and violins in a closely spaced chordal setting), to capture the listener's attention in preparation for the composition's impending conclusion.

Debussy usually avoids such calculated treatment in his songs. Because the voice cannot readily handle octave transpositions, we should not be surprised that the technique is absent from vocal lines, but Debussy also avoids it in piano accompaniments. A rare exception is "Pour ce que Plaisance est morte" (*Trois chansons de France*), whose introductory motive (in the piano) is fixed on d^1 for its first three appearances before being reassigned to a higher octave for the last statement, three bars before the end (ex. 14.1K).

Many of the foregoing examples illustrate another feature of Debussy's treatment of reprised materials: his tendency to alter their contexts. In "Des pas sur la neige," for example, the second appearance of the ostinato (in the original register assignment) brings an expansion of the register compass (from [2] at m. 1/beat 1 to [22] at m. 8/beat 1) as well as a significant downward shift of mean placement (from d^1 to e). "La fille aux cheveux de lin" shows comparable changes: register spans for its theme's three statements are [0], [21], and [50], respectively, while mean placements are d^2, eb^1, and db^1. Similar changes may be seen in example 14.1C–K. Those of the quartet are especially cogent; the theme's placement (at mm. 9, 13, 25, 107) vis-à-vis its setting changes from highest voice to lowest and back again, without any change in assignment.[4]

TENDENCY TOWARDS EXPANSION

Another common feature is the tendency for register spans to widen by stages throughout a work. Often local expansions are rested within ones of longer range.

This hierarchic process, in which the overall tendency is replicated repeatedly at lower architectonic levels, also contributes to a composition's kinetic form, since progressively wider spans lead towards a climactic maximum.

"Des pas sur la neige"

Figure 14.1 displays the register span of "Des pas sur la neige" from one bar to the next. The graph plots, for every bar, the first and last notes of each outer part, which it displays in two-semitone increments as points on a vertical axis that extends up and down from c^1. The horizontal axis represents the composition's time span delineated in segments that correspond to bars. The points that represent register are located at the beginning and middle of each measure's segment.[5] Gaps in either outer register indicate rests. The chart provides an index of register extremes from moment to moment that permits observation of general trends and tendencies not readily apparent in the score.

A common surface pattern is the vacillation across a m3 (d^1–f^1) embodied in the ostinato itself, heard in mm. 8–11 and mm. 26–27, where the ostinato constitutes the treble extreme. This pattern also appears in the bass, mm. 16–18 (transposed to g–b♭).

The piece divides into four periods of expansion indicated by the vertical lines that section the graph at mm. 8, 16, and 26. Of these, the first concludes with a partial compression where the upper extreme falls back to its original register, and the third features a partial compression in both extremes. In spite of these, the overall result is a significantly wider register span at the end of each section compared with its beginning. The two compressions—and other, local compressions such as those at mm. 3, 8, 18, and 28 (to cite only a few)—contribute to a rich and complex register surface without detracting from the larger trends that their countertendencies merely delay.

The piece as a whole exhibits a hierarchic tendency towards register expansion seen in the diverging lines that connect the extremes in the outer parts. The successively wider spans of the first two periods contribute in a progressive fashion to this tendency, which is fulfilled in the fourth period's apogee at m. 36. The third period's more modest apogee (m. 24) contradicts the tendency, temporarily, and thereby replicates across the work as a whole similar countertendencies found within each period.

A downward shift in mean placement from the composition's beginning to its end is seen in a comparison of the first and final positions of the broken line. Slight shifts of a placement from beginning to end are typical and contrast with the practice of Debussy's tonal predecessors, who tend to return to (or retain) the initial mean register placement by observing obligatory register.

Like register compass, mean placement tends to fluctuate considerably from moment to moment. In "Des pas sur la neige," these fluctuations form two similar patterns: the first unfolds during the initial and second periods and consists of a cycle of ascent-descent-ascent (its initial and endpoints are different and replicate the shift shown by mean placement overall); the second pattern encompasses the

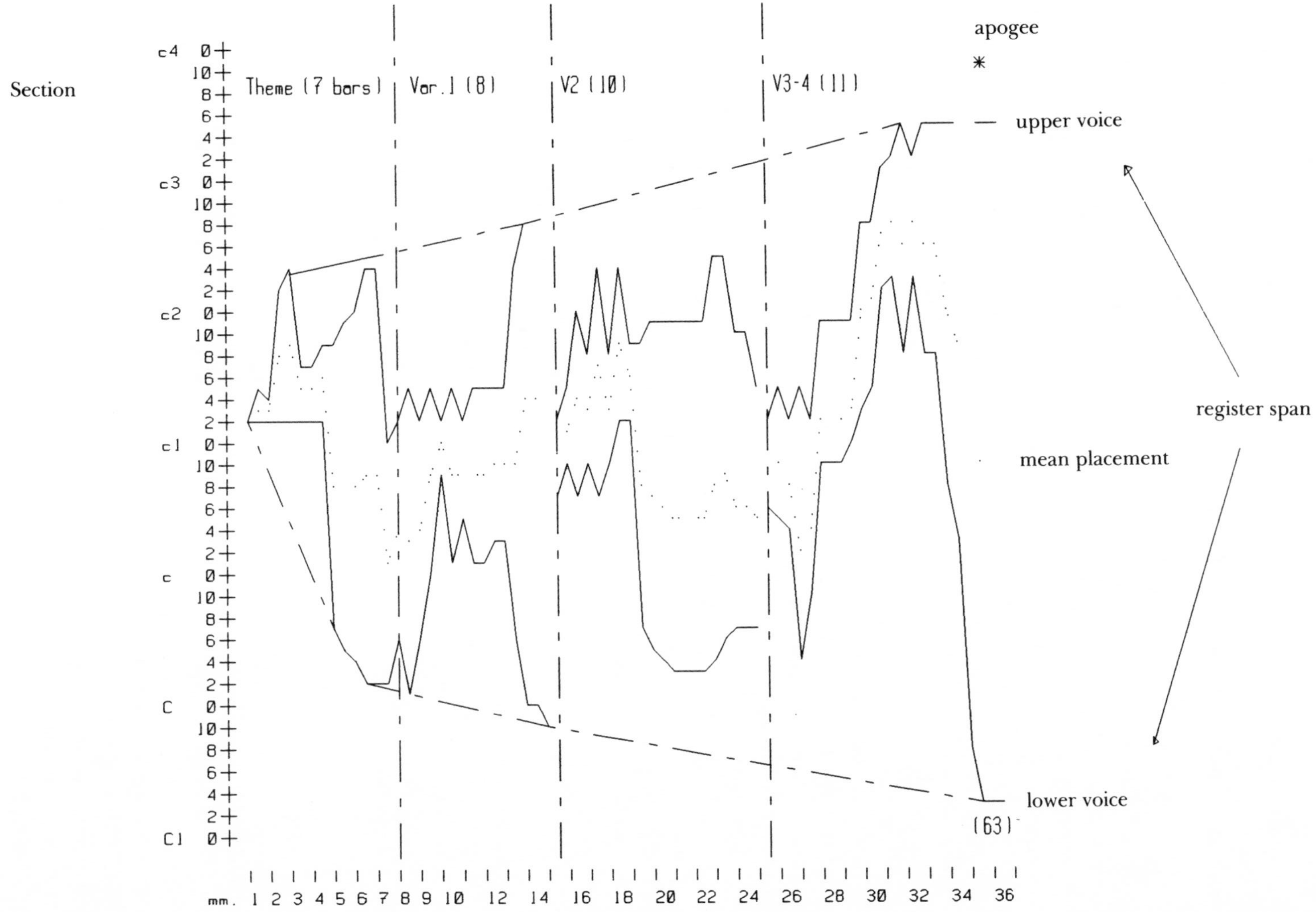

Figure 14.1. Register compass and mean placement in "Des pas sur la neige"

third and fourth periods and extends the preceding cycle by half (again, the overall placement shifts slightly from initial to endpoint).

Fluctuations in mean placement occur only when motion between the outer parts is unequal (since exact contrary motion expands or contracts the register compass in both directions equally). Stable mean placements are most likely to occur towards the middle and at the very end of formal units; they are least likely to occur at the beginning.

The prelude's first gesture reveals the principle of register expansion in this, the first musical thought, for the ostinato's two rhythmic components expand from a unison to a second, and then to a third. In the domain of register, as in others, structural principles and resources are integrated across hierarchic levels. They are also integrated progressively across temporal spans. Thus, in "Des pas sur la neige," the principle of stepped registral expansion that is first revealed as a surface feature manifests itself gradually on intermediate structural levels (across sections) and, eventually, at the highest level (across the piece as a whole).[6]

The overall range of register extremes for this prelude extends from [0] to [63] ($5\frac{1}{3}$ octaves), about average for the piano works; indeed, it is the norm for chamber and orchestral works as well.

EXPANSION FOLLOWED BY COMPRESSION

Another common pattern is one in which register expansion is followed by gradual contraction. "La fille aux cheveux de lin" and *Prélude à "L'après-midi d'un faune"* both illustrate this principle.

"La fille aux cheveux de lin"

Figure 14.2 graphically represents fluctuant register span and mean placement in the same manner as figure 14.1. The prelude's three main sections plus coda are indicated by vertical lines. Short horizontal brackets delineate the first four phrases; the long bracket over the middle of the figure indicates the apogee of register expansion, which occurs here not as a moment, but as a span of fifteen bars.

The widest register compass is [50], achieved first at the end of m. 15 and again in mm. 28–29 (hence the wide apogee). Within the apogee the compass fluctuates but tends to be significantly wider than before m. 15 or after m. 29. The passages that lead to m. 15 expand progressively: [0] to [24] (mm. 1–4); [0] to [36] (mm. 4–6); [0] to [29] (mm. 8–11); [31] to [48] (mm. 11–13). The regressive expansion across mm. 8–11 (compared with its antecedent) reminds us that such counter-tending passages are typical of Debussy's rich surfaces. Three of these four phrases feature at least a partial compression following their apogees, and the last two place the apogee at very nearly the center. In this they replicate the nearly symmetrical placement of the overall apogee, which spans mm. 15–29, set within thirty-nine bars overall.

"La fille aux cheveux de lin" incorporates more parallel motion than does "Des

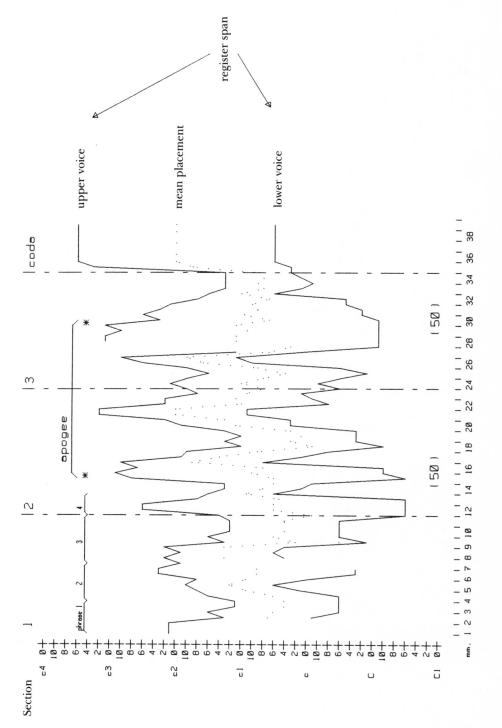

Figure 14.2. Register compass and mean placement in "La fille aux cheveux de lin"

pas sur la neige" (especially mm. 17–18, 19–22, 24–27, and 35–39); as a result, its mean placement is even more fluctuant, especially mm. 13–27. Like "Des pas sur la neige," "La fille aux cheveux de lin" exhibits a typical shift in mean placement, this time to a higher placement at the end, as is seen in a comparison of the first and last positions of the dotted horizontal line.

Prélude à "L'après-midi d'un faune"

The *Prélude à "L'après-midi d'un faune"* also embodies a cycle of expansion and contraction in its fluctuant register space (ex. 14.2), from [0] to [60] to [28].[7] The apogee is preceded by a gradual but considerable expansion that begins with the opening flute solo and is followed by a steady though less dramatic contraction to the end. Typical are the subtle asymmetries that result from the apogee's placement twelve bars after the composition's center (at almost exactly the work's Golden Section) and the shift in mean placement.

Closer to the musical surface, fluctuations in compass and mean across mm. 1–10 mimic the sloped, elliptical shape of the overall pattern. In general, many of the composition's lowest-level formal units replicate these patterns; others maintain a more stable compass and placement, as in mm. 37–50. This is the second allusion to connections between register and form and it leads to the next topic: alignment of design features in the domain of register with those in the domain of form.

REGISTER FLUCTUATION AND FORMAL BOUNDARIES

In general, patterns of fluctuation in register span align with formal boundaries, as is readily apparent in the excerpts quoted in example 14.1. The first movement of the Sonata for flute, viola, and harp illustrates this feature well (ex. 14.3A). The initial gesture (mm. 1–2), which begins with harp alone and enfolds the flute after the fourth note, expands from [0] to [20] and then gradually contracts to [9]. This asymmetrical ellipse, with its lovely surface undulations, is at once twice imitated, in a simpler form, by the flute's flourishes over the harp's quiet accompaniment. The basic elliptical pattern recurs in myriad permutations throughout the work; each time, the pattern's completion signals the end of a motive, phrase, or section. In addition, pronounced shifts of mean placement initiate new formal units at higher structural levels—at m. 9/beat 2, again at m. 14, at m. 18, m. 26, m. 48, and

Example 14.2. Register extremes in *Prélude à "L'après-midi d'un faune"*

A. Replication of a register pattern in the first two motives

B. Mean register placement and formal boundaries

Example 14.3. Register and form in the Sonata for flute, viola, and harp, I

elsewhere. (Example 14.3B shows only the boundary at m. 9.) This is not to say that changes in mean placement define all of the movement's formal boundaries, but they certainly contribute to many.

"De l'aube à midi sur la mer"

"De l'aube à midi sur la mer" (*La mer* I) illustrates the same principle on a larger scale. Example 14.4A shows the register spans at either boundary of every section as well as each section's clear pattern of expansion or contraction. The first two exhibit dramatic expansions, as may be seen in the tallies of semitones under the bass staff. For both, the apogees coincide with points of climax towards the ends of the sections.[8]

Sections 3, 4, and 5 are linked by common spans at shared boundaries. Here register follows other parameters in which connections are forged across formal partitions. Section 5 reverses the tendency towards expansion manifest within sections 1, 2, and 3; its register span contracts across the section's ten bars. Section 4 adumbrates this reversal by its own small contraction, but compared with the other sections its register compass is relatively stable. Linked by compass and mean, the contours that arise from fluctuations in register throughout sections 4, 5, and 6 conjoin to form an ellipse (though the low mean of m. 84 distorts its symmetry).

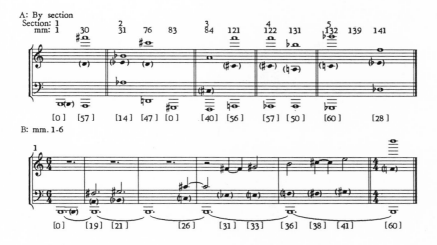

Example 14.4. Register expansion in "De l'aube à midi sur la mer"

Formal dynamism is manifest across the movement in the fluctuations of compass and mean placement. The unequivocal tendency towards expansion in sections 1 and 2 places intermediate climaxes at the ends of those formal units; of the two, the climax of section 1 is greater. Section 3 proceeds in the same fashion, but its climax is deferred (and heightened thereby) until the beginning of section 5 by the sustained compass and placement throughout section 4.[9] That register and form interact in a hierarchic fashion is demonstrated by the nesting of sectional patterns within one that spans several sections, and in the creation of a superior register climax in m. 132 compared with subsidiary apogees at mm. 30, 76, and 121. These connections keyed to middle and deep formal levels have a counterpart on the musical surface. Example 14.4B shows the dramatic expansion and mean ascent that occurs in the movement's first five bars.[10] Its pattern, which exhibits an expansion from [0] (in m. 1) to [60] (in m. 6), and an ascent in mean placement of over two octaves, from D to f[1], replicates that of section 1 and of the movement as a whole.

REGISTER AS A DEVICE OF TEXT EXPRESSION

In general, Debussy associates certain registers with particular dramatic situations: intense emotions, for example, with higher mean placements (though despair and ominous portent usually employ lower placements than moments of rage or erotic passion); intense but constrained emotions find expression in narrow register spans with intermediate mean placements; calmer, benign emotions such as affection usually find higher mean placements and moderate to wide spans. Voice ranges affect mean placements to some extent; in *Pelléas et Mélisande*, for example, when Arkel expresses affection for Mélisande, the mean placement tends to be relatively low to accommodate his bass range.

A few examples from act IV, scene 4, must suffice to illustrate the foregoing. (Example 14.5 shows compasses and mean placements for several passages identified by page and bar number in the orchestral score.)

The instrumental music that accompanies Pelléas's entrance (p. 319/11) is set in a low, narrow register; its compass is [33] with a mean placement on B♭. The mood is gloomy as Pelléas considers his circumstances, namely, his futile love for Mélisande which now forces him to leave Allemonde. Within a few bars (p. 321/2), as the level of emotional intensity increases commensurate with his declaration "I will flee weeping with joy and with despair like a blind person who would flee from his burning home,"[11] the register span increases to [53] centered on b.

Just before Mélisande's crucial entrance (p. 324/3); the register span narrows to [35] while the mean placement rises to e². This reflects the tension Pelléas feels, for although Mélisande agreed (at the end of scene 2) to this final meeting, he is not sure that she will come.

Their declaration of love (p. 332/4–6), which is famous for its constrained setting (unaccompanied and almost whispered), occupies the narrowest possible register compass of [0] in a tessitura that lies between e and e¹. This fits the dramatic situation perfectly: the sense of feelings suspended momentarily, emotions held under extraordinarily tight rein as the lovers absorb the implications of their declarations. Thereafter, emotional energy builds quickly and bursts forth in the orchestra (p. 333/6) after Mélisande confides that she has loved him "since always, since I first saw you,"[12] and the compass expands for an instant to [62] placed about c♯¹. At p. 341/1 (*tres animé*), the culmination of the scene's eroticism (Pelléas's words are "And now I have found you"),[13] the mean placement rises further, to d♯¹, within a moderately wide compass of [45].

The moment (p. 362/5) where Golaud falls on the pair and murders Pelléas is set in a high, narrow compass of [27] placed about d♯³.

Throughout this scene, register span and mean placement are in constant flux, consistent with the ever-shifting character of the drama, at times anticipating events, at others underscoring them, and sometimes reacting to them. The expressive role of register is no different from that of pitch or orchestration; all serve to heighten and clarify the drama's emotional content from moment to moment.

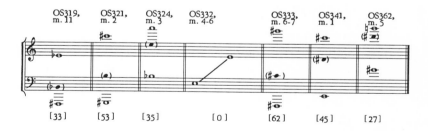

Example 14.5. Register compass and mean placement in *Pelléas et Mélisande*, act IV, scene 4

REGISTER AS A MEDIUM FOR DISPARITIES IN OTHER DOMAINS

Register provides an alternative medium to temporality for separating disparate elements while maintaining proximity; two pc set genera, for example, can be superimposed in different registers rather than juxtaposed.

"Pour les degrés chromatiques" (Douze études II) furnishes a felicitous example. Its pc materials embody a dichotomy between the chromatic genus on one hand, contrasted by turns with diatonic, whole-tone, and octatonic genera on the other. Sometimes temporal juxtaposition projects the dichotomy, but more often register is the medium, with chromatic pc sets assigned to higher registers and those of the other genera assigned to lower ones, as in example 14.6A.

A more subtle example occurs in the first movement of the Sonata for flute, viola, and harp, m. 12, where diatonic pc sets in the harp (doubled in the viola) are pitted against 8–17/18/19–complex sets in the flute (ex. 14.6B). The registers overlap to some extent, and so instrumental color and figuration assist in distinguishing one genus from another. Nevertheless, opposing register assignments facilitate aural separation and comparison.

Register also separates conflicting metric schemes, as in "Les sons et les parfums tournent dans l'air du soir," where the metric scheme that governs the recurrent low pedal A is independent of that of the other pc materials set in higher registers.

Register's structural role is difficult to verify aurally because it is not easy to separate the parameter of register from pitch class. The same problem obtains in verifying structural roles for timbre and meter, which also are inextricably conjoined to pc relations. It is possible, however, to suppress the customary preoccupation with pitch manifest in tunes and chords in order to concentrate on register, instrumental color and texture, metric accents and their matrix of relations, fluctuant pc fields, and the incredibly complex contrapuntal concatenation of rhythms that their synthesis engenders.

For every issue this study addresses, it raises new ones. What, for example, is the nature of temporal perception? Do we sense durational proportions in the same way as spatial proportions? Do they have the same aesthetic meaning? Do we hear pc sets and complement relations because we identify them, or vice versa? Can we experience a composition's structural multifariousness, or only marvel at it? Is the relation between intra- and extramusical meaning universal, culturally and historically bound, autosuggestive, or behaviorally conditioned by the composer? Such questions provide sufficient impetus for several books.

It is impossible to summarize the ideas explored in these pages in a few paragraphs without resorting to banalities. However, two recurrent features merit comment: the music's pervasive multifariousness and its kinetic properties as a focus of invention.

Multifariousness pervades the general as well as the specific. It is present in pc resources that lend themselves to multiple interpretations (such as the opening

A. "Pour les degrés chromatiques"

B. Sonata for flute, viola, and harp, I

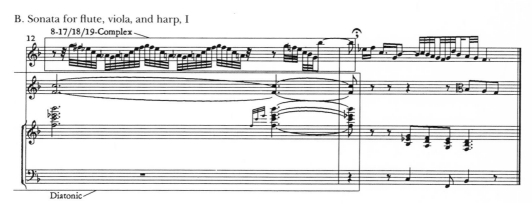

Example 14.6. Register used to separate genera

gesture of "Evantail") and resides as well in structural principles—morphological versus kinetic form, and tonal versus pc set relations—that allow the same musical events to be heard in contradictory ways. Multifariousness is also manifest in details: in sets, for example, that belong to two or more genera and require contextual features to clarify them.

A key to Debussy's extraordinary originality vis-à-vis his predecessors and contemporaries, and comparing his own late works with earlier ones, is his emphasis in invention on kinetic, processive principles rather than constructs; for principles can be applied in ever-new ways and can create ever-new contexts. The principle of mutation is applicable to any pair of internally homogeneous, externally heterogeneous pc set groups; the expressive principle that associates distinct musical features as symbols for extramusical dramatic meaning can be applied to any musical parameter; the formal principle of transformation versus return can generate innumerable schemes. These principles led to new constructs that became hallmarks of Debussy's style and the stuff of his musical language.

LIST OF PITCH-CLASS SETSa WITH SUCCESSIVE-INTERVAL ARRAYS (SIAS) AND INTERVAL VECTORS (IVS)

Set	SIA	IV	Set	SIA	IV
2–1	1–11	100000	10–1	1–1–1–1–1–1–1–1–1–3	988884
2–2	2–10	010000	10–2	1–1–1–1–1–1–1–1–2–2	898884
2–3	3–9	001000	10–3	1–1–1–1–1–1–1–2–1–2	889884
2–4	4–8	000100	10–4	1–1–1–1–1–1–2–1–1–2	888984
2–5	5–7	000010	10–5	1–1–1–1–1–2–1–1–1–2	888894
2–6	6–6	000001	10–6	1–1–1–1–2–1–1–1–1–2	888885
3–1*	1–1–10	210000	9–1*	1–1–1–1–1–1–1–1–4	876663
3–2	1–2–9	111000	9–2	1–1–1–1–1–1–1–2–3	777663
3–3	1–3–8	101100	9–3	1–1–1–1–1–1–2–1–3	767763
3–4	1–4–7	100110	9–4	1–1–1–1–1–2–1–1–3	766773
3–5	1–5–6	100011	9–5	1–1–1–1–2–1–1–1–3	766674
3–6*	2–2–8	020100	9–6*	1–1–1–1–1–1–2–2–2	686763
3–7	2–3–7	011010	9–7	1–1–1–1–2–1–2–2	677673
3–8	2–4–6	010101	9–8	1–1–1–2–1–2–2	676764
3–9*	2–5–5	010020	9–9*	1–1–2–1–1–1–2–2	676683
3–10*	3–3–6	002001	9–10*	1–1–1–2–1–2–1–2	668664
3–11	3–4–5	001110	9–11	1–1–2–1–1–2–1–2	667773
3–12*	4–4–4	000300	9–12*	1–1–2–1–1–2–1–1–2	666963
4–1*	1–1–1–9	321000	8–1*	1–1–1–1–1–1–1–5	765442
4–2	1–1–2–8	221100	8–2	1–1–1–1–1–1–2–4	665542
4–3*	1–2–1–8	212100	8–3*	1–1–1–1–1–1–3–3	656542
4–4	1–1–3–7	211110	8–4	1–1–1–1–1–2–1–4	655552
4–5	1–1–4–6	210111	8–5	1–1–1–1–2–1–1–4	654553
4–6*	1–1–5–5	210021	8–6*	1–1–2–1–1–1–4	654463
4–7*	1–3–1–4	201210	8–7*	1–1–1–1–3–1–3	645652
4–8*	1–4–1–3	200121	8–8*	1–1–1–3–1–1–3	644563
4–9*	1–5–1–5	200022	8–9*	1–1–3–1–1–1–3	644464
4–10*	2–1–2–7	122010	8–10*	2–1–1–1–1–2–3	566452
4–11	1–2–2–7	121110	8–11	1–1–1–1–2–2–3	565552
4–12	2–1–3–6	112101	8–12	1–2–1–1–1–2–3	556543
4–13	1–2–3–6	112011	8–13	1–1–1–2–1–2–3	556453
4–14	2–1–4–5	111120	8–14	1–1–2–1–1–2–3	555562
4–Z15	1–3–2–6	111111	8–Z15	1–1–1–1–2–2–1–3	555553
4–16	1–4–2–5	110121	8–16	1–1–1–2–2–1–1–3	554563

Set	SIA	IV	Set	SIA	IV
4–17*	3–1–3–5	102210	8–17*	1–2–1–1–1–2–1–3	546652
4–18	1–3–3–5	102111	8–18	1–1–1–2–1–2–1–3	546553
4–19	1–3–4–4	101310	8–19	1–1–2–1–1–2–1–3	545752
4–20*	1–4–3–4	101220	8–20*	1–1–2–1–2–1–1–3	545662
4–21*	2–2–2–6	030201	8–21*	1–1–1–1–2–2–2–2	474643
4–22	2–2–3–5	021120	8–22	1–1–1–2–1–2–2–2	465562
4–23*	2–3–2–5	021030	8–23*	1–1–1–2–2–1–2–2	465472
4–24*	2–2–4–4	020301	8–24*	1–1–2–1–1–2–2–2	464743
4–25*	2–4–2–4	020202	8–25*	1–1–2–2–1–1–2–2	464644
4–26*	3–2–3–4	012120	8–26*	1–1–2–1–2–2–1–2	456562
4–27	2–3–3–4	012111	8–27	1–1–2–1–2–1–2–2	456553
4–28*	3–3–3–3	004002	8–28*	1–2–1–2–1–2–1–2	448444
4–Z29	1–2–4–5	111111	8–Z29	1–1–1–2–1–1–2–3	555553
5–1*	1–1–1–1–8	432100	7–1*	1–1–1–1–1–1–6	654321
5–2	1–1–1–2–7	332110	7–2	1–1–1–1–1–2–5	554331
5–3	1–1–2–1–7	322210	7–3	1–1–1–1–1–3–4	544431
5–4	1–1–1–3–6	322111	7–4	1–1–1–1–2–1–5	544332
5–5	1–1–1–4–5	321121	7–5	1–1–1–2–1–1–5	543342
5–6	1–1–3–1–6	311221	7–6	1–1–1–1–3–1–4	533442
5–7	1–1–4–1–5	310132	7–7	1–1–1–3–1–1–4	532353
5–8*	2–1–1–2–6	232201	7–8*	2–1–1–1–1–2–4	454422
5–9	1–1–2–2–6	231211	7–9	1–1–1–1–2–2–4	453432
5–10	1–2–1–2–6	223111	7–10	1–1–1–1–2–3–3	445332
5–11	2–1–1–3–5	222220	7–11	1–2–1–1–1–2–4	444441
5–Z12*	1–2–2–1–6	222121	7–Z12*	1–1–1–1–3–2–3	444342
5–13	1–1–2–4–4	221311	7–13	1–1–2–1–1–2–4	443532
5–14	1–1–3–2–5	221131	7–14	1–1–1–2–2–1–4	443352
5–15*	1–1–4–2–4	220222	7–15*	1–1–2–2–1–1–4	442443
5–16	1–2–1–3–5	213211	7–16	1–1–1–2–1–3–3	435432
5–Z17*	1–2–1–4–4	212320	7–Z17*	1–1–2–1–1–3–3	434541
5–Z18	1–3–1–2–5	212221	7–Z18	1–1–1–2–3–1–3	434442
5–19	1–2–3–1–5	212122	7–19	1–1–1–3–1–2–3	434343
5–20	1–2–4–1–4	211231	7–20	1–1–2–3–1–1–3	433452
5–21	1–3–1–3–4	202420	7–21	1–1–2–1–3–1–3	424641
5–22*	1–3–3–1–4	202321	7–22*	1–1–3–1–2–1–3	424542
5–23	2–1–2–2–5	132130	7–23	2–1–1–1–2–2–3	354351
5–24	1–2–2–2–5	131221	7–24	1–1–1–2–2–2–3	353442
5–25	2–1–2–3–4	123121	7–25	2–1–1–2–1–2–3	345342
5–26	2–2–1–3–4	122311	7–26	1–2–1–1–2–2–3	344532
5–27	1–2–2–3–4	122230	7–27	1–1–2–1–2–2–3	344451
5–28	2–1–3–2–4	122212	7–28	1–2–2–1–1–2–3	344433
5–29	1–2–3–2–4	122131	7–29	1–1–2–2–1–2–3	344352
5–30	1–3–2–2–4	121321	7–30	1–1–2–2–2–1–3	343542
5–31	1–2–3–3–3	114112	7–31	1–2–1–2–1–2–3	336333
5–32	1–3–2–3–3	113221	7–32	1–2–1–2–2–1–3	335442
5–33*	2–2–2–2–4	040402	7–33*	1–1–2–2–2–2–2	262623
5–34*	2–2–2–3–3	032221	7–34*	1–2–1–2–2–2–2	254442
5–35*	2–2–3–2–3	032140	7–35*	1–2–2–1–2–2–2	254361
5–Z36	1–1–2–3–5	222121	7–Z36	1–1–1–2–1–2–4	444342
5–Z37*	3–1–1–3–4	212320	7–Z37*	1–2–1–1–2–1–4	434541
5–Z38	1–1–3–3–4	212221	7–Z38	1–1–2–1–2–1–4	434442

Set	SIA	IV	Set	SIA	IV
6–1*	1–1–1–1–1–7	543210			
6–2	1–1–1–1–2–6	443211			
6–Z3	1–1–1–2–1–6	433221	6–Z36	1–1–1–1–3–5	
6–Z4*	1–1–2–1–1–6	432321	6–Z37*	1–1–1–1–4–4	
6–5	1–1–1–3–1–5	422232			
6–Z6*	1–1–3–1–1–5	421242	6–Z38*	1–1–1–4–1–4	
6–7*	1–1–4–1–1–4	420243			
6–8*	2–1–1–1–2–5	343230			
6–9	1–1–1–2–2–5	342231			
6–Z10	1–2–1–1–2–5	333321	6–Z39	2–1–1–1–3–4	
6–Z11	1–1–2–1–2–5	333231	6–Z40	1–1–1–2–3–4	
6–Z12	1–1–2–2–1–5	332232	6–Z41	1–1–1–3–2–4	
6–Z13*	1–2–1–2–1–5	324222	6–Z42*	1–1–1–3–3–3	
6–14	1–2–1–1–3–4	323430			
6–15	1–1–2–1–3–4	323421			
6–16	1–3–1–1–2–4	322431			
6–Z17	1–1–2–3–1–4	322332	6–Z43	1–1–3–1–2–4	
6–18	1–1–3–2–1–4	322242			
6–Z19	1–2–1–3–1–4	313431	6–Z44	1–1–3–1–3–3	
6–20*	1–3–1–3–1–3	303630			
6–21	2–1–1–2–2–4	242412			
6–22	1–1–2–2–2–4	241422			
6–Z23*	2–1–2–1–2–4	234222	6–Z45*	2–1–1–2–3–3	
6–Z24	1–2–1–2–2–4	233331	6–Z46	1–1–2–2–3–3	
6–Z25	1–2–2–1–2–4	233241	6–Z47	1–1–2–3–2–3	
6–Z26*	1–2–2–2–1–4	232341	6–Z48*	1–1–3–2–2–3	
6–27	1–2–1–2–3–3	225222			
6–Z28*	1–2–2–1–3–3	224322	6–Z49*	1–2–1–3–2–3	
6–Z29*	1–2–3–2–1–3	224232	6–Z50*	1–3–2–1–2–3	
6–30*	1–2–3–1–2–3	224223			
6–31	1–2–2–3–1–3	223431			
6–32*	2–2–1–2–2–3	143250			
6–33	2–1–2–2–2–3	143241			
6–34	1–2–2–2–2–3	142422			
6–35*	2–2–2–2–2–2	060603			

[a]Arranged in best normal order after Forte, *Structure*, 179–81. Symmetrical sets are identified by asterisks following set names.

THE DIATONIC GENUS OF PC SETS

Set	SIA	IV	Set	SIA	IV
2−1	1−11	100000			
2−2	2−10	010000	10−2	1−1−1−1−1−1−1−1−2−2	898884
2−3	3−9	001000	10−3	1−1−1−1−1−1−1−2−1−2	889884
2−4	4−8	000100	10−4	1−1−1−1−1−1−2−1−1−2	888984
2−5	5−7	000010	10−5	1−1−1−1−1−2−1−1−1−2	888894
2−6	6−6	000001			
3−2	1−2−9	111000			
3−4	1−4−7	100110			
3−5	1−5−6	100011			
3−6*	2−2−8	020100	9−6*	1−1−1−1−1−1−2−2−2	686763
3−7	2−3−7	011010	9−7	1−1−1−1−1−2−1−2−2	677673
3−8	2−4−6	010101			
3−9*	2−5−5	010020	9−9*	1−1−1−2−1−1−1−2−2	676683
3−10*	3−3−6	002001			
3−11	3−4−5	001110	9−11	1−1−1−2−1−1−2−1−2	667773
4−8*	1−4−1−3	200121			
4−10*	2−1−2−7	122010			
4−11	1−2−2−7	121110			
4−13	1−2−3−6	112011			
4−14	2−1−4−5	111120			
4−16	1−4−2−5	110121			
4−20*	1−4−3−4	101220			
4−21*	2−2−2−6	030201			
4−22	2−2−3−5	021120	8−22	1−1−1−2−1−2−2−2	465562
4−23*	2−3−2−5	021030	8−23*	1−1−1−2−2−1−2−2	465472
4−26*	3−2−3−4	012120	8−26*	1−1−2−1−2−2−1−2	456562
4−27	2−3−3−4	012111			
4−Z29	1−2−4−5	111111			
(4−Z15)	1−3−2−6	111111			
5−Z12*	1−2−2−1−6	222121			
5−20	1−2−4−1−4	211231			
5−23	2−1−2−2−5	132130			
5−24	1−2−2−2−5	131221			

Set	SIA	IV	Set	SIA	IV
5–25	2–1–2–3–4	123121			
5–27	1–2–2–3–4	122230			
5–29	1–2–3–2–4	122131			
5–34*	2–2–2–3–3	032221			
5–35*	2–2–3–2–3	032140	7–35*	1–2–2–1–2–2–2	254361
(5–Z36)	1–1–2–3–5	222121			
6–Z25	1–2–2–1–2–4	233241	(6–Z47)	1–1–2–3–2–3	
6–Z26*	1–2–2–2–1–4	232341	(6–Z48)*	1–1–3–2–2–3	
6–32*	2–2–1–2–2–3	143250			
6–33	2–1–2–2–2–3	143241			

THE WHOLE-TONE GENUS OF PC SETS

Set	SIA	IV	Set	SIA	IV
2–2	2–10	010000	10–2	1–1–1–1–1–1–1–1–2–2	898884
2–4	4–8	000100	10–4	1–1–1–1–1–1–2–1–1–2	888984
2–6	6–6	000001	10–6	1–1–1–1–2–1–1–1–1–2	888885
3–6*	2–2–8	020100	9–6*	1–1–1–1–1–1–2–2–2	686763
3–8	2–4–6	010101	9–8	1–1–1–2–1–1–2–2	676764
3–12*	4–4–4	000300	9–12*	1–1–2–1–1–2–1–1–2	666963
4–21*	2–2–2–6	030201	8–21*	1–1–1–1–2–2–2–2	474643
4–24*	2–2–4–4	020301	8–24*	1–1–2–1–1–2–2–2	464743
4–25*	2–4–2–4	020202	8–25*	1–1–2–2–1–1–2–2	464644
5–33*	2–2–2–2–4	040402	7–33*	1–1–2–2–2–2–2	262623
6–35*	2–2–2–2–2–2	060603			

THE CHROMATIC GENUS OF PC SETS

Set	SIA	IV	Set	SIA	IV
2–1	1–11	100000	10–1	1–1–1–1–1–1–1–1–1–3	988884
2–2	2–10	010000	10–2	1–1–1–1–1–1–1–1–2–2	898884
(2–3)	3–9	001000	10–3	1–1–1–1–1–1–1–2–1–2	889884
(2–4)	4–8	000100	10–4	1–1–1–1–1–1–2–1–1–2	888984
(2–5)	5–7	000010	10–5	1–1–1–1–1–2–1–1–1–2	888894
(2–6)	6–6	000001	10–6	1–1–1–1–2–1–1–1–1–2	888885
3–1*	1–1–10	210000	9–1*	1–1–1–1–1–1–1–1–4	876663
3–2	1–2–9	111000	9–2	1–1–1–1–1–1–1–2–3	777663
(3–3)	1–3–8	101100	9–3	1–1–1–1–1–1–2–1–3	767763
(3–4)	1–4–7	100110	9–4	1–1–1–1–1–2–1–1–3	766773
(3–5)	1–5–6	100011	9–5	1–1–1–1–2–1–1–1–3	766674
4–1*	1–1–1–9	321000	8–1*	1–1–1–1–1–1–1–5	765442
4–2	1–1–2–8	221100	8–2	1–1–1–1–1–1–2–4	665542
4–3*	1–2–1–8	212100	(8–3)*	1–1–1–1–1–1–3–3	656542
(4–4)	1–1–3–7	211110	8–4	1–1–1–1–1–2–1–4	655552
(4–5)	1–1–4–6	210111	8–5	1–1–1–1–2–1–1–4	654553
(4–6)*	1–1–5–5	210021	8–6*	1–1–1–2–1–1–1–4	654463
(4–7)*	1–3–1–4	201210	(8–7)*	1–1–1–1–3–1–3	645652
(4–8)*	1–4–1–3	200121	(8–8)*	1–1–1–3–1–1–3	644563
(4–9)*	1–5–1–5	200022	(8–9)*	1–1–3–1–1–1–3	644464
5–1*	1–1–1–1–8	432100	7–1*	1–1–1–1–1–1–6	654321
5–2	1–1–1–2–7	332110	7–2	1–1–1–1–1–2–5	554331
5–3	1–1–2–1–7	322210	(7–3)	1–1–1–1–1–3–4	544431
(5–4)	1–1–1–3–6	322111	7–4	1–1–1–1–2–1–5	544332
(5–5)	1–1–1–4–5	321121	7–5	1–1–1–2–1–1–5	543342
(5–6)	1–1–3–1–6	311221	(7–6)	1–1–1–1–3–1–4	533442
(5–7)	1–1–4–1–5	310132	(7–7)	1–1–1–3–1–1–4	532353
6–1*	1–1–1–1–1–7	543210			
6–2	1–1–1–1–2–6	443211			
6–Z3	1–1–1–2–1–6	433221	(6–Z36)	1–1–1–1–3–5	
6–Z4*	1–1–2–1–1–6	432321	(6–Z37)*	1–1–1–1–4–4	
(6–5)	1–1–1–3–1–5	422232			
(6–Z6)*	1–1–3–1–1–5	421242	(6–Z38)*	1–1–1–4–1–4	
(6–7)*	1–1–4–1–1–4	420243			

THE OCTATONIC GENUS OF PC SETS

Set	SIA	IV	Set	SIA	IV
2–1	1–11	100000			
2–2	2–10	010000			
2–3	3–9	001000	10–3	1–1–1–1–1–1–1–2–1–2	889884
2–4	4–8	000100			
2–5	5–7	000010			
2–6	6–6	000001	10–6	1–1–1–1–2–1–1–1–1–2	888885
3–2	1–2–9	111000			
3–3	1–3–8	101100			
3–5	1–5–6	100011			
3–7	2–3–7	011010			
3–8	2–4–6	010101			
3–10*	3–3–6	002001	9–10*	1–1–1–1–2–1–2–1–2	668664
3–11	3–4–5	001110			
4–3*	1–2–1–8	212100			
4–9*	1–5–1–5	200022			
4–10*	2–1–2–7	122010			
4–12	2–1–3–6	112101			
4–13	1–2–3–6	112011			
4–Z15	1–3–2–6	111111			
4–17*	3–1–3–5	102210			
4–18	1–3–3–5	102111			
4–25*	2–4–2–4	020202			
4–26*	3–2–3–4	012120			
4–27	2–3–3–4	012111			
4–28*	3–3–3–3	004002	8–28*	1–2–1–2–1–2–1–2	448444
4–Z29	1–2–4–5	111111			
5–10	1–2–1–2–6	223111			
5–16	1–2–1–3–5	213211			
5–19	1–2–3–1–5	212122			
5–25	2–1–2–3–4	123121			
5–28	2–1–3–2–4	122212			
5–31	1–2–3–3–3	114112	7–31	1–2–1–2–1–2–3	336333
5–32	1–3–2–3–3	113221			
6–Z13*	1–2–1–2–1–5	324222	(6–Z42)*	1–1–1–3–3–3	
6–Z23*	2–1–2–1–2–4	234222	(6–Z45)*	2–1–1–2–3–3	
6–27	1–2–1–2–3–3	225222			
(6–Z28)*	1–2–2–1–3–3	224322	6–Z49*	1–2–1–3–2–3	
(6–Z29)*	1–2–3–2–1–3	224232	6–Z50*	1–3–2–1–2–3	
6–30*	1–2–3–1–2–3	224223			

APPENDIX SIX
THE 8–17/18/19–COMPLEX GENUS OF PC SETS

An X in any of the three columns labeled "8–17/18/19" means that the given set is a subset or superset of that octachord. For example, an X in the "18" column for set 4–9 means that set 4–9 is a subset of 8–18, and the absence of X's in the "17" and "19" columns means that 4–9 is not a subset of octachords 8–17 or 8–19.

Set	SIA	IV	8–17/18/19
2–1	1–11	100000	X X
2–2	2–10	010000	X X X
2–3	3–9	001000	X X X X
2–4	4–8	000100	X X X X
2–5	5–7	000010	X X X X
2–6	6–6	000001	X X X
3–1*	1–1–10	210000	X X X
3–2	1–2–9	111000	X X X
3–3	1–3–8	101100	X X X X
3–4	1–4–7	100110	X X X X
3–5	1–5–6	100011	X X X X
3–6*	2–2–8	020100	X X X X
3–7	2–3–7	011010	X X X X
3–8	2–4–6	010101	X X X X
3–9*	2–5–5	010020	X X X X
3–10*	3–3–6	002001	X X X X
3–11	3–4–5	001110	X X X X
3–12*	4–4–4	000300	X X
4–1*	1–1–1–9	321000	X X
4–2	1–1–2–8	221100	X X X X
4–3*	1–2–1–8	212100	X X X X
4–4	1–1–3–7	211110	X X X X
4–5	1–1–4–6	210111	X X X
4–6*	1–1–5–5	210021	X
4–7*	1–3–1–4	201210	X X X X
4–8*	1–4–1–3	200121	X X X
4–9*	1–5–1–5	200022	X
4–10*	2–1–2–7	122010	X X X
4–11	1–2–2–7	121110	X X X X
4–12	2–1–3–6	112101	X X X X
4–13	2–2–3–6	112011	X X X X
4–14	2–1–4–5	111120	X X X X
4–Z15	1–3–2–6	111111	X X X X
4–16	1–4–2–5	110121	X X X X
4–17*	3–1–3–5	102210	X X X X
4–18	1–3–3–5	102111	X X X X
4–19	1–3–4–4	101310	X X X

Set	SIA	IV	8–17/18/19
10–1	1–1–1–1–1–1–1–1–1–3	988884	X X X
10–3	1–1–1–1–1–1–2–1–2	889884	X X X X
10–4	1–1–1–1–1–2–1–1–2	888984	X X X X
10–5	1–1–1–1–2–1–1–1–2	888894	X X X X
10–6	1–1–1–1–2–1–1–1–2	888885	X
9–3	1–1–1–1–1–2–1–1–3	767763	X X
9–4	1–1–1–1–2–1–1–3	766773	X X X
9–5	1–1–1–2–1–1–1–3	766674	X
9–10*	1–1–1–2–1–2–1–2	668664	X
9–11	1–1–2–1–1–2–1–2	667773	X X X
9–12*	1–2–1–1–2–1–1–2	666963	X
8–17*	1–2–1–1–1–2–1–3	546652	X X X
8–18	1–1–1–2–2–1–3	546553	X X X
8–19	1–1–2–1–1–2–1–3	545752	X X

			X marks
4–20*	1–4–3–4	101220	X X
4–21*	2–2–2–6	030201	X X
4–22	2–2–3–5	021120	X X X
4–23*	2–3–2–5	021030	X X X X
4–24*	2–2–4–4	020301	X
4–25*	2–4–2–4	020202	X X X X
4–26*	3–2–3–4	012120	X X X X
4–27	2–3–3–4	012111	X X X
4–28*	3–3–3–3	004002	X X X
4–Z29	1–2–4–5	111111	X X

			X marks
5–2	1–1–1–2–7	332110	X X X
5–3	1–1–2–1–7	322210	X X X
5–4	1–1–1–3–6	322111	X X
5–5	1–1–1–4–5	321121	X X X
5–6	1–1–3–1–6	311221	X X
5–7	1–1–4–1–5	310132	X X
5–8*	2–1–1–2–6	232201	X X
5–9	1–1–2–2–6	231211	X X
5–10	1–2–1–2–6	223111	X X
5–11	2–1–1–3–5	222220	X X
5–Z12*	1–2–2–1–6	222121	X X X
5–13	1–1–2–4–4	221311	X X
5–14	1–1–3–2–5	221131	X X X
5–15*	1–1–4–2–4	220222	X X X X
5–16	1–2–1–3–5	213211	X X X
5–Z17*	1–2–1–4–4	212320	X X X X
5–Z18	1–3–1–2–5	212221	X X
5–19	1–2–3–1–5	212122	X X X
5–20	1–2–4–1–4	211231	X
5–21	1–3–1–3–4	202420	X X X
5–22*	1–3–3–1–4	202321	X X X
5–23	2–1–2–2–5	132130	X X X
5–24	1–2–2–2–5	131221	X X X
5–25	2–1–2–3–4	123121	X X X
5–26	2–2–1–3–4	122311	X X X
5–27	1–2–2–3–4	122230	X X X
5–28	2–1–3–2–4	122212	X X
5–29	1–2–3–2–4	122131	X X
5–30	1–3–2–2–4	121321	X X
5–31	1–2–3–3–3	114112	X X

			X marks
7–11	1–2–1–1–1–2–4	444441	X
7–13	1–1–2–1–1–2–4	443532	X
7–16	1–1–1–2–1–3–3	435432	X X
7–Z17*	1–1–2–1–1–3–3	434541	X X
7–Z18	1–1–1–2–3–1–3	434442	X
7–19	1–1–1–3–1–2–3	434343	X
7–21	1–1–2–1–3–1–3	424641	X X
7–22*	1–1–3–1–2–1–3	424542	X X
7–26	1–2–1–1–2–2–3	344532	X
7–30	1–1–2–2–2–1–3	343542	X
7–31	1–2–1–2–1–2–3	336333	X

Set	SIA	IV	8–17/18/19	Set	SIA	IV	8–17/18/19
5-32	1-3-2-3-3	113221	X X	7-32	1-2-1-2-2-1-3	335442	X X
5-33*	2-2-2-2-4	040402	X				
5-34*	2-2-2-3-3	032221	X				
5-Z36	1-1-2-3-5	222121	X	7-Z36	1-1-1-2-1-2-4	444342	X
5-Z37*	3-1-1-3-4	212320	X X	7-Z37*	1-2-1-1-2-1-4	434541	X
5-Z38	1-1-3-3-4	212221	X X	7-Z38	1-1-2-1-2-1-4	434442	X
6-Z3	1-1-1-2-1-6	433221	X X	(6-Z36)	1-1-1-1-3-5		
6-Z4*	1-1-2-1-1-6	432321	X	(6-Z37)*	1-1-1-1-4-4		
6-5	1-1-1-3-1-5	422232	X				
6-8*	2-1-1-1-2-5	343230	X				
6-Z10	1-2-1-1-2-5	333321	X	6-Z39	2-1-1-1-3-4		X X
6-Z11	1-1-2-1-2-5	333231	X	6-Z40	1-1-1-2-3-4		X
(6-Z12)	1-1-2-2-1-5	332232		6-Z41	1-1-1-3-2-4		X
6-Z13*	1-2-1-2-1-5	324222	X	6-Z42*	1-1-1-3-3-3		X X
6-14	1-2-1-1-3-4	323430	X X				
6-15	1-1-2-1-3-4	323421	X X				
6-16	1-3-1-1-2-4	322431	X				
6-Z17	1-1-2-3-1-4	322332	X X	6-Z43	1-1-3-1-2-4		X X
6-18	1-1-3-2-1-4	322242	X X				
6-Z19	1-2-1-3-1-4	313431	X X	6-Z44	1-1-3-1-3-3		X X X
6-20*	1-3-1-3-1-3	303630	X				
6-21	2-1-1-2-2-4	242412	X				
6-22	1-2-1-2-2-4	241422	X				
6-Z23*	2-1-1-2-3-3	234222	X	(6-Z45)*	2-1-1-2-3-3		
6-Z24	1-2-1-2-3-3	233331	X X	6-Z46	1-1-2-2-3-3		X
6-Z25	1-2-1-2-1-4	233241	X X				
6-Z26*	1-2-2-1-1-4	232341	X	(6-Z48)*	1-1-3-2-2-3		
6-27	1-2-1-2-3-3	225222	X X				
6-Z28*	1-2-2-1-3-3	224322	X X	6-Z49*	1-2-1-3-2-3		X X
6-Z29*	1-2-3-2-1-3	224232	X X	6-Z50*	1-3-2-1-2-3		X
6-30*	1-2-3-1-2-3	224223	X				
6-31	1-2-2-3-1-3	223431	X X				
6-34	1-2-2-2-2-3	142422	X				

DURATIONS BY COMMON UNIT
FOR "DE L'AUBE À MIDI SUR LA MER"

Section 1	Section 2	Section 3	Section 4	Section 5
65 durations	107 durations	152 durations	60 durations	74 durations

Key: 1 duration = 1 half note of the original tempo, m. 1

NOTES

Preface

1. Edward Lockspeiser, *Debussy: His Life and Mind*, 2 vols., rev. ed. (Cambridge: Cambridge University Press, 1978) is still the most comprehensive biography and includes valuable indices, lists of works, and bibliographies. Marcel Dietschy, *La passion de Claude Debussy* (Neuchâtel: La Baconnière, 1962) is also an excellent source as is Léon Vallas, *Claude Debussy: Hs Life and Works*, trans. Maire and Grace O'Brien (Oxford: Oxford University Press, 1933; reprint, New York: Dover, 1973). Debussy's published letters and critical writings are dispersed among a number of sources, including *Debussy Letters*, selected and edited by François Lesure and Roger Nichols, translated by Roger Nichols (Cambridge, Mass.: Harvard University Press, 1987), and *Debussy on Music*, edited by Lesure, translated and annotated by Richard Langham Smith (New York: Alfred A. Knopf, 1977). Excellent studies of the history and documents pertaining to specific works include David A. Grayson, *The Genesis of Debussy's "Pelléas et Mélisande"* (Ann Arbor: UMI Research Press, 1986), and Robert Orledge, *Debussy and the Theatre* (Cambridge: Cambridge University Press, 1982). A valuable (though dated) catalog of source locations and publication history is Lesure, *Catalogue de l'oeuvre de Claude Debussy* (Geneva: Minkoff, 1977). Studies devoted to the composer's autographs include Denis-François Raus, "Le terrible finale: Les sources manuscrites de la sonate pour violon et piano de Claude Debussy et la genèse du troisième mouvement," *Cahiers Debussy*, n.s. 2 (1978):30–62; Marie Rolf, "Debussy's 'La Mer': A Critical Analysis in the Light of Early Sketches and Editions" (Ph.D. diss., University of Rochester, 1976); and, by the same author, "Orchestral Manuscripts of Claude Debussy: 1895–1905." *Musical Quarterly* 70 (1984): 538–66. Two important studies of Debussy's relations with the symbolists and symbolism are Stefan Jarocinski, *Debussy: Impressionism and Symbolism*, trans Rollo Myers (London: Eulenburg, 1976) and Arthur B. Wenk, *Debussy and the Poets* (Berkeley: University of California Press, 1976). Many of the above contain extensive bibliographies, but the most comprehensive and best organized (though dated) tool is Claude Abravanel, *Claude Debussy: A Bibliography* (Detroit: Information Coordinators, 1974). *Cahiers Debussy* (Saint-Germain-en-Laye: Centre de documentation Claude Debussy, 1974–76), new series (Geneva: Minkoff, 1977–) is an important source of current scholarly research.

2. Allen Forte, *The Structure of Atonal Music* (New Haven: Yale University Press, 1973).

3. In particular, Wallace Berry's *Structural Functions in Music* (Englewood Cliffs, N.J.: Prentice-Hall, 1976) has stimulated my thinking about nonpitch issues and provided practical solutions to analytical problems.

4. Forte, *Atonal Music*, pp. 3–4.

Chapter 1. Harmony and Voice Leading

1. See James Baker, "Schenkerian Analysis and Post-Tonal Music," in David Beach, ed., *Aspects of Schenkerian Theory* (New Haven: Yale University Press, 1983), 153–86; William E. Benjamin, " 'Pour les Sixtes': An Analysis," *Journal of Music Theory* 22 (1978):253–90; Robert Gauldin, "An Analysis" [of

"Pour les Sixtes"], ibid. 241–51 (Gauldin's voice-leading graphs imply an acceptance of Salzer's emendations to Schenker; see n. 2 below); Michael L. Friedmann, "Approaching Debussy's 'Ondine,'" *Cahiers Debussy,* n.s. 6 (1982):22–35 (combines tonal and set-theoretic approaches); Adele Katz, *Challenge to Musical Tradition,* (New York: Alfred A. Knopf, 1945; reprint, New York: Da Capo, 1972), 248–93; Arthur B. Wenk, *Claude Debussy and Twentieth-Century Music* (Boston: Twayne, 1983); and Felix Salzer, *Structural Hearing: Tonal Coherence in Music,* 2 vols. (New York: Boni, 1952; reprint, New York: Dover 1962). Salzer analyses "Bruyères" (Préludes II) in its entirety (1:222–23) and a portion of *Prélude à "L'après-midi d'un faune"* (1:209–10).

2. Heinrich Schenker, *Harmony,* edited by Oswald Jonas, translated by Elizabeth Mann Borgese (Chicago: University of Chicago Press, 1954), v–xxiv. In *Structural Hearing* (1:27, 204–05), Salzer had hypothesized that pc collections other than V, which he called *contrapuntal-structural chords,* could occur as intermediate structural elements wherever the dominant was absent. Jonas disagreed: "Such an attempt was possible only through misinterpretation of Schenker's basic theories, first of all his concept of tonality, and therefore is doomed to fail" (Schenker, *Harmony,* viii). Despite the argument's attractions, an extension of Schenker's concept of the *Ursatz* that embraces nontonic-related and nondiatonic pc collections as intermediate structural elements opens a Pandora's box of logical inconsistencies. In the Schenkerian model, the significance of the structural V is that its root, which supports the passing second scale degree in the upper voice, unfolds the tonic triad's fifth and thus transforms the passing tone into a consonance by means of a bass note that refers back to the tonic itself. The linear function of the *Urlinie* passing tone is enriched by its acquired harmonic function, whose autonomy also partitions the overall structure (with ramifications for form). Diatonicism within the Ursatz is crucial because it identifies concretely the possible scale steps for any key. William E. Benjamin notes the necessity of making a clear distinction between linear elements (which move stepwise) and harmonic elements (which skip), for if harmonic elements may include seconds without constraints, then the distinction between harmony and line is effaced and function can no longer be determined ("Tonality Without Fifths: Remarks on the First Movement of Stravinsky's Concerto for Piano and Wind Instruments," *In Theory Only* [1976–77]:58). Even though context plays a large determining role, the relativism of Schenker's theory is constrained by clear definitions and functional roles for structural levels, consonance and dissonance, diatonicism and chromaticism, which combine to provide analyst and listener with clues to the possible meaning of each note. To "liberalize" Schenkerian theory is to obliterate the constraints within which Schenker's relativism operates so that *anything* is potentially structural or elaborative, and an element's function becomes wholly a matter of interpretation. See Baker, "Schenkerian Analysis and Post-Tonal Music," 153–86, for a survey and critique of relevant literature.

3. Schenker's comments about Stravinsky come to mind in this regard; see "Thirteen Essays from the Three Yearbooks *Das Meisterwerk in der Musik* by Heinrich Schenker: An Annotated Translation," trans. Silvan Kalib, 3 vols. (Ph.D. diss., Northwestern University, 1977), 2:212–16.

4. Lesure (*Catalogue,* 66) gives this date but expresses doubt, remarking that it is attested neither in writing nor by witnesses.

5. Lesure dates "Nuit d'étoiles" around 1880 (*Catalogue,* 21). This song will be examined in detail in chap. 8.

6. Though the motive is notated in the middleground (rather than the foreground), the tetrachord is a unit in the foreground, owing to the divider that occurs there. The divider is a middleground event, caused by the disjunction between two unfoldings: $a^2-f\sharp^2$ (m. 5) and $e^2-g\sharp^2$ (mm. 6–7).

7. For a discussion of this phenomenon in Webern, see William E. Benjamin, "Ideas of Order in Motivic Music," *Music Theory Spectrum* 1 (1979):24–25.

8. Lesure, *Catalogue,* 85.

9. As we shall see, the V^9 sonority occupies a favored position in Debussy's sonorous vocabulary.

10. The fair copy is among the manuscripts that constitute the Lehman Deposit (Provenance Cortot) in the Pierpont Morgan Library, New York.

11. Katz, *Challenge,* 254–59.

12. Jeffrey Kresky, *Tonal Music: Twelve Analytic Studies,* (Bloomington: Indiana University Press, 1977) devotes a chapter to "La fille aux cheveux de lin." He, too, asserts the importance of the D♭–E♭–D♭ neighbor-note motion and the triadic content of the theme and harmony in mm. 1–3, which he considers seminal for the work's tonal aspects as well as for shaping many of its surface motives.

13. Lesure, *Catalogue,* 146. Debussy composed two versions: one for solo voice and piano, pub-

lished by Durand in 1916, and another for children's choir and piano, which remains unpublished. Lockspeiser (*Debussy*, 2:204–25) poignantly describes Debussy's ordeals during this difficult period.

14. Lesure, *Catalogue*, 144.

15. The chromatic upper line unfolds a diminished triad, a^1–c^2–eb^2, in its series of quadruplets that resemble those of mm. 1–4. The result of superimposing this triad over the theme's D minor triad is an enigmatic ninth-chord that is incongruent with subdominant function.

16. See Richard S. Parks, "Tonal Analogues as Atonal Resources and Their Relation to Form in Debussy's Chromatic Etude," *Journal of Music Theory* 29 (1985):33–60, for a separate study of this piece that concentrates on pc set-theoretic relations.

17. A representative list of additional examples includes "Clair de lune" from *Suite bergamasque* (dated 1890–1905), "Doctor Gradus ad Parnassum" from *Children's Corner* (1906–08), "Minstrels" from Préludes II (1909–10), and "Pour les tierces" from Douze études II (1915). There are many tonal diatonic passages in *Pelléas et Mélisande* (1893–1902), though I believe that the evidence resists attempts to make a convincing case for harmony and voice leading as the ultimate source of control over the opera's pitch materials. For information about primary sources and dates, see Lesure, *Catalogue*, 74, 89, 118, 121, and 144.

18. Debussy was not the first composer who exhibited a special interest in the subdominant, of course; many nineteenth-century composers seem to have shared this predilection, including Chopin, Schumann, Brahms, and Liszt. For example, Schumann's "Romanze" from the *Fassingschwanck aus Wien* exploits the enigmatic relationship between subdominant and tonic in the roles occupied by C on the surface (mm. 1–2) and in the middleground (mm. 9–17).

Chapter 2. Tonality Imposed through Other Means

1. In the example, referential pcs 10,1,3,6 are notated using open noteheads; nonreferential pcs use filled noteheads.

2. Parks, "Tonal Analogues."

3. Vallas, *Claude Debussy*, 19–20, describes the occasion in 1883 when Théodore Dubois, a harmony teacher at the Paris Conservatoire (where Debussy was a student) and organist at the Madeleine, improvised an accompaniment to a verse of the Magnificat "in the Debussy manner" using mutation stops to produce parallel chords through doublings at various intervals.

4. Phrases are defined by full and half cadences.

5. Note that fluctuations in the degree of pc saturation by a referential collection may or may not involve modulation. In conventionally tonal music such fluctuations characterize modulations, but in musics that eschew diatonic deep structures, modulation is not necessarily a concomitant feature.

6. The statistical tallies include doublings. The voice-leading graphs of example 1.5 show registral placement.

7. Dated 12 Dec. 1909 in the fair copy (Lehman Deposit, Pierpont Morgan Library, New York).

8. George Perle characterizes it as a "naive" example of serial technique without discussing its tonal aspect (*Serial Technique and Atonality*, 3d ed. [Berkeley: University of California Press, 1972], 40–41). Katz (*Challenge*, 284–88) attaches much importance to the augmented triads (especially the form [0,4,8], which she sees unfolded throughout the work) and to the incongruously omnipresent Bb_1 pedal. Apropos of tonality—how and, indeed, whether the piece is tonal—she is ambivalent. Lockspeiser (*Debussy*, 2:234) alludes to "ambiguities of key" and assigns the piece variously to A minor (?) and C major. He, too, considers the Bb_1 pedal an enigma.

9. Tripartite schemes in which the last section synthesizes contrasting features from the preceding two occur in a number of other works, such as "Pour les arpèges composés" (Douze études II).

10. Exceptions are mm. 31–32, especially m. 31, where referential pcs 6,8,10 are *not* focal points except in the inner voice, which briefly interjects new pcs 1,7. The avoidance of referential pcs and the interjection of two new pcs conjoin with crescendos, a ritard followed by a ceasura, a pronounced increase in activity seen in the number of notes struck, and the second widest register span of the piece (Bb_1–d^3) to make this one of the composition's two climactic moments. (The other occurs at m. 44.) Their placement at the approximate center of the piece will be discussed in part 5.

11. Exchanges of this sort will be discussed in part 2.

12. Lesure, *Catalogue*, 94.

13. "unis avec la blanche cire qui est douce à mes lèvres comme le miel."

14. Wenk's *Debussy and the Poets* contains repeated allusions to this idea. See, for example, his comments on Debussy's settings of Banville, Baudelaire, and Verlaine (pp. 7–8) and his concluding chapter (272–77).

15. Debussy's own *Proses lyriques* (1892–93) are far less adventurous musically and poetically than the *Cinq poèmes de Baudelaire* of 1887–89, the *Chansons de Bilitis*, or the *Trois poèmes de Stéphane Mallarmé* of 1913. (Dates from Lesure, *Catalogue*, 84, 64, and 127).

16. Lesure, *Catalogue*, 86.

17. Dated 1915 (Lesure, *Catalogue*, 144).

18. The cyclic variation technique employed throughout the quartet is well known, as is Debussy's debt to Franck for its model (see, for example, Lockspeiser, *Debussy*, 1:125–26). But the quartet's "theme" is basically morphological; contour, harmony, and durational proportion are features whose superficies vary but whose structural shapes remain. In *Prélude à "L'après-midi d'un faune,"* Debussy turns away from morphological features as constants, towards processive features.

19. Deborah Stein, "The Expansion of the Subdominant in the Late Nineteenth Century," *Journal of Music Theory* 27 (1983):153–80, provides a good overview of the increasing structural importance accorded to the subdominant by late nineteenth-century composers, especially Hugo Wolf.

20. The implication of this conjecture will be explored more fully in part 2.

21. Julia D'Almendra, *Les modes grégoriens dans l'oeuvre de Claude Debussy* (Paris: Gabriel Enoult, 1950) is an exhaustive study of modes and their use.

22. Allen Forte, "Schenker's Conception of Musical Structure," *Journal of Music Theory* 3 (1959): 28–30, includes a discussion of voice leading within "parallel chords" in "La cathédrale engloutie."

Chapter 3. Four Genera

1. Vocal works will receive extensive coverage in part 3.

2. See, for example, Forte, *Atonal Music*, and Richard Chrisman, "Describing Structural Aspects of Pitch-Class Sets Using Successive Interval Arrays," *Journal of Music Theory* 21 (1977):1–28.

3. Sets are ordered and labled according to Forte's list (*Atonal Music*, 179–81).

4. "C major," for example, denotes a specific manifestation (for whose matrix of pc relations pc C serves as focus) of the general concept of "tonality and key," but C major may also be regarded as a specific manifestation of the general concept of "diatonic tonal collection," for which "C major scale" denotes the constituent pcs.

5. By "diatonic" is meant the collection of seven pcs that generates the major and natural minor scales; expressed in terms of pc sets, this would be set 7–35 plus all of its subsets and supersets.

6. Other diatonic piano pieces include "La cathédrale engloutie" (Préludes I), "Bruyères" (Préludes II), "Pagodes" (*Les estampes*), "Pour invoquer Pan, dieu du vent d'été" (*Six épigraphes antiques*), "Doctor Gradus ad Parnassum" (*Children's Corner*), and "Pour les huit doigts" (Douze études I). His early songs (through 1888) are wholly diatonic, as are many later ones, including his last song, "Noël des enfants qui n'ont plus de maisons" (1916).

7. Despite unwanted connotations of regularity and standard length (of about four bars), the term *phrase* conveniently invokes the notion of small, coherent formal units, which is the sense in which I use it.

8. The reader who resists hearing the arpeggiated tetrachord of motive A as conjoined to the eighth-note chord at the end of the bar may be won over by a glance at mm. 28–30, where the return of the theme (an octave higher) is first prepared by articulating a C-flat major triad. This triad is then sustained for three measures under the theme itself, where, in spite of registral partitioning, it would be difficult to avoid associating the two elements.

9. They are forms of set 4–27, which is not important in this piece, though it is a prominant constituent of Debussy's harmonic vocabulary.

10. Sets 4–26 and 5–35 belong to the special category of symmetrical sets whose inversion forms replicate each other. Set 5–35 as (0,2,4,7,9), for example, yields the same pc content under inversion followed by transposition (where t=4): $I(0,2,4,7,9) = (0,10,8,5,3)$; $T(t_4(0,10,8,5,3)) = (4,2,0,9,7)$.

11. Sets 4–11 and 6–32 do not participate wholly in the invariance relations.

12. Kresky, *Tonal Music*, 158, suggests that the linear trichord comprised of a M2 and a m3 (set 3–7), which saturates this brief gesture, derives from the neighbor-note motion E♭–D♭ over B♭ (and G♭) in the cadence of mm. 2–3. Set 3–7 appears as a trichordal subset of sets 4–11, 4–26, 5–27, 5–35, 6–

32, and 7–35 more times than any other trichord; hence its ubiquity in diatonic music should not surprise us.

13. This return of pcs and sets points to m. 24 (rather than m. 28) as the beginning of the reprise.

14. The sketch appears on p. 104 of the Debussy sketchbook date 1909–11. It is held in the Robert Owen Lehman Collection on deposit in the Pierpont Morgan Library, and is reproduced courtesy of the Pierpont Morgan Library.

15. Though certainly germane to an analytical study, the evidence in autographs and sketches is far too large a topic to include here. Excellent documentary studies include, in addition to those of Grayson, Raus, and Rolf mentioned in the notes to the Preface: James Robert Briscoe, "Debussy's Earliest Songs," *College Music Symposium* 24 (1984):81–95; and Briscoe, "The Compositions of Claude Debussy's Formative Years (1879–1887)" (Ph.D. diss., University of North Carolina, 1979).

16. Some diatonic sets (set 7–35 included) evoke associations with the tonal repertoire through their sonorous properties alone (though in Debussy's music such associations may mislead, since they can be thwarted by context). Parks, "Tonal Analogues" takes this problem as its point of departure.

17. See for example, Milton Babbitt, "Set Structure as a Compositional Determinant," *Journal of Music Theory* 5 (1961):72–94; Richmond Browne, "Tonal Implications of the Diatonic Set," *In Theory Only* 5/6–7 (July–Aug. 1981): 3–21; John Clough: "Aspects of Diatonic Sets," *Journal of Music Theory* 23 (1979):45–61; Clough, "Diatonic Interval Sets and Transformational Structures," *Perspectives of New Music* 18 (1979–80):461–82; and Clough and Gerald Myerson, "Variety and Multiplicity in Diatonic Systems," *Journal of Music Theory* 29 (1985):249–70.

18. Because all two- and ten-note sets are symmetrical, there is no need to identify them as such on the table.

19. Sets 8–23, 9–9, and 10–5 are also "quartal" and exhibit similarities in relative numbers of entries across their ivs. But whereas for the smaller sets, a concentration of entries in a few ics also limits severely the number of possible entries for other ics, for the larger sets, the dramatic increase in overall ic content militates against an exceptional concentration within any one ic. As a consequence, sets 8–23, 9–9, and 10–5 are significantly less distinctively diatonic then are their counterparts of three to seven pcs.

20. In chapter 2. Ethan Haimo, "Generated Collections and Interval Control in Debussy's Preludes," *In Theory Only* 4/8 (Feb.–March 1979): 3–15, discusses this invariant relation with reference to the transition from pentatonic/diatonic mm. 43–47 back to whole-tone mm. 48–64.

21. The dramatic crescendo and use of high register coupled with increases in notes struck per beat and texture-density are other components of the climax.

22. The reader will note that I use the term *acceleration* here in the same sense as Wallace Berry, "Rhythmic Accelerations in Beethoven," *Journal of Music Theory* 22 (1978):177–240.

23. Dated in the manuscript fair copy, Lehman Deposit, Morgan Library, New York.

24. E. Robert Schmitz, *The Piano Works of Claude Debussy* (London: Duell, Sloan and Pearce, 1950; reprint, New York: Dover, 1966), 133–36; George Perle, *Serial Composition and Atonality*, 3d ed. (Berkeley: University of California Press, 1972), 5–6, 40–41; and Arnold Whittall, "Tonality and the Whole-Tone Scale in the Music of Debussy," *Music Review* 36 (1975):261–71. Schmitz's traditional approach identifies (p. 133) what he calls "tonic" and "dominant" "teams" (G♯–C–E and F♯–D–B♭, respectively) and the pedal B♭$_1$ that "links the entire prelude" (p. 134), through which he attempts to ascribe hierarchic function to specific pcs. For Schmitz, B♭ is not a "tonic" but a member of the dominant "team." Perle (p. 41) dismisses any tonal implications in favor of a primitive form of serialism. He does not consider organization overall nor the relationship of whole-tone to pentatonic materials. Whittall (p. 282) identifies three "weaknesses" in "Voiles": its opposition of "static and dynamic harmonic entities," by which he means the whole-tone scale and the pentatonic scale; the use of only one transposition of the whole-tone scale; and the lack of integration of the two scales. Why these are "weaknesses" remains unexplained.

25. It is exactly these kinds of transformations (sometimes complicated by transposition) that occur in "Jimbo's Lullaby," which we will examine next.

26. Maurice Emmanuel recorded the following remark made by Debussy during a conversation in 1889 with his former harmony teacher, Ernest Guiraud: "The tonal scale must be enriched by other scales" (Lockspeiser, *Debussy*, 1:206).

27. Lesure, *Catalogue*, 118.

28. Whittall, "Tonality and the Whole-Tone Scale," 282.

29. "Chromatic collections" are sets whose chief characteristic is a predominance of ic 1 in their ivs

and sias. Chromatic sets in Debussy's music more nearly exhibit order relations because they are usually disposed in successions of adjacent semitones.

30. It occurs as the linear tetrachord that spans degrees 4–7 in the major scale.

31. The forms of diatonic cynosural set 7–35 that contain subset 5–35 (as 5,7,9,0,2) correspond to the major scales for C, F, and Bb major, to which Db (pc 1) is foreign.

32. The pc content for Ab major (and its relative minor) is 7–35 (= 8,10,0,*1,3,5,7*); for Bb and Ab melodic minor it is 7–34 (= 10,0,*1,3,5,7*,9 and 8,10,11,*1,3,5,7*, respectively).

33. A more conventional way to account for pc 6 is through traditional harmonic analysis. F is a tonicized dominant of Bb major (to which it resolves in the next section), complicated by mixture (the Gb triad can be heard as Bb minor's submediant).

34. "Octatonic" refers to the eight-note scale of alternating whole and half steps. Sets 4–12 and 5–31 are subsets of that scale. The octatonic genus is discussed below.

35. A prominent complement results from the new pcs interjected in m. 53: the pc content of mm. 49–53 forms set 8–22, whereas the two upper lines of mm. 49–52 form tetrachord 4–22.

36. Though trichord 3–12 appears in tonal music, its usage as an altered chord severely restricted by voice-leading imperatives makes it rare.

37. Though it is neither diatonic nor chromatic, the summary set, 8–11, exhibits ties with both genera.

38. Exceptions are mm. 39–46, which are entirely whole-tone, and mm. 54–56, which connect Gb from m. 53 to Eb of m. 57 by chromatic passing motion in the bass.

39. The two anomalous octatonic pc sets cited in mm. 34 and 37–38 are fleeting external references to yet another genus.

40. This is the kind of ambiguity to which Whittall refers (Tonality and the Whole-Tone Scale," 282).

41. See Parks, "Tonal Analogues," for a detailed study of this piece.

42. The forms of 7–35 that hold the pentatonic theme's pcs (5,7,9,0,2) as a subset include (9,10,0,2,3,5,7), (4,5,7,9,10,0,2), and (11,0,2,4,5,7,9). The first of these is the melody's most likely reference given the key signature and the course of subsequent pitch events.

43. Lesure (*Catalogue*, 128–29) gives 1910–12 as the dates of composition for the second book of Préludes. According to Roy Howat and Claude Helffer, Debussy gave the premiere on 5 March 1913 (*Oeuvres complètes de Claude Debussy*, series 1, vol. 5 [Paris: Durand-Costallat, 1985], xii). It seems likely that "Feuilles mortes" was completed towards the end of 1912, but it is impossible to date the piece more precisely.

44. That the melodic line is itself diatonic (5–23 as 11,1,2,4,6) is possible because of the octatonic modulations in mm. 2–3, a feature to be examined shortly.

45. I call the three transposition forms of set 8–28 types A (= pcs 0,1,3,4,6,7,9,10), B (= pcs 1,2,4,5,7,8,10,11), and C (= pcs 2,3,5,6,8,9,11,0). The two represented in the pc set materials of theme A are type A (mm. 1,3) and type B (m. 2).

46. The scale for m. 8 corresponds to E major. Scales for mm. 9 and 10–14 can only be conjectured, since hexachord 6–32 could occur as a subset in either of two forms of 7–35 (D major or G major) and set 9–7 contains two forms of set 7–35 as subsets (C major or G major). The familiar tonal ambiguity of an implied tonic that is promised but never delivered has its set-theoretic counterpart here.

47. There are, of course, only two distinct whole-tone scales, related by transposition where t = 1.

48. Subdivisions 1/1, 2/3, 3/6, and 5/10 contain six of these pcs, and 2/4 contains all seven; conversely, subdivisions 1/2, 3/7, 4/8, 8/14, 9/15, and 9/16 contain as many or more pcs excluded from this form of 7–35 as are included in it. Note that tonal referents need not be tied to a particular genus. Here, indeed, they manifest interconnections with two different genera: diatonic and octatonic. Also, controlled fluctuation between referential and nonreferential pcs constitutes one of the composition's dynamic processes. (An analogy with modulations to distant keys is not far-fetched.)

49. James Baker, *The Music of Alexander Scriabin* (New Haven: Yale University Press, 1986) does not mention octatonicism as such, but identifies 8–28 as a source of harmonic organization. Arther Berger, "Problems with Pitch Organization in Stravinsky," in Benjamin Boretz and Edward T. Cune, eds., *Perspectives on Schoenberg and Stravinsky* (Princeton, N.J.: Princeton University Press, 1968), 123–54, demonstrates the octatonic scale's importance as pitch resource in several of Stravinsky's works. Phillip Russom, "A Theory of Pitch Organization for the Early Music of Maurice Ravel" (Ph.D. diss., Yale University, 1985) includes the octatonic scale among several scales that he identifies as resources

for Ravel's pitch materials. Pieter C. van den Toorn, *The Music of Igor Stravinsky* (New Haven: Yale University Press, 1983) examines the scale's use as a pitch resource throughout Stravinsky's oeuvre.

50. I discussed Debussy's use of octatonic collections in "Pitch Organization in Debussy: 'Unordered Sets in 'Brouillards,'" *Music Theory Spectrum* 2 (1980):119–34. Other pieces in Préludes II that employ the octatonic genus include "Les fées sont d'exquises danseuses," "La terrasse des audiences du clair de lune," and "Ondine."

51. Enharmonic equivalents count as only one scale.

52. D minor passages, for example, usually utilize the diatonic C (of the relative-major key) as well as the new (key-defining) pc, C♯.

53. Transposition of the whole-tone scale returns either all pcs as invariants (where t = ic 2,4,6)—in which case the effect is insignificant—or no pcs (where t = ic 1,3,5).

54. Transposition of 8–28 by ics 1,2,4,5 returns four invariants in each case, all forms of set 4–28.

Chapter 4. The Pc Set Genera in Early Works

1. Lesure, *Catalogue*, 64–65.

2. Ibid., 80.

3. Ibid., 83–84.

4. Exceptions are the sprinkling of wholly diatonic pieces, which eschew extensive chromaticism, that appear throughout his oeuvre, including "La fille aux cheveux de lin," "Bruyères," and "Noël des enfants qui n'ont plus de maisons."

5. This song is frequently used to illustrate connections between Debussy and Wagner. Robin Holloway, *Debussy and Wagner* (London: Eulenberg, 1979), 44–47, cites resemblances between "Recueillement" and the beginning of *Tristan und Isolde*, act II. Roger Nichols, *Debussy* (Oxford: Oxford University Press, 1973), 9–11, rightly observes that the sound of mm. 10–11 is Wagnerian. However, his assertion that "the harmony is largely triadic, but within a range of keys that the older professors at the Conservatoire perhaps found disturbing" does not do justice to the song's more radical attributes.

6. Fluctuant phrase length is typical of all except the earliest of Debussy's songs. Normative phrase lengths will be taken up in part 5.

7. "Aquarelles 2: Spleen" (*Ariettes oubliées*), which antedates "Recueillement" slightly, conspicuously employs octatonic pentachord 5–31 in inversely equivalent, interlocking forms at mm. 3–4 and again at m. 12. The pentachord is disposed as a chord (4,7,10,0,1) and in the right hand alone (7,8,10,1,4). The nondiatonic pcs are E and G, and while the G can be related through voice leading to the preceding harmony on G♭, E submits less gracefully to this rationale. I assume that Debussy sought out this unusual harmony for its own sonorous attractions and, given its dual disposition in inversely equivalent forms, that he was more than casually aware of its characteristic ic contents. The pc materials of the song's remainder are typically post-Romantic and unremarkable. My observations are based on the first version of the song published in Paris by E. Girod in 1888. Howat, *Debussy*, 34–36, discusses aspects of the form and proportion of the song, and credits the harmonies I have cited to "tritonal juxtaposition (G♭ to C)." He assigns to this piece the place of importance in Debussy's evolution that I would reserve for "Recueillement" and "Le jet d'eau."

8. Its forms span major-scale degrees 2–3–4–5–6–7 and 5–6–7–8–1–2.

9. Any transposition of trichord 3–11 in its major-triad form is a subset of three rcs, as is its inversely equivalent minor-triad form.

10. These bars in particular are cited by Holloway (*Debussy and Wagner*, 44–47) and Nichols (*Debussy*, 9–11) in their discussions of Debussy's "Wagnerian" tendencies.

11. The invariants (11,1,3,5) form the ambiguous tetrachord 4–21 encountered in "Jimbo's Lullaby," where it plays a similar role as a link between the same diatonic and whole-tone pentachordal representatives.

12. Yniold's scene with the sheep, for example (*Pelléas et Mélisande*, act IV, scene 3), makes much of set 6–27 as well as 6–34, which will be discussed shortly.

13. Set 6–34 is the *Prometheus* or "mystic" chord of Scriabin. Simms, *Music of the Twentieth Century* (New York: Schriner Books, 1986), 40–41, calls it the "nearly-whole-tone" hexachord and discusses its ubiquity in early twentieth-century music. Baker, *Scriabin*, discusses it extensively. See also H. H. Stuckenschmidt, "Debussy or Berg? The Mystery of a Chord Progression," *Musical Quarterly* 51 (1965):453–59.

14. "La gerbe d'eau qui berce / Ses mille fleurs, . . . Tombe comme une averse / De larges pleurs."

15. "Reste longtemps sans les rouvrir, / Dans cette pose nonchalante / Où t'a surprise le plaisir."

16. Set 4–25 is also whole-tone; set 4–27 is also diatonic.

17. Lockspeiser, *Debussy,* 1:206–07.

18. Louis Laloy, "*Claude Debussy et le Debussysme,*" *S.I.M. Revue musicale mensuelle* 6 (1910):511–14: "L'invention remonte aux anciens Grecs; elle a duré jusqu'à nos jours. Ainsi le son cesse d'être un son pour devenir une note, c'est-à-dire un numéro d'ordre; à l'entendre, on n'éprouve aucune impression particulière, mais on le reconnaît pour le premier, le troisième ou le sixième degré d'une certaine gamme. . . . Et fréquemment ses mélodies n'emploient d'autres notes que celles de la gamme majeure, ses accords sont ceux d'un ton déterminé: elle retrouve ainsi le système classique, mais sans avoir eu l'intention préméditée de s'y conformer, et seulement parce que cette disposition est celle même de sa fantaisie. Elle en retrouve également de tout autres: on croit entendre tantôt l'écho de modes anciens, ceux du chant grégorien ou de la musique grecque, tantôt les gammes chinoises sans demi-tons, puis des gammes chromatiques, toutes en demi-tons, des gammes par tons entiers, d'autres encore, avec des altérations, jusqu'ici inconnues, du quatrième, du cinquième et du septième degré. . . . Il y a plus: nous arrivons à une époque où tout accord, quelle qu'en soit la composition et même si on ne peut le réduire à des sons harmoniques, pourra compter comme consonance. Un accord n'a plus aucune preuve à nous fournir de sa légitimité; c'est une sonorité, qui, bien employée, contentera pleinement notre oreille, sera donc justifiée. De la combinaison des sons, un autre son d'ensemble résulte, comme de la juxtaposition des couleurs, une autre couleur."

19. "d'autres encore, avec des altérations, jusqu'ici inconnues, . . ."

20. Forte, *Atonal Music,* 63.

21. I have used Charles Lord's measures, where the range is 1–5 and the smaller the number, the greater the similarity. See Lord, "Intervallic Similarity Relations in Atonal Set Analysis," *Journal of Music Theory* 25 (1981):91–111.

22. A glance at sias on the complete list of 210 pc sets (appendix 1) will place this information in perspective. We need not consider the last interval for trichordal sias since the first two intervals connect all three pcs. Trichordal patterns *not* found in characteristic 8–17/18/19–complex sets include 1–5, 1–6, 2–3, 2–4, 2–5, 2–6, 3–5, 3–6, 4–4 (except for 4–19), and 4–5. Of these, 2–2 and 2–3 are prominent in the sias of diatonic sets, while 2–2, 2–4, and 4–4 are prominent among those of the whole-tone genus.

23. The octatonic genus appears in "Recueillement," which is one of Debussy's first works to use the pc set genera, and the 8–17/18/19–complex genus appears in *Jeux.*

Chapter 5. The PC Set Genera in Later Works

1. For information see: Lockspeiser, *Debussy,* 2:173–76; and Orledge, *Debussy and the Theatre,* 149 and 162–76. Orledge's account is very thorough.

2. Jann Pasler, "Debussy, *Jeux:* Playing with Time and Form," *19th Century Music* 6 (1982):60–75, is an excellent analytical study that concentrates on the issue of dramatic expression achieved musically through manipulation of meter, tempo, form, and instrumental color.

3. The form of hexachord 6–Z44 that embodies the pc content of m. 192 is associated with two forms of cynosural set 8–18; however, their common subset, which contains that form of 6–Z44, is 7–22 (0,1,2,5,6,8,9). In cases where two (or more) forms of a cynosural octachord are inferable as supersets of a genus's representative, and evidence does not permit one to be selected over the other, the largest common (invariant) subset represents them as a referential collection. Hence, 7–22 in its form (0,1,2,5,6,8,9) represents both forms of 8–18 inferable for m. 192. The situation is similar for m. 193; two forms of 8–18 are inferable as cynosural supersets for 6–Z19, and so 7–22 in its form (3,4,6,7,10,11,0) represents them.

4. Herbert Eimert, "Debussy's *Jeux,*" translated by Leo Black in *Die Reihe* 5:3–20 (Bryn Mawr, Penn.: Presser, 1959): traces motivic derivations through a process that he calls "endless variation" and "endless melody."

5. "Le lien qui les relient [les divers épisodes] est peut-être subtil mais il existe pourtant?" (letter to Gabriel Pierné dated 5 March 1914, in Debussy, *Lettres,* ed. François Lesure [Paris: Hermann, 1980], 251). Pasler, *Jeux,* 69, interprets this as a reference primarily to metric and tempo relations. Orledge's assertion is weakened somewhat by the interrogative form of the quotation (I am indebted to Mr.

Harry Haskell for pointing this out), which suggests that perhaps the "awareness" was more intuitive than conscious.

6. This feature of *Jeux* will be examined in more detail in part 5.

7. Set 3–7 is one of two trichordal subsets of set 4–23; the other is 3–9. Both occur in two forms each.

8. Judith Shatin Allen, "Tonal Allusion and Illusion: Debussy's Sonata for Flute, Viola and Harp," *Cahiers Debussy,* n.s. 7 (1983):38–48, mixes traditional harmonic analysis and Schenkerian theory in her approach to the issue of tonality in this work.

Chapter 6. Complement Relations

1. Dated "Winter 1894" by the composer on the autograph (Lehman Deposit, Pierpont Morgan Library, New York). The date will serve to distinguish this set of *Images* from the two later sets, *Images* I and II.

2. The sets that provide the harmonies of m. 39 are, in order, 4–27 (6,8,11,2), 4–24 (twice: 5,7,9,1 and 2,4,6,10), and 3–5. The outer parts form sets 3–7 (6,9,11) and 5–4 (4,7,8,9,10). Each is associated with two or more genera, but only the 8–17/18/19–complex genus holds them all, along with the summary set, 10–3.

3. See example 4.1 for a complete pc reduction.

4. The other pairs are 6–Z25/(6–Z47), 6–Z26/(6–Z48), 2–2/10–2, 2–3/10–3, 2–4/10–4, and 2–5/10–5. The sets listed parenthetically are not subsets of 7–35.

5. See Constantin Brailoiu, "Pentatony in Debussy's Music," *Studia Memoriae Belae Bartok Sacra* (London: Boosey and Hawkes, 1958), 377–417, for an exhaustive study of this feature.

6. Two pc constructs integral to Debussy's musical language appear in every genre and saturate his entire oeuvre: trichord 3–7, used both harmonically and melodically, and the M2 used as a harmonic interval. Set 3–7 is source for the connection that Jarocinski (*Debussy,* 112) recognizes among the opening of "Nuit d'étoiles," Mélisande's motif, *La damoiselle élue,* and "De fleurs" (*Proses lyriques*). In fact, the trichord is conspicuous everywhere in Debussy's music.

In "Tonal Analogues," 55, I noted the ubiquity of the M2 dyad as a harmonic construct throughout "Pour les degrés chromatiques." In fact, M2s are omnipresent in Debussy's music, and the chromatic etude is merely typical.

7. Appendix 3 includes all pairs for this genus.

8. See appendix 5 for the hexachordal pairs. In general, hexachordal complements are rare in Debussy.

9. See appendix 4.

10. See appendix 6.

11. David Lewin, "Some Instances of Parallel Voice-Leading in Debussy," *19th Century Music* 11 (1987):59–72, discusses the parallel fifths, harmonic progression, and modulations of these bars.

12. Other pairs follow: in mm. 4–10 the pc content yields set 7–26, whose complement is found in mm. 8–9 in the horns (pc 10 serves an embellishing function and is "nonharmonic" to the set); in mm. 11–12, the pc content forms set 9–3 with its complement disposed in the violas and clarinets.

13. Lesure, *Catalogue,* 132–33.

14. Lewin, "Parallel Voice-Leading," 59–62, proposes a perspicuous reading for the parallels in the opening bars that suggests an origin for the enigmatic obligato line of mm. 61–64.

15. An exception is "Voiles," mm. 42–47, where the anhematonic pentatonic scale alone accounts for all pcs.

16. As in the closing chord of the fanfare that precedes "Le concile des faux dieux" (*Le martyre de Saint-Sébastien* III); "Danseuses de Delphes," m. 16/beat 2; and "La cathédrale engloutie," mm. 23–24.

Chapter 7. *Pelléas et Mélisande*

1. Grayson, *Genesis* is a thorough, comprehensive, and readable source of information about the history and documents related to this, Debussy's largest work. Lockspeiser uses the completion of the opera as the dividing point between the two volumes of his study.

2. Leonard Meyer discusses the general relationship of emotion to music stimulus in *Emotion and*

Meaning in Music (Chicago: University of Chicago Press, 1956), 256–72. See also Manfred Clynes, *Sentics: The Touch of Emotions* (New York: Anchor Press/Doubleday, 1978), esp. chap. 8, "Music and Sentics: Music as a Sentic Mirror." Clynes proposes a theory that correlates melodic shapes to various emotions as part of a general theory of emotion and aesthetic perception. He does not address the issue of the relation between harmonic sonority and emotion.

3. I do not wish to imply that only two psychological domains are subject to manipulation by pc materials, nor that affect must always be general in nature.

4. Although the focus throughout this chapter is on pc materials, I do not mean to imply that other musical elements are not affective. Indeed, some will receive at least cursory treatment in part 5.

5. It is in this area that Clynes's work falls. In *Sentics*, 226–34, he discusses motivic shapes in keyboard works by Bach, Beethoven, Chopin, Mozart, and Schubert, which he links to specific emotions as aural correlates to spatial and temporal patterns from other sensory domains.

6. Grayson (*Genesis*, esp. 225–75) examines the corpus of autographs, proofs, and annotated scores in order to trace leitmotivs through Debussy's many revisions. His perspicacious account provides a wealth of information about Debussy's evolving views of the characters as well as insights regarding subtler uses of leitmotivs for expressive purposes. Orledge (*Debussy and the Theatre*, 81–96) discusses leitmotivs and their transformations. Nichols (*Debussy*, 43–44) lists transformations of a motive associated with Golaud. Mary Jean van Appledorn, "A Stylistic Study of Claude Debussy's Opera, Pelléas et Mélisande" (Ph.D. diss., University of Rochester, 1966), 406–34, lists thirty-two leitmotivs and traces their appearances and transformations throughout the opera. Other sources that enumerate leitmotivs include Antoine Goléa, *Pelléas et Mélisande: Analyse poétique et musicale,* (Paris: Château-Rouge, 1952); Maurice Emmanuel, *Pelléas et Mélisande de Debussy: Etude et analyse* (Paris: Mellottée, 1925); Michel-Dimitri Calvocoressi, "Debussy and the Leitmotiv," *Musical Times* 66 (1935): 695–97; and Lawrence Gilman, *Debussy's "Pelléas et Mélisande": A Guide to the Opera* (New York: Schirmer, 1907).

7. Virgil Thomson, *The Musical Scene* (New York: Alfred A. Knopf, 1945), 165–67, provides charming character sketches of Mélisande and Golaud in a review of a 1944 Metropolitan Opera production. He considers Golaud's actions to be those of a sane and forthright (if brutal) member of the nineteenth-century French middle class.

8. Claude Debussy, *Pelléas et Mélisande* (Paris: Durand, 1957). See Grayson, *Genesis*, 133–95, for information about the differences among editions. The International, Dover reprint, and Durand editions use identical pagination and measure numbers.

9. "J'ai tué sans raison!"

10. "Est ce que ce n'est pas à faire pleurer les pierres! Ils s'étaient embrassés comme des petits enfants."

11. "Et moi, moi tout de suite!"

12. "Est-ce le soleil qui se couche?"

13. "Oui; c'est le soleil qui se couche sur la mer; il est tard."

14. "Je n'ai jamais été mieux portante."

15. "Que dis-tu?"

16. "Je ne dis plus ce que je veux."

17. "Je suis tout heureux de t'entendre parler ainsi . . ."

18. Set 7–32 is one of those two large sets (the other is 7–34) that correspond to minor-scale inventories.

19. "il y a encore le médecin"

20. "Et puis il y a encore quelqu'un."

21. "Qui est-ce?"

22. "C'est ton mari, c'est Golaud."

23. "Golaud est ici? Pourquoi ne vient-il pas près de moi?"

24. "Est-ce vous, Golaud?"

25. "Je ne vous reconnaissais presque plus."

26. "C'est que j'ai le soleil du soir dans les yeux."

27. This is an anomaly since most pairs of diatonic rcs form cynosural supersets.

28. "Pourquoi regardez-vous le murs? Vous avez maigri et vieilli."

29. "Je voudrais lui dire quelque chose . . ."

30. "Je suis un malheureux."

31. Orledge, *Debussy and the Theatre*, 54–55. See also Grayson, *Genesis*, 113–32.

32. "Je ne puis pas te dire le mal que je t'ai fait. Mais je le vois, je le vois si clairement aujourd'hui depuis le premier jour."

33. "Oh! vous êtes belle."

34. "Voyons, ne pleurez pas ainsi."

35. "C'est que j'ai le soleil du soir dans les yeux."

36. At p. 379/2, as at most crucial dramatic moments, a striking complement relation occurs: the vocal line overlaps the diatonic passage of p. 378/11–p. 379/2 with the 8–17/18/19–complex passage of p. 379/3–10. The connecting note, d♯², added to the pc content of the latter passage, yields set 8–Z15 (7–30 as 0,1,2,4,6,8,9, + pc 3), whose Z-complement (4–Z29) is embedded prominently in the accompaniment ostinato figuration of the violas.

37. Although Golaud does not specifically address his misdeeds here, he does elsewhere, most poignantly near the end of act V, following Mélisande's death, when he declares (p. 402/5): "It is not my fault!" ("Ce n'est pas ma faute!")

38. Register, sonorous density, dynamic level, accent, and attenuation of overall activity conjoin to make this an especially piquant passage. Also, embedded complements appear in profusion here, as the harmonies are all forms of 5–34 that pair to produce forms of 7–34.

39. "Mon petit bras n'est pas assez long, et cette pierre ne veut pas être soulevée."

40. Whole-tone superset 8–24 provides the pc content of p. 311/1–6, in which 5–33 is the most conspicuous harmony. Other important sets include 6–34 and 7–30, both associated with the 8–17/18/19–complex genus.

41. "J'entends pleurer les moutons."

42. "Il n'y a plus de soleil."

43. "Ils ont peur du noir. Ils se serrent! Ils pleurent et ils vont vite!"

44. Hexachord 6–27 is prominent throughout p. 313/1–4.

45. Orledge, *Debussy and the Theatre* 64, 350–51n24 attributes the rumor to Albert Carré, the director of the Opéra Comique at the time of the first production. His view is supported by David A. Grayson, "Debussy in the Opera House: An Unpublished Letter Concerning Yniold and Mélisande," *Cahiers Debussy*, n.s. 9 (1985):17–28, who confirms Carré's role and presents evidence (in the form of a letter from Debussy to a subsequent Opéra director, Pierre Barthélemy Gheusi) that, at least so far as the composer was concerned, practical considerations led to the cut and nothing more.

46. Most will agree, for example, that the piano reduction possesses much (though certainly not all) of the expressive impact of the orchestra version.

Chapter 8. A Survey of Text Expression in Early, Middle, and Late Works

1. Lockspeiser (*Debussy*, 2:228) dates it to 1876. Lesure (*Catalogue*, 21) considers this much too early and places it around 1880. Margaret Cobb, *The Poetic Debussy: A Collection of His Song Texts and Selected Letters* (Boston: Northeastern University Press, 1982), 12–13n, agrees with Lesure. The Peters edition gives 1876 or 1878 as possible dates; see Debussy, *Frühe Lieder nach verschiedenen Dichtern*, ed. Reiner Zimmerman (Leipzig: Peters, 1976), 41.

2. All pc replacements that result from diatonic modulations involve semitonal shifts, which are also characteristic of Debussy's technique of mutation and modulation among the nondiatonic pc set genera. Surely his awareness of this relation embodied in traditional materials contributed impetus to extend the principle to nondiatonic materials.

3. Observe, for example, the use of wider and higher registers in the vocal line of the more agitated "B" sections compared with the less agitated "A" sections.

4. Set 7–32 (pcs 4,5,7,8,10,0,1 in mm. 13–17), for example, generates the F♮ harmonic minor scale. That 7–32 and 6–Z40 are both indigenous to the 8–17/18/19–complex genus suggests yet another traditional source for this genus. Debussy may have discovered his sonic inventories through improvisation and experimentation, but his point of departure was the harmonic language of his tonal antecessors.

5. Later songs that are predominantly tonal employ the same means for text expression as "Nuit d'étoiles." Debussy's last song, "Noël des enfants qui n'ont plus de maisons," is an example in point.

6. See figure 2.3 for a formal plan aligned with the text.

7. "Il est tard; voici le chant des grenouilles vertes qui commence avec la nuit."

8. Lesure (*Catalogue*, 109 and 107) gives 1904 as the date for "Les ingénus" and "Colloque

sentimental" from *Fêtes galantes* II, and for "Pour ce que Plaisance est morte" from *Trois chansons de France*.

9. "Les hauts talons luttaient avec les longues jupes, / En sorte que, selon le terrain et le vent, / Parfois luisaient des bas de jambes, . . ."

10. ". . . trop souvent Interceptés!"

11. ". . . —et nous aimions ce jeu de dupes. / Parfois aussi le dard d'un insecte jaloux / Inquiétait le col des belles sous le branches . . ."

12. ". . . est morte . . ."

13. "Que doy, pour faire devoir."

14. "Le temps ces nouvelles porte . . ."

15. See Lesure, *Catalogue*, 130–31, for information regarding dates and sources. The work has been a focus of controversy for many reasons. An important issue is the extent to which André Caplet (Debussy's friend and assistant for a number of projects) was involved in its composition. It was rumored that Caplet was more collaborator than aide, and that he had in fact composed portions of the work, in particular the chorus of part 5. Lockspeiser (*Debussy*, 2:157–67) discusses the matter in detail and considers it unlikely that Caplet did more than simply carry out Debussy's instructions for much of the orchestration. Orledge (*Debussy and the Theatre*, 217–36) agrees and asserts (p. 226) that Debussy orchestrated part 5 himself (during the rehearsals).

16. See Grayson, *Genesis*, 13–38, for a detailed reconstruction of the opera's compositional chronology.

17. Orledge (*Debussy and the Theatre*, 61–62) identifies all of the added passages—for example, OS p. 25/3–p. 28/8.

18. Claude Debussy, *Le martyre de Saint-Sébastien*, piano-vocal score by André Caplet, trans. Hermann Klein (Paris: Durand, 1911–14), 67–72.

19. "Renversez les torches, . . ."

20. "Il descend vers les noires Portes! Tout ce qui est beau l'Hadès morne l'emporte."

21. "Eros! Pleurez!"

22. "Le laurier blessé" (part 4, no. 3) contains passages that employ the octatonic set 9–10, and in which 8–28 may be heard as well. The emphasis, however, is on small sets such as 3–10, 4–3, 4–10, and 4–28, which the octatonic and 8–17/18/19–complex genera share.

23. Lesure, *Catalogue*, 136, and Cobb *The Poetic Debussy*, 175n.

24. Modulations are too numerous to include on the concise formal plan of figure 8.3 (they occur at one-half-bar intervals in mm. 13.5–17).

Chapter 9. Form and Proportion

1. According to Lockspeiser (*Debussy;* 2:230–31), "Since an advanced stage in harmonic development had been reached the older forms of music could not be maintained." The stance of Debussy's chief biographer is typical; Lockspeiser does not explain what replaced the "older forms," beyond asserting that "development" is integral to them. Eric Salzman, *Twentieth-Century Music: An Introduction*, 2d ed. (Englewood Cliffs, N.J.: Prentice-Hall, 1974), 21, observes that "Debussy was able . . . to organize these new relationships [of melody, harmony, rhythm, and color] into new forms," but he avoids confronting the nature of the relationships. Arthur Wenk, *Claude Debussy and Twentieth-Century Music* (Boston: G. K. Hall, 1983), 120–21, speaks of "circular," "symmetrical," and "global" forms as Debussy's alternatives, but his discussion is too general to clarify exactly how these forms differ from older principles. Eimert ("Debussy's *Jeux*," 3) suggests that "one can see what Debussy's form no longer is; much harder to say what it is. One makes least progress if one tries to apply to Debussy the standard concepts of musical theory. It is a mistake even to refer to themes, periods or paragraphs. The same applies to traditional formal schemes."

2. But see Maria Porten, *Zum Problem der "Form" bei Debussy: Untersuchungen am Beispiel der Klavierwerk* (Munich: Emil Katzbichler, 1974). Porten's study focuses, first, on problems of grouping, by which a composition's continuum may be demarcated into formal units of large and small scale, and, second, on formal paradigms that account for form types in Debussy's piano works. Although her mode of explication derives from traditional harmonic and formal theories that are not always well suited to Debussy's nontraditional idiom, her attitude is fresh and her ideas find echos in the recent work of several Debussy scholars. The semiological approach has generated a rather substantial literature in recent years, including Marcelle Guertin, "Différence et similitude dans les Préludes pour

piano de Claude Debussy," *Canadian University Music Review* 2 (1981):56–83; Michel Imberty, "La *Cathédrale engloutie* de Claude Debussy: De la perception au sens," ibid. 6 (1985):90–161; Imberty, *Signification and Meaning in Music: On Debussy's Préludes pour le piano,* trans. Jean-Jacques Nattiez (Montreal: Groupe de recherches en sémiologie musicale, Faculté de musique, Université de Montréal, 1976); Nattiez and Louise Harbour-Paquette, "Analyse musicale et sémiologie à propos du Prélude de *Pelléas,*" *Musique en jeu* 10 (1973):42–69; Nattiez, "From Taxonomic Analysis to Stylistic Characterization: Debussy's *Syrinx,*" *Proceedings of the First International Congress on Semiotics of Music, Belgrade, 1973,* ed. Gino Stefani (Pesaro: Centro di Iniziativa Culturale, 1975), 83–112; Nicholas Ruwet, "Notes sur les duplications dans l'oeuvre de Claude Debussy," *Revue belge de musicologie* 16 (1962):57–70; and Arthur B. Wenk, "Parsing Debussy: A Proposal for a Grammar of His Melodic Practices," *In Theory Only* 9/8 (1987):5–20 (which includes a good bibliography of sources in semiotics and linguistics).

3. Although a given intermediate or higher-level formal unit may not be divided into lower-level units, other units within its level must be subdivided, since there cannot be a higher level if there is no lower level.

4. Meter in its more profound sense is the subject of chap. 13.

5. See Manfred Clynes and Janice Walker, "Music as Time's Measure," *Music Perception* 4 (1986): 85–119, for an intriguing study of the performer's instinctive tendency to compensate for adjustments in tempo in order to replicate execution times from one performance to the next.

6. Thematic/motivic resources and repetition/recurrence complement and overlap. Assignments to architectonic levels must reflect their relatedness and ensure that a given feature is not counted twice.

7. The complex role of orchestration is the subject of chap. 12.

8. Register is the subject of chap. 14.

9. As yet there are no studies that address the issue of listeners' ability to sense proportion in the temporal domain, and so we can only conjecture whether listeners measure and compare time spans in a manner analogous to the way they measure and compare spaces; the cognitive significance of temporal proportion must therefore remain, for now, in the realm of speculation. There is, nonetheless, an aspect of spatial cognition to the physical layout of a *score,* and, certainly, to the *concept* of a temporal span that the score represents, which permits a composer to include spatial proportion among the means of compositional control. Much empirical evidence exists to support the notion that symmetrical and asymmetrical proportional schemes, which arise from the varied lengths of formal units, are an important structural feature in Debussy's music.

10. Lesure, *Catalogue,* 23.

11. See Lockspeiser, *Debussy,* 2:272–77.

12. But see Howat, *Debussy,* 163–81.

13. The vastness of this topic's scope precludes a proper bibliography, but for those who wish to pursue it, two representative sources are H. E. Huntley, *The Divine Proportion: A Study in Mathematical Beauty* (New York: Dover, 1970) and D'Arcy Wentworth Thompson, *On Growth and Form* (Cambridge: Cambridge University Press, 1917). Howat (*Debussy,* 1–22) provides a good introduction and bibliography.

14. Howat (*Debussy,* 77 and 97) illustrates nested proportions by means of spiral diagrams in his formal plans for "De l'aube à midi sur la mer" and "Dialogue du vent et de la mer."

15. Regarding Golden Section and summation series in music, see Howat, *Debussy,* 1–10; J. H. Douglas Webster, "Golden-Mean Form in Music," *Music and Letters* 31 (1950):238–48; Jonathan D. Kramer, "The Fibonacci Series in Twentieth-Century Music," *Journal of Music Theory* 17 (1973):110–48; Paul Larson, "The Golden Section in the Earliest Notated Western Music," *Fibonacci Quarterly* 16 (1968):513–15; Erno Lendvai, *Béla Bartók: An Analysis of His Style* (London: Kahn and Averill, 1971); Newman W. Powell, "Fibonacci and the Golden Mean: Rabbits, Rhumbas, and Rondeaux," *Journal of Music Theory* 23 (1979):227–73; and Margaret Vardell Sandresky, "The Golden Section in Three Byzantine Motets of Dufay," *Journal of Music Theory* 25 (1981):291–306.

Chapter 10. Morphological Forms and Proportion

1. Lesure, *Catalogue,* 39.

2. "Positive" Golden Section places the longer segment of the line first; "Negative" Golden Section places the shorter segment first.

3. If all seventy measures of "Mandoline" were in 6/8 meter, the total number of durations (measured in eighth notes) would be 420, for which the negative Golden Section is 160.44, following approximately the fifth eighth note of m. 26. The 3/8 bar reduces the total number of eighths to 417, for which the Golden Section is 159.29, which follows the end of m. 27.

4. This overall proportional scheme is valid only if the marked tempo change of the coda (mm. 183–94) and all other tempo changes are ignored in calculations. In other words, here the nature of the proportional scheme is truly spatial (embodied in the score) rather than temporal (embodied in the music as heard).

5. Eimert, "Debussy's *Jeux*," 3–20.

6. Measure 24 corresponds to the point of Golden Section for the piece as a whole. If the composition's length is taken as 115 quarter-note beats (omitting from consideration the two quarter rests of final m. 39), the Golden Section occurs after 71.07 beats, or $23\frac{2}{3}$ measures.

7. The fourth variation begins at the composition's center (m. 55); the third variation begins at the Golden Section (m. 31) of the duration measured from the beginning to the composition's center. Howat (*Debussy*, 149–53) discusses form and porportion in this piece. So does Jean Barraqué, "An Experiment Crowned With Success," *Debussy, Prélude to "The Afternoon of a Faun*," trans. and ed. William Austin (New York: Norton, 1970), 162–65. Barraqué views the design as a synthesis of several form types, chiefly sonata design and song form (though he also mentions variation procedure).

8. *La mer* is cyclic in its reuse of themes across movements; in particular, the third movement incorporates thematic material from the first two.

9. Howat, *Debussy*, has this premise as his thesis throughout.

10. Howat (*Debussy*, 56) discusses other occurrences of the Golden Section in *Pelléas et Mélisande*.

11. Translation of tempo and meter changes into durational units equivalent to the original eighth notes is straightforward for the most part, though there is one refractory passage: mm. 21–25, where the meter signature changes from 7/8 to 8/8 to 9/8, complicated by a *molto ritard* following an *animando*. For each of the 8/8 bars and the first 9/8 bar, I assume progressively shorter durations (in eighth notes) and, accordingly, I assign durations equal to or slightly less than the previous 7/8 bars; I recognize the molto ritard by doubling the durations for each of its bars. I ignore minor tempo changes such as ritards at cadences.

12. Howat, *Debussy*, 162. The compositions we have examined reveal a more pervasive use of summation series in early works than Howat (pp. 30–45) seems willing to concede. Howat identifies "Spleen" (ca. 1885–88) as the first of Debussy's songs to manifest a Golden Section proportional scheme, and dismisses the "Arabesques" as "devoid of . . . any sign of consistent proportional structure in their forms." Yet "Mandoline," which antedates "Spleen" by at least three years, embodies a complex scheme based on the Lucas series that encompasses most of the song (though it excludes the introduction and coda), and both "Arabesques" reveal such series spanning each of their main sections. For the first "Arabesque," my differences with Howat issue, in part, from alternative interpretations for certain partitions. I accord higher status, for example, to the division between the third and fourth periods of the B section of the first "Arabesque," since the modulation to C major effects a radical (and dramatic) change in pc content. Howat focuses mainly on schemes that comprehensively control events of both long and short span as found in Debussy's mature works. The early works make more use of local schemes.

13. Howat (*Debussy*, 64–135) thoroughly examines proportion in *La mer*.

Chapter 11. Kinetic Forms

1. Pasler ("*Jeux*, 72, 74–75) makes the crucial point that in the ballet, Debussy gives the treatment of time distinct characteristics that vary from section to section, and thereby uses time as an element to create form.

2. Roy Howat, "Dramatic Shape and Form in *Jeux de vagues*, and Its Relationship to *Pelléas, Jeux* and Other Scores," *Cahiers Debussy*, n.s. 7 (1983):7–23, assumes this posture. Howat, *Debussy*, also focuses on kinetic form, though here it is subsidiary to his interest in morphological form.

3. For many of the concepts in this and the following chapters, I owe a substantial debt to Wallace Berry, in particular to *Structural Functions in Music* (Englewood Cliffs, N.J.: Prentice-Hall, 1976), esp. 301–424; "Rhythmic Accelerations in Beethoven," *Journal of Music Theory* 22 (1978):177–236; and "Metric and Rhythmic Articulation in Music," *Music Theory Spectrum* 7 (1985):7–33.

4. A sudden decrease in the number of notes struck per beat, for example—say, from sixteenths to quarters—may, of itself, suggest "slowing down." But if this occurs in a series of brief passages

(defined in other ways) that follow a longer one with more notes per beat (assuming equal beats), the listener may yet perceive the music as livelier and faster-paced owing to the quickened rate of section changes. It depends upon whether one hears changes in the durations of sections as more affective than changes in the numbers of notes struck, or vice versa.

5. Debussy, *La mer* (Paris: Durand, 1909; reprint New York: Kalmus, [n.d.]). Howat (*Debussy*, 64–67) discusses sources briefly. Rolf, "Debussy's *La mer*," 236–81, includes a thorough study of editions. The 1909 edition contains a few changes by Debussy; most notably, mm. 83–84 of the 1905 edition are condensed into a single bar (m. 83). Readers will want to be sure their reference scores contain the 1909 revisions.

6. Debussy, *La mer* (Paris: Durand, 1938). The piano reduction is based on the 1905 Durand edition.

7. As in so many other pieces, trichord 3–7 is ubiquitous in "De l'aube à midi sur la mer," embedded in its crucial thematic resources as well as in subsidiary materials. See, for example, mm. 12–16, 33, 35, 43, 67, 76, 84, and 85ff. Bars 93–97 furnish a clear example of the use of set 3–7 in ostinati. The trichord sometimes links adjacent passages (as in the treble line, mm. 46–47).

The M2 interval also permeates the movement's sonorities, conspicuous alike in melodic lines and supporting ostinati. It serves as a crucial unifying device as well, in the form of invariant dyads that cross adjacent formal units. (See, for example, mm. 6–13 and 17–30 [pcs 9,11]; mm. 31–45 [pcs 8,10]; and mm. 110–18 [pcs 8,10].)

8. Both Howat (*Debussy*, 84) and Rolf ("Debussy's *La mer*," 158–66) propose formal plans for "De l'aube à midi sur la mer," and the literature includes others (Rolf's measure numbers correspond to the 1905 edition). Most agree on the main partitions (though not on appropriate labels for sections), but there are many differences at the level of detail. Howat, pp. 76–86, discusses symmetry and Golden Section proportions in this movement.

9. See Howat, *Debussy*, 84. For the most part I have adopted his correspondences between passages set in different meters and tempos, but I take issue with his handling of mm. 84–85, where he makes no adjustment for the radical change of tempo (from dotted quarter note = ca. 116 in m. 83 to quarter note = 69 in mm. 84–85, before changing to quarter note = 104 for the remainder of the section). An appropriate adjustment yields six durations each for mm. 84–85, instead of four durations as found in mm. 86–121. A table that compares proportional durations for each section appears in appendix 7.

10. Howat, *Debussy*, 70.

11. Asterisks above the horizontal axis for section 3 mark, respectively, the movement's negative Golden Section; the movement's midpoint; the midpoint of section 3; the mean between the movement's midpoint and its positive Golden Section; and the positive Golden Section.

12. Though these nonchromatic sets may be missed on a first hearing, since they are concealed, their accessibility increases as we acquire familiarity with the composition's pitch materials.

13. Howat, *Debussy*, 151–52.

14. Lesure, *Catalogue*, 95.

15. They are: mm. 13, rc = A♭ major; m. 14, rc = E♭ major; m. 17, rc = C major; m. 19, rc = A♭ major; m. 21, rc = C major; m. 29, rc = D major; and m. 31, rc = C major.

16. They are: m. 33, rc = 8–19 (11,0,2,3,4,6,7,8); m. 35, rc = 8–19 (1,2,4,5,6,8,9,10); m. 39, rc = 7–32 (0,2,4,5,7,8,11); m. 42, rc = 8–19 (1,2,4,5,6,8,9,10); and m. 43, rc = 8–18 (10,11,1,2,4,5,6,7). Set 7–29 at mm. 37–38 is anomalous; its prominent subset, 6–33 (2,4,5,7,9,11), is diatonic, for which the B♭ acts as a suspension or appoggiatura.

17. In their perceptive commentary on register in "Nuages," Cogan and Escot (*Sonic Design*, 385–97) observe that the recurrent English horn solo's placement is at the center of the register span occupied by this movement.

18. This places its morphological form among those derived from strophic variations such as the *Prélude à "L'après-midi d'un faune"* and the etudes "Pour les degrés chromatiques" and "Pour les notes répétées."

19. Their ivs and sias are: 5–34 [032221] 2–2–2–3–3; 6–34 [142422] 1–2–2–2–2–3; and 7–34 [254442] 1–2–1–2–2–2–2.

Chapter 12. Orchestration, Instrumental Effect, and Structure

1. Perhaps the best discussion of Debussy's *technique* of orchestration is found in Jarocinski, *Debussy*, 138.

2. The instrumentation comprises six horns, four C-trumpets, three trombones, tuba, and timbales in F, G, B♭, and C.

3. Additional examples include "Jeux de vagues" (*La mer* II), rehearsal number (#) 26 + 2 bars (trumpets 1,2); "Dialogue du vent et de la mer" (*La mer* III), #52 + 5 bars; and "Par les rues et par les chemins," "Ibéria," I (*Images pour orchestre* II), #19 + 3.

4. Eimert ("Debussy's *Jeux*," 14–20) discusses aspects of orchestration in *Jeux*, which he asserts are form defining (though he does not explain how).

5. Several authors have drawn parallels between the cyclic treatment of themes in the String Quartet and Franck's D minor Symphony (e.g., Lockspeiser, *Debussy*, 1:125–26). *Nocturnes* shows Debussy still able to profit from this principle, as does *La mer* a few years later.

6. The motto-theme in "Sirènes" also appears once in the English horn (mm. 133–34).

7. The latter is distorted by pc 8, which joins pcs 9,11,1,3,5 to form set 6–34, a familiar 8–17/18/19–complex hexachord that shares sia characteristics with the whole-tone and diatonic genera. At mm. 127–28 the diatonic/whole-tone dichotomy is manifest in a familiar juxtaposition of diatonic 5–34 against whole-tone 5–33.

8. Diatonic pentachord 5–25 (as 6,9,11,0,2), whose pcs are disposed to project diatonic subsets 3–8, 3–11, 4–26 and 4–Z29, provides the motive's harmonic setting. The motive itself adds two pcs: pc 4, which aligns with the diatonic genus (rc = G major); and pc 8, which distorts the genus by combining with the hexachord to form set 7–34. From a kinesthetic viewpoint, the distortion is only a semitonal adjustment away from the whole-tone scale: a transposition of dyad 9,11 to 10,0 (or to 8,10) would yield a whole-tone scale (0,2,4,6,8,10).

9. Two authors who address the issue are Orledge (*Debussy and the Theatre*, 97–99), who discusses technical details of orchestration vis-à-vis the drama; and Wenk (*Debussy and Twentieth-Century Music*, 43–44), who provides a table of associations between dramatic features and solo instrumental timbres.

10. While passivity is the conspicuous feature of Mélisande's demeanor, she is, nonetheless, decisively active at crucial moments that shape the course of the drama. For example, she continually encourages Pelléas, though coyly, and implies that she actively manipulates Golaud, though covertly. (Consider her comment in act IV, scene 4 [OS p. 336/2]: "Non, je ne mens jamais, je ne mens qu'à ton frère" ("No, I never lie; I lie only to your brother").

11. "Oh! vous êtes belle."

12. "Je suis tout heureux de t'entendre parler ainsi . . ."

13. "Oui, oui, je te pardonne."

14. "Je te donnerai quelque che demain. . . . Un carquois et des flèches."

15. "De grandes flèches?"

16. "J'ai tué sans raison! Est-ce que ce n'est pas à faire pleurer les pierres!"

17. "Ils s'étaient embrassés comme des petits enfants. Ils étaient frère et soeur."

18. "Et moi, moi tout de suite!"

19. Their function here is also practical, as they help to raise the loudness level to maximum intensity.

20. Performers should avoid vibrato in these passages so that their timbres may blend properly.

21. The performance tradition that advocates a dry sonority accomplished through greater use of the sostenuto pedal poses an important obstacle for the listener, who must be able to hear the larger harmonic context within which details occur in order to decipher their pc-set-generic meaning. The "dry" tradition seems to have originated in the 1920s and 1930s with performers such as Alfred Cortot and E. Robert Schmitz, was carried forward by Walter Gieseking and Robert Casadesus, among others, and is very much alive today. Pianists (and listeners) are better served by a technique that strives for clear articulation within an overall sonority that blurs together large harmonic blocks in a manner consistent with Debussy's notation. Paul Jacobs, "On Playing the Piano Music of Debussy," *Cahiers Debussy*, n.s. 3 (1979):39–44, corroborates this view. Jacobs notes that Debussy did not have a sostenuto pedal on his pianos and so the damper pedal sufficed for all sustaining, and that long note values often serve as pedal indications (wherever the notes to which they are attached could not be sustained by holding the keys). Jacobs's recordings of Debussy attest eloquently to the efficacy of his ideas; moreover, they are consistent with Debussy's own recorded performances of 1913, included in "The Welte Legacy of Piano Treasures: Great Composers/Pianists Perform Their Own Compositions," vols. 3 and 4, Recorded Treasures GCP 771A–3 and GCP 771A–44.

Chapter 13. Meter

1. A brief list of sources includes Berry, *Structural Functions*, 301–424; Berry, "Metric and Rhythmic Articulation"; William E. Benjamin, "A Theory of Musical Meter," *Music Perception* 1 (1984):355–413; Grosvenor Cooper and Leonard B. Meyer, *The Rhythmic Structure of Music* (Chicago: University of Chicago Press, 1963); and Maury Yeston, *The Stratification of Musical Rhythm* (New Haven: Yale University Press, 1976). The best available bibliographic source is Jonathan D. Kramer, "Studies of Time and Motion: A Bibliography," *Music Theory Spectrum* 7 (1985):72–106.

2. "Field" because time-length, tempo, and internal fluctuations such as rubato normally vary from one performance to the next.

3. Cooper and Meyer, *Rhythmic Structure*, 4.

4. Berry, "Metric and Rhythmic Articulation" discusses metric accents of all types. The concept of middle- and end-accented units poses special problems for the verification of unit boundaries.

5. Metric levels are often congruent with (though not the same as) formal levels, where the weight of a partition determines the formal unit's hierarchic assignment.

6. Debussy's music has received little attention in this area, though in her treatment of form, Porten, *"Form" bei Debussy*, focuses on relations that I consider metric.

7. The remaining L_1 metric units are indicated by the shortest vertical lines that rise perpendicular to the topmost horizontal axis in figure 13.1.

8. Indicated by the intermediate perpendicular lines that intersect the horizontal axis of figure 13.1.

9. Other L_3 metric units are indicated by the highest vertical lines that intersect the horizontal axis.

10. Lesure, *Catalogue*, 104.

11. The beginning of stanza 2 coincides exactly with the composition's negative Golden Section at m. 21, and the last word of the phrase "our mad young eyes" ("nos jeunes yeux de fous") aligns with the positive Golden Section at m. 33/beat 3.

12. "Interceptés!"

13. The 8–17/18/19–complex and diatonic genera are also used for exaggerated effect, the former in mockery to evoke an aura of malignancy at the song's beginning, the latter to mock frenzied passion at mm. 27–36.

14. "Et c'étaient des éclairs soudains de nuques blanches . . ."

15. "Les belles, se pendant reveuses à nos bras . . ."

16. The grace notes within L_2 are unmeasured and so the durations of their metric units are approximate.

17. Note that L_1 metric units are withheld altogether until m. 5.

18. This composition's fluctuant tempo poses problems, especially the *en serrant* in mm. 7–9. I have assumed that acceleration occurs through these bars, and that "eighth note = 184" doubles the tempo, and I have accordingly adjusted durations in the figure.

19. Lesure, *Catalogue*, 126–27.

Chapter 14. Register

1. Debussy studies that consider register include Wenk, *Debussy and Twentieth-Century Music*; Porten, *"Form" bei Debussy*; Dieter Schnebel, "Brouillards: Tendencies in Debussy," trans. Margaret Schenfield, *Die Reihe* 6:33–39 (Bryn Mawr, Penn.: Presser, 1964); Cogan and Escot, *Sonic Design*. The studies by Schnebel, Porten, and Wenk are suggestive, though they do not examine systematically or comprehensively the nonpitch parameters they embrace. Cogan and Escot (pp. 92–101) point to the importance of register in the course of their discussion of "Syrinx," and they develop an effective analytical approach for identifying and comparing register spaces in their perspicuous study of "Nuages" (*Nocturnes* I) (pp. 385–97). For a general study that treats register and timbre as structural determinants (and includes a discussion of "Nuages"), see Robert Cogan, *New Images of Musical Sound* (Cambridge, Mass.: Harvard University Press, 1984).

2. An earlier discussion of the morphological form of "La fille aux cheveux de lin" (chap. 3)

distinguished between reprises of pc content (m. 24) and theme (m. 28); the reprise of the pc content occurs in the original register.

3. In many respects we may regard "Bruyères" (Préludes II) as a recomposition of "La fille aux cheveux de lin," with which it shares a pervasive diatonicism that emphasizes complementary pairs of pc sets, a morphological formal structure that undergoes a process of continuous development until its late reprise, an unaccompanied opening, and a conspicuous use of V^{11}–I cadences on various scale steps. "Bruyères" also moves its opening theme to a higher octave in its reprise (m. 44) shortly before the conclusion a few bars later.

4. Even when the register disposition remains the same, the contrapuntal-harmonic details of the setting are modified. Note changes in the viola part, for example, at mm. 5 and 9.

5. Most of the data are straightforward but sometimes they are refractory, as in mm. 14 and 17, where the first highest *sound* of each bar is $f\sharp^1$ and d^1, respectively. Yet common sense argues for e^2 and c^2, respectively, as first highest notes, which are necessarily delayed owing to pianistic limitations.

6. "Canope" (Préludes II) provides yet another example of a piece whose register compass expands over its course. It also illustrates the principle of reassigning its initial theme to a higher octave for its final statement just prior to the composition's conclusion.

7. Slightly wider spans occur at mm. 21 and 23 ([68] and [74], respectively), but they result from the apexes of harp glissandi with only fleeting effect.

8. The second section's register span falls back to a narrower compass after m. 76, in preparation for the next section, but the anticlimatic, codetta-like character of these few measures distinguishes this contraction as a superficial countertendency that prepares for the next section's initially narrow compass and does not contradict the overall tendency towards expansion.

9. The climax is further heightened by the initially low mean placement of the beginning of section 3.

10. Bars 1–5 constitute a surface-level formal unit that is antecedent to the consequent phrase which precedes the first statement of the motto theme at rehearsal number 1.

11. "Je vais fuir en criant de joie et de douleur comme un aveugle qui fuirait l'incendie de sa maison."

12. "Depuis toujours. Depuis que je t'ai vu."

13. "Et maintenant je t'ai trouvée."

BIBLIOGRAPHY

I. Historical, Biographical, and Bibliographical Sources and Editions

A. Primary Sources, Autograph Studies, and Editions

Briscoe, James Robert. "Debussy's Earliest Songs." *College Music Symposium* 24 (1984): 81–95.

———. "The Compositions of Claude Debussy's Formative Years (1879–1887)." Ph.D. diss., University of North Carolina, 1979.

Cobb, Margaret. *The Poetic Debussy: A Collection of His Song Texts and Selected Letters.* Boston: Northeastern University Press, 1982.

Debussy, Claude. "Aquarelles." No. 2. "Spleen." *Ariettes oubliées* VI. Paris: E. Girod, 1888.

———. *Correspondance de Claude Debussy et Pierre Louÿs (1893–1904).* Ed. Henri Borgeaud. Paris: José Corti, 1945.

———. *Debussy Letters.* Edited by François Lesure and Roger Nichols. Translated by Roger Nichols. Cambridge, Mass.: Harvard University Press, 1987.

———. *Debussy on Music.* Edited by François Lesure. Translated and annotated by Richard Langham Smith. New York: Alfred A. Knopf, 1977.

———. *Lettres, 1884–1918.* Ed. François Lesure. Paris: Hermann, 1980.

———. *La mer.* Paris: Durand, 1909.

———. *La mer.* Piano transcription by Lucien Garban. Paris: Durand, 1938.

———. *Le martyre de Saint-Sébastien.* Paris: Durand, 1911.

———. *Le martyre de Saint-Sébastien.* Piano-vocal reduction by André Caplet. Paris: Durand, 1911–14.

———. "Nuit d'étoiles." *Frühe Lieder nach verschiedenen Dichtern.* Ed. Reiner Zimmerman. Leipzig: Peters, 1976.

———. *Pelléas et Mélisande.* Full score. Paris: Durand, 1957.

———. Préludes. Books 1 and 2. Ed. Roy Howat and Claude Helffer. *Oeuvres complètes de Claude Debussy.* Series 1, vol. 5. Paris: Durand-Costellat, 1985.

———. "The Welte Legacy of Piano Treasures: Great Composers/Pianists Perform Their Own Compositions." Vols. 3 and 4. Nos. GCP 771A-3 and 771A-4. North Hollywood, Calif.: Recorded Treasures, n.d.

Raus, Denis-François. "Le terrible finale: Les sources manuscrites de la Sonate pour violon et piano de Claude Debussy et la genèse du troisième mouvement." *Cahiers Debussy*, n.s. 2 (1978): 30–62.

Rolf, Marie. "Debussy's 'La Mer': A Critical Analysis in the Light of Early Sketches and Editions." Ph.D. diss., University of Rochester, 1976.

———. "Orchestral Manuscripts of Claude Debussy: 1895–1905." *Musical Quarterly* 70 (1984): 538–66.

353

B. Secondary Sources: Historical Studies, Bibliographies, and Reference Works

Abravanel, Claude. *Claude Debussy: A Bibliography.* Detroit Studies in Music Bibliography 29. Detroit: Information Coordinators, 1974. Though dated, this is a very useful tool, for both its comprehensiveness and its thoughtful organization.

Austin, William. *Music in the Twentieth Century: From Debussy through Stravinsky.* New York: W. W. Norton, 1966. Chapters 1–3 are devoted wholly or largely to Debussy. Good bibliography, though dated.

Calvocoressi, Michel-Dimitri. "Debussy and the Leitmotiv." *Musical Times* 66 (1935): 695–97.

Debussy, Claude. *Prelude to "The Afternoon of a Faun": An Authoritative Score, Mallarmé's Poem, Backgrounds and Sources, Criticism and Analysis.* Ed. William W. Austin. New York: W. W. Norton, 1970. Includes analyses by Austin and Jean Barraqué.

Dietschy, Marcel. *La passion de Claude Debussy.* Neuchâtel: La Baconnière, 1962.

Gilman, Lawrence. *Debussy's "Pelléas et Mélisande": A Guide to the Opera.* New York: Schirmer, 1907. Includes catalogue of leitmotivs.

Grayson, David A. "Debussy in the Opera House: An Unpublished Letter Concerning Yniold and Mélisande." *Cahiers Debussy.* n.s. 9 (1985): 17–28.

———. *The Genesis of Debussy's "Pelléas et Mélisande."* Ann Arbor: UMI Research Press, 1986. Includes an extensive bibliography.

Holloway, Robin. *Debussy and Wagner.* London: Eulenberg, 1979.

Jacobs, Paul. "On Playing the Piano Music of Debussy." *Cahiers Debussy,* n.s. 3 (1979): 39–44.

Jarocinski, Stefan. *Debussy: Impressionism and Symbolism.* Trans. Rollo Myers. London: Eulenburg, 1976.

Laloy, Louis. "*Claude Debussy et le Debussysme,*" *S.I.M. Revue musicale mensuelle* 6 (1910): 507–19.

Lesure, François. *Catalogue de l'oeuvre de Claude Debussy.* Geneva: Minkoff, 1977. Though dated, this source still contains much valuable information about sources and their locations.

Lockspeiser, Edward. *Debussy: His Life and Mind.* 2 vols. 2d ed. London: Cassell, 1965–66. Reprint with corrections. Cambridge: Cambridge University Press, 1978. Still the definitive biography. Includes valuable indices, lists of works, and bibliographies.

Nichols, Roger. *Debussy.* London: Oxford University Press, 1973.

Orledge, Robert. *Debussy and the Theatre.* Cambridge: Cambridge University Press, 1982.

Salzman, Eric. *Twentieth-Century Music: An Introduction.* 2d ed. Englewood Cliffs, N.J.: Prentice-Hall, 1974.

Thomson, Virgil. "Mélisande." *The Musical Scene.* New York: Alfred A. Knopf, 1945.

Vallas, Léon. *Claude Debussy: His Life and Works.* Trans. Maire and Grace O'Brien. Oxford: Oxford University Press, 1933. Reprint. New York: Dover, 1973. An important early biography by a contemporary of the composer.

Wenk, Arthur B. *Debussy and the Poets.* Berkeley: University of California Press, 1976.

II. Theoretical and Analytical Studies and Sources

A. On Debussy

Allen, Judith Shatin. "Tonal Allusion and Illusion: Debussy's Sonata for Flute, Viola and Harp. *Cahiers Debussy,* n.s. 7 (1983):38–48.

Benjamin, William E. "'Pour les sixtes': An Analysis." *Journal of Music Theory* 22 (1978): 253–90.

Brailoiu, Constantin. "Pentatony in Debussy's Music." *Studia Memoriae Belae Bartok Sacra,* 377–417. London: Boosey and Hawkes, 1958.

Cogan, Robert. *New Images of Musical Sound.* Cambridge, Mass.: Harvard University Press, 1984. Includes a discussion of "Nuages" (*Nocturnes* I).

Cogan, Robert, and Pozzi Escot. *Sonic Design: The Nature of Sound and Music.* Englewood Cliffs, N.J.: Prentice-Hall, 1976. Includes analyses of "Nuages" (*Nocturnes* I) and "Syrinx."

D'Almendra, Julia. *Les modes grégoriens dans l'oeuvre de Claude Debussy.* Paris: Gabriel Enoult, 1950.

Deliège, Célestin. "La relation forme-contenu dans l'oeuvre de Debussy." *Revue belge de musicologie* 16 (1962):71–96. Discusses the Baudelaire songs.

Eimert, Herbert. "Debussy's *Jeux.*" Trans. Leo Black. *Die Reihe* 5:3–20. Bryn Mawr, Penn.: Presser, 1959.

Emmanuel, Maurice. *Pelléas et Mélisande de Debussy: Etude et analyse.* Paris: Mellottée, 1925. Includes a catalogue of leitmotivs.

Forte, Allen. "Foreground Rhythm in Early Twentieth-Century Music." *Music Analysis* 2 (1983):239–68. Includes a study of "Voiles" (Préludes I) that identifies its rhythmic motives and their synthesis.

———. "Schenker's Conception of Musical Structure." *Journal of Music Theory* 3 (1959):1–30. Includes a discussion of voice leading within "parallel chords" in "La cathédrale engloutie" (Préludes I).

Friedmann, Michael L. "Approaching Debussy's 'Ondine.'" *Cahiers Debussy,* n.s. 6 (1982): 22–35. Combines tonal and atonal approaches.

Gauldin, Robert. "An Analysis" [of "Pour les sixtes"]. *Journal of Music Theory* 22 (1978):241–51. Gauldin's voice-leading graphs imply an acceptance of Salzer's emendations to Schenker.

Goléa, Antoine. *Pelléas et Mélisande: Analyse poétique et musicale.* Paris: Château-Rouge, 1952.

Guertin, Marcelle. "Différence et similitude dans les Préludes pour piano de Claude Debussy." *Canadian University Music Review* 2 (1981):56–83 A semiotic study.

Haimo, Ethan. "Generated Collections and Interval Control in Debussy's Preludes." *In Theory Only* 4/8 (Feb./March 1979):3–15.

Hepokoski, James. "Formulaic Openings in Debussy." *19th Century Music* 8 (1984):44–59.

Howat, Roy. "Dramatic Shape in *Jeux de vagues,* and Its Relationship to *Pelléas, Jeux* and Other Scores." *Cahiers Debussy,* n.s. 7 (1983):7–23.

———. *Debussy in Proportion.* Cambridge: Cambridge University Press, 1983.

———. Debussy, Ravel and Bartok: Toward Some New Concepts of Form." *Music and Letters* 58 (1977):285–93.

Imberty, Michel. "La *Cathédrale engloutie* de Claude Debussy: De la perception au sens." *Canadian University Music Review* 6 (1985):90–161. Combines psychological-perceptual and semiotic perspectives.

———. *Signification and Meaning in Music: On Debussy's Préludes pour le piano.* Trans. Jean-Jacques Nattiez. Montreal: Groupe de recherches en sémiologie musicale, Faculté de musique, Université de Montréal, 1976. A semiological study that presents a theory of musical semantics.

Katz, Adele. *Challenge to Musical Tradition.* New York: Alfred A. Knopf, 1945. Reprint. New York: Da Capo, 1972. Katz follows Salzer's attempt to extend Schenkerian principles in order to account for Debussy's idiomatic tonality. She analyses "La fille aux cheveux de lin" in some detail.

Kresky, Jeffrey. *Tonal Music: Twelve Analytic Studies.* Bloomington: Indiana University Press, 1977. Includes an analysis of "La fille aux cheveux de lin."

Lenormand, René. *A Study of Twentieth-Century Harmony.* Trans. Herbert Antcliffe. London: Joseph Williams, 1915. Reprint. New York: Da Capo, 1976. An early, pioneering study that attempted to characterize and catalog Debussy's innovations either as traditional sonorities and part writing placed in novel contexts, or as exoticisms culled from folk and Eastern musics.

Lewin, David. "Some Instances of Parallel Voice-Leading in Debussy." *19th Century Music* 11 (1987):59–72. Examines portions of the Violin Sonata, "Le vent dans la plaine," and "Canope," and presents alternative readings to parallel voice leading that reveal origins of motives and large-scale pitch structures.

Moevs, Robert. "Intervallic Procedures in Debussy: Serenade from the Sonata for Cello and Piano, 1915." *Perspectives of New Music* 8 (1969):82–101.

Nattiez, Jean-Jacques. "From Taxonomic Analysis to Stylistic Characterization. Debussy's *Syrinx*." *Proceedings of the First International Congress on Semiotics of Music, Belgrade, 1973*. Ed. Gino Stefani. Pesaro: Centro di Iniziativa Culturale, 1975. A semiotic approach.

Nattiez, Jean-Jacques, and Louise Harbour-Paquette. "Analyse musicale et sémiologie à propos du Prélude de *Pelléas*." *Musique en jeu* 10 (1973):42–69.

Parks, Richard S. "Pitch Organization in Debussy: Unordered Sets in 'Brouillards.'" *Music Theory Spectrum* 2 (1980):119–34.

———. "Tonal Analogues as Atonal Resources and Their Relation to Form in Debussy's Chromatic Etude." *Journal of Music Theory* 29 (1985):33–60.

Pasler, Jann. "Debussy, *Jeux:* Playing with Time and Form." *19th Century Music* 6 (1982):60–75.

Porten, Maria. *Zum Problem der "Form" bei Debussy: Untersuchungen am Beispiel der Klavierwerk*. Munich: Emil Katzbichler, 1974.

Ruwet, Nicholas. "Notes sur les duplications dans l'oeuvre de Claude Debussy." *Revue belge de musicologie* 16 (1962):57–70. Treats form and problems of segmentation.

Salzer, Felix. *Structural Hearing: Tonal Coherence in Music*. 2 vols. New York: Boni, 1952. Reprint. New York: Dover, 1962. Salzer analyses two pieces by Debussy: a portion of *Prélude à "L'après-midi d'un faune"* (1: 209–10) and "Bruyères" in its entirety (1: 222–23).

Schmitz, E. Robert. *The Piano Works of Claude Debussy*. N.p.: Duell, Sloan & Pearce, 1950. Reprint. New York: Dover, 1966. Intended for pianists, with many suggestions for interpretation, Schmitz's analytical approach is pragmatic and traditional. There are some errors in matters such as key designations.

Schnebel, Dieter. "Brouillards: Tendencies in Debussy." Trans. Margaret Schenfield. *Die Reihe* 6:33–39. Bryn Mawr, Penn.: Presser, 1964.

Stuckenschmidt, H. H. "Debussy or Berg? The Mystery of a Chord Progression." *Musical Quarterly* 51 (1965):453–59.

Van Appledorn, Mary Jeanne. "A Stylistic Study of Claude Debussy's Opera *Pelléas et Mélisande*." Ph.D. diss., University of Rochester, 1966. An enormous statistical study of the sonorities employed in the opera. An appendix catalogs leitmotivs.

Wenk, Arthur B. "Parsing Debussy: Proposal for a Grammer of His Melodic Practices." *In Theory Only* 9/8 (1987):5–20. Invokes linguistic concepts to formulate a general theory of melody. Includes a good bibliography of sources in semiotics and linguistics.

———. *Claude Debussy and Twentieth-Century Music*. Boston: Twayne, 1983. Includes a good, brief bibliography.

Whittall, Arnold. "Tonality and the Whole-Tone Scale in the Music of Debussy." *Music Review* 36 (1975):261–71.

B. Other

Babbitt, Milton. "Set Structure as a Compositional Determinant." *Journal of Music Theory* 5 (1961):72–94.

Baker, James. "Schenkerian Analysis and Post-Tonal Music." In David Beach, ed. *Aspects of Schenkerian Theory*. New Haven: Yale University Press, 1983.

———. *The Music of Alexander Scriabin*. New Haven: Yale University Press, 1986.

Benjamin, William E. "A Theory of Musical Meter." *Music Perception* 1 (1984):355–413.

———. "Ideas of Order in Motivic Music." *Music Theory Spectrum* 1 (1979):24–25.

———. "Tonality without Fifths: Remarks on the First Movement of Stravinsky's Concerto for Piano and Wind Instruments." *In Theory Only* 2/11–12 (1976–77):53–70; 3/2 (1977/78):9–31.

Berger, Arthur. "Problems with Pitch Organization in Stravinsky." In *Perspectives on Schoenberg and Stravinsky*. Ed. Benjamin Boretz and Edward T. Cone. Princeton, N.J.: Princeton University Press, 1968.

Berry, Wallace. "Metric and Rhythmic Articulation in Music." *Music Theory Spectrum* 7 (1985):7–33.

———. "Rhythmic Accelerations in Beethoven." *Journal of Music Theory* 22 (1978):177–236.

———. *Structural Functions in Music*. Englewood Cliffs, N.J.: Prentice-Hall, 1976.

Browne, Richmond. "Tonal Implications of the Diatonic Set." *In Theory Only* 5/6–7 (1981): 3–21.

Chrisman, Richard. "Describing Structural Aspects of Pitch-Class Sets Using Successive Interval Arrays." *Journal of Music Theory* 21 (1977):1–28.

Clough, John. "Aspects of Diatonic Sets." *Journal of Music Theory* 23 (1979):45–61.

———. "Diatonic Interval Sets and Transformational Structures." *Perspectives of New Music* 18 (1979–80):461–82.

Clough, John, and Gerald Myerson. "Variety and Multiplicity in Diatonic Systems." *Journal of Music Theory* 29 (1985):249–70.

Clynes, Manfred. *Sentics: The Touch of Emotions*. New York: Anchor Press/Doubleday, 1978.

Clynes, Manfred, and Janice Walker. "Music as Time's Measure." *Music Perception* 4 (1986): 85–119.

Cooper, Grosvenor, and Leonard B. Meyer. *The Rhythmic Structure of Music*. Chicago: University of Chicago Press, 1963.

Forte, Allen. "Pitch-Class Set Genera and the Origin of Modern Harmonic Species." *Journal of Music Theory* (forthcoming).

———. *The Structure of Atonal Music*. New Haven: Yale University Press, 1973.

Huntley, H. E. *The Divine Proportion: A Study in Mathematical Beauty*. New York: Dover, 1970.

Kramer, Jonathan D. "Studies of Time and Music: A Bibliography." *Music Theory Spectrum* 7 (1985):72–106.

———. "The Fibonacci Series in Twentieth-Century Music." *Journal of Music Theory* 17 (1973):110–48.

Larson, Paul. "The Golden Section in the Earliest Notated Western Music." *Fibonacci Quarterly* 16 (1968):513–15.

Lendvai, Erno. *Béla Bartók: An Analysis of His Style*. London: Kahn and Averill, 1971.

Lord, Charles. "Intervallic Similarity Relations in Atonal Set Analysis." *Journal of Music Theory* 25 (1981):91–111.

Meyer, Leonard. *Emotion and Meaning in Music*. Chicago: University of Chicago Press, 1956.

Perle, George. *Serial Technique and Atonality*. 3d ed. Berkeley: University of California Press, 1972.

Powell, Newman W. "Fibonacci and the Golden Mean: Rabbits, Rhumbas, and Rondeaux." *Journal of Music Theory* 23 (1979):227–73.

Russom, Phillip. "A Theory of Pitch Organization for the Early Music of Maurice Ravel." Ph.D. diss., Yale University, 1985.

Sandresky, Margaret Vardell. "The Golden Section in Three Byzantine Motets of Dufay." *Journal of Music Theory* 25 (1981):291–306.

Schenker, Heinrich. "Resumption of *Urlinie* Considerations." Trans. Silvan Kalib. In "Thirteen Essays from the Three Yearbooks *Das Meisterwerk in der Musik* by Heinrich Schenker: An Annotated Translation." Ph.D. diss., Northwestern University, 1977.

———. *Harmony*. Edited and annotated by Oswald Jonas. Translated by Elizabeth Mann Borgese. Chicago: University of Chicago Press, 1954.

Simms, Bryan. *Music of the Twentieth Century*. New York: Schirmer Books, 1986.

Stein, Deborah. "The Expansion of the Subdominant in the Late Nineteenth Century." *Journal of Music Theory* 27 (1983):153–80.

Thompson, D'Arcy Wentworth. *On Growth and Form*. Cambridge: Cambridge University Press, 1917.

Van den Toorn, Pieter C. *The Music of Igor Stravinsky*. New Haven: Yale University Press, 1983.

Webster, J. H. Douglas. "Golden-Mean Form in Music." *Music and Letters* 31 (1950):238–48.

Yeston, Maury. *The Stratification of Musical Rhythm*. New Haven: Yale University Press, 1976.

INDEX OF WORKS

GENERAL INDEX